Mandy Magro lives in Cairns, Far North Queensland, with her daughter, Chloe Rose. With pristine aqua-blue coastline in one direction and sweeping rural landscapes in the other, she describes her home as heaven on earth. A passionate woman and a romantic at heart, she loves writing about soul-deep love, the Australian rural way of life and all the wonderful characters who live there.

www.facebook.com/mandymagroauthor

www.mandymagro.com

Also by Mandy Magro

MANDY MAGRO

A Country Mile

First Published 2018
Second Australian Paperback Edition 2022
ISBN 9781867255888

A COUNTRY MILE
© 2018 by Mandy Magro
Australian Copyright 2018
New Zealand Copyright 2018

Published by
An imprint of Harlequin Enterprises (Australia) Pty Limited (ABN 47 001 180 918), a subsidiary of HarperCollins Publishers Australia Pty Limited (ABN 36 009 913 517)
Level 13, 201 Elizabeth St
SYDNEY NSW 2000
AUSTRALIA

® and TM (apart from those relating to FSC ®) are trademarks of Harlequin Enterprises Limited or its corporate affiliates. Trademarks indicated with ® are registered in Australia, New Zealand and in other countries.

A catalogue record for this book is available from the National Library of Australia
www.librariesaustralia.nla.gov.au

Printed and bound in Australia by McPherson's Printing Group

MIX
Paper | Supporting
responsible forestry
FSC® C001695

Secrets. Everyone harbours at least one. And lies, well, it would be a big fat lie for a person to say they'd never told one. It's often difficult to distinguish one from the other, because secrets create lies and lies create secrets. It can become a vicious circle, a whirlwind of deceit that sends everyone involved into a spin. A little white lie to avoid hurting somebody's feelings is socially acceptable. Then there are the secrets someone pleaded with you to keep, and for the sake of loyalty you felt obligated to, and quite often have to lie to keep it buried. Then there are those secrets where lying goes hand in hand. These are the type that, if discovered, have the power to create a tidal wave that will leave people gasping for air and struggling to stay afloat.

Just remember, everything isn't always as it seems.

CHAPTER

1

Stone's Throw, North Queensland

Stealing a peek into the guest room, Faith Stone breathed a small sigh of relief. Grace, her twelve-year-old, high-spirited niece was finally asleep, with her headphones on. As much as Faith loved her coming to stay over the school holidays, as Grace had for the past couple of years, trying to keep her volatile husband's temper under wraps while Grace was about was wearing her out. The last thing she wanted was for her niece to witness the horrors she went through on a daily basis, and then go home with stories of the dark secrets that were hidden beneath this roof. And she didn't want to worry her sister, either. With her husband fighting in Afghanistan, and a demanding job as a midwife – quite often with back-to-back shifts – Kimmy had enough on her plate.

Next door to Grace's room, she paused by her nine-year-old son's bed. He looked so peaceful, and yet so fragile, a polar opposite to when he was awake. Her heart ached with immense love for him, and also deep guilt for the life he had to put up with, all because she'd made a bad decision the night she'd fallen head over heels for his father. Oh how foolish she'd been as a seventeen-year-old girl. Not long now and she would free him of it. Then she would give her son the life he deserved, far away from here and his insufferable father. Leaning in, she gently brushed a kiss over his cheek, tears stinging her eyes as she did.

She padded to the kitchen and started to make a coffee. She needed something to keep her awake. Her husband, Don, would blow his stack if she didn't wait up to have dinner with him. Tossing the teaspoon in the sink, she cradled her mug, drawing warmth from it. Glancing out the kitchen window, she took comfort in the panorama of nothingness that was her backyard. Although only twenty acres, and not big enough to make a living from, it was her country heaven by the sea. After spending the past thirteen years of her life here, she would miss this place, as would Dylan. But it just had to be done. How else were they meant to get away from the brutality of his father, her husband? The velvet-black sky glimmered with stars, the dazzling show warming her aching soul. She recalled her dear mother telling her each star was a person's dream, waiting to be reached and made into a reality. If that were true, all of her own dreams must still hang there. Lady Luck certainly hadn't been on her side so far.

The glow of the moon cast shadows across the lawn, the branches of the towering gum trees mimicking clawed hands reaching for her. But there was nothing to fear outside – the real danger lived within these four walls. Turning, she rested against the kitchen sink. She used to be a glass-half-full kind of girl. Not anymore. Her father's guitar, her pride and joy and the only keepsake of his she had, lay battered and broken near the back door. A flashback of last night, when Dylan and Grace had been having a sleepover at Sophie Copinni's place, flooded her mind. She had watched the son of a bitch bash it against the wall, helpless to stop him for fear of it being her head meeting the wall next. When she had enough money, she would take it to be fixed, but there were more important things to save for first. Tears threatened to fall, the memory of her father giving it to her on his deathbed five years ago plaguing her. Cancer was a bitch. But she blinked the tears back. *No use crying over spilt milk*, as her dad would always say. His memory would live within her heart forever.

Needing to move, she began to wander. Lightly touching the sketch taped to the fridge door, she smiled proudly. Her boy had talent – the way he'd shaded the tiger's face brought it to three-dimensional animation. She ached to give him the future he deserved, and finally it was possible thanks to her best friend's idea. It had taken a while to put everything into place, but the miracle she'd been praying for had arrived in more ways than one. She finally had her and her boy's ticket out of this fear-filled existence. The first part of the plan had transpired, now it was time to plot their getaway. If Don found out what she was up to, or caught her trying to escape, she was sure he'd kill her and Dylan, and then kill himself. He'd promised as much many times over. Not a man to face up to his wrongdoings, Don would opt for the coward's way out. So she had to tread very carefully. Watch her every move. Keep her secret buried. Act like nothing was unusual. As hard as this was proving to be, she had no other choice. She just hoped to God Gina and her sister, Marie, could do the same. Nobody could hear of this. Not now. Not ever. That was the deal. They had thought out ways around everything, devised answers to the questions the locals would undoubtedly ask, and they'd come up with a solution to every problem that could arise. Now they all had to stick to the plan.

It was close to midnight when Don finally staggered in. They sat at the dining table in the same chairs they always sat in. Her appetite non-existent, Faith fought every mouthful down, trying not to look nauseous. Instinctively, her hand went beneath the table and to her belly. For the first time in years she felt worthwhile – the life inside of her giving her reason, substance. So much could go wrong. But then so much could go right. Nevertheless, dark thoughts plagued her. Her heavy heart sank deeper. Panic coursed through her. Silently, she tried to calm herself. She had to keep it together. She looked to where his pistol sat, drawn from the holster and beside his dinner plate. It was a pathetic way to make himself feel bigger and somehow better than her. He knew she hated it being there, knew it made her nervous, but he didn't care. After all these years, she'd grown to accept that was just the way it was. Don Stone did what he wanted, when he wanted, how he wanted – end of story. When they'd first met, she'd found his strength and self-assurance attractive. That was until he married her and she discovered that behind closed doors he was a narcissist.

Shoving in a mouthful of food, Don looked her way and smirked. Forcing a smile, she wondered what he was thinking, and prayed to God he didn't want to have sex with her tonight. It was a chore she fulfilled out of fear and obligation, and certainly not because she wanted to. The silence was unnerving and his presence, as always, intimidating. Every tick of the clock above the stove felt like a bomb dropping. She should have thought to put the radio on, but she wasn't going to risk doing that now. No one got up from the table unless he said so. And with the dangerous mood he was in, she knew she was destined for trouble if she disobeyed his rules.

'Did you enjoy yourself at the pistol range today?' She kept her tone soft, careful.

Bloodshot eyes came to meet hers once more, fierce and challenging. 'What's it to you?'

'Sorry.' Focusing back on the dinner that had spoiled while waiting for him to return home, she sighed. He reeked of stale alcohol – nothing unusual there. 'Catch up with many people at the pub?'

'Why you bloody well asking?' He sucked air through his teeth. A habit she loathed.

'I just gathered you had because you're home so late.' The words left her lips before she'd even thought about the way they could be taken.

He drew in a slow, measured breath. 'Are you accusing me of cheating?' His voice was a low growl. There was a familiar glint in his eye. He was up for a fight. Her fight or flight instincts kicked in. Did he know? Was he playing with her?

She fought the urge to run from the room. 'No, of course not, I was just trying to have a conversation with you. You know, show interest in your day. That's all.'

'Are you saying I can't communicate?' His eyes narrowed. His nostrils flared. The red blotches on his cheeks from years of drinking seemed to grow darker.

She quickly shook her head. 'That's not what I meant.'

'Well that's what it sounded like from where I'm sitting.'

'Maybe you're just overtired and overthinking things.' She forced her shaky lips to smile.

'Am I, now? Or are you just being a bitch?'

The sudden urge to throw up for the umpteenth time that day overcame her. *Please, not now.* But the feeling increased. She jumped out of the chair, urgently needing the sanctuary of the toilet. It was an instinctive move that she regretted immediately.

Don's hand latched onto her arm, painfully tight. 'Sit the fuck down.'

'I feel like I'm going to be sick.'

He squeezed even tighter and then let go of her. 'Liar!'

'I'm not lying. I think I've got a stomach bug.' She took wary steps towards the hallway, her hand over her mouth. Unable to hold it back any longer, she grabbed the bin and falling to her knees beside him, hurled up the few mouthfuls of dinner she'd succeeded in getting down.

Don's fist connected with her jaw in an eruption of pain, sending her sprawling to the floor. Lights flashed inside her head like firecrackers. She bit her lip to stop from screaming. She was not going to allow him the satisfaction of hearing her cry out in pain. She was beyond that, the years of abuse hardening her beyond the naïve woman she once was.

Hands smashed down upon the table as his six-foot frame rose, sending cutlery and the gun crashing to the floor. 'You stupid woman!' he roared. 'You made me do that. When are you ever going to learn?'

She watched his gun slide across the tiles. With bated breath she expected him to pick it up, but with his eyes on her he remained oblivious. She breathed a small sigh of relief.

He jabbed her stomach with his steel-cap boot. 'Say sorry, and I might help you up.'

A red-rage stole away her ability to think rationally. 'To hell with you, you horrible man!' she hissed.

'You dare talk back to me, woman?' He rubbed at his beard, the glint in his eye increasing. 'You're going to regret that.'

Her arms instinctively went around her stomach as his boot met with her forearms. Twice. Three times. Four times. She cowered into a ball. He stepped over her and kicked her in the back. He went to kick her again but she grabbed his leg. Overthrowing him, she sent him crashing to the floor, praying to God neither Dylan nor Grace could hear them.

His face now only inches from hers, she watched the blood trickle from his split lip. He sneered, the hatred in his eyes immeasurable. 'You wanna play rough, huh?'

Panic and fear overrode her newly found courage. On her hands and knees, she tried to scramble away from him. He caught her ankle and dragged her back. She struggled but her small build was nothing against his goliath one.

'You know I love it when you play rough. It turns me on every single time.' Grabbing his zipper, he tugged it down, his hand going within. 'I'm hard already just thinking about what I'm going to do with you.'

On her back now, all she could think of was protecting the innocent unborn. She kicked out, her foot connecting with his cheekbone. She'd never struck him before. He barely flinched. His dark gaze raked over her, warning her of what was about to unfold. It unearthed a fear deep within her, more so than she'd ever felt before.

'I'll fucking kill you for that, you bitch!' Fury contorted his face and bloody spittle flew from his lips.

Before she could roll away he launched on top of her. His weight on her stomach, his knees pressed into her chest and arms, making it hard to draw breath. Kicking and bucking beneath him, she tried to fight him off. But it was useless. He had her exactly where he wanted her, and there would be no getting away. Not this time. He wrapped his hands around her throat and, to her horror, began to squeeze the life out of her. Dylan's face flashed before her eyes. If she died tonight, what would become of her beautiful boy? He needed her. She was all he had. She had to live. Her eyes met the gun, less than a few feet away. If she were lucky enough to get to it, could she really pull the trigger? Yes, she could. It was kill or be killed. She tried to pull her arm free as she struggled against the darkness overcoming her. She gasped. Wheezed. Her lungs burnt. She fought as best she could as she begged God to help her.

CHAPTER

2

Stratford-upon-Avon, England, twenty years later

It was a picture-perfect Sunday afternoon in Shakespeare's hometown. Birds were chirping, the sun was putting on a dazzling show, and the temperature was a balmy twenty-five degrees. It was the kind of day friends and families gathered to embrace the arrival of summer along the banks of the beautiful Avon River. Even the swans had returned to bask in the glory of it all. The chance to shrug off the wintery blues so typical of Britain was rarely disregarded.

But that wasn't the case for Sophie Copinni.

No. It. Wasn't.

Today was the day her world had been completely and utterly turned upside down, for the second time in her life. As if once wasn't bloody well enough. She felt like a madwoman as her boyfriend's favourite golf club connected with everything in its path. Her anguished cries filled the room and echoed off the double-glazed windows as if slapping her in the face. The fine crystal whiskey decanter and one of the matching tumblers she'd bought him for Christmas crashed to the floor, smashing among what had been his meticulously organised paperwork. Halting in her tracks, she stared with wild eyes at the framed photo beside his computer. The one she'd put there to try to remind him of the spark they'd felt when they'd first crossed paths in the London subway; the very spark that had led her to believe they were in love, led her to stupidly think moving here with him, a million miles from her home, was a great idea. Led her to believe he was her happily ever after, and they would marry and have a tribe of kids. That was eight long years ago. What a fool she'd been.

Turning away to try to shield herself from any more heartache, she caught her reflection in the mirror hanging above the chaise longue they'd bought in Italy. With mascara smudged all over her cheeks and her usually perfectly styled platinum hair now unruly, she looked as shocking as she felt. And she looked old, way beyond her twenty-nine years. Gone was the smiling, carefree, country-loving young woman she'd once been, and all that was left was a burnt-out shell dressed in clothes she never would have been seen dead in back home. He'd done this to her, with his constant condescending comments and endless demands. The bastard. She'd had so much going for her when she'd met him. She'd just graduated with honours in her Bachelor of Arts degree and had her whole life ahead of her. And now, other than material wealth, she had nothing. No real friends, no potential husband, no children to love, and not one ounce of optimism for her future. Then again, it took two to tango, and she had a mind of her own. She should have known better than to succumb to a man, to believe his promise of one day marrying her, of committing to making a life together.

A threatening letter from a woman she'd stupidly classed as a dear friend had made her run from Australia, and from the arms of her first true love. Vulnerability had allowed her to be swept off her feet by a suave Englishman used to always getting what he wanted. Seething with anger, at him and herself, and with Grace for putting her in this position in the first place, she lifted her weapon of choice and swung it again and again and again.

'Go to hell,' she screamed, as she swiped what was left on his desk to the floor.

Why had she chosen to ignore the elephant in the room? Fool her, believing he was out of town on a business trip, and for an entire week. How convenient that it got him out of attending her cousin's wedding in Australia too. It made her wonder how many times he'd told her he was working when instead he was making love to another woman in some mind-blowingly expensive hotel room while she stayed home and played the happy little housewife. Typical bloody Zachary – crafty and shrewd. He'd certainly pulled the wool over her eyes. A cocktail of anger and hurt, fuelled by adrenaline, coursed through her. She brought the golf club down even harder.

Realisation washed over her, and then the reality of it all hit her like a punch to the chest. He'd clearly had no plans of marrying her. They'd lived together for seven years, and separation now would mean an equal separation of assets, and there were plenty of those. So instead he kept her hoping, longing, pining for the picket-fence dream, stringing her along so he got what he *needed* from her, and all while he went behind her back and got what he *wanted*. She was the perfect woman. She cooked, cleaned, washed, ironed, shopped, massaged his feet when he was tired, held lavish dinner parties for him on a whim, and had learnt to smile at endless gala dinners where the conversations honestly bored her to death. And this was all after she fulfilled her duty as a freelance editor.

Maybe she needed to look at this as Zachary having done her a huge favour, as heartbreaking as it was. She had been feeling extremely homesick and craving for the life she once knew back in Australia. Grace had passed away eight months ago, and as tragic and sad as her death was, it might give Sophie the chance to finally tell her family and Dylan what she knew – if she could summon up the courage. Revealing the two secrets she carried would have massive consequences and hurt the ones she loved dearly, she was sure of it. But the truth needed to be told. She couldn't bear the weight of the secrets any longer. So maybe this *was* the sign she needed to pack her bags and return home permanently. What she'd give to pull on a pair of jeans and boots each day, to ride her horse wild and free across the paddocks of the family farm, or stand among friends and family at a barbeque eating her fill of fresh seafood and snags while talking about anything but the damn weather. The English she mixed with were so consumed by it. She missed the golden shores of the family farm, the saltiness that lingered in the air there, the feeling of the sand between her toes when she wandered around her front yard, the easy-going Australian lifestyle, and most of all the love of her tight-knit family. And she secretly had to admit, she missed *him* too. One hell of a lot.

What was she doing even thinking about him right now?

Sophie tried to shake the thoughts of Dylan Stone away. Breathless, sobbing and with nothing else left to strike, she fought to remain upright in her skyscraper heels. Taking the last slug of whiskey from the tumbler she'd filled to the brim, she screwed her face up and then threw the glass to the floor, taking comfort as it shattered. The liquor hit her empty stomach like a lit match. Nausea engulfed her and she stumbled towards the wastepaper bin, barely making it as her breakfast came back up. Not a big drinker, other than the occasional glass of wine, the alcohol was wreaking havoc on her shock-ridden stomach. Leaning against the wall for support, and with the offending golf stick still in hand, she eyed what was now left of her cheating, no-good boyfriend's home office. She'd always thought the morbidly drab room needed a woman's touch, just maybe not so much a woman scorned. She almost laughed at the absurdity of it.

How had he kept this from her so easily and so callously? Yes, she had her own colossal secrets, ones she'd been aching to tell to those back home. But this, this was different. At twenty-one years young, after taking Grace's threatening letter very seriously, she'd made a heartbreaking decision to run to protect those she loved – Dylan, her mum and dad, her sisters, and even Faith. Zachary, on the other hand, had acted out of self-centredness, and broken her heart into a million little pieces in the process.

Her sister. She needed to talk to Amy. Now. She looked at her watch and did the maths. It was only five-thirty in the morning in Shorefield. She couldn't ring now. Could she? Defeated, and feeling completely alone, she kicked off her high heels, slid down the wall and sat cross-legged. The red haze that had descended upon her three hours ago was dissipating, allowing some of her usual common sense to return. How she'd come from the Berkshire Hotel back to her home was a complete blur. Although, the image of Zachary and his twenty-four-year-old blonde bombshell of a secretary canoodling in the hotel foyer as they'd waited for the lift (to go up!) was now etched in her brain forever, as if scorched there with a branding iron.

One to embrace the notion that everything happens for a reason, she believed fate had brought her right to them. She had never stepped foot in the swanky hotel until today, and the only reason was to use the ladies' toilets – give her a hotel's toilets over the public ones in Birmingham any day. And she'd only driven to Birmingham, which was almost an hour away, by chance – an advertisement for a new European deli had lured her there in search of her childhood favourites, *imqaret* (date filled pastries) and *ghadam tal-mejtin* (almond cookies). Her father being Maltese and her mum having embraced his traditions, Sophie had grown up with a healthy appreciation of good food – not that her size ten figure spoke anything of that. Her fast metabolism was a godsend. At least she had that going for her, she thought with a heavy sigh.

Glancing down at her white blouse now pulled free of her linen skirt, she grimaced at the fresh stain of whiskey. What a state she'd got herself into. In hindsight, she wished she'd walked right up to Zachary and slapped him in the face, told him just what she thought of him, and then given his scantily clad mistress what-for too. But, in a frenzied panic, she'd run for her life – just as she had nearly nine years ago. History damn well repeated. She needed to learn to stop running. Thank God they hadn't seen her leaving like a dog with its tail between its legs because underneath her fragility she knew she was stronger than that. Much stronger. A Copinni never gave up, or gave in. But that part of her had long gone – somehow left on the shores of Australia when she'd received that damn letter and moved here. She needed to find herself again and stand strong.

Now that she was thinking more clearly, she knew she couldn't lay total blame on Zachary for the breakdown of their relationship. It wasn't entirely his fault she'd lost her way. She was a big girl and had made her choices. It was time she took control. Being so far from her loved ones and her home had taken a toll on her happiness, and she'd become dependent on him in a way she was not proud of, nor pleased with. And beneath it all, she would always secretly love another man – a man she couldn't be with at the time because she needed to protect him. But that didn't give Zachary an excuse to cheat on her. Oh. No. It. Didn't.

Tears fell and she dropped her face into her hands. A yearning to be with the only people in her life who truly loved her unconditionally overcame her. How were they going to react when they found out her life had fallen apart, especially when theirs were so perfect? She sobbed harder. She felt like a failure – hollow, vulnerable, and so very stupid. The lure of adventure, an escape from the secrets she hid deep down in her soul, along with what was now a myriad of broken promises by Zachary, had led her here, into this lifestyle that was nothing like her. She retrieved her mobile phone from where she'd thrown it against the wall and quickly dialled Amy's number.

It took four rings. 'Hello.' Amy's voice was heavy with sleep.

'Sorry to wake you, sis, but …' That was all Sophie could get out before she wept uncontrollably.

'Oh my God, Sophie, is everything okay?' All traces of sleepiness had vanished from Amy's tender voice.

'No, not really,' she choked out.

'What's happened?'

'It's Zach …'

'Oh no, has he been in an accident?'

'No, nothing like that.' Sophie drew in a shuddering breath. 'Everyone is alive and well.'

'Thank God.'

'I miss you, Amy.' It was a little slurred.

'I miss you too, sis. Are you drunk?'

Even though Amy couldn't see her, Sophie nodded. 'A little …'

'That's not like you … What's happened?'

'Zachary is having an affair.' Sophie hated hearing the words roll off her tongue because it made it all the more real.

'Oh, Sophie, I'm so sorry. The bastard.' The phone line muffled and Amy mumbled something.

Sophie could picture her younger sister, her jaw clenched and her dark eyes fierce as she reiterated what had just been said to her husband.

'Sorry, Soph, Kurt was in my ear.'

'Eavesdropper,' Sophie said lightheartedly. It felt good to have a little joke amidst the commotion.

'Ha-ha, yup, suppose we can't really blame him, though, seeing as he's lying beside me.'

'Yeah, true that.' Sophie sniffled. 'Say hi to him for me.'

Amy did as asked. 'Kurt says hi, and bye. He's getting up and at 'em.'

'But it's only just gone six o'clock there, hasn't it? I thought he didn't start work at the hardware shop until nine.'

'He's been hitting the gym before work, trying to lose the extra kilos he doesn't need. Mind you, he's still stuffing his face with ice-cream every night and because he's drinking light beer he thinks he can drink twice as many of them.' Amy huffed. 'Men, the weird bloody creatures they are.'

'You got that right, Amy.'

'Does Zach need reminding of how much you gave up to be with him?'

'Probably, but I don't really need to be reminded of the fact right now.'

'I'm sorry, Soph. It just makes my blood boil. If he was standing in front of me I'd punch him in the balls.'

Kurt laughed in the background, and for the first time that day Sophie let go and laughed too. 'You would, wouldn't you, Ames?'

'My bloody oath I would. I'd even consider ripping them off and shoving them down his throat, but then that's no way to act like a lady.'

'Oh yeah, because that's what you are, hey, a *lady*.' It was said with a smile.

'Oi, I've got feelings, you know.' Amy chuckled. 'All jokes aside, though, Soph, how did you find out he was doing the dirty on you?'

'Long story short, I caught him red-handed, but I'll fill you in on all the sordid details when I get there. I don't really feel up to going over it all again right now.'

'Okay, I understand. Can I ask who with, though?'

'His secretary.'

Amy whistled through her teeth. 'Go fucking figure. How did he react when you caught him?'

'He doesn't know I have yet.'

'But I thought you said you caught him red-handed?'

'I did.' Sophie grimaced as she remembered running out the hotel's doors, and the wave of shame engulfed her once again.

'Right, well, okay. I don't really understand how it all went down but yes, you can explain it when you get here. Did you suspect anything was going on?'

'If I'm being perfectly honest, then in a way, yes … He's been going away more and more for work lately, and he doesn't touch me as much as he used to. I'm lucky to get a kiss goodbye in the mornings.'

'Did you try talking to him about all this?'

'Not really.'

'Why the hell not?'

'Because I was worried I was imagining things, and with everything feeling like it's on eggshells here lately I didn't want to make it any worse.'

'Oh, Soph, I didn't know you guys were having such a hard time. From the way you were talking everything sounded hunky-dory.'

'I didn't want to worry you guys back home.'

'Don't be stupid. It's our job to be here for you. You should have talked to me or Tania. That's what sisters are meant to do, to be there for one another. We're blood, Soph, always have been and always will be. Nothing will ever change that.'

Amy spoke with gusto and so much love that the need to reveal her deep dark secret overcame Sophie, but as she had for years, she pushed it back down. It was something she could only say to her face to face. 'How is Tania?'

'Yeah, she's good.'

'Has she found another job yet?'

'Yeah, she has.'

'Are you going to tell me what it is?'

'She's teaching pole-dancing classes at the local gym.'

Sophie bit back a chuckle. 'At least her few months as a stripper have come in handy. How does Dad feel about it?'

'I'm not sure she's going to tell him the whole truth.'

'What *has* she told him then?'

'That she's a fitness instructor at the gym.'

'Fair enough. A little bit of a white lie never hurt anyone, I suppose. Her secret is safe with me.'

'Good, and don't tell her I told you either. Wait until she tells you herself before you say anything about it.'

'Will do. I've tried ringing her a couple of times the past few weeks and left a few messages on her voicemail, but she's shocking at returning calls. She's sent me a couple of short texts, basically telling me she's still alive and kicking and making sure I am too, and that's about it.'

'Yeah, she is a bit of a slacko at keeping in touch, but that's Tania. If I didn't see myself every time I looked at her, I wouldn't even know she and I were twins half the time. Don't take it personally; you know how much she hates talking on the phone.' She sighed. 'And I'm just as bad when it comes to keeping in touch. With both of our lives so damn busy I barely see her, and she only lives half an hour's drive from me. I really should make more of an effort.'

'Don't be too hard on yourself, Ames. Life gets away from all of us.'

'Yes, I know. At least she seems really happy when I do see her. She made mention of a new love interest a few months back, but so far I'm yet to meet him. I'm actually starting to wonder if she's deliberately keeping him away from me and the family.'

Sophie chuckled. 'Can you blame her, with us crazy lot?'

'Ha-ha, good point.' Amy drew a noisy breath and then sighed it away. 'But, anyway, as slack as she is, Tania loves you to bits … never forget that. And I know she will want to be there for you when she hears what Zachary has done.'

'Well, in three days from now you can both be there for me, but I don't really want everyone else knowing for now, okay?'

'Why not, Soph?'

'Because I feel like a failure.'

'You're not a failure because your boyfriend cheated on you.'

'If you say so.'

'I do say so.'

'I can't even get falling pregnant right, Ames.'

'Who said it's your fault you can't fall pregnant? Maybe it's Zachary's bits and bobs that aren't working properly.'

'Yeah, maybe … he won't go to the doctor to find out, though.'

'Of course he won't, just in case he's told he has a glitch in his system. Please stop beating yourself up, Soph. It's not warranted and it'll only make you more upset.'

'I'll try, but I ain't promising anything.' Sophie sighed, suddenly feeling completely exhausted.

'I can't wait to have you back where you belong so I can give you a hug. We all miss you like crazy.'

'Ditto, Ames, and with all of this going down, I'm thinking I might make it a permanent trip this time round.'

'Oh my God, yay.' Amy almost jumped through the phone. 'Please don't say you're pulling my leg, Soph. I'd do anything to have you living back here, as would Mum and Dad and Tania.'

'Nah, I'm being serious. There's nothing here for me now Zachary and I are over, and I can basically do my work wherever I am.'

'I'm sorry you've gone through what you have to get to this point, but I can't lie, I'm over the moon you're coming home for good, Soph. Can you believe it's been almost two years since you've been back here?'

'I know, Ames, I'm so sorry. Life just got away from me.'

'Don't apologise, Sophie. We all get busy. We'll make up for lost time when you get here, okay?'

'We sure will. I'm looking forward to it.'

'Daniela's hens' night is going to be loads of fun, so don't forget to bring your dancing shoes. We'll get happy drunk like the good old times and sing our hearts out to "Khe Sanh".'

'I can't drink like I used to and there is no way I'm getting up on stage for a karaoke session.' Sophie chuckled. 'I sound like I'm choking a chicken when I sing.'

'There's no way you're *not* getting up and singing karaoke.'

'You'll have to drag me kicking and screaming.'

'Oh, trust me, I will do just that if I have to.' The two women laughed and then Amy sighed softly. 'What happened to my crazy big sis? You've gone all staid and proper over there.'

'I have not.'

'Have too,' Amy teased.

'Well, I promise I'll try to shake it off.' Amy was right. She'd lost her fire and sparkle. 'So what are the blokes doing for the bucks' night?'

'They're going to the other pub for some pool competition and then maybe meeting up with us all at the end of the night.'

Sophie's heart stalled. 'Oh, right. I thought the hens' night was meant to be just that … for the girls.'

'You can't avoid him forever, Soph. You're going to have to face him sooner or later seeing as he's a groomsman and you're a bridesmaid at Daniela's wedding.'

'I know, I know. I just still feel so guilty, leaving him the way I did. The last time I saw him, at your wedding, he barely spoke two words to me.' She sucked in a shuddering breath. 'It was as if he hated me, and to be honest I couldn't blame him if he did. I hate myself for hurting him so badly.'

'The wedding was five years ago, Soph, and he was still hung up on you back then. A lot of life has gone on since then, for all of us. I think I'd be safe in saying that after … how long is it? Nearly nine years, he'd be well and truly over it all, don't you think?'

'Maybe, but I broke his heart, Amy.'

'Yes, you did hurt him but that's life. I'm sure you had your reasons for what you did, even though every time I've asked what they were you've only given me half-hearted answers, like you've got some secret or something.'

If only you knew, Sophie wanted to say. 'Yes, I did have my reasons.' She pressed her lips together to not say any more. Her mind went to the letter she'd hidden away in her bedroom back home in Queensland, and as much as it still enraged her, she also felt so terribly sad as she thought about Grace dying from a drug overdose. A wild child when they were growing up, Grace had obviously fallen in with the wrong crowd in Kings Cross. Poor Dylan and his family had to deal with the tragedy. Life could be so cruel.

There was a pause and a heavy breath before Amy continued. 'Can I ask what those reasons *really* were now we're on the subject?'

'I've already told you …' Sophie's tone was defensive but she couldn't help it. It was a very touchy subject. 'I wanted to spread my wings and travel. Simple as that.'

'Oh, come on, Sophie. You loved him with every inch of you. I don't believe you gave him up because you had itchy feet, because I have no shadow of a doubt that if you'd asked him to join you, he would have. That man would have gone to the ends of the earth for you and then some.'

Sophie's heart squeezed tight. 'Please, I really don't want to talk about it.'

'Why won't you ever tell me, Soph? I'm your sister, I'm not going to judge you, no matter what it is or what you may have done.'

'Please, Amy, just drop it.' With her emotions raging, Sophie was struggling to breathe.

There was a weighty sigh followed by an extended silence. 'Okay, all right, I'm sorry. I'll drop it. Regardless of why you did it, things don't always turn out peachy perfect, and I'm sure Dylan has come to understand that. It's high time you both moved on, really.'

'Yes, we do need to move past it. And I hope you're right, Ames. I was such a bitch, leaving him the way I did.'

'For goodness sake, stop being so hard on yourself, Sophie. Sadly, your lives just took different paths. It happens. If you'd come back here after a year, like you'd planned, maybe you and Dylan might have worked things out, but you'll never know that now. It's not your fault you met an arsehole along your travels that promised you the world and then didn't deliver.'

'Please don't do the whole "I told you so" right now, Ames. I know you've never really liked Zach.'

'Righto, I'll zip it and save that speech for later, when you're feeling better.'

'Oh, please don't.'

Amy chuckled. 'I'm only kidding. I love you, my big, beautiful, at times bossy, sister.'

'Ha-ha, love you too, Ames.'

'Look, time heals, Soph. Dylan's a good man and not the kind of bloke to hold a grudge for too long. So you need to suck it up and try to make peace with him … at the very least I'm sure you could both be friends again, if you tried. Daniela will want her wedding day to be relaxed and calm, with no usual Copinni family quarrels. *Capisci?*'

Sophie grinned. 'Daniela might be wanting the impossible … you know what our mob can be like when all put under one roof.'

'Yeah, true. And just for the record, before I forget to mention it, Dylan is currently single.'

A thunderbolt struck Sophie in the stomach. 'He is? Seriously?' Memories of Dylan as a fine-looking young man with that mischievous grin flashed through her mind.

'Yes, seriously.'

What was she doing even harbouring the thought? Reality crumbled on top of Sophie like a tonne of bricks. 'Don't start playing cupid, Ames.'

'Who said anything about playing cupid?'

'Uh-huh.' Sophie shook her head. 'Anyway, I have bigger things to worry about than running into Dylan. Like the fact my whole life has turned to shit and I'm going to need a damn good lawyer to get what I deserve out of Zachary.'

'Daniela is apparently cutthroat in the courtroom. Maybe you should talk to her about it.'

'Yeah, maybe I should, but I'll let her get over the stress and hype of the wedding first.'

'Yeah, good idea … it's not going to be easy, Soph, and it's going to take time to sort everything out, but I hope Zachary plays fair.'

'I doubt it but miracles do happen.' Sophie groaned. 'Oh my God, there's just so much to think about.' She rubbed at the sharp ache behind her eyes. 'And I really don't want to think about it all right now.' Tears slid down her cheeks. 'It's just all too much.'

'Oh, sis, don't cry. I'm sorry I can't just come over and give you a damn good hug.'

'I know, I'm sorry you can't too.' Pushing scattered paperwork out of the way, Sophie plucked a tissue from the upturned box. 'By the way, I've smashed his office to smithereens.'

'You've what?'

'I got his golf club and smashed everything. I lost it, Ames.'

'Oh go you good thing! You've got to get the anger and frustration out somehow, so what better way than to do just that.'

'Lucky his beloved Audi wasn't parked outside or I'd probably have gone to town on that too.' She grimaced. 'Then I would have been in really deep shit.'

'You could still hunt it down,' Amy said lightheartedly.

'Oh, stop it. You're a bad influence.'

Amy chuckled. 'Someone has to be.'

Silence hung between them as Sophie blew her nose.

'I know you're going through hell right now and there's a lot to sort out, but it will do you good to get your butt home. You can clear your head in some clean Aussie country air.'

'That it will, Ames. Can you do me a favour and not tell Mum and Dad it's a more permanent move? I want to do it when I get there.'

'Sure. Of course.'

'Thanks. And have you made sure not to let slip I'm arriving a day earlier so we can surprise them?'

'Yup, mission accomplished.'

Sobered from the conversation, Sophie stood on more grounded legs. 'I better let you go get ready for work.'

'Yeah, I better go. The hospital is short staffed so I don't want to be late. I'll give you a call tonight, Soph.'

'Thanks, Ames, talk then … Love you.'

'Love you too.'

Ending the call, Sophie felt a wave of renewed strength. Amy always had a way of making her feel like she could conquer anything. She took a deep breath, tipped her chin up and straightened her shoulders. She could do this. She just had to. She and Zachary had been unhappy for a very long time. They'd been holding on to something that had gone way past its use-by date. It was time to let it go. Fate had shown her the way; now she just had to trust it, wherever it was going to lead her. Her mind went to the letter that had sent her running from everything and everyone she'd ever known. She didn't need to read it again – after doing so countless times she knew it word for damning word.

CHAPTER
3

Kings Cross, Sydney

Dylan Stone felt as if he could slice through the tension in the room with a knife. His boss looked nervous as hell. Something wasn't right. Actually, something was very, *very* wrong. He could feel it in his bones and his instincts were telling him to get out before the shit hit the fan. But, not wanting to dramatise the situation, he was doing his best to try to convince himself otherwise. There was no proof of anything untoward going on. So what did he have to worry about? Maybe he was making a mountain out of a molehill. Maybe his reservations about heading back to Shorefield tomorrow and seeing her for the first time in five years was clouding his judgement, throwing off his usually spot-on instincts. Damn his overactive mind for giving him every possible scenario of his homecoming while he'd fought sleeplessness last night. He'd been lucky to get a solid two hours' rest, and his weariness wasn't helping him think rationally now. Rolling his head from side to side, he clutched the back of his neck. This was going to be one long-arse day. Lucky he had four weeks' holiday up his sleeve … he was going to enjoy every last second of it.

Turning his attention back to the job at hand, he tried to focus. All the legalities were done. He'd checked her ID to make sure she was of age, and had her sign the indemnity forms. Now it was time for the action to take place. With the meticulous preparation second nature to him, Dylan went through the motions as if on autopilot. After six years at the job the familiarity was a small reprieve from what was going on in his head. But frustration with not being able to put his finger on what was bothering him amplified as the minutes ticked by. Like his Aunt Kimmy had said over breakfast this morning, a holiday up north was going to do him the world of good. He felt guilty about leaving her, though, with his uncle, Kimmy's husband, recently back fighting a never-ending war as an army general, and with Grace having passed away only eight months ago. But he desperately needed a break from the craziness that was the big smoke, and his best mate's wedding was the perfect excuse to escape from it. It was going to be great to spend some quality time with his mum during her holidays, back where life was slower and a country mile separated him from his neighbours. He couldn't wait to shrug off the urban lifestyle he'd never grown accustomed to. He would gallop his stockhorse, Gunner, across the paddocks of Stone's Throw, and his wide-brimmed hat was finally going to get some good use. Sydney was not really a place to wear it.

Her shirt off and positioned on the bed at an angle to allow him easy access, the young woman tucked her jet-black hair behind her ears, revealing a row of piercings, and smiled nervously. 'It's going to hurt like a bitch, isn't it?'

Eyeing her three facial piercings – lip, brow and cheek – Dylan smiled. 'Put it this way, it's not going to tickle, but I'm guessing you're a tough nut so I reckon you'll be right.'

She followed his gaze. 'Oh, these things …' She pointed to her face. 'Done when I was under the influence. So trust me when I say, looks can be deceiving.' She laughed like it was cool to be wasted.

Dylan hoped she was referring to alcohol. After losing his cousin Grace to an accidental drug overdose, and seeing the devastation her death left behind for his poor aunt and uncle, as well as his own heartbreak, he hated drugs and the bastards who sold them. 'You're not under the influence now, are you?' His tone was probably a little sterner than it should have been.

'Nope. Straight as a die.' She looked as though one of her parents had just busted her with a stash.

Dylan remained serious, taking a few moments to come to his own conclusion. As far as he could tell, she looked totally with it. 'Good, otherwise I wouldn't be touching you. A person can't make smart decisions when they're not thinking rationally, and what you're about to do is for life.'

'Fair point, I suppose.' She wiped her palms on the towel beneath her. 'I'm so nervous I swear it feels like my heart is going to leap out of my chest.'

'Like I said, you'll be right.' Having seen the fear of a first timer so often, Dylan did his best to comfort her. 'But don't worry, if it's hurting too much I'll stop and give you a breather, okay? There's no need to act tough with me.' He made sure his tone was calm.

She nodded and then started texting on her mobile phone.

He looked down at her hands. 'Probably not a good idea.'

'Why not?'

'It'll make you wriggle around too much.'

She sighed and placed the phone down beside her. 'Four hours without my phone is going to be hell.'

'I'm sure you'll survive.' Dylan groaned inwardly. What was with people's attachment to the blasted things? He owned a mobile phone under protest – it was the way of this busy world. Most of the time he had it on silent. Too many people spent their lives staring down at their screens instead of taking in the world around them, or communicating with the person sitting opposite them. It gave him a feeling of remaining anonymous in a technology-obsessed world – Facebook, Twitter and Instagram held not one bit of interest for him. Pulling on the latex gloves, he pointed at the muted television anchored to the ceiling. 'Watch that instead, it'll help take your mind off it.'

'But I can't hear it.'

'Doesn't matter.' He shrugged. 'The distraction of the picture helps, trust me.'

'Oh, right. Thanks for the tip.'

He positioned himself so his back didn't start to ache too soon. With what she was hoping for, he was going to be at it for a good part of the afternoon. 'Ready?'

'Ready as I'll ever be,' she said softly, her eyes already glued to the screen.

The needle bar assembled and his little pots of ink lined up, Dylan pressed the foot pedal. He hoped the hum of the machine would send him to the place he always went while tattooing – a place where everything else faded away while he got to live out his passion for sketching. It was his way of meditating. But today, it wasn't to be.

While he started on the outline of a black rose, his mind wandered and took him back to the day he'd stood at the crossroads of his life. After telling him she didn't want to be with him anymore, that she wanted to be free and single to travel the world, Sophie Copinni wiped her hands of him, just like that, as if their love had meant nothing. She'd shattered his heart into a million pieces – some of the fragments he was yet to put back together, even after all these years. Driving home from her house, his old banger of a car had broken down, black smoke billowing from under the rusty bonnet. He'd exploded from the driver's seat, kicked at the gravel, punched the nearest tree – he still had a scar on his knuckles to prove it – and had told the world to go and get fucked as loudly as he could. Then, totally defeated, he'd fallen to his knees and for the very first time in his life he'd cried his heart out.

It was a day he preferred to forget.

Six days after Sophie Copinni had broken his world, he'd made the decision to pack his bags and go live with his Aunt Kimmy, Uncle Gary and Grace in Sydney. Now, nearly nine years later, he was itching to return to his roots up north, to make a life back in Shorefield, but he was battling with the fact he'd have to leave his aunt on her own to do it. He was sure she'd be supportive if she knew what he wanted to do, but he still felt obligated to be there for her. Kimmy was on the road to recovery, if there was such a thing after losing a child she'd always seen as her own, but she still had a way to go.

And then, without warning, his mind swerved back to the day Grace had first tried to kiss him. It had thrown him for a six. After only spending a few school holidays together and with their contact having waned as they'd become adults with responsibilities, one day, out of the blue, Grace had come to visit. He was twenty-one and she was twenty-five. They'd been sitting by the dam; both of them shrivelled up like a pair of prunes after swimming for hours, when she'd looked at him like a cousin never should – even though they were related only through marriage. Grace was Gary's baby daughter before he'd met and married Kimmy. Nevertheless, in Dylan's eyes she was still family. Before he could stop her, she leant in and pressed her mouth against his. Shocked, he'd recoiled from her, wiping his lips. Not only were they family – he looked on her like the sister he'd never had – he was also in love with Sophie. He'd quickly tried to explain how wrong it was, in both senses.

Shamefaced, Grace had burst into tears, saying how sorry she was, and then blamed it on the couple of bottles of beer she'd drunk. Feeling awful, he'd tried to hug her, but she shoved him away, and then ran all the way back to the cottage. The next day she'd acted like it had never happened, and so he went with the flow, grateful she didn't make a big deal of it. There had been a couple of moments since then, when Grace had looked at him in the very same way, and where her lips had lingered on his cheek that bit too long when they'd shared a hug. But he'd tried to brush it off, to pretend he was ignorant to her advances. He'd cared for her as a cousin, and hadn't wanted to hurt her like he had back at the dam. His heart ached with the memories. If only she hadn't fallen in with the wrong crowd. He missed her so much.

The young woman squirmed as the needle moved over one of her ribs, and Dylan's mind shot back to the present. 'You doing okay there?'

'Yeah, sorry ... I'll try and keep still.'

'No worries, hey. The ribs are the worst part. You want a rest?'

'No. But thanks. I'd rather you kept going so we can get it over with.' It was said through gritted teeth.

He tried to catch her eyes but she squeezed them shut. 'Righto, but don't be afraid to stop me if you need to.'

'Yup, will do.'

Dylan made himself stay in the moment by heightening his senses. The strong scent of antiseptic lingered. Metallica's 'Nothing Else Matters' boomed from the speakers. It was early afternoon and every seat in the Kings Cross tattoo parlour was taken. Only the best artists worked here, and people travelled from all around New South Wales to come and have their skin adorned with ink. Dylan was grateful for the chance he'd been given and he didn't take his role as shop manager lightly. Most people feared his boss, Angus McDonald, who at six foot five, tattooed from head to toe and with more piercings than a pincushion, did not look like a man you'd want to meet in a dark alley. But Dylan knew that he had a heart somewhere beneath his armour. He'd had a glimpse of it once, and that was more than most ever got. Recalling the night he'd crossed paths with the brawny Scotsman, he smiled. Across a seedy bar at one of the Kings Cross strip joints, Angus had offered him a legitimate way out of his shitty job as a barman in an establishment he hated. Now a couple of years out of his tattoo apprenticeship, Dylan knew he had a lot to be thankful for.

As if reading his thoughts, Angus gave him a tight-lipped smile from where he sat at the front desk. Dylan returned the gesture, at the same time wondering why Angus was here. With another tattoo parlour in the city that Angus managed, it was rare to see him in at the Cross. Dylan hoped it had nothing to do with his management of the shop – he went above and beyond to make sure it was a smooth sailing ship.

The front door swung open. Two burly blokes dressed in black suits walked in. They looked out of place. Angus stood and shook their hands. With a few words quietly spoken, he invited them behind the desk and then led them past Dylan. With dark sunglasses, solemn faces and don't-fuck-with-me personas, they reeked of wrongdoings. Dylan couldn't help but stop for a second and stare at them. Angus met his eye as he passed, the warning to look away brazen. Dylan sucked in an irritated breath. As much as this was Angus's establishment, Dylan saw it as his turf to protect. He didn't like things going on that he wasn't privy to.

The door of the back office clicked shut. Trying to remain focused on the job at hand, Dylan's jaw clenched. Something seedy was going on and his instincts told him it was something he didn't want to be a part of. But how could he not be when it was happening in the shop he managed? And what was he meant to do, storm in there and tell them all to bugger off? Not if he wanted to keep his job. It had to be a dodgy deal and most likely drugs. Grace's face flashed before his eyes and hot rage shot through him. The drug trade was a multimillion dollar business, and with the company Angus was clearly keeping, Dylan wondered if maybe the man he admired was just like the rest of them. His mind flashed back to the news report he'd watched only last night, the journalist speaking of how a homeless twelve-year-old girl had died after overdosing on ice. It sickened him to think someone had sold it to her to make a buck. He hated drug dealers; they were morally culpable murderers, the scum of the earth. It was a godsend he was heading off tomorrow. Hopefully when he returned, this, whatever this was, would all be over with.

'How's it looking?' The young woman's voice pulled him from his thoughts.

'I've only done the outline of the roses so far. You want me to grab a mirror so you can have a look?'

'Nope, after what I've heard about your work, I trust you.' She smiled. 'I want to look at it once it's all done.'

'Sounds like a plan.' Dylan couldn't help but take satisfaction in her words as he got back to it. He prided himself on his reputation as a highly sought-out tattoo artist.

'Dylan, you got a minute, mate.' Angus's deep Scottish lilt came from behind him.

The three other tattoo artists glanced up before thinking better of it and focusing back on their clients. As he took his foot off the pedal, the tattoo gun quietened. Annoyed with the unusual interruption, Dylan did his best to hide his irritation. 'Not really, Angus. Can it wait until I'm finished here?'

'Sorry, but no, it can't.' It was sharp and to the point. Angus loomed at his side, his eyes boring a hole into Dylan's. He placed a hand on the young woman's leg. 'Sorry to interrupt, but this will only take a minute.' He smiled, but it was forced. 'Be a good excuse for a breather.'

'Okay.' The woman nodded then grabbed her mobile phone as if her life depended on it.

'Sorry about this, back in a sec.'

'No worries.' She didn't even look at him, her attention in phone land.

Standing, Dylan yanked off his gloves and tossed them into the bin, the entire time his gaze never leaving Angus's. He really didn't want to see what was going on in the office. Because if his instincts were right, not only was it against everything he believed in, it would alter his perception of Angus forever and make him question his job here. He just wanted to get his work done and get the hell out of here for a few weeks. Was that too much to bloody well ask?

Angus gestured for him to hurry up. The two men moved out of earshot, behind a cane wall divider, the heavy metal blaring from the speakers drowning out their lowered voices. 'What's so bloody urgent?' Dylan grumbled.

'I just need you to witness something. It'll only take a second.' Angus turned to walk off.

Dylan placed a hand on his shoulder, making him spin back around. Angus swiped his shoulder as though there was dirt on it. He didn't look happy. 'What the fuck?'

'I really don't want to get involved in your private business dealings.'

'Bit too late for that.' Angus's voice was serious. 'You work here.'

Folding his arms, Dylan held his ground. 'Yeah, tattooing.'

Angus cracked his knuckles. 'And as my manager, anything else I might need you to do while you're under this roof. Or would you prefer me to fire your sorry arse?'

Dylan's jaw clenched. 'Are you threatening me?'

'Nothing of the sort.' Angus's demeanour softened and he offered a grim smile. He leant in, dropping his voice. 'Look, sorry, mate, but I have nobody else in here I trust and this has to be done now or I'm going to lose out, big time. With what the courts have awarded the fucking ex, I need this.' Desperation laced his every word. 'Please, Dylan, I could lose everything if I don't do something drastic. You just need to stand back and witness the exchange. That's it.' He held his hands up and shrugged. 'There ain't nothing illegal with that now, is there?'

'Yeah, there is. I'll be an accessory to whatever you're doing.'

'Oh, come on, lighten up. People do this all the time. Your name won't even be mentioned if I get busted, which I won't. I'm too clever for that.'

'Don't get so cocky, mate. People get busted for doing illegal shit all the time.' Dylan shook his head, the respect he'd held for Angus now feeling as if it were all based on a facade. 'Is it drugs, Angus?'

'Yeah, but what's it to you?'

'Drug dealers are the scum of the earth, and you don't want to be classed as one of them. Isn't there some other way?'

Angus's eyes flashed with fury. 'If there was, I'd do it, trust me. But there ain't. I have two weeks to come up with two hundred grand, or I'll have to sell everything to pay the bitch out. And I've worked too damn hard for everything to go to shit.'

Dylan's hackles rose and not only because a drug deal was taking place right here, right now. Angus's ex-wife had been a tattoo artist here in the Kings Cross shop when he'd first started, and she'd always been kind to him. She was a good woman. But angry, after finding out her husband had been cheating on her for years. She'd worked hard for all they had too, so what did Angus expect? 'Oh come on, Angus. That woman you're referring to is the mother of your three kids.'

Angus puffed his chest out, his nostrils flaring. 'Now's not the time to be raising your moral issues with me, Dylan. I don't need this shit. I've got enough to fucking deal with.'

Not comfortable with how close Angus was standing, Dylan took a step back. 'Sorry, but there's always another way so count me out of it, I don't want to get involved.'

Angus grabbed Dylan's collar and pulled him chest to chest, his voice now more of a snarl. 'You owe me this much after all

I've done for you, so don't disappoint me. I know what's near and dear to you.' It was said extremely quietly, but with chilling conviction.

'What's that supposed to mean?'

Angus tapped his temple. 'Your secret is safe with me, as it always has been, but only if you do this one little thing. Otherwise, I might just have a slip of the tongue, and you wouldn't want that, would you? Just imagine what might happen to your mum, and you, if the truth got out. And besides all of that, if you want your job here, you better do as I tell you or you can kiss it goodbye.'

'You bastard.' Shoving Angus away, Dylan stepped back, his eyes narrowing. 'I thought you were better than this, fucking fool me.'

With his fists clenched at his sides, Angus matched Dylan's hostile stance. 'Office. Now.' He turned on his heel and headed towards the closed door before Dylan had time to respond. 'Do as you're told and get your arse back here … or there'll be consequences.'

Dylan hesitated. This felt wrong in so many ways, but not only that – the thought of having a drug conviction terrified him. It would ruin his dream of owning his own tattoo shop one day; a prerequisite for a tattoo licence was to not have any hard drug convictions for ten years. He really didn't want to do this, but he wasn't taking Angus's threat lightly. Nobody could know the truth of what happened the night his father died. He had to protect those he loved. Why the hell he'd thought Angus could be trusted with such sensitive information was beyond him now.

Standing at the door, Angus glared at him. So many things passed between them without a word uttered. Dylan was about to turn his back to the man but then thought better of it. If it were anyone else grabbing him by the collar and making threats, he would have taught them a damn good lesson. Tomorrow he'd be riding out of here and that thought gave him some kind of comfort. Maybe he needed to consider it being more of a permanent thing. He didn't like this one little bit. But with Angus knowing about the skeletons hiding in his closet, leaving on bad terms just wasn't an option.

CHAPTER

4

Cairns, North Queensland

Twenty-nine hours after she'd dragged her weary, sorry self to Heathrow Airport Sophie had finally reached Aussie soil – and felt she'd found a new lease on life. Very soon she would be back among those who truly loved her and the countryside that owned her heart. Now the real healing could begin. She tried to imagine what Zachary would do when he came home to find her personal belongings gone, her letter explaining why, and his office destroyed. It wasn't going to be pretty, she knew that much. But he'd made his bed, now the bastard had to sleep in it. She was done, dusted. There'd be no talking her around, either. She wasn't a woman who'd forgive a man who cheated. Ever. Although downtrodden, she had more self-respect than that – and she knew that a leopard never changed his spots.

Stretching out in her business-class seat, she looked out the cabin window as the plane descended. Home, sweet home. Her heart swelled with the thought. The world below was golden and bright, stunningly so. Pristine blue water and brilliant white sand met wide squares of deep green sugarcane, which made the landscape appear as if it were a patchwork quilt. Gone were the grey stone buildings and cobble streets she'd grown accustomed to, and although pretty in their own right, she couldn't be happier about it.

As soon as the plane came to a stop at the terminal, seatbelts clicked and butts rose from seats before the seatbelt light had even been switched off. There were stern looks from the flight attendants but nobody cared. As if their lives depended on it, overhead baggage was quickly claimed and people filled the aisles in their eagerness to get out after flying for more than thirteen hours. Sophie took her time; rushing was not going to help her disembark quickly considering the number of passengers in front of her. The cabin door was swung open, and even though it was officially winter in Cairns, the humidity hit her like a hot towel. And it felt damn good.

So ecstatic to be back on Aussie soil, Sophie almost kissed the tarmac when she stepped down from the Boeing 747. Unlike the previous times she'd flown home from England, once for Amy's wedding and twice for Christmas, when she'd suffered with jetlag for days, she felt like a million bucks. Although ludicrously expensive, the business-class ticket had been well worth it. The poached lobster tail in saffron reduction was to die for, the service had been impeccable, and the cocktails had been delish. It had been an experience beyond her wildest dreams, and one that had left her feeling a little more empowered than she was two days ago. Usually one to fly economy, she'd splashed out and upgraded at the airport. It was her little way of making the bastard pay, literally, after what he'd done. He had tried to call her a few times over the past couple of days, but she'd let him go to message bank. Until he returned to their apartment on his own, without his secretary, she didn't want to talk to him.

Trying to rid her thoughts of Zachary so she didn't burst into tears the minute she saw her family, she focused on imagining her parents' faces when she arrived home. She couldn't wait to wrap her arms around each of them. Phone calls, Skype and Facebook could only cover so much. Butterflies fluttered in her belly as she stepped into the arrivals hall. Straining her eyes, she tried to spot Amy, Tania and her aunt, Gina. Immediately she saw the bright red hair and equally bright orange outfit gleaming like gemstones amidst the crowd of people. Unlike her mother, Aunt Gina was never one to shy away from standing out. Beside her, Amy, who much like Sophie herself was dressed in jeans and a simple t-shirt, had her phone pressed up against her ear. She was looking stunning as always. Tania was nowhere to be seen.

With a sudden desperate need to be held by someone who loved her, Sophie picked up the pace until she was running towards them. The lump in her throat was growing by the second and she was struggling to hold back the tears. Almost within reach, Gina blinked owlishly through her glasses, then threw her arms out, pulling Sophie into a tight embrace. It was a gesture Sophie had gained so much comfort from over the years, and Gina's citrus-scented perfume was wonderfully familiar. Amy squealed then wrapped her arms around the pair of them. When they finally untangled, they said their hellos amid sniffles and smiles.

Somewhat recovered, Sophie wiped her teary eyes. 'Where's Tania?'

'She's just ducked off to the loo. She shouldn't be too far away,' Gina said with a smile.

'Oh good, for a second I thought she hadn't made it.'

'She almost didn't,' Amy said. 'When I got to her place to pick her up she was still snoozing. I'm sure she could sleep for all of Australia.' She placed her hand on Sophie's arm, her brown eyes meeting Sophie's hazel ones. 'Considering you've just travelled fifteen thousand kilometres with a broken heart, you're looking pretty good, sis.' Her glossy lips quivered. 'God, I've missed you so much.'

'I've missed you too, Ames, big time.' And they began to cry again.

Laughing through her emotion, Sophie rifled through her handbag for tissues.

In the blink of an eye, Gina pulled two from the depths of her bra. Handing them to Sophie and Amy, she then wiped her own watery eyes and sniffled. 'Oh, stop it, you two. You're going to make my mascara run.'

'I can't believe you still keep tissues down there, Aunt Gina.' Sophie shook her head. 'You used to pluck them out as fast as speeding bullets whenever we were hurt or upset as kids.'

'Bad habit really. Daniela and Gino are mortified when I do it for them now.' Gina glanced down at her ample cleavage. 'But you have to admit these babies are pretty handy when you want to store stuff. Sometimes I even keep my phone down there.'

'They are big.' Sophie couldn't help but laugh.

'I know,' Gina said, grinning. 'But at least they're what God gave me and I didn't pay a fortune for them.' She leant in to whisper to the girls. 'Mind you, when I'm not wearing my bra they hang down to my bloody waist these days.'

Amy and Sophie cackled with laughter.

'It feels so good to be laughing all together again.' Amy gave Sophie's arm a squeeze. 'I'm so glad you're home, sis.'

'Me too, Ames, it's been a long time coming.'

'Look at your luggage,' Gina said, nodding at the four bags. 'You honestly don't need to bring the kitchen sink every time you visit, Soph, we do have them over here, you know,' she added with a cheeky wink.

'Yeah, but you know me, I'm an in-case kind of gal. And I've brought you all presents too.' Sophie's voice was way too chirpy. She tried to smile her way out of it but failed – Gina noticed instantly. She held Sophie's gaze, as if peeking into her soul.

'What is it, love?'

'Nothing.'

Gina didn't budge. 'Don't fib to me. I know something's bothering you.'

Sophie sighed; there was no keeping anything from Gina. 'Zachary and I have broken up, hence the reason I have so many bags.'

'Oh, love, I'm so sorry.' Gina reached out and took her by the hand and gave it a gentle squeeze. 'What's happened?'

'It's a long story, but the short of it is, he cheated and I left.'

'Well, as much as I hate to see you hurt, good for you leaving, because once a cheater, always a cheater.'

'My thoughts exactly.'

'Has he tried to talk his way out of it?'

'He doesn't know I know yet.'

'Oh.' Gina's face showed her confusion. 'How's that?'

'Like I said, long story.'

A squeal sounded from behind them and Sophie turned to see Tania legging it towards them, her arms and eyes equally wide. 'Oh my beautiful big blister, you're really here.'

With Sophie smiling at her nickname, Tania gave her a tight hug. More tears fell. Sophie was the first to pull away and she looked into Tania's big brown eyes. 'Have you been looking after yourself, Tans?' Sophie asked, noticing the dark rings around them.

Tania groaned. 'Yes, I am looking after myself, mother hen.'

'Really?'

'Yes, really. I've just had a few late nights and they've caught up with me, that's all.'

Sophie looked Tania up and down, stopping and smiling when she spotted Tania's footwear. 'Why in the hell are you wearing slippers?'

'I was fast asleep when Amy and Gina pulled up, and neither of them gave me any time to get ready. You're lucky I'm not still in my pyjamas with the way they were ushering me out the door. I jumped in the car without thinking to put shoes on.' She pointed down at the fluffy balls of pink. 'These ugly things were the only form of footwear Aunt Gina had in her car. I tried to go barefoot but neither of them would let me out of the car until I'd put them on.'

Sophie giggled. 'The craziness of this family, I've missed it.' She tipped her head to the side. 'So who's the new love interest?'

'Oh, you know, just someone I met at work.'

'No, I don't know. What's their name?'

'Alex.'

'Hmmm, Alex hey, nice strong name … is he buff?'

Tania was looking mighty uncomfortable. 'You could say that.'

Sophie wasn't letting up. 'There's that look in your eyes that's telling me you're hiding something. So spill …'

'Nothing to spill.' Mimicking Sophie's stance, Tania folded her arms and looked her sister up and down. 'And I could say the same about you. You might be all refreshed after your business-class flight, and thanks for the text to rub that minor detail in, but you can't fool me, blister. So how about you do the spilling, huh?'

Was there nothing she could hide from this family? Sophie wondered. 'Zachary and I have broken up.'

'Oh my God, when?'

'Two days ago.'

'Oh, blister, what happened?' Tania reached out and took her hands.

Sophie felt herself choking up, and took a moment to gather herself.

'Long story,' Gina piped in, saving Sophie. 'But let's just say he's a cheating mongrel and leave it at that for now.' She patted Sophie's arm. 'You two keep yakking, Amy and I will grab your bags and we'll go out to the car.'

'That son of a bitch, doing that to you.'

Sophie smiled through her hurt. 'Uh-huh.'

Tania offered a loving smile. 'Well, we will all make you feel much better, blister, don't you worry about that.'

'I don't doubt that for a second.' Sophie reached out and tapped Tania's nose ring. 'When did you get this?'

'A couple of weeks ago … you like?'

'Yeah, it suits you.'

Tania lifted up her ankle-length boho skirt to reveal a thigh tattoo of an angel. 'You like this little beauty too?'

'Holy crap, did that hurt?' Sophie reached out and lightly touched it, as though afraid she was going to inflict more pain on Tania by doing so.

'Like you wouldn't believe.' She dropped the skirt back down. 'But it was worth it.'

'I love it. I've always wanted to get a tattoo, but I'm too afraid of passing out from the pain. One day I might find the guts.'

'It's a cinch ... kind of a good pain once you get used to it.'

'I'll take your word for it, Tans.' Sophie smiled. 'What does Dad think of it?'

'Haven't shown him yet.'

'Ha-ha, I wonder why ...'

Tania shook her head. 'Yeah, I know the spiel, that no man will ever want to marry us if we have tattoos and blah, blah, blah.' She shrugged. 'I don't really care. I'm old enough to do my own thing. Dad will just have to suck it up.'

Sophie folded her arms. 'Oh, really, I dare you to tell him that.'

Tania raised her chin. 'I will if it comes to it.'

'Uh-huh.' Sophie interlaced her arm in Tania's as she tugged her sister forwards. 'Now come on, let's go. I could use a nice strong drink.'

'That's the best damn thing I've heard all day,' Tania said with a wicked grin.

CHAPTER
5

Shorefield

They finally reached the outskirts of Shorefield. Not far now and they'd be at her parents' elite horse agistment and training property, Rosewood Farm. The clear blue sky and the rolling landscape dotted with fruit trees, sugarcane fields, cattle and horses flashed past the passenger window, the distance between each house a beautiful country mile – so unlike the crowded street Sophie had lived in back in the UK. An hour's drive from Cairns airport, the conversation had tapered off with both Amy and Tania now glued to their mobile phones. Having always been a nervous driver, Gina was sitting forward, almost pushing against the steering wheel as she carefully approached a T-intersection. The very one Sophie had once overshot and ended up in the paddock opposite, in her trusty old Holden ute when she was still a P-plate driver. Thank God there hadn't been a fence like there was now or she wouldn't have walked away from it unscathed.

Making sure to check both ways a few times before she drove off again, Gina turned down the long winding road that led to Sophie's one and only real home. She'd learnt the alphabet there; learnt how to ride horses there, and also how painful it was to fall off a horse many times; learnt the magic of a first kiss with the one and only Dylan Stone up by the top dam; and also learnt how hard it was to walk away from it all when she packed her bags and left for London. It felt damn good to be coming home.

With the beach now in sight, Sophie rolled down her window and filled her lungs with sea air, feeling as if she'd been holding her breath for years. A yacht glided across the bay, its white sails up and foamy water glittering in its wake. The tropical warmth spread through her and into her soul. Some of the burden she was carrying lifted, making her feel lighter, more at peace. Soaring palm trees, heavy with coconuts, swayed in the breeze. She briefly shut her eyes as the salty aroma gave rise to goosebumps and a gentle smile. When she opened them again she noticed that the tide was slowly moving in. The sound of the waves crashing on the shore was music to her ears. She imagined strolling along the waterline, the pull of the ocean carrying away all her problems as it washed over her bare feet. She peered beyond the shore. The calm aqua blue seemed to stretch on forever, appearing to drop off the edge of the earth beyond the horizon. To the south, the lush green hills curved gently down to the sea and to the north were mountains that soared into the sky. Unlike British beaches, which were either pebbly or had mud-coloured sand, and where she needed a thick wetsuit, neoprene hood, gloves and boots just to swim, this, right here, was her kind of heaven. It was where she felt the *real* her. Where she truly felt alive.

They drove past a familiar driveway; the rustic timber sign hanging from the fence announcing it was Stone's Throw – Dylan's home. So many times she'd gone down that driveway to see him, and had walked down there hand in hand with him, so in love, so happy, so positive about their future together. It was years ago but she remembered it as if it were only yesterday. Thinking of him being there now, her heart lurched into her throat. How was she going to handle seeing him again? Before she could torture herself with the *what ifs*, she saw it, the grand, two-storey, Queenslander-style homestead rising up from the cliff, the wide timber verandahs facing the sea. She'd spent many a good day out there on the hammock with a book. The scent of the golden wattles that lined the back fence of the property lingered, bringing back memories of riding through the scrub.

Easing her new car over a cattle grid as if it were made of glass, Gina brought it to a stop near the security gates, which were necessary to keep the highly prized horses and Angus cattle safe. Putting it in park, Gina undid her seatbelt, turned down the Pink song playing on the radio, removed her sunglasses, and then hung halfway out the window to punch in the security code, much to the amusement of the three girls.

'Oi, you lot. Being short has its handicaps, but I'll have you know it comes with pluses too.' Grinning, she sat down again and tugged her Gucci sunnies back on as she waited for the gates to swing open.

'And what might they be?' Sophie asked with a grin. With her long legs she was usually the one people would ask to get something down off the top of a grocery shelf.

'Well, let me see.' Gina drummed the dash as she thought about it. 'Like having plenty of leg room on planes, more probability of winning a game of limbo, and the chance of becoming a jockey if you want to, and that's just the tip of the iceberg.'

'Trust you to come up with all of that.' Tania laughed and shook her head. 'And speaking from experience, great things come in small packages too, hey, Aunt Gina?'

'They certainly do, sweetheart.' Gina chuckled as she crawled along at five kilometres an hour.

Sophie caught the sound of hearty laughter. Two men rested on the railings of a roundyard, their butts very appealing in their tight jeans, but it was the fine looking horses that drew her attention and the barking of a kelpie from the back of one of the utes that made her smile. She was feeling more and more at home by the second.

Pulling to a stop at the side of the house, beneath a giant mango tree, Gina switched off the engine. After all four of them piled out, Gina blipped the car locked and chuckled. 'I really don't know why I do that; it's not like anyone's going to nick it here. Habit of living in town, I suppose. We'll come back for the suitcases soon, Soph.' She clapped her hands excitedly. 'Let's go give your oldies the surprise of their lives first.'

Following one another up a pathway lined with tropical plants, they headed towards the front door. Pulling the flyscreen open ever so quietly, then the timber door, they tiptoed inside. And were met with silence.

'Are you sure they're home?' Sophie whispered.

Gina shrugged. 'Your guess is as good as mine.'

'Maybe they're down at the stables?' Tania said.

Amy glanced at her watch. 'Nah, it's just gone afternoon teatime and they're both creatures of habit. They're usually sitting at the table by three-thirty sharp with their slices of buttered fruit cake and coffees.'

Reaching the end of the hallway, Tania walked into the open-plan lounge and dining room, spinning this way and that. 'Maybe we should just call out?'

'No, I want to see their faces when they see me,' Sophie said as she plonked down in a leather lounge chair, wishing the curtains were open so she could admire the unobstructed ocean view. She loved this room with its warm mahogany furniture and the many shelves of books. As a teenager, it had been her hidey-hole, a place to escape the outside world and lose herself in one of her favourite western novels.

With the room shrouded in dusky darkness, Gina switched on a lamp by the couch. All their eyes went to what was on the coffee table. Two empty wine glasses, one with pink lipstick on the rim, and a plate of half-eaten cheese and biscuits. On the arm of the couch hung a pair of what looked like men's underpants and draped over the back of the lounge was a lacy red bra.

Sophie shot to standing and took a few steps back, as though the undergarments were going to bite her. 'Eww. That's just a little bit too much information.'

Hands on hips, Tania edged closer to her sisters. 'A big hell yeah to what Sophie just said.'

The three of them looked to Gina, who threw her hands up in the air. 'Why are you lot looking at me? They may be nearing sixty but they're still human, you know.'

A loud thump was swiftly followed by a man's voice yelping as if in pain.

Sophie took off in a sprint. 'Oh my God. Dad!'

The other two followed. Reaching their parents' bedroom door, they stopped.

Sophie tried the handle but the door was locked. 'Dad, are you okay in there?'

'Sophie, is that you?' Frank Copinni's voice was strained.

'Yes. Surprise! Are you okay?'

'Oh God, don't come in here,' Frank shouted.

'Hi, Sophie darling, how wonderful you've arrived early,' Marie Copinni called out. 'And like your father said, best not to come in here.'

Imagining what she might see on the other side, Sophie screwed her face up. 'Okay, we're not going to.'

'Who's we?' Frank asked.

'Oh, Amy and Tania are here too. And Aunt Gina … they all picked me up from the airport. I wanted to surprise you.'

'Gina's here too?'

There was a collective 'yes' from the four women as Gina walked up the hall.

'Hi, Frank. Hi, Marie,' she called, stifling a chuckle.

'Oh, how wonderful. Hi, Gina.' Marie's reply was a little squeaky. 'Hi, Tania and Amy.'

'Hey, Mum,' the two said in unison.

Another loud, painful groan sounded, followed by muffled laughter.

'Come on, you two, we're worried,' Sophie called out.

'We're all okay in here. You just go and fix yourselves a drink or something, and we'll be out in a jiffy,' Marie said, through bursts of laughter.

'Righto then,' Sophie called back.

Exchanging looks that spoke of their desire to do no such thing, the women pushed their ears up against the bedroom door.

'It's not funny, Marie,' Frank said. 'I think I've thrown my back out.'

'I'm sorry, Frank, it's just ...' Marie cackled with laughter. 'I told you you're not meant to go past your pain threshold. Kama Sutra is not something you can perfect from the get go. It takes time.'

Sophie, Tania and Amy looked to each other with absolute disgust, Tania even going as far as to simulate barfing. Gina covered her mouth to stop the laughter. Sophie slapped her on the arm and told her to shush. Amy covered her eyes as if she were witnessing what was going on the other side of the door.

'Yeah, well, I was trying to impress you, Marie. Here, you have to try and help me up. I'm not going to have our three girls and your sister see me lying naked on the bedroom floor.'

More laughs, both from their father and mother.

'We really should go and get ourselves that drink,' Amy said, looking a little pale. 'I honestly can't listen to any more of this. Parents aren't meant to have sex. And they especially aren't meant to be performing Kama Sutra.' She visibly shuddered. 'They've got a better sex life than Kurt and I do.'

Gina rolled her eyes. 'Just because we're old doesn't mean we've shut up shop.'

Tania threw her hands over her ears. 'Oh yuck, wayyyyy too much information.'

'Are you lot still standing out there?' Frank called out.

They all shot off down the hallway. Once in the kitchen, they eyed each other silently then tried to muffle hooting laughter.

'Oh my God. Who would have thought our mum and dad would even speak the words *Kama Sutra*, let alone be trying it out?' Sophie said between her mirth-filled snorts. 'I've always painted them as more old-fashioned types, especially considering how strict they were with us when we were growing up.'

Amy nodded. 'Yeah, we were barely allowed to have an inch of skin showing whenever we went on a date. I'm surprised Dad didn't demand we wear a burqa.'

'I still don't want to think about what's going on behind that door, thank you very much,' Tania said, holding her hands up.

Now somewhat composed, Sophie went in search of wine glasses and hopefully some good red wine, which was pretty much a sure thing in her parents' house. The Maltese loved their vino, perhaps even more than their food. 'Good on them, I think. I wish Zachary and I had that kind of love life, then he might not have …' She stopped, not wanting to put a downer on the cheery vibe. This trip was about the joy of a wedding, not the misery of her devastated love life.

All three women gave her a look of tender compassion.

Sophie pulled open the fridge door, desperate to veer away from the shitty situation she'd left behind. 'Holy crap.'

'What now?' Tania asked. 'Don't tell me, there's a dead body in there.'

'I don't think I've ever seen Mum and Dad's fridge full of so much healthy stuff.' Sophie held the door right open so everyone could see the goodies within. 'It's usually full of so many carbs my hips grow bigger just looking at it.'

Amy walked in with a bottle of wine in hand. 'Holy shit, who are these people and where have they hidden our parents?' She joined Sophie at the fridge. 'And look, the crisper drawers are full to the brim with fruit and veg, and there's even yoghurt and weird looking dips and some jar of stuff called ...' She turned the large bottle around so she could read it. '"Love Peace and Vegetables Super Kraut". What the heck?'

'Now that's my kind of fridge.' Tania dashed to Sophie's side, grabbing the jar from her hand. Twisting the lid off, she smiled. 'Yum, I freaking love this stuff. I get it from the markets every week. It's mouth-wateringly tasty, and to make it even better it's really good for your gut too. Kinda like probiotics, but better.'

'Probiwhatics?' Gina asked.

Tania grabbed a fork from the drawer and tried a mouthful of the pickled cabbage, talking between chews. 'You know, good bacteria.'

Sophie threw her hand over her nose. 'Far out, what is that smell?' She looked around suspiciously as she placed a beetroot and feta dip on the bench. 'Okay, which one of you let a sneaky one loose?'

'Not me,' Gina and Amy said in unison.

Tania held the jar up. 'It's this stuff, Soph. Pretty potent, huh? Just imagine what your farts smell like once you've eaten some.'

Sophie laughed and shook her head. 'Oh lord help us, Tans, because you're the master farter at the best of times.'

'Oh, if my memory serves me right I don't know about that, Soph. I reckon you might take the cake there,' Amy called over her shoulder as she opened the wine and poured six substantial glasses.

'What's all this talk about butt yodelling?' Frank hobbled into the kitchen, followed by the smell of Tiger Balm, his smile stretching from ear to ear and his hair still damp from a shower. 'Your mother will be out in a minute.'

'Dad!' Sophie swamped him with an almighty hug. Amy and Tania joined in until there was no sign of Frank Copinni beneath all the limbs.

'My three girls.' Frank laughed. 'And as much as I love you all, I've pinched a nerve in my back so be gentle with me.'

'Don't suffocate the poor bugger,' Gina said.

Emerging from the tangle of arms, Frank kissed each of his girls on the cheek. 'Oh, my beautiful daughters, I'm so happy to have all of us together again now Sophie is here.' He looked to Sophie. 'And coming a day early to surprise me too, you cheeky bugger.'

'Yes, well, I didn't think I'd be surprised as much as you were.' Sophie leant against the marble kitchen bench, smirking.

Tania, Sophie and Gina mumbled their agreement before taking sips from their glasses of wine.

The room fell silent, all of them but Frank smiling. His face was turning a brighter shade of red by the second.

'Now, now, you lot,' Frank muttered as he rubbed the bottom of his back. 'That'll be enough of that.'

Even though her dad's skin was dark olive, thanks to genes and many years in the sun, Sophie could still see the traces of embarrassment on his cheeks as he seized a glass of wine. Gesturing to chink glasses, he cheered in Maltese, '*Sahha.*'

'*Sahha,*' Gina and the girls replied.

Frank pointed at Tania. 'Did you know there's a piece of metal hanging out of your nose? If you're not careful a cattle farmer might come and put a rope in it.'

Tania groaned. 'Oh come on, Dad, that one's getting old.'

'Why don't you show him your tattoo?' Sophie whispered in passing. 'He'd love to see it.'

Tania reached out and slapped her.

'I think the nose ring looks beautiful.' A happy voice pulled their attention to the doorway.

'Mum!' Sophie leapt to her.

'Oh, my darling, it's so good to see you.' Marie pulled her in tightly. 'I've missed you so much my heart hurt every time I thought about you.'

Sophie choked back sobs. There was something about her mother's hugs that always brought everything to the surface. But she wasn't going to let anything cloud such a happy moment.

Marie pulled her back at arm's length. 'Is everything okay, Soph? You look a little out of sorts.'

'Yeah, Mum, I'm all good.' She wiped a couple of tears from her cheek. 'Just happy to see you and Dad, that's all.'

Marie tipped her head to the side. 'You sure?'

'Positive.'

'So where are we all dining tonight? Here or out?' Amy gave Sophie a sideways glance as if to say, 'I'll save you from answering that.'

Sophie thanked her with a small smile.

'Well, I would have cooked up a storm if I'd known you lot were going to be here today,' Marie said, 'but seeing as it's almost four o'clock, do you want to just go and eat at our favourite spot instead?'

'At La Luna's?' Amy said.

Marie nodded.

Sophie's mouth watered. 'Oh, yes. Yum! I hope they still have their crab-filled ravioli with burnt butter and sage sauce.'

'And their garlic prawns are to die for,' Amy added. 'Kurt and I go there on special occasions, which isn't often enough, and I have them every time.'

Pulling a sleeve of tablets from his pocket, Frank popped two pills out. 'I'm fairly certain their menu hasn't changed in all the years we've been going there, Soph, so they should still have your crab ravioli.' Tumbler glass in hand, he filled it with water from the tap. 'Are you happy to go out for dinner, Tania?'

'Yeah, and I don't care where we eat. I'm that hungry I could almost chew my own arm off.' As if on cue, her belly grumbled loudly.

'Do you want to bring Alex along, love? We're all dying to meet him,' Marie said.

'Yes, we certainly are,' Amy said.

'Oh no, but thanks for the invitation. Alex is working tonight.'

'Alex is always working,' Frank said. 'I hope he's made sure to have the day off for Daniela's wedding.'

'I hope so too, otherwise I'll be dateless.' Tania laughed a little too loudly, attracting weird looks from Sophie and Amy. She quickly turned away from her sisters. 'Are you sure you're up for going out, Dad? You're walking a bit ... uncomfortably.'

'I'll be right. The painkillers and red wine will kick in soon enough. And besides ...' He gently prodded Tania in the belly. 'Sounds like that thing needs feeding, so you girls best get ready.'

'I'll have a quick shower,' Sophie said.

'While you're doing that I'll give Kurt a ring and tell him to meet us there after he closes the store.'

'Right then, that was easy.' Frank turned to Gina. 'Do you and Vinnie want to join us?'

'We'd love to but I'm afraid we can't tonight, Frank. Daniela and I are going over the last few details for the seating plan – with some people who can't bear the sight of each other and the rifts between some of Mark's family, it's been a bloody nightmare to sort out.'

'Oh you should have seen us trying to do Amy and Kurt's …
it was horrendous,' Marie said. 'I was pulling my hair out by the
end of it.'

Amy started to protest while Gina and Marie went on to
talk about how stressful weddings were to organise, and Frank
and Tania discussed the menu and the best dish to order at the
restaurant. Remaining quiet, Sophie just enjoyed being in their
company again, as if it had only been yesterday that they'd last
caught up.

Amy's phone buzzed a message and she pulled it from her back
pocket. 'Oh, speak of the devil. Kurt's just sent a text to tell
me they're having a suit fitting. Says he's keen to catch up with
Dylan for a beer afterwards. I'll text him back about dinner now.'
She glanced up at Sophie. 'Should I ask him to invite Dylan too?'
There was a cheeky glint in her eyes.

'No way.' She couldn't hide the panic from her face.

'I'm just kidding, Soph. Breathe before you pass out.'

Sophie's belly had backflipped – if simply the mention of
Dylan's name could do that to her, she could only imagine how
she would feel when she saw him. Grabbing her glass of wine,
she took a long drink. The next few weeks were going to be very
interesting.

CHAPTER

6

Stone's Throw

After two long days on the road, Dylan felt like death warmed up. His back ached like buggery and his head throbbed because he'd replayed the events at the tattoo shop over and over in his mind. Before he'd left, his Aunt Kimmy had noticed his anxious mood over their usual Friday fish and chip night. Shoving a few chips in his mouth, he'd gently shrugged off her concern by telling her he'd had a hectic day at work. He was fairly certain she hadn't believed him. But she didn't push the subject; instead she'd given him a look as if to say, 'If you need to talk about it, I'm here.' He could never tell her what he'd seen at the shop, or how he'd done nothing about it when he damn well wanted to. But what could he have done? He couldn't risk Angus revealing the secret he'd told him. Why the hell had he trusted the man with such damning information? And he couldn't do anything about what he'd seen in the office as he'd be an accessory to it and if that got out, then his dream of opening his own tattoo shop would be over before it had even begun. He gripped the handlebars tighter, his jaw aching as he clenched his teeth.

Angus fucking McDonald can go to hell …

Angus was once a man he'd greatly respected and regarded as a father figure in some ways; now Dylan would be happy if he never saw McDonald again. Just like his own deadbeat father, the lowlife bastard had failed him. The position Angus had put him in could not have been worse – Dylan had walked into the office to see millions of dollars worth of ecstasy pills on the table. It was the same drug that had killed Grace. He was an accessory now, a man who knew too much. Thank Christ he was putting miles between them. After seeing what was going on he couldn't get away quick enough. And Angus knew it. His last few words to Dylan before he'd stepped out of the tattoo parlour had been both callous and cautionary. 'Shame, I thought you would have been more supportive of my new business venture, Dylan. Just remember, I know where you live and I know your dirty little secret, so make sure those lips of yours stay well and truly sealed, you hear me?'

Fuck you, Dylan had wanted to say, but instead he'd replied, 'Loud and clear, catch ya …' Funny how things could change in the blink of an eye. Now he had to think long and hard about what he was going to do for work, because over his dead body would he ever set foot in the tattoo shop again. Maybe, just maybe, he could look at opening his own shop back in Shorefield. But what would Kimmy do without him?

There were too many maybes …

Half an hour later Dylan sat staring out of the window of the last roadhouse before the home stretch. The late lunch of a steak burger and chips had hit the spot nicely and given him some fuel to get through the next hour of riding. Thank God for small mercies. Watching a cloud of dust rise as a b-double truck filled with cattle pulled up out the front, he huffed. He needed to shake it all off. Needed to try to let it all go. He wanted to concentrate on spending time with his mum, and the joy of the wedding. To hell with everything else. There was no point going over and over it. It was done. Dusted. Gone. Finished. To get past it he needed to focus on what was ahead, not what he was leaving behind. The wedding of one of his long-time best mates was something to be celebrated. He was sure he just needed a decent night's sleep to shift his mood. After rolling out of the uncomfortable motel bed halfway through the night, pulling on his jeans and boots, tossing his backpack over his shoulder and getting on the road again, he was buggered.

Downing the last of his black coffee, he smiled at the pretty waitress. He wasn't interested, but manners cost nothing. Her come-get-me eyes did nothing for him, and neither did her perfectly curvaceous figure. He needed a lover with substance, and fiery passion, a woman who knew exactly who she was, played a little hard to get, and would love him fiercely once he won her over, just as he would her – that's the kind of woman who attracted him. Frustratingly, he'd only ever come across someone like that once in his life and she'd gone and ruined it, had crushed him without any hesitation. As much as he tried not to think about it, the memory of her beautiful face claimed his mind. It had been five years since he'd laid eyes on Sophie, and he'd barely been able to talk to her for fear of breaking. Would he be any different this time round? Could he move past what she'd done to him? Love claimed his heart and a mixture of emotions sat in the pit of his stomach. He had so many questions, but there was only one he was going to ask her, when the time was right. And he hoped to God she gave him an honest answer. He felt he deserved one. Then he might finally have the closure he needed.

Paying his bill, he made sure to leave a tip, something he'd learnt to do in the United States when Angus had sent him to a tattoo convention there. Walking to the front door, he felt all eyes on him. He was used to the rubberneckers, especially in the smaller towns. A six-foot-four goliath with an assortment of tattoos tended to attract it. He just took it in his stride. Little did they realise that he was a bit of a softy beneath his tough exterior, not that he was keen to let many know that fact. Squinting as he stepped out into the glorious afternoon sunshine, he pulled his sunglasses from the pocket of his leather jacket and slipped them on. Then he headed for the payphone and dialled his mum's number. Leaning up against the glass, he waited. Four rings and Faith Stone's soft voice answered. 'Hello.'

'Hey, Mum.'

'Oh, Dylan, thank goodness. I've been worried sick knowing you're on the road, and so has your Aunt Kimmy.'

He chuckled. 'You two worry about me too much, Mum.'

'That's our job, to worry about you.' She sighed. 'I've been ringing your mobile for two days now and it keeps going straight to message bank. I was starting to think something terrible had happened.'

'Yeah, sorry 'bout that. It's gone flat. I forgot to charge it before I left Sydney.'

'Well, I suppose I should have guessed. You're shocking with that thing. And if it is charged it's normally on silent anyway.'

She sighed again. 'At least you're okay, that's the main thing. I'll let Kimmy know, too.'

'Thanks, Mum. I'm all good, other than a crook back from riding two days straight.'

'You'll have to get yourself a massage. I know a really good lady in town.'

'Yeah, maybe.'

'Before I forget to mention it, Angus has rung here twice looking for you.'

'Has he? I didn't think he'd have your number.' Dylan's heart took off in a wild gallop.

'Yes, and he says it's pretty urgent he gets hold of you. He sounded a little bit agitated, Dylan. He also called around to Kimmy's last night, asking if you'd already left and wanting to know the phone number here. Kimmy said he seemed really on edge.'

'He did?' The thought of Angus going anywhere near his family made Dylan's stomach coil with rage.

'Is there something you need to tell me, Dylan? Are you in some sort of trouble?'

'No, Mum, it's probably just got to do with something at work, that's all.' He tried to keep his voice calm and steady while raw, hot anger coursed through him. He needed to change the subject, and fast, before his mother cottoned on to the fact he wasn't telling her the whole truth. 'I'm only about an hour away now, so I'll be there before you know it.'

'Oh yay, I can't wait to see you … it's been way too long between visits this time round.'

'Yeah, I know. Can't wait to see you, too, Mum.' He watched an overweight truck driver struggle as he made his way up the side steps and into the cab of a long road train. 'I better go. Catch you soon.'

'Okay, love you.'

'Love you too.' After returning the receiver with a thump, Dylan stormed out of the phone booth. He quickly made his way over to his motorbike, wanting to hit the road first before the road train pulled out.

What in hell was Angus doing? A visit to his home in Sydney and then a call to his mum's place could only mean trouble. Dylan couldn't call him now because he didn't know his number – it was stored in his flat mobile. And here he was thinking he could leave it all behind him. It was the story of his life; the past never really let go of him. If only he was half the hardarse bastard most people thought he was, he might be able to shrug things off and not give a damn. But he wasn't, and he couldn't.

Grabbing his open-face helmet from the seat, he tugged it on and buckled it up. With practised ease he threw his leg over and straddled the iron beast he'd worked his guts out to rebuild in his time off from the shop. His bike, along with his home gym, had been the only way he'd been able to deal with the lack of paddocks to gallop over. A true cowboy at heart, he was born to ride. Horses were his preference, but when living in the big smoke a motorbike was the next best thing. The steel-grey Indian Chief Vintage grunted like a wild animal as he kicked it to life. Pulling out onto the highway, he patted the gas tank as if it were a horse about to set off. He needed to clear his mind and this was the best way to do it.

Soon he was chasing the white lines. He'd always liked this road. It felt safe, familiar and, unlike the streets of Sydney, it was built with gentle curves to forgive a tired driver's mistakes.

He pressed the throttle harder. The speedometer needle jumped from eighty to a hundred, to a hundred and ten. He glanced away for a split second, checking his rear-view mirror for any sign of the cops, and then looked back at the road. A speeding ticket was not at the top of his wish list, and he didn't want to bring any attention to himself. The white tip of the needle quivered at a hundred and thirty-five. The speed made his mind vanish, allowed him time to breathe away the complications of his life. But only for a few brief seconds before he lay off the throttle and came back to earth.

Fuck Angus McDonald.

Twenty minutes into the ride and the paddocks began to get smaller, the houses closer together. He knew he wasn't far now. A sign pronounced the drop in speed limit and he slowed. He cornered the familiar sharp bend, the wheels caressing the road smoothly as his knee barely missed the blacktop. It may have been almost five years since he'd ridden this stretch of road, but he still knew it like the back of his hand. The highway now widening before him, he opened the throttle; the feeling of the wind whipping past him was invigorating. He once again broke the speed limit. He couldn't help himself. Not the twenty-one-year-old that had left here, he wondered what the townsfolk were going to think of the man he'd become. Now tattooed and broad-shouldered, with his string-bean days long behind him, he chuckled as he pondered the fact they most probably wouldn't even recognise him.

The highway took him up a soft rise. Shorefield finally came into view. Rolling landscape met with a glistening pewter sea, surrounded by emerald mountains. His breath caught. A hidden gem in the beauty of North Queensland, he'd forgotten how

stunning it was. And then a wailing siren caught his attention.
He looked down at his speedometer. He was doing ten kilometres
over the speed limit. He swore under his breath. Not a good
start. His hand gripped the throttle. Part of him wanted to wind
it down and take off again. But he didn't want to tangle with
the local town copper. So, he slowed, eyeing off a truck stop just
up ahead as the only safe place to pull over. He glanced in his
rear-view mirror at the red and blue lights flashing. He could
just imagine his mother now, rolling her eyes at his misfortune.
'Why does trouble always follow you, Dylan Stone?' She would
say it with a half-hearted grin. Bless her big beautiful heart. She'd
visited him in Sydney so often over all these years so he didn't
have to make the trip back here, always saying it was a good
excuse for her to see her sister at the same time.

He flicked on his indicator, as if to say to the copper, 'See, I
can be careful', and pulled off the road. The cop car pulled in
close behind him. A door slammed. Heavy footfalls approached.
The stern-faced, middle-aged cop stood with hands on hips. 'Off
the bike, sir.'

Sir, hey. Dylan almost laughed. He hadn't been called that ever.
But he did as he was told.

'Is there a fire?' the copper asked.

'Nope.'

'Accident?'

'Nope.'

'Someone's dying.'

'Not that I know of.' Dylan had to bite his lip to stop from
smirking.

The cop folded his arms. 'Funny bugger, hey?'

'Sometimes.'

Silence hung. The copper huffed. 'Licence.'

'Yup, I'll just grab it.' Opening the saddlebags, Dylan took a few moments to find it. When he turned back around, the copper had his hand resting on the gun at his hip. 'Worried I was going to pull something else out, officer?' He held out the licence.

'Can never let your guard down on this job.'

'Is it because of how I look?'

'Nope.' The copper reached out and took the card, the expression on his face saying otherwise. When he glanced back up, he shook his head. 'Well, I'll be damned.'

'What did I miss?'

'You Faith Stone's son?'

'Yes, the one and only ... why you asking?'

'She said you're a bit of a livewire.' He looked Dylan up and down. 'And she wasn't kidding.'

'You should never judge a book by its cover.' Dylan leant in to read the copper's nametag. 'Sergeant Tucker.' It was his turn to fold his arms, to defend his turf. 'So how do you know my mother?'

'Ah, yeah. She's giving my son guitar lessons. Clever lady.'

'That she is.' Dylan couldn't help but grin proudly. His mum had come such a long way over the years. Now working as a part-time music teacher at the high school, she also offered lessons at home to make enough money to live comfortably.

The copper tapped the licence against his palm as he eyed Dylan, and then handed it back. 'Take this as a warning, Stone. If I catch you speeding again, I won't hesitate in booking you. Understand?'

'Yeah, thanks, but why are you letting me off? I didn't think you coppers had it in you to be lenient.'

Sergeant Tucker shrugged. 'I owe your mum a favour.'

'Right.' What sort of favour, Dylan was dying to ask, but he bit his tongue. *Choose your battles, Dylan*, his mother's voice rang out in his head again. 'Well, lucky me.'

The copper half smiled. 'You could say that.'

Dylan tossed his leg over the motorbike. 'Might catch you around the traps.'

Tucker nodded, the smirk tugging at the corners of his lips becoming a little more noticeable. 'I have no doubt.'

Great vote of confidence, Dylan thought as he carefully pulled back out onto the highway. Damn coppers, they always zeroed in on him.

❦

Half an hour later, Dylan had bypassed the main street of Shorefield and was coming close to his one true home, no matter what dark memories still lingered there. Making sure to stick to the speed limit, he crested a rise, unconsciously holding his breath. He knew what he'd see at the top, but that didn't make him any less apprehensive. The seemingly never-ending timber fence line of the Copinnis' prestigious property came into view, and just beyond it was the glimmer of the iron roof of his mum's cottage, the small acreage of Stone's Throw nestled nicely between Shorefield National Park, Rosewood Farm and Horseshoe Bay. He caught sight of the Copinnis' welcome sign, *Rosewood Farm – Frank and Marie Copinni*. Just seeing Sophie's last name etched into the timber sign posted at the gate to the flash-looking driveway made his heart quicken. Small town, small world – there'd be no getting away from her here. Hesitation rippled through him, but he shook it off. He stared out at the land he had so longed to come back to, and now here he was. Although there had been a dark day at Stone's Throw what seemed like eons ago, and a secret had been buried that night, there were still many happy memories to hold dear, and that's what he needed to focus on. As much as he felt it might ease his burden if the truth of his father's death came out, he'd made a promise to his mother that he never would tell anyone. What would happen to her if the law knew the truth?

Cruising past the extravagant security gates that led to Sophie's home he then slowed to almost walking pace as he came up to Stone's Throw. Blooming bougainvillea and blood red roses hugged either side of the rusty front gate – his mother had always had a green thumb. The same small sign he'd known as a child hung from a large paperbark tree, stating the name of the property. Rolling along, he removed his helmet and slung it from the handlebar, enjoying the feeling of the gentle breeze against his skin. Passing the same old mailbox, an old milk urn, he bounced over a cattle grid. In the neighbouring paddock, fat black cattle were grazing, their coats gleaming. Dylan had to give credit where credit was due – Frank Copinni took great care of his animals.

The dirt drive was long, flat and windy. His mum always kept the place looking immaculate. It was a testament to her hardworking nature. He drank in the picturesque surrounds as he rode towards his mother's modest cottage shaded by the yellow blooms of the wattle trees and the jacaranda trees flowering purple. On either side of the driveway lush green pastures were dotted with towering ghost gums. Beneath their draping limbs, white egrets strode between the horses and cattle. Sun glinted off the dam just beyond and his skin prickled in anticipation of jumping in and having a swim. With no traffic whizzing past, no sirens, no horns blaring, no high-rises blocking the view and no houses shoulder to shoulder, there was just so much to appreciate in the vastness of beautiful nothingness. God, how he'd missed this.

The verandah at the front of the cottage sagged a little and the white trellis that laced the edge of it had seen better days, but the weariness gave the place a certain kind of character. Give him something loved and lived in over a grand house any day. The land surrounding the homestead was gentle, welcoming, just like his beautiful mum. The old tobacco barn off to the right of the cottage used to be his bachelor pad, before he'd moved away. He had loved the place. A rush of nostalgia came over him, followed by a deep desire to never leave again. It felt damn good to be home, back to his roots. He slowed even more, wanting to drink in every detail. The bike rumbled beneath him, more of a purr now, but still the noise was in such sharp contrast to the peaceful surrounds.

He could almost smell the tack room at the back of his mother's house, all leather and horse. Just in front of him, a flock of chickens scattered from the gravel driveway, squawking in protest at being disrupted. And then he spotted a black and white duck running for him full pelt. It looked like it meant business. The front door swung open and his mother stepped out. Her bohemian-style dress floated at her ankles and her sandy coloured, waist-length hair framed a face that spoke of many experiences, and many smiles. 'Plucka, you stop right there, buddy!'

What a name – Plucka. It reminded him of the old *Hey Hey It's Saturday* days, when he and his mum would get comfy on the couch with a bar of chocolate and watch the show together. The Muscovy duck skidded to a stop just shy of the motorbike. Dylan couldn't wipe the smile from his face.

Faith hurried down the path, waggling a finger in the duck's direction. The bell anklet Dylan had given her for Christmas tinkled with her every step. He loved how wherever his mum was, a melody followed her. 'Don't you dare attack my son, or I'll have you for dinner.'

The duck recoiled as if it understood every word. It quacked, twice, eyed Dylan as if in a stand-off with him, and then waddled off with a strut to make a supermodel jealous.

The hullaballoo over, Dylan dismounted and looked at his mother, laughing. He opened his arms wide to catch her just as she reached him. 'Mum!' Arms entwined, and with her forehead only reaching his chest, he lifted her from the ground and spun her around – as always, she felt as light as a feather. He placed her back down and smiled; the scent of her perfume oil was comfortingly familiar.

'It's so good to see you, Dylan.' Faith looked up at him, her smile warm and tender.

Admiring his mother's youthfulness, albeit at fifty-three years, Dylan leant in and kissed her on the cheek. 'Yeah, you too, Mum.' He gestured to where Plucka was now chasing one of the chickens. 'He's a bloody handful.'

She rolled eyes that matched the colour of his baby blues. 'Tell me about it. I saved him from a bloke down the road when they were going to roast him after he succeeded in making their dog too scared to come near the house.'

Chuckling, he shook his head. 'You've always been a sucker for saving animals, Mum.'

'I know, I can't help myself. No wonder I'm a vegetarian.'

'You got to give it to him, though, he's a damn good guard dog.'

Faith grinned. 'That he is.' She shook her head as she watched her chickens running for their lives. 'Plucka, stop chasing poor Ruby … at this rate I won't have any eggs for a week.'

Plucka did as he was told and Faith looked back at Dylan. 'He's getting better than he used to be. Nobody could get anywhere near me at first, but Plucka is learning it's bad manners to chase the visitors away. Mind you, it's only ever really the men he's still suss on. He tends to like the women.'

'I like his way of thinking.' Dylan shoved his hands in his pockets as he watched the duck watching him. 'Plucka and I might become firm friends after all.'

'You won't be here long enough to win him over completely, but you can try. You've always liked a challenge.' Faith reached out and gave his arm a squeeze. 'Come on then, come inside. I'll make us a cuppa.'

'Sounds good, Mum, just let me grab my stuff.' Groaning from the ache in his back, Dylan yanked his saddlebags from the bike and slung them over his shoulder. 'Any more rescued creatures I should know about before I step inside?'

'Now that you mention it …' A playful smile claimed Faith's lips.

'What is it? Not a bloody snake again, I hope. You know how much I hate the bastard things.' He recalled all the times he woke up with his mum's pet tree snake, one she'd rescued from the side of the road, coiled around his bedhead. For some reason the three-metre serpent had loved the spot.

'No, nothing like that.' She waved her hand through the air, her many bangles jingling. 'I'm looking after an orphaned joey at the moment. I've named him Sir Bouncealot. He's going to the local zoo in a couple of days and I'll really miss him when he's gone.'

'Sir Bouncealot?'

'He can't sit still, so that's where the name came from. Ants in his pants is something you two have in common, I reckon.' Her smile was filled with so much warmth. She gestured to the saddlebags and his backpack. 'Is that all you've brought for four weeks?'

'Yeah, you have a washing machine, don't you?'

'Of course I do.' She gave him a playful slap on the arm.

'I can't wait to tuck into your famous passionfruit sponge cake.'

'How did you know I'd made it?'

'You always make it when you're getting visitors; why would I be any different?

'You know me all too well, my boy.' Faith patted his face tenderly and then wrapped her arm in his, tugging him forwards.

The fragrance of the bush lemon trees growing at one corner of the white picket fence drifted towards him, as did the scent of blossoming jasmines dotted through the garden as they headed down the pebbled path towards the front verandah. Climbing the five steps, Dylan spotted his old feathered mate, Bluey. True to form, the sulphur-crested cockatoo screamed abuse from its perch. 'Bugger off, dickhead, we don't want any.'

Dylan chuckled. 'I see you still haven't taught him any manners.'

'Can't teach an old dog new tricks, I'm afraid. Bob Jones was a cantankerous old coot, and his bird's no different. Twelve years under the same roof as the old bugger and there's no changing

Bluey. I gave up trying and have learnt to accept he is who he is, through gritted teeth sometimes, mind you.'

Nodding in agreement, Dylan grinned at the bird. 'Nice to see you too, Bluey.'

'Get stuffed,' the cocky squawked.

'You get stuffed,' Dylan said. 'You're lucky Mum took you in when your owner kicked the bucket, so show some appreciation, why don't ya?'

'Get stuffed,' the cocky said again.

'You're all class, Bluey.' Dropping his bags on the well-used cane settee, Dylan warily stroked the snowy feathers.

The bird cocked his head and fanned out his yellow crest.

Faith rested her hand on Dylan's back. 'Other than me, you're still the only one he'll let pet him.'

'That's because he remembers I'm the only one that feeds him biscuits.'

'Cocky wants a biscuit,' the bird squawked as it danced along its perch.

'Not until you say please,' Dylan replied.

Faith flicked off her thongs on the doormat that playfully read, *Enter with Caution*. 'I'll go and put on the kettle.' Opening the flyscreen door, it screeched wearily.

'Some WD40 will do the trick on that.' Dylan followed her in.

'I have a can of it in the laundry cupboard. But it doesn't need it. That sound adds character.'

'Uh-huh.' Hearing one of his mum's favourite sayings made Dylan grin.

The scent of burning incense instantly made him feel at home. His eyes adjusting to the change in light, Dylan swept his gaze over the lounge room with its mismatched couches, two beanbags that had survived him as a teenager, and scatter cushions his mother had bought while on a meditation retreat in Bali. He loved how she was a hippy from way back; her unconventional spirit was what made her all the more special. The room felt warm and welcoming, real and unpretentious. Buddha statues, oil burners and candles were placed in strategic spots, as too were framed photos of him and his mum, along with snaps of Faith and Kimmy, and one of them with Grace, Sophie and himself, their grins wide. A pang of heartache stabbed him with his cousin's memory, but he shook it off. At this moment he wanted to focus on all that was good in life.

He released the breath he'd been holding since leaving Sydney. He was back. And hopefully his return was going to be a peaceful one. Something told him that would all depend on what Angus had to say, which he would find out as soon as he'd had a cuppa with his mum and recharged his phone. He prayed to God it wasn't anything too drastic, but with what the man had got himself involved in and the company he was keeping, Dylan wasn't holding out much hope. His thoughts were distracted when a furry torpedo bounded past him.

He pointed down the hallway where a grey tail disappeared into the laundry. 'Sir Bouncealot, I gather?'

'That most certainly was.' A bleating sounded from the back verandah. 'Oh, and I forgot to mention, I'm babysitting a goat too. Just until tomorrow.'

'Ah, home sweet home.'

Faith smiled, the corners of her eyes crinkling. 'Come on, let's have some cake, and then I'll think about putting dinner on.'

It was only after he'd devoured two slices of his mother's mouth-watering sponge cake that Dylan felt satisfied. Licking the icing from his fingers, he sat back in his chair, legs stretched out and folded at the ankle.

'So you enjoying being the big boss at the tattoo shop now?' Faith asked.

'Yeah, most of the time.' Dylan tried to laugh off his white lie.

'You've come so far, son, I'm proud of you.'

'Thanks, Mum.'

She took a sip of tea before gently placing her cup down. 'So tell me, now you can't hide behind the phone, how's Kimmy *really* doing?' When Dylan remained silent she continued. 'She keeps telling me she's okay, as do you, but I can hear in her voice she's not coping as well as she likes to make out.'

He sighed. 'Some days she's okay, other days I can tell she's been crying, even though she denies it, and she's working way too much, in my opinion.'

'How much?'

'Almost double the shifts she used to do. Sometimes I don't see her for a couple of days, in between her roster and mine.'

Faith's brows knitted together, her usually sparkling eyes filled with sadness. 'Oh, really? With Gary's army pay, I don't think they'd be in any financial difficulty.'

'Nah, I don't think so either. I reckon it's just her way of coping with Grace's death – keeping busy so she doesn't have to deal with it like she would if she was sitting at home. I wish I could do something to help her, but I don't know what.'

'Oh, Dylan, I'm so sorry. This shouldn't be your concern.' Faith's eyes were wet with tears. 'I really should go down there more often – to help her through.'

'Don't beat yourself up, Mum, you can't leave your work – you do as much as you can. I want to be there for her, it's just ...' He paused, biting the rest of the sentence back.

Faith reached out and placed her hand over his, stopping his fingers from drumming on the table. 'What is it?'

'I really miss it here; miss you, that's all. I'm not cut out for the city lifestyle. It's way too claustrophobic for me. But with Gary away so much, I don't want to leave her high and dry, and living in an empty house.'

'Oh, son, as much as you love your aunty, as I love her, you have your own life to live. You've always been a country boy … and for the record I miss having you here very much too.' She sighed as though the weight of the world had just landed on her shoulders. 'Gary might have to have a hard think about retiring, as much as he loves his job.' Faith shook her head. 'Christ knows they don't need the money, and he'd be on a healthy pension for the rest of his life considering the number of years he's given fighting for his country.'

'Yeah, easier said than done, though, I think.' Dylan took the last sip from his mug. 'Gary lives for the army.'

'Yes, I know, but maybe he needs to prioritise, for Kimmy's sake.' Faith straightened out a crease in the tablecloth. 'Has she packed up Grace's room yet?'

Dylan shook his head.

'Oh my poor darling baby sister. I tried to gently let her know I would help her with it when I was there for Christmas, but she was resolute she'd do it when she was ready.'

'I think she's holding on to anything she can.' Dylan folded his hands on the table. 'She sometimes sleeps in Grace's bed.'

'Poor Kimmy.' The welling tears fell. 'I'll give her a call later, remind her how much I love her.'

Dylan's heart broke – he hated seeing his mum upset. She'd cried enough tears when his damn father was alive to last a lifetime. 'Oh, Mum, please don't cry.'

'I'm sorry.' She wiped at her eyes. 'I just feel so helpless up here.'

'Well, if it makes you feel any better, I'm seriously considering moving home – as long as Aunt Kimmy will be okay on her own.'

'Are you serious?' A smile shone through her sorrow.

'Of course.'

'Wouldn't that be throwing away a job you love?'

'Yes and no … I'd look at opening a tattoo shop in town, seeing there isn't one here yet.'

'What a wonderful idea.' Faith shot up and wrapped him in her arms. 'Oh, Dylan, that would make me the happiest mother alive.' She held him back and looked at him. 'The old menswear shop is empty and up for rent now. It would be the perfect spot for a tattoo parlour seeing as it's right beside the agriculture shop.'

Dylan grinned, loving her enthusiasm. 'We've got to talk to Kimmy first because I'm not leaving her on her own if she needs me there. She's been like a second mother to me.'

Faith sat back down, her expression serious. 'Of course, leave it with me.'

Sir Bouncealot jumped in and stood there as if wanting attention.

Giving the joey a scratch behind the ears, Dylan's smile stretched from ear to ear. 'He's an adorable little brute.'

'He sure is. Can you hold him while I heat up his bottle?'

'Love to.'

Sir Bouncealot nestled into Dylan's lap, his beady eyes wide as he took in the stranger. 'Hey, buddy.' Dylan gave his belly a scratch and the joey stretched out, clearly loving the attention.

'I've cleaned up the tobacco shed, like you asked, and made your bed in there …' Faith said, glancing over her shoulder. 'But you do know you're welcome to stay here, in the cottage, don't you?'

'Yeah, I know, Mum, thanks, but I think it would be better if we both had our own space – especially if I'm going to make it a permanent base. It's got everything I need.' He grinned. 'And like when I used to live there before moving to Sydney, I'll just come back over here and dump my washing basket when it's full, eat all the food out of your fridge, have parties when you're not home, and steal your toilet paper.' He was kidding and she knew it. She'd raised him to stand on his own two feet and work hard for what he had. And he appreciated that now ... maybe not so much as a teenager.

She tossed a tea towel at him. 'You'll do no such thing, Dylan Stone.'

'Only one way to find out,' he said lightheartedly.

Faith smiled. 'It'd be so nice to have you around longer than a few weeks. I hate you living down in the city where there are murders and bashings all the time.'

'There are bad things happening everywhere, Mum, not just in the city. People are being bashed and murdered all the time – even right here in the country.' Dylan instantly regretted his choice of words when he watched her eyes dart to *that* spot.

He followed her gaze to the area of the kitchen floor where Don Stone had lost his life, and his heart stalled. He stole a sideways glance back at his mother's paling face. Even twenty-odd years on, the fear and horror of that night were still so raw, for both of them.

'I really wish we could erase that night from our memories, son.' She didn't look at him and spoke softly, as though a million miles away.

'Me too, but I've come to accept that's an impossibility.'

'Mmm.' Her eyes were still locked on the spot his father's blood had pooled.

'We just have to keep doing what we've been doing, and move on with life as best we can, Mum, that's all we *can* do.'

Faith smiled sadly. 'Yes, you're right.' She wandered back to the table and began gathering the plates as though on autopilot. 'You still haven't told anyone what happened here, have you? I don't really want anyone other than us, and of course Kimmy, knowing.'

'Kimmy never speaks of it, and neither did Grace over the years. I think it was as traumatising for Grace as it was for us, seeing as she was here the night it happened.' He so wanted to say, no, he hadn't told a soul, but he couldn't lie. 'I kind of let it slip to Angus over a few beers last year, though.' He grimaced.

Shock made Faith appear even paler. The two plates she was holding crashed to the floor and shattered. 'You what?' She gripped the chair so hard her knuckles were white. 'What's going to happen if he lets it slip?'

Dylan jumped to her side. Kneeling on the floor, they both picked up the shattered pieces. 'I'm so sorry, Mum. I just needed to talk to someone about it. A secret like that is a massive burden to carry.'

'I know, I carry it around every day too, Dylan.' She looked him square in the eye. 'You could have talked to me, or even Kimmy if you needed to.'

'Yes, I know, but it's too late for that now.'

'Well, let's hope our secret is safe with him, then, hey?'

Dylan nodded, knowing damn well it wasn't.

CHAPTER

7

Rosewood Farm

Fingers of dawn sunlight light crept beneath the curtains and into the bedroom. Reaching over, Sophie grabbed her fitness tracker from the bedside table, a gadget she found annoying because it reminded her how much she needed to walk more. Pressing a button, the screen lit up. It was a few minutes to six. Although tired, she felt a bubble of anticipation of what might lie ahead over the next few days. She looked to where the curtains fluttered softly in the salty sea breeze. The sound of the waves spilling against the shore, as relaxing and peaceful as it was, hadn't even been enough to lull her to sleep.

After a delicious dinner, great conversation, and one too many wines, she'd climbed into bed with the hope of a good night's rest. But the darkness of her bedroom seemed to only bring with it images of Zachary and his secretary doing things that tore her already broken heart to shreds. She'd come to the conclusion it wasn't so much the loss of Zachary, she'd lost him ages ago, it was more the loss of a dream of settling down and making a family. Nearing thirty, it was something she'd expected to achieve way before this. She wasn't sure how much longer she could keep the news of the break-up from her parents. Pretending everything was hunky-dory was not proving to be easy, and she couldn't help but beat herself up – feeling as if she were the disappointment of the family. Amy was happily married; Tania was in love with Alex, whoever he was; and here she was, the eldest, and her relationship had fallen apart. A few times last night she'd found herself fighting tears at the dinner table, and warding off the desire to spill everything about her shitty life back in England. A few hand-squeezes beneath the table from Amy had given her the strength to move past it. A dinner table was neither the time nor place to divulge such things.

With the dull ache behind her eyes becoming more of a throb, she pushed the covers off and sat on the side of her tussled bed. Stretching her arms high, she willed her weary body to life. Besides her overactive mind, the time difference between England and Australia wasn't doing her any favours. Right about now she'd be climbing into bed, not dragging herself out of it. She'd even tried counting sheep at some ungodly hour last night, but being a lover of lamb it had only made her hungry and she'd got up in search of a midnight snack. The pepperoni and pecorino cheese had gone down a treat, followed by some coco pops – her dad's favourite. She groaned wearily. Maybe the jetlag had finally caught up? The ocean would give her the get-up-and-go she needed, especially if she was going to survive a full day of bridesmaid festivities, followed by the hens' party tonight.

So the sooner she sunk her feet into the sand, and her body into the sea, the better.

She glanced around her room, smiling at how it was basically as she'd left it nine years ago. Other than the upgrade to a new queen-size ensemble to replace her squeaky old single bed, along with matching bedside tables, all the other furniture remained the same. Pictures of her favourite horses and the trophies she'd won riding them at gymkhanas still adorned the walls and shelves of her room. Her dresser still held a photo of her sisters and her from fifteen years ago – her with braces and Amy and Tania clinging to either side of her, their perfect, straight-teeth smiles wide and their silky black hair a sharp contrast to her platinum blonde. The frame sat on one of her mum's prized doilies; they were everywhere throughout the house, lacy little bits under each and every photo, ornament or lamp. It was like stepping back in time, but it gave Sophie a sense of familiarity she'd never felt anywhere else.

Looking beyond the photo, her reflection met her. She grimaced. Dark rings circled her hazel eyes, her smile lines at the corners seeming more pronounced than usual. Talk about looking like death warmed up. She gazed to where her boobs sagged a little beneath the sheer cotton of her white singlet. Aging and gravity were not her friends. She grabbed each breast and lugged them up, imagining what it would be like if they just stayed there without the aid of a bra. She visualised all the pretty backless dresses she could wear, and the off-the-shoulder boho tops she adored on everyone else but herself. Sighing, she let them drop. She knew she needed to snap out of her self-loathing, but after what Zachary had done it was not proving to be easy. She puckered her lips, donning the best duck face ever, before sucking in her cheeks. If only she had Amy and Tania's pronounced cheekbones, wouldn't that be nice. She hated feeling so down but it was a matter of circumstance right now. Besides being sceptical about her appearance, she also felt lost, wretched and older than her years on the inside. 'Come on, universe,' she mumbled, 'give me something to feel like I've got a purpose.' And then she sat, looking this way and that, waiting for a sign to miraculously appear in her lap. She huffed when it didn't. Then rolled her eyes. She was being an idiot.

Running her fingers through her mane of blonde hair (something she was extremely thankful for) she yanked it up and into a ponytail, pulling the hair tie from around her wrist to secure it in place. Standing up from the bed, she went to the closet. She'd unpacked her clothes and toiletries at two this morning, in a bid to try to wear herself out – it hadn't worked. Opening a dresser drawer, her eyes were instantly drawn to where she'd tucked the threatening letter from Grace beneath a pile of haphazardly folded knickers. She would need it for proof of why she did what she did when the truth came out. And by hook or by crook, it was going to. Sooner or later she would have to face up to the past she'd run from.

Grabbing her turquoise bikini and a matching sarong, she tugged off her pyjamas and got dressed for an early morning swim. A glimpse of her old jewellery box had her reaching on her tippy toes to retrieve it from the top shelf of her bookcase. Scenes from her youth flashed before her and a smile played on her lips. Although it had been one of her favourite possessions, a gift from her parents for her nineteenth birthday, she'd forgotten all about it.

She walked over to her bed and placed it down. Sitting, she flicked open the latch and lifted the lid. A chuckle caught in her throat when she spotted the array of cheap jewellery inside. She sorted through it all – laughing at the number of chokers and mood rings she'd had back then – they'd been all the rage. Mind you, chokers were coming back now. Each piece brought back memories, reminding her that she did, in fact, have a life before Zachary. In a weird way, it gave her hope. Grabbing a pair of long feather earrings, she held them up. They were pretty and would match the dress she'd brought along for the hens' party. If she were game, she might even wear them with it. They were very different from what she'd usually wear when she was going out with Zachary; pearls were more the style for his fancy-nancy dinners, but tonight, she could be herself and wear what she damn well pleased. And these earrings pleased her. A lot.

She put them down beside her, recalling the last time she'd slipped them on – her very first date with the magnificent Dylan Stone when she was just shy of turning seventeen. He had stolen her heart in a matter of seconds, without even realising it. She sighed dreamily. Unexpectedly, she remembered him giving her a yin and yang necklace that night – it was designed to snap in two so they could each wear a piece of it. She'd found it such a romantic gesture, and still did. She looked through the jewellery box in search of it, grinning when she found the half she'd worn for almost four years. It had meant more to her than diamonds or gold. Ah, sweet love. She'd been so young and free and happy back then. She wondered if Dylan would ever truly forgive her for leaving him heartbroken. If only he knew why she left he might understand her reason – this was a freedom Grace's death had given her. But her timing of when she revealed the truth, to him and everyone dear to her, was going to be pivotal.

With all the contents now emptied onto the bed, a note lodged at the bottom of the jewellery box caught her eye. She carefully unfolded it. Smiling gently, she ran her fingers over the cursive letters, somehow feeling as though she were sitting beside her seventeen-year-old self as she did. She spoke the words softly as she read it …

Things I want to achieve before I'm thirty
Eat something disgusting
Skinny dip
Dance Coyote Ugly style on a bar
Get on the back of a motorbike
Get a tattoo
Dance in the rain
Sleep under the stars
Tell Mum and Dad I know
Tell Amy and Tania the truth
Stand at the altar with Dylan Stone

She took in a sharp breath. Covering her mouth, her eyes welled with tears. As much as some things on the list made her laugh, two of them scared the living daylights out of her. Was this the sign she'd just asked for, the universe showing her the path she should be taking? Standing at the altar with Dylan was certainly out of the question. But the other nine, they *were* possible if she somehow found the guts to face her fears.

She quickly folded the note up, put it back where it had come from, and tossed the jewellery back on top of it. Then she hid the jewellery box on the floor of her closet, covered by a jumper, and dashed out of her bedroom, downstairs and out the back door of the homestead, relieved she'd found no other sign of life in the house along the way. Her mum and dad would already be out checking on the horses by now, before ducking back home for breakfast. She was looking forward to joining them for bacon and eggs once she'd had a swim to try to clear her mind. Not that she believed that was going to be at all possible with all the *what ifs* and *should Is* whirling in it right now.

Wandering along the path, through the gardens blooming with a multitude of flowers, mainly birds of paradise and wild gingers, she arrived at the steps that led down to Horseshoe Bay. She spotted her father's fishing boat bobbing at their private jetty. Beyond it, the aqua-blue ocean opened up before her, disappearing off the horizon. The scene was something that belonged on a postcard. She took in a long, deep breath, and then licked at the saltiness already upon her lips. This was absolute heaven. She was so blessed to be able to call this her home. Damn the secrets that had made her run from here all those years ago. Anger bubbled in her mind but she shoved it back down. She felt ripped off that she'd missed out on so much life with her family, and a possible love-filled future with the man of her dreams, all because she'd run from a problem that wasn't really hers to begin with. But dwelling on it wasn't going to help her now.

Focusing instead on the glorious moment, her heart sang as she jogged down the steps. The very second her feet sunk into the white sand her soul fired to life. She made a beeline towards the water, laughing at her own expense when she noticed how pale her usually olive complexion had become. Untying her sarong, she dropped it to the sand and ran for the water, arms up high. Splashing in, she took in a sharp breath at the unexpected coolness of it, and then dived beneath the waves.

Rising to the surface, the secrets she'd pushed down all those years ago rose to the surface too. There was no such thing as a coincidence. There was a reason she'd found her seventeen-year-old bucket list, and only a month off turning thirty. She was going to do her very best to tick off nearly all the things on the list, mindful that walking down the aisle with the love of her life was one thing she simply could not achieve. Maybe she could jump out of a plane to make up for it? She dived down again, enjoying the sound of the water beneath the waves. And just like that, everything seemed to fall into place. She knew what had to be done, and as hard as it was going to be, she trusted she could get through it somehow.

Feeling like she had a purpose now, she rose from the surf a new woman in strength and spirit. The salt stung her eyes when she flicked them open but she didn't care. She paddled out further and then floated on her back as she allowed the ebb and flow to ease her worries. She was doing the right thing; she just had to believe it. She watched as a few clouds began to creep in, gradually blocking out the glorious sunshine. Eventually, she swam back to shore, cursing when she realised she'd forgotten to bring a towel. Picking her sarong up from the sand, she wrapped it around herself. Combing her wet hair back with her fingers, she ran to the steps and climbed them, two at a time, feeling as though she were finally ascending from the hole she'd confined herself to more than eight long years ago.

CHAPTER

8

Stone's Throw

Sir Bouncealot was in his favourite spot, hung from the back of a kitchen chair in his hessian pouch, his head drooping over the side of it as he slept. After devouring a cream biscuit, Bluey was nodding off on his perch. The am radio station hummed in the background, the announcer saying something about it being a ripper of a day ahead. Dylan wished the day ahead was all he had to think about – but instead he was engrossed in his past. He'd had a rough night, much of it spent out on the back verandah staring up at the half moon while wishing he could wash away on his racing thoughts. Some were of his father and what had happened here that night; some were of Sophie and how he would feel when he saw her again; but mostly, his thoughts were about Angus. After calling his phone numerous times over the past twenty-four hours, with no answer or reply to the many voice and text messages Dylan had left, the feeling of unease that had sat in the pit of his stomach yesterday had now turned into full-scale panic. He'd barely been able to eat the bacon and eggs his mum had made him this morning, and it was one of his favourite meals of all time. He was doing his very best to keep his cool, not wanting to worry her, but he wasn't sure how much longer he could fool his mother and keep her thinking there was nothing wrong. She'd asked him over breakfast if everything was okay and he'd changed the subject. He could never successfully hide anything from her for too long.

Sighing, he popped another dish in the draining rack while gazing out the kitchen window. A few kangaroos bounded along the fence line and then disappeared down the back gully. Galahs squawked from their perches in the mango trees that lined the fence, the birds' rose-coloured chests a striking contrast to the dark green leaves. He could make out the silhouettes of his mother's two horses, Skye and Wizard, and his bad boy, Gunner, not far behind them, against the radiance of the morning sunshine. He couldn't wait to go for a gallop – it was on the cards for today. There was so much to be grateful for here and he was annoyed he couldn't fully relax to be able to enjoy it all. As if on cue his mobile phone burst to life from the windowsill. With sud-covered hands, he reached out and grabbed it, irritated it was a private number.

'Hello.'

'Dylan, it's me, Angus.' He sounded out of breath.

'Hey, I've been trying to get a hold of you. Why's your number private?'

'Because I'm calling from a pay phone.'

'Why?'

'I'm keeping a low profile and I don't want to use my phone in case it's tapped.'

'Okay.' Dylan moved as far out of earshot from his mother as he could without looking suspicious. 'Where are you? What's going on?'

'The stash has gone missing from the tattoo shop. You wouldn't have anything to do with it, would you?'

What the fuck?

'Just hang on a minute, would you; I can't hear you properly in here. I don't think I've got good service in the house.'

'Yeah, righto, but hurry it up, I haven't got all day.'

He had perfect phone service but with his mother walking into the kitchen, he needed an out. He stepped outside and down the back steps. Him? Stealing Angus's stash of drugs? The idiot had to be kidding. Dylan felt like telling him what for, but he bit his tongue.

'What the hell is going on, Angus?' He kept his voice low and a smile plastered to his dial, well aware his mother was watching him out the window as she washed up the rest of the breakfast dishes.

'Like I said, did you have anything to do with my stuff going missing?' It was said with a low growl.

'I told you, I don't want a bar of it, so why would I steal it?'

'Bit of a fucking coincidence, don't ya reckon, that you leave and the shit goes AWOL?'

'Think whatever the hell you like, Angus.'

'You listen, and you listen good, Stone. I left the pills in the safe that only you and I know the combination to, and when I went back to get them early the next morning, before the shop opened, the back door had been bashed in and they were fucking gone. Looks pretty bloody suss to me.'

'As if I'd have anything to do with it … you know how I feel about drugs and the people who sell them. And why in the hell would I bash the back door in when I have a set of keys?'

'To make it look like it was someone else.'

'Oh for Christ's sake, Angus.' Dylan felt like he was hitting his head against a brick wall. 'Someone else stole your stash. What about the security camera out back? Just watch the footage and you'll find out who it was.'

'Yeah, I would, except for the fact the camera was smashed to pieces.'

'Right, well, whatever the case, I had nothing to do with it. End of story.'

'Don't go fucking lying to me, Stone. I know your dirty little secret and I'm not afraid to go to the police with it.'

'I'm not lying, Angus, so don't go threatening me.' Although unnerved by the thought, Dylan choked back a sarcastic laugh. 'And it's not as if you're in any shape to go to the cops right now anyway.'

'Don't try me, because there's more than one way to skin a fucking cat. I got my ways, Dylan … and if you've crossed me, I'm bloody well going to cross you too.'

'You seriously think I took the shit and ran, do you?'

'Stranger things have happened.'

'You son of a bitch, you can shove your fucking job where it fits.' Dylan couldn't help himself.

'As if I was going to let you back near the place now.' Angus laughed mockingly.

'Look, Angus, I don't have your gear, okay … so can you just leave me and my family in peace.' Dylan could hear the anger in his voice.

'Yeah, whatever, I don't believe a damn word that comes out of your mouth, buddy.' The sound of traffic whizzing past wherever Angus was standing almost drowned out his voice.

Dylan was leaning against the back fence now, well out of earshot of his mum, staring out towards where he knew the sea hid behind the tree line. 'Don't buddy me, McDonald. I'm no friend of yours anymore.'

'You obviously never were. I'll forgive you for making a stupid fucking mistake if you just get the shit back to me.'

'You're barking up the wrong damn tree, McDonald. Go to hell.' Hitting the end button, Dylan had to fight from throwing his mobile phone into the scrub. This was bad. If it weren't for the wedding, he would pack his bags and leave now. Go undercover somewhere until all this blew over. But he couldn't. And he was tired of running. He wanted to stand his ground this time and deal with it. He was telling the truth. He just had to pray to God everything would work itself out soon, and whoever took the drugs was caught. He couldn't have Angus leaking his secret to the police.

'Everything all right, Dylan?'

He plastered a smile on his lips before he spun around. 'Yeah, all good, Angus is just having trouble with some of the staff, that's all. Goes with the territory.'

'Oh, right.' Faith looked at him carefully. 'Well, I'm going into town to pick up some groceries and feed for the horses and all the critters. You want to come for a run?'

Dylan wasn't in the mood for small talk with all the locals he hadn't seen for years. And with Angus's bullshit to worry about he wasn't ready to catch up with his mates yet either. Kurt and Mark were both keen to meet for a beer, but that could wait until the dinner tomorrow night. 'I might stay here and go for a ride on Gunner, if that's okay with you, Mum.' Striding across the back lawn, he climbed the steps and met her at the door.

'Yeah, of course it is.' She reached out and touched his cheek. 'You sure everything's okay?'

'Yeah, all good.' He stepped past her and held the door open for her to follow. 'Age before beauty.' He grinned cheekily and she gave him a firm but playful slap on the arm.

Just as Dylan latched the fly screen shut, the crunch of tyres on gravel pulled his attention to the driveway. A cop car appeared from around a bend and Dylan's stomach backflipped. Had Angus already done what he threatened? What was going to happen to his mum if he had? The bastard. Suddenly light-headed and dizzy, he found it hard to draw a decent breath. Time stood still. When his mother started to walk out to the front yard he almost grabbed her arm and pulled her back. But then she smiled and waved to whoever was behind the wheel.

Sweet baby Jesus.

A wave came from the open driver's window just before the cop car pulled to a stop. 'Hey there, Faith.'

When Dylan saw the copper who had pulled him over yesterday, his nerves subsided, but they didn't leave completely.

'Hi, Jim.' Faith had a spring in her step, the bells around her ankle jingling. 'To what do I owe this visit?' Dylan couldn't help but notice that her voice was more singsong than usual.

'I was just over at Frank's place, dropping off some paperwork for one of his workers that had his car stolen, so I thought I'd pop in to say g'day.'

Out of nowhere, Plucka swooped in, but there was none of the commotion of yesterday. He quacked as he waddled past the front of the car, and Sergeant Tucker called out hello to the feathered guard dog as though they were long-time friends. Dylan took note of their familiarity with one another, bird and man, and it made him wonder how often Jim Tucker called out here to see his mum. Interesting. Something told him it wasn't just for guitar lessons for his son.

'Well that's nice of you to come by and check on me, Jim.' She gestured to Dylan with a sweep of her arm. 'This is my son, Dylan.'

'I know, we've already met.' Sergeant Tucker graced him with a nod and a knowing smirk. 'Hey there, Dylan.'

Now leaning on the verandah rail, Dylan gave him a brisk nod. 'G'day.'

Faith pointed from one to the other. 'So how have you two met already?'

'I think Dylan was in a bit of a hurry to get here and see you yesterday, and I pulled him over for speeding.' He smiled at Faith in a way that suggested more than friendship. 'But seeing as he was your boy I let him off with a warning.' He shot a cautionary glance in Dylan's direction. 'This time, but next time he won't be so lucky.'

'Dylan.' Faith tutted in his direction, her arms folded.

Dylan grinned at the fact his mother still treated him as though he were a teenager. 'Don't you worry, Sergeant Tucker, there won't be a next time. I learnt my lesson good and proper.'

'Good, that's what I like to hear,' he said. 'So you still okay for Jason's guitar lesson tomorrow arvy?'

Faith nodded, smiled broadly, and then said something Dylan couldn't quite hear.

'That'd be lovely, thanks, Faith.'

'My pleasure, Jim.'

'Right then, I better be off. Catch you both tomorrow.'

Faith stepped back from the cop car. 'Yes, see you then.'

Both men exchanged a nod, and as Jim Tucker drove away, Dylan couldn't help but wonder what in the hell was going on between the pair. Having a copper around was not the best of things. Not only because of what was happening right now, but also because of what happened here twenty-odd years ago.

ॐ

Daniela had to get back to work straight after the dress fitting, so it was just Sophie and her sisters at the table. She pointed to an item on the menu, her gag reflex already kicking in to full force. She swallowed down hard, determined to do this. 'I'll have the crumbed lamb's brains, please.' She smiled up at the waiter who nodded and jotted it down on his notepad like it wasn't a big deal. 'Does it come with any sauce on the side?' *Oh, please, dear lord, let it come with a sauce to drown it in*, she thought.

'Yes, it does, ma'am. A piquant herb sauce.'

'Oh right, what's that?'

'It's a foamy butter reduction with capers, parsley, mint and dill.'

'Okay, well, that sounds divine.'

Looking at her with bewilderment, Tania and Amy ordered the same as each other, mussels in a white wine and garlic cream sauce. Twins just couldn't seem to help doing many things the same.

Once the waiter had dashed off to place their order, Tania gave her a look of absolute horror. 'Why are you ordering lamb's brains? That's majorly disgusting.'

Amy mimicked her sister's grossed-out expression. 'Yeah, you wouldn't even eat oxtail stew growing up. What have they done to you in jolly old England?'

Sophie shrugged. 'I just feel like trying something new, that's all.'

Tania and Amy turned to each other, their shocked expressions worth a thousand words. Amy was the first to turn back to her. 'You never try anything new.'

'There's always a first time for everything.' Needing to look away, Sophie gazed out at the glimmering ocean beneath a bright blue sky. The view from the new seaside restaurant was very impressive.

'I'm not buying it.' Amy took a sip of her pink champagne, eyeing Sophie the entire time over the rim of her glass. Placing it back down, she lifted a brow. 'Come on, spill … who dared you to eat lamb's brains?'

'Nobody did.'

Amy remained silent, her eyes never leaving Sophie's as she waited for her sister to crack.

True to form, Sophie did. Slumping forward, she rested her chin on her hands, her elbows dug into the table. 'All right. You got me. I found a list I'd written when I was about seventeen of things I wanted to achieve before I was thirty, and eating something disgusting was one of them.' She smiled. 'Happy now, Little Miss I Need to Know Everything?'

Amy sat back and smiled smugly. 'I knew there was something behind it.'

'Oooo, a bucket list.' Tania sat forwards, mimicking Sophie's posture. 'Do tell.'

Sophie feigned ignorance. 'Do tell what?'

'Do tell what else is on the list,' Tania said.

Shit, think quickly … 'Oh, nothing too exciting, just things like this, and then skinny dipping, sleeping out under the stars, dancing in the rain.' She shrugged. 'Things like that.'

Tania clapped her hands. 'Oh my God, that sounds like fun.'

'Sure does, and it'll do you good to let your hair down and do things you wouldn't normally,' Amy said. 'Might help you get over Mister I Can't Keep It In My Pants.'

'Amy!' Sophie shot her sister a disapproving look.

Amy grimaced. 'Sorry. I don't have a filter.'

'No, you don't,' Tania said with an equally disapproving look. 'Do Mum and Dad know yet, Soph?'

Sophie shook her head.

'Well, I think you should tell them sooner rather than later.'

'I know, it's just, I feel like such a failure.'

'Why, sis?' Tania's voice was filled with compassion.

'Because I moved my whole life to be with Zachary, and Mum and Dad warned me it was too soon to know if we'd work as a couple, but I did it anyway, and now look where I am. Almost nine years later, still not married and still no children.' She choked back tears, not wanting to sob like a baby in the middle of the restaurant.

'You're nowhere near a failure, Sophie Copinni, so don't even say that out loud,' Amy said, her eyes fierce. 'You're a well-regarded freelance editor and you've travelled the world. God, Tania and I haven't even left Queensland, like, never.'

'Yeah,' Tania chimed in. 'And look at me go, I'm a pole-dancing instructor.'

'You are?' Sophie tried to feign not knowing, even though Amy had filled her in.

'I am.' Tania smiled. 'And to be honest, I love my job.'

'That's good, Tans, and I bet you're very good at it too.' Even though she was smiling now, a tear escaped and Sophie quickly wiped it away before either of her sisters noticed.

'But don't tell Mum and Dad. They think I'm a fitness instructor.'

Sophie pretended to zip her lips.

Amy drank the last of her champagne and sat back. 'Well, while we're all being honest, I really don't like my job.'

Sophie gasped. 'You don't? I thought you loved being a nurse.'

'I used to, but now I just want to stay home and make babies.'

'Fair enough, Ames, me too.' Sophie looked to Tania. 'How about you, you want to stay home with Alex and make babies?'

Tania looked mortified with the thought. 'Oh, no thank you ... too much hard work involved with kids for me.'

Sophie looked from one sister to the other. 'Twins in a lot of ways, huh, but chalk and cheese in others.'

'Yup,' Amy and Tania said in unison.

'Thank you for being such amazing sisters.' Sophie smiled at the two women sitting opposite her. She had kept a massive secret from them all these years, and looking at them now the feeling of guilt inside her was growing even stronger.

'You're an amazing sister too,' Amy said.

'Yes, you most certainly are,' Tania agreed.

The guilt festered. Wanting to move the attention away from her, Sophie quickly changed the course of the conversation to something that had been playing on her mind since arriving home yesterday. 'So what do you think is going on with Mum and Dad? They're acting like a pair of lovesick teenagers and the fridge ...' She held her hands up and shook her head. 'Don't even get me started on what we found in the fridge.'

'I've been wondering the same thing. I caught them both coming out of the doctor's surgery a few weeks back, and when I asked what they were doing there, together of all things, they both said it was just a routine yearly check-up,' Amy said. 'I didn't think much of it at the time, but when I think back to it, they were acting a little strange. I hope neither of them has something seriously wrong where they've had to change their diet.' Clutching her refilled champagne flute, Amy paused with it raised to her lips. 'Or then again, maybe it's as simple as they're both having a mid-life crisis.'

'Maybe,' Tania added. 'But I reckon there's something they're not telling us. That jar of probiotic sauerkraut is a dead set giveaway that either our parents have been brainwashed by aliens, or there's something serious going on.'

'Maybe we should sit them down and ask them,' Sophie suggested.

'Ask them why they're practising Kama Sutra?' Tania looked horrified. 'No, thank you.'

'No, Tans, ask them if they're both healthy and well.'

'You really think it might be serious?' Tania looked extremely worried now.

'I don't think so. But there's no harm in asking, is there?'

'Nope. Let's do it,' Tania and Amy said in unison, once again.

The meals arrived, bringing the conversation to an end. Sophie was quite happy to see that the crumbs made the brains look edible. But only just.

'Well, come on then, Soph, tuck in.' Tania shoved a mussel in her mouth and grinned.

Amy jiggled in her seat. 'Eww, I can't wait to see this.'

Piercing one of the golden morsels with her fork, Sophie dunked it in the sauce and then, closing her eyes (she didn't know why because it wasn't going to help the taste), she shoved it in her mouth and chewed. She gagged a little with the texture, which reminded her of a cross between tofu and scrambled eggs. Then the custard-like creaminess threatened to overcome her need to behave in the classy restaurant and not spit it out. And then there was the taste. Ah, the taste – a combination of rich umami and pork, her least favourite meat. With a strength she didn't know she had, she forced it down her throat. Opening her mouth, she showed her sisters the feat was accomplished. Tania and Amy both clapped, drawing the attention of most of the people lunching around them.

Sophie felt her cheeks glow red as she sculled her glass of champagne, shaking the glass out in front of her to indicate it needed refilling, and fast. Amy did the honours.

Tania wiped her lips with her napkin. 'So, what do you think?'

'Not my favourite, and I won't be eating the rest of them, but at least that's one thing I can tick off my bucket list.'

'Do you want some of my mussels, sis?' Tania pushed her bowl towards Sophie.

Her appetite destroyed after one mouthful of brains, Sophie gently pushed the bowl back. 'Thanks, but no thanks.' She eyed the crusty bread in the middle of the table that she'd chosen not to tuck into earlier. 'I might just have some of this with a bit of butter.'

'That bad, huh?' Amy said with a giggle.

'Yup, that bad.' Sophie grinned but at the same time she was thinking that this tick off her bucket list was probably the easiest one of the lot.

CHAPTER

9

Rosewood Farm

Daniela Copinni pulled up out the front of the homestead. Turning the Tim McGraw song down, she left the engine running and put the car in park. Undoing her seatbelt and then leaning over to the passenger side, she and Sophie brushed kisses on each other's cheeks. 'Thank you for all your help today, Soph. I couldn't have got it all done without you."

'My pleasure, any time.' Sophie grabbed her handbag from the floor.

'I'll see you at the pre-wedding dinner tomorrow night then.'

Sophie's breath caught. 'There's a dinner?' This meant she would most probably be seeing Dylan sooner rather than later.

'Yeah, your mum came up with the idea.' Daniela looked concerned as she noticed Sophie's confusion. 'It's at your place, so I thought you'd already know about it.'

'Nope, nobody's mentioned it.'

'Oh crap, really?'

'Really.'

'That's strange. Could you just make sure your mum is still keen for it? Or maybe I got the dates wrong, or something. My head's all over the place with this wedding, sorry, Soph, and Mum's no better. She's been running around like a chook with her head cut off lately.'

'Sure,' Sophie choked out. 'I'll ring you later and confirm.'

'Groovy.' Daniela gave a megawatt smile.

'Cool beans.' Sophie paused, wondering whether to ask what was on the tip of her tongue, and then curiosity got the better of her. 'Is Dylan coming tomorrow night?'

Daniela looked at her like she was clueless. 'Of course, he's the best man.'

'Oh, yeah, stupid question.' Sophie tried to act nonchalant but knew she was failing miserably.

'Oh, Soph, I thought you two would've been able to move past all that now without a problem.'

'Yes, we should be able to, it's just that I feel so bad about what I did to him.'

Daniela rolled her eyes. 'You were young and silly way back when, but you're mature adults now … you'll be fine, trust me.'

Sophie nodded. 'Let's hope so, hey?'

'Dylan is a good man, with a kind heart – he will be nothing but respectful towards you, especially in your own home.'

'Yes, you're right. I need to stop worrying so much.'

'Don't stress the small stuff, Sophie. Life is too short.'

'Okay, I'll try not to.' She went to slide out of the car, but Daniela grabbed her hand. 'Mum told me about you and Zachary.'

'Oh for God's sake, there really is nothing secret in this family, is there?' She said it with a lighthearted edge.

'No, of course not … you should know that by now.' Daniela grinned. 'I just wanted to tell you I'm happy to go over all the legalities of a separation, when you're ready, of course. But don't leave it too long or Zachary will get the upper hand.'

'Thanks, Daniela, I really appreciate it.'

'My services will be free of charge too.'

Sophie held her hand up. 'No, I won't hear of it.'

'Sophie, please, that's what family do, we take care of each other.'

Sophie bit back tears. Goddamn it, she was crying at the drop of a hat lately. 'Thanks.'

'It will be my absolute pleasure; the cheating bastard won't know what's hit him when I'm done.'

'I just want what's fair, that's all.'

Daniela nodded, her smile warm. 'I know, and that's what you'll get.'

Stepping out, Sophie slung her handbag over her shoulder. As she'd clicked the door shut Daniela gave her a quick wave and sped off, leaving her standing in a cloud of dust. *Definitely not a car made for a dirt driveway*, she thought as she watched the red sports car disappear around a bend. Daniela was a livewire, just like her mum, Gina.

Turning on her heel and heading towards the house, Sophie heaved a weary sigh. With another dress fitting, finalising the flower and cake details, and shopping for the rest of the decorations for the hall, most of the day had gone, but she had enjoyed every second of it. Time with her family, no matter what they were doing, was time well spent. Reaching the front door, she paused to take in the view. Tangerine and crimson were just beginning to spill across the cloud-scattered sky. She needed to get changed quick smart if she wanted a dip in the ocean before the sun disappeared.

Five minutes flat and she was making her way down the back steps and towards the ocean. The scene was something right out of a movie, the setting sun painting golden trails across the shimmering water. When her bare feet hit the sand she stopped and squished her toes into it, a happy sigh escaping her. She'd spent countless hours sitting on the beach, staring out at this view with her sisters by her side. Life had seemed so free and easy back then. Now, here she stood, years later, pondering who she was and what she wanted from her life, and also the fact that she was about to run stark naked into the water.

Was she really going to do this?

She looked left and right, relieved to see there wasn't another soul in sight. She'd die of embarrassment if she were caught out. She made her way towards the water while staring out across the vast expanse of sea. Two beach stone-curlews dipped into the ocean as they fished for their dinner. Way out on the horizon, a freightliner languidly made its way to port. She wondered if they had clear sight to the beach, and if they did, if they would be horrified at what they were about to see. She soothed herself by thinking they'd need super-dooper binoculars to home in on her. Clutching her sarong around her, she ran to where the small waves spilled onto the shore, depositing a variety of shells and seaweed. Overhead a fleet of pelicans flew past, wings outstretched. Looked like the only spectators she would have were the birds, and she was okay with that. Lord help her if anything bit her private parts.

Just as she was about to rip the silky material from her, to reveal her nakedness beneath, a voice sounded from behind. Her cheeks flared to what she guessed was the brightest shade of red ever seen upon human skin. Spinning around as if she'd just been busted doing the unthinkable, she grinned into friendly eyes and a sunbaked face. Bob Watson, the family's gardener for the past fifteen years, smiled back at her. A half-smoked rollie hung from his lips. How could she not have seen him approaching? Talk about stealth.

'Going for a twilight dip, Sophie?' He was carrying a bucket and a fishing pole.

'Was thinking about it. You catch anything?' She tried to peer into his bucket, but a puff of tobacco smoke made her pull back quick smart.

He pulled the rollie from his lips and blew another stream of smoke upwards. 'Sure did.' He tipped the bucket so she could look inside. A massive clawed creature with beady little eyes stared back at her.

'Oh, wow, a mud crab.'

'Yup. Missus Watson is going to think all her Christmases have come at once.' He looked proud as punch. 'I've got some crab traps in down yonder.' He thumbed over his shoulder. 'And this is the first little blighter I've caught in over a month.' He grinned. 'I can't wait to get him in my belly.'

Sophie shuddered at the thought of having to kill the poor thing. 'Well, enjoy, and say hi to Missus Watson for me, won't you?'

'Will do.' He gestured to the water with a tip of his head. 'Make sure you don't swim out too far. It'll be dark soon.'

'I won't. I just want a quick dip before dinner, to wash the day off.'

'Well, I'll be off then, let you enjoy it.'

'Bye, Bob.'

He gave her a wave over his shoulder as he trudged through the sand and up the steps. She waited until he was out of sight, and then before her nerves could get the better of her she pulled the sarong off and ran for the water, cursing when she remembered she hadn't brought a towel. Again.

After riding until his growling stomach had dragged him home for an afternoon snack, and then doing some odd jobs around the cottage for his mum, including conquering the squeaky front door because he couldn't stand it a minute longer, the day had got away from Dylan. It was close to five-thirty before he found himself back at the stables. The ride this morning had been that good he was coming back for more. An afternoon trot along the beach to watch the sun set into the ocean was his idea of an afternoon well spent – and it would help take his mind off his dramas with Angus, and the dinner tomorrow night.

Gunner stood patiently as Dylan checked the girth strap, fixed the corner of the saddle blanket and then hoisted himself up. The horse neighed softly as Dylan relaxed into the seat of his trusty old saddle. Even though the events of yesterday had upended him, he couldn't help but smile. Being on a horse, back in the arms of Stone's Throw, gave him a strong sense of arriving home, and he liked it one hell of a lot.

Grabbing his sunglasses from the rim of his wide-brimmed hat, he slipped them on. 'Right, buddy, let's hit the beach.'

Heading away from the stables, he nudged the old boy into a canter and down a soft slope that led to a small flat. Bringing Gunner to a stop once they'd reached it, he admired the expanse of sparkling ocean before him. It was so flat it looked like a sheet of glass. Steep cliffs separated them from the beach below – but that wasn't going to stop them. It never had before. He breathed in deeply, liking the taste of sea salt on the breeze. Sitting forward in the saddle, he guided Gunner on, towards the steep but familiar descent to the glorious golden sand.

While enjoying the sway from side to side as Gunner made his way over the rocky terrain, Dylan's mind wandered back to this morning, to the visit from the town copper. He couldn't help but notice the way his mother had blushed. In all his years he'd never seen her like that with a bloke. Although it was nice to know that she was on cloud nine, it also worried him that the copper might find out about the night Don Stone died. Police took an oath to abide by the law under any circumstance, and Jim Tucker would be no different, so there would be implications, he was sure of it. He didn't want to see anything happen to his mum because of the lies she'd told.

That fateful night crashed into his mind. As if it were only yesterday he remembered running to his mother and clutching her like his life depended on it, with Grace sobbing beside them. He'd almost lost his mother that night, once again at the hands of his father, and the terror he'd felt was the kind of fear he wouldn't wish on his worst enemy. Then all three of them had stood, hand in hand, staring down at the bullet hole in his father's chest. There was shock in Don Stone's lifeless eyes. The blood had seeped out, leaving a growing puddle beneath his body. Dylan had felt nothing but relief in that moment; his father could no longer hurt either of them. Don Stone had done enough damage, had stolen enough of their happiness, had left bruises on his mother too many times. It was high time he repented his sins before God. Grabbing the phone, his mum had rung the police while he and Grace had tried to console each other. His mother was sobbing, her body trembling and covered in splatters of his father's blood. Dylan remembered wishing he could take her pain away. The scent of gunfire still hung in the air, strong and pungent. The blood had puddled at his feet, and he and Grace stepped back, away from it. The call over, his mum had dragged him and Grace from the kitchen, her shaking hands trying to cover their eyes as if to rid them of the sight already burnt into their memories. The next month had been a blur of police investigations. The light among all the darkness had been Aunt Kimmy. She took a month off to come up and be with them. She was their rock, their confidant, and along with Grace, the keeper of their secret all these years.

Dylan came back from the past and shivered despite the warmth of the sun on his back. The dark shadows from that time were still long enough to reach out and overwhelm him, but they weren't scary enough to claim his every waking moment anymore. And that was one hell of a giant step forwards. As Gunner's hooves hit the sand, Dylan gave a slight squeeze of his thighs to entice him into a canter. Then, wanting more, he gave his equine mate permission to break into a gallop. As if flooring an accelerator, the horse took his cue and leapt forward. Sand flew up from his hooves in an arc behind them, a trail of hoof prints left in the sand. Gunner neared the lacy fringes of the waves, and splashed speckles of water into the glow of the setting sun with each thunderous step, the droplets shining like tiny diamonds on the sea breeze. Dylan steered him further in, and as the ground disappeared beneath them the horse plunged forwards, snorting excitedly. With Gunner now swimming, Dylan felt as if he were floating on air. The small waves parted before them as the horse swam out deeper. He tried to lure Gunner back to shore, but like a child reluctant to leave the fun of the surf the horse did another circle, only then heading back in.

Returning to the sand, Gunner broke into a gallop at Dylan's urging. The exhilaration of being full throttle in the saddle swept over him, and he closed his eyes to heighten the sensation, only to open them to a sight he was completely unprepared for. Although some distance away, the reflection of the sun off the woman's long, silky blonde hair was achingly familiar. So much so he instinctively wanted to reach out and touch it, as he used to all those years ago. As she rose from the water goddess-like and completely naked, he couldn't help but admire her beautiful breasts, long legs and luscious curves in all the right places. Still completely unaware of him, she wrapped her sarong around herself, and then shook the water from her hair. He felt the punch to his stomach and the stab to his heart – feelings he'd tried to convince himself he wouldn't have when he saw her again.

She began to walk towards where he knew steps led up to her parents' place. He stood up and stretched to his height from the stirrups, and the horse adjusted his gait smoothly to help balance him. 'Sophie?' Her name left his lips as a whisper. It felt strange rolling off his tongue because he hadn't spoken it in almost five years – not since Amy and Kurt's wedding. Not even once. At first it was because of the hurt she'd caused him, and the anger he felt towards her for it, and then it was his way of coping, of pretending she didn't exist.

But here she was, as beautiful as ever, stealing his breath from him.

'Woo now, mate.' Gunner cocked his ears back to listen as Dylan brought him to a trot and then a slow walk.

Her foot on the first step, Sophie stopped and then spun round. Dylan wanted to look away but he couldn't. Her eyes found his face, and her mouth fell open in complete shock. 'Dylan.' He couldn't hear her but he could easily read the lips he had kissed hundreds if not thousands of times.

Now only metres from her, he acknowledged her with a tip of his hat, doing his very best to come across as lighthearted and confident. 'G'day. Long time no see.' It felt a little lame but what else was he meant to say?

Sophie smiled warily, and he felt the tug of the invisible cord that had always bonded them, the one he'd stupidly thought he'd severed. In a split second she stepped from his past to his present and he could feel his heart reaching out for hers. As much as he was still hurt by what she'd done all those years ago, he was, as he used to be, mesmerised by the unusual blue-green shade of her arresting eyes.

She stopped a few feet short of him and tilted her head back slightly to meet his gaze. She gave him a curious look, which quickly dissolved into a broader smile than the last. 'Howdy, stranger … it's really nice to see you.' Quickly switching her focus to the horse, she reached out and stroked Gunner's muzzle.

Her smile was so familiar and so warm as she acquainted herself with her old horsey mate. It somehow erased the years and brought Dylan back to times he wasn't ready to relive. His girl of then was a mature, *spoken for* woman now, and even more gorgeous than he remembered.

'Oh, and it's good to see you too, Dylan.' She looked back up at him and grinned playfully.

'It's nice to …' He cleared his throat. 'Bump into you too.'

As if suddenly realising he may have seen her starkers, Sophie sucked in a sharp breath and covered her mouth. 'Oh my God, did you see me coming out of the water?' She had a slight lilt of a British accent and that irritated him. Not only did Zachary get to enjoy all there was to love about her these past eight years, he'd also marked her with his haughtiness.

'I did.' Dylan couldn't help the wayward grin that surfaced. 'Was the water nice?' Her lips, now trembling a little, still reminded him of a luscious ripe strawberry ready to be tasted. As he imagined what it would be like to kiss her again, he couldn't help but wonder what she thought of the man he'd become.

Her gaze skipped over the tattoos on each of his forearms. 'The water was beautiful.' She flicked the wet hair from her face. Hair he used to run his fingers through as he kissed her and made love to her. 'I'm really embarrassed you busted me, though. I don't usually do that kind of stuff.' Her face was glowing a bright shade of red but she was still smiling – only now the curl of her mouth hinted at the cheekiness she'd harboured all those years ago.

'What's happened to your Aussie accent? You sound like a pom now.' He didn't like looking down on her, so he eased himself out of the saddle and onto the sand. Gunner stood perfectly still beside him. When he focused back on her, her expression had changed to one of poorly concealed hurt. 'Sorry, I didn't mean anything by that,' he said.

'Yeah, well, I can't help taking on some of the English accent after living there for so bloody long, hey?' She wasn't smiling as widely now and what lingered of it, he could tell, was forced. He wondered what she really wanted to say if she put aside the niceties that were expected when running into someone for the first time in years.

'Fair point.' He recalled her last words to him, spoken in the darkness at the front of her house, and the stab in his heart was just as sharp and deep as it had been back then. 'How's life treating you in the UK?'

'Yeah, good, I suppose.' It sounded unconvincing.

Something about the sad look in her eyes made him want to take her into his arms and soothe whatever it was away. But he couldn't. Wouldn't. There was a line in the sand, and he wasn't going to cross it. 'That's good.' He didn't want to feel anything when he looked at her, but that wasn't the case. She reminded him of a time when he believed in love and a happily ever after, and she also reminded him of the fact that could end in the blink of an eye. Like a smoker stubbing out a cigarette, she'd crushed his dreams in seconds, and then acted as if he'd never meant a thing to her.

An uncomfortable silence settled.

He made damn sure that his expression gave nothing away. She didn't deserve his heartache, and didn't deserve this feeling of tenderness he still held for her either. 'Must be good seeing the family, hey?'

'It sure is.' She stared past him to the waves crashing against the shore and when she looked back her eyes were even sadder than before. 'The wedding should be nice.'

'Yeah, I'm really looking forward to it. About time, seeing Daniela and Mark have been together since high school.' He paused, but only for a split second. 'At least one couple lasted the distance.' A low blow but he couldn't help himself.

'Yeah, true.' Stepping from foot to foot, she looked at him as if she were trying to climb inside of his soul. 'I'm so sorry about what happened, Dylan. I never meant to hurt you the way I did.' Tears welled in her beautiful, soulful eyes.

Shock hit him like a freight train. How was he meant to respond? Nicely or truthfully? 'Thanks for apologising, because you did hurt me, a hell of a lot, Sophie.'

She looked down at her bare feet. 'I know, and I live with the guilt of that every waking day.'

'I don't want you to live with guilt. It's in the past and we can't change it. But what I do want is to ask you something that's been bugging me all these years …'

'Then please, ask me.'

'Why?'

'Why what?' Her expression told him she knew exactly what he meant.

'Oh come on, Sophie, you know what I'm asking. Why did you do it? Why did you leave me?'

She shifted uneasily beneath his gaze, pressing her lips together the way she always did when she was uncomfortable. 'I wasn't thinking straight, and I was desperate to travel. I made a really bad decision that I wish I could take back.'

'I'm sorry but I don't believe you.' Dylan shook his head.

'I don't know what else to tell you.' She drew in a shuddering breath, biting her bottom lip between her teeth.

There was something in her eyes and her defensive stance that made him a hundred percent sure she was hiding something from him. 'The truth would be a good start.'

She remained silent. He could see she was holding her breath, and yet her chest was rising and falling rapidly. She reached across the chasm that separated them and squeezed his hand.

'You aren't going to tell me the truth, are you?' He didn't respond to her gesture, but he also didn't withdraw from it.

Her lips clamped shut even tighter.

'Rightio, well that's that then.'

'I'm sorry, Dylan.'

'Stop saying sorry.' He drew in a slow, steady breath. 'I just have to get over it.'

'I feel terrible.' She bit her lip and her eyes teared up again.

As much as he was cross with her, and disappointed she didn't offer the answer that would give him some kind of closure, he still had a place in his heart for this woman, and he felt like an arsehole making her cry. Reaching out, he finally gave in to his longing to do so, and pulled her to him. At first she hesitated, but then she melted into him. 'Let's try and start afresh, and be mates, hey?' he whispered against her golden hair.

Her head now buried in his chest, she nodded. They remained like that for a few moments, and then sniffling, she pulled back from him. 'Thank you, Dylan.'

'It's better than being bitter – makes for an unhappy life.'

'That's it.' She gave him an appreciative smile. 'Well, it'll be dark very soon, so I better head off and let you get home too. I'll catch you tomorrow night at the dinner?'

'Yeah, you will.'

She gave him a little wave. 'Bye, Dylan.'

'Bye, Soph.'

She climbed the steps two at a time, as though desperate to get away from him. He stood and watched her go, the deep sense of loss he'd felt all those years ago returning. She didn't turn back, and that cut his already bleeding heart, even though it shouldn't have. He made sure she was at the top safely, her graceful silhouette disappearing over the rise, before climbing up and back into the saddle. He meant what he said. He wanted to try to at least be mates. If not for their sakes, then for Daniela and Mark's – they didn't need tension in their bridal party on their wedding day. Maybe one day, when the time was right, Sophie would be able to explain why she'd left him. Until then, he just had to learn to live with the fact she would never ever be his again.

CHAPTER
10

Rosewood Farm

Sophie sat at the dining table, unaware she was drumming her fingers. One of her all time favourites, her mother's homemade lasagne, sat uneaten on the plate in front of her. She stared out the large bay windows towards the star-studded sky that was putting on a dazzling show worthy of an ovation. Below, the moonlight reflected off the water as if it were a mirror. She imagined floating among the beauty of it all and letting all her worries drain away.

For the past few hours, she'd tried to stop wondering, tried to stop asking herself how things would have transpired if she'd blurted it all out to Dylan this afternoon. But it just hadn't felt like the right moment to do so. Her mind was scattered and her heart ached beyond belief; she needed to take action, somehow, to ease some of the burden, some of the heartache. But that was going to take courage, courage she didn't have the strength for right now. She wanted answers, closure, a fresh start, and she felt that unless she dealt with the past, she was never going to achieve that.

As much as she felt she deserved it, it had hurt not seeing the spark in Dylan's beautiful blue eyes, the one that had been there when he'd loved her so deeply. She missed him; so much more than she'd allowed herself to believe these past years. But seeing him today, in all his mannish gorgeousness and still wearing his heart on his sleeve, she'd almost crumbled to the sand in tears. Ridiculously tall and with a bad-boy, good-man persona, he'd struck a match inside her instantly. It had been a feat holding his gaze while keeping her pulse from careening out of control. What she would have given to feel his lips press against hers in greeting. She remembered what his kiss tasted like, could still recall in detail what it had felt like the first time they'd made love down on the very beach she was looking out over. Unawares, her fingers trailed across her lips as a sigh escaped her.

'Are you all right, sweetheart?' Her mother's gentle voice snapped Sophie from her thoughts and she looked down at her uneaten meal. 'Yeah, sorry, I've just got a few things on my mind.'

'We're all ears if you want to talk about it, Soph.' Her father gave her a look that implied he might already know something. Maybe Amy or Tania had told them about the break-up.

Instantly choked up, Sophie burst into tears.

Marie leapt to her feet and dashed around to take her into her arms. 'Oh, love, what is it?'

Hugging her mum like her life depended it, Sophie wept harder. There was something to be said about a mother's hug and the magical power it had. 'I don't want to ruin the wedding with all my dramas.'

Marie pulled back a little, but only enough to look her daughter in the eye. 'Don't be silly, Soph. Please tell us what's wrong.' She paled, her eyes wide. 'You're not sick, are you?'

'No, nothing like that.'

'Then what is it?'

Sophie looked over her mother's shoulder to her dad, and then back down to her plate. 'I caught Zachary cheating on me.' She almost whispered it.

'Oh, love, why didn't you tell us before now?'

'Because I feel like a disappointment.'

'Sophie, don't say such silly things.' Marie's eyes were filled with compassion.

Her father's hand slammed the table with an almighty crash. 'That son of a bitch ... I knew he was no good. I warned you, Sophie, didn't I, that he wouldn't treat you right?'

Marie shot him a warning glance. 'Frank, now's not the time for "I told you so".'

'Yes, you're right.' He looked to Sophie. 'Sorry, love, I just hate knowing you gave up so much to be with him, and now he's gone and done this to you.'

'I know you're just being protective, Dad.'

Frank gripped his fork tightly. 'So what does he have to say for himself?'

'I don't know.' Sophie shrugged.

Frank shook his head. 'You haven't confronted him?'

'No, not yet. I wanted time to get my head around what I was going to do first.'

'Right, and what are you going to do?' He eyed her warily. 'I hope you're not considering staying with him?'

'No, of course not, I just wanted time to be level headed when I tell him I'm leaving. Although, he would have worked it out for himself by now, after he read the letter I left him on the table.' Her mum handed her a tissue and she wiped at the tears rolling down her cheeks.

'I'm so sorry he's done this to you,' Marie said. 'You deserve much better than that, Soph. You must live here with us until you find your feet, and forget he ever existed.'

'I want to, but it's not that cut and dry, Mum.'

'Yes, it is.'

'My freelancing business is based there, and we own the apartment together ...' Her voice trailed off. A sick feeling settled in her stomach when she thought about all the things she had to sort out. Thank God she had Daniela there to help her, once the wedding was all over, that was.

'I'm sure you can move your business here, love, I've no doubt you'll get lots of work in Australia with your credentials.' Her dad's brown eyes grew even darker. 'And let me just say ... he's damn lucky he's so far away because if I could get my hands on him I'd teach him a bloody good lesson.'

Marie tutted. 'Frank, violence never fixed anything.'

'There's always a first time, Marie.'

Sophie gave her mum a little smile. 'He's just being caring in his own way, Mum.' A sudden urge to spill the beans to her parents about what she knew overcame her. She sucked in a breath and went with it. 'There's something else I need to tell you both, too.'

'What is it?' her parents said in unison.

The house phone rang. They all looked at each other. Her father glanced towards where it sat on the side table. Maybe the universe was intervening, telling her now *wasn't* the time. She followed her dad's gaze. 'Do you want to get it?' she asked.

'I better.' The chair scraped as he stood and then strode over to answer it, his hand resting on where he'd hurt his lower back. Sophie tried not to think about *how* he'd done it.

'Hello, Copinni residence.'

There was a pause, and then her father let rip, in English at first and then Maltese. It was something he always did when he was extremely angry, which wasn't very often. Hurt his girls and the protective father came out swinging. She understood every word he was saying, but knew the man at the other end wouldn't have a clue. It was probably a good thing. Her father spun around to face her, red rage hinting through the deep olive of his cheeks. 'Well, I really don't know if she wants to talk to you.'

She nodded and waved for the phone. 'I'll talk to him.'

Her mother stopped her from standing, her hand pressing down upon her shoulder. 'Are you sure, love?'

'I'm going to have to at some point, so why not now?'

Her father reluctantly handed her the phone. Marie stood and her parents busied themselves clearing the table, but she could clearly tell their ears were wide open. She drew in a slow, calming breath and then held the phone to her ear. 'Zachary.' She paused, waiting.

'Why aren't you answering your mobile, Sophie, and what's up with your dad? I couldn't understand a word he was saying.'

'He's just looking after me, that's all.'

'Okay, I don't get why but there you go – your family has always been a little weird.'

Sophie bit her tongue.

'I've called to let you know I've just arrived home to find my office smashed to smithereens.' His tone was short, sharp, curt. 'Someone must have broken in with both of us away, but oddly there's nothing missing. It will cost an absolute fortune to fix it. I am going to call the police after I talk to you, and report it.'

'I was the one who smashed your office.' Not even a mention of the note she'd left on the kitchen table that said they were over, although she hadn't explained why. She'd saved that for when he called her, which she knew he would as soon as he saw his office or the note, or both.

'What the hell? Why would you do such a thing, Sophie?' Zachary's voice was shrill.

She watched her parents comfortably working together, packing the dishwasher and cleaning up. That's what she wanted, a marriage like theirs. 'Because I felt like it, just like you felt like sleeping with your secretary.'

'Have you lost your marbles? What the hell are you on about?'

Now he was going to try to treat her like a fool, talk his way out of it. It was something he did often and well. Her anger shot up a few more notches. 'Did you find my note?'

'What note?'

She huffed. 'The one saying we were over.'

'What? No. And why are we over?'

'Because you're having an affair.'

'No, I'm not.'

'Oh, please, I saw it with my own eyes, Zachary, so don't try to weasel your way out of this. At the very least show me a little bit of respect and own up to what you've done to me, would you?'

'I'm not owning up to something I haven't done.' He groaned like she was an annoying child. 'Humour me, would you, and tell me what makes you think I'm sleeping with my secretary.'

She made sure her voice was calm and steady. 'Oh, just the small fact that I watched you kiss her and then drag her off into the elevator of the hotel and up to your room.'

She was met with silence. She could just picture him racking his brain, trying to come up with an excuse, a lie, a reason this was all her fault. 'Well?'

'We were going up to meet a client in his room.'

'Oh, really? A threesome, was it?' Both Frank and Marie shot her stunned glances. Sophie squirmed in her seat.

'Oh, for Christ's sake, Sophie. Okay, yes, I slept with my secretary. But only this once and only because I'm tired of all the pressure you've put on me about wanting more of a commitment from me.'

Bam! There it was. 'So my wanting to settle down gives you reason to go stick your wick in somewhere else, does it?'

'Good God, woman, you sound like one of them already and you've only been back in Australia for a few days.'

'You're a bloody piece of work, Zachary, putting all this on me and then having a dig at me about my Australian heritage.' Her dad shot her a look that showed he was about to grab the phone, but she shook her head and turned her back to him.

'Well, it's the truth! You're all so, what do you call it, ocker over there.'

Sophie made her way into the privacy of the lounge room. 'Are we really? Well, how about you go fuck yourself then.'

'Oh nice, just lovely.' Zachary's aristocratic accent grated on her nerves.

'So not even a word of an apology, Zachary?'

'I'm sorry, Sophie, but I think we both know we were over a long time ago.'

'That's no excuse for infidelity.' It was the most unapologetic apology she'd ever heard. 'My lawyer will be in touch.' She choked her words out, the need to burst into tears gaining momentum by the second, but she wasn't about to let him hear her cry.

'Your what?' There was a hint of sarcasm in his voice.

'My lawyer. Bye, Zachary.' Hanging up, she tossed the phone to the opposite lounge chair and then hung her head in her hands and cried for everything she'd lost and everything she was about to go through.

❧

From her seat in the saddle, Sophie gazed out across the top paddock, past the cattle and towards where the sun appeared to be sinking behind the mountains. It had been almost twenty-four hours since she'd spoken to Zachary, and there hadn't been another word from him – which she was both hurt and happy about. Break-ups really sucked. All in all, it had been a nice day – a great suggestion of her dad's to help him with exercising a few of the horses. She'd needed the distraction, and felt much better for it. Horses had always had a special way of calming her and helping her to clear her mind.

Last night's conversation with Zachary, although painful, had reminded her how heartless he'd become over the years. When she'd met him, he'd been fresh out of law school and had a zest for life, and a zest for her, but over the years, his work had darkened him. The countless hours in the courtroom had made him an angry, unhappy man. He used to be giving and keen to be romantic, but now everything was about him, and had been for a very long time. Blindsided by the fact she longed for the family life she'd grown up in, she hadn't seen the truth beyond her rose-coloured glasses. But she did now, and with blinding clarity. Although she was deeply hurt that he'd cheated on her, she couldn't continue to hate him for it. Peas from very different pods, they just weren't meant to be together. Accepting this gave her a deep sense of understanding.

The palomino mare tossed her head a little as they headed towards home. Sophie gave a gentle pull on the reins, letting the horse know she was still in control. The mare heeded her subtle warning and Sophie smiled. 'Good girl.' The horse's ears pricked as her voice was carried away on the sea breeze. After spending most of the day in the saddle, she was keen to stand under a steaming shower. Although riding was something she loved, and had missed terribly in England, she'd forgotten just how taxing it was. Her back was aching, as were her thighs and legs – she was going to be sore tomorrow.

Half an hour later and the palomino was hosed down and back in her paddock. Wiping her dirty hands on her jeans, Sophie took a slug from her water bottle. Then, hoisting the saddle on her hip, she tramped across the yard and towards the stables. Storing it in the tack room, she grabbed the quartered apple from where she'd left it and headed for the stalls. Candy, her very own buckskin horse, which she'd had since she was nineteen, had been brought in from the paddocks and was in the Hilton of all horse stalls. She seemed to be growing fatter every day, and Sophie couldn't wait to meet the new foal. She stroked the mare's neck and Candy curled her lip up and gave her best horsey smile before dunking her head back into the feed bucket.

Sophie grinned. 'I've got something way better than that for you, my girl.'

Picking up on the scent, Candy lifted her head and nudged Sophie's leg with her muzzle. Piece by piece, Sophie fed her horse her favourite treat and then stroked her belly softly. 'Never mind, you'll soon get your figure back.' Candy neighed a response. After giving her a cuddle around the neck, Sophie left her to it, wanting to get back to the homestead for a quick shower before the dinner started at seven. She had a little over an hour – plenty of time to freshen up and look nice before everyone arrived.

As she wandered across the yard and towards the verandah, galahs squabbled in the gum trees, making her laugh. She kicked off her dusty boots at the top of the stairs and walked inside, catching her reflection in the mirror by the back door. Streaks of dirt lined her cheeks and her hair was in complete disarray. Tossing her hat on the hook near the door, she tugged off her socks. Grinning at her unkempt state, one she would have never got herself into back in the UK, she pulled her grimy shirt from the waistband of her jeans and let it hang.

The scent of roast lamb wafted from the kitchen and her mouth watered as she wandered down the hallway. Hearing Amy and Tania laughing with her mum, Sophie felt warmth fill her heart – this was what *home* was all about. She was just about to go into the kitchen when a man's voice stopped her in her tracks. As if avoiding an assassin, she jumped back and pinned herself up against the hallway wall, her heart in her throat. Why was he so damn early? And then she heard Daniela's voice, followed by Mark's hearty chuckle. Had she really heard Dylan? She honed her ears, trying to hear over the babble that was her family. Tania and Amy were debating whether white or red wine was better, her parents were playfully arguing over who was going to cut the lamb, Gina and Vinnie were discussing the best order of the speeches for the wedding, along with Daniela, and then there was Mark talking to Dylan.

'Yeah, I couldn't believe it,' Dylan said.

'Trust you to get pulled over on your way into town, buddy,' Mark replied.

She glanced down at her grubby shirt and jeans, grimacing as she recalled her reflection. Peeling herself off the wall, she started to tiptoe down the hallway to the bathroom when Dylan's unmistakable husky voice called her name.

Mid-step, she halted. Plastering the biggest smile she could muster on her lips, she turned to face him. 'Oh, hi. I didn't know you were here already.'

He thumbed over his shoulder. 'It's mayhem in there. When are you going to come and save me?'

Her hands itching to smooth her mop of hair, she instead shoved them in her pockets. 'Soon. First I have to get cleaned up.'

'You look fine.' He gave her a smile that would make even the most steadfast woman buckle at the knees, and she almost did. Almost.

She shrugged. 'Thank you.'

He took a step towards her and she nearly retreated. Not because of him, but because he smelt so damn good and she knew she smelt like horse shit and anything else she'd wiped on her jeans throughout the day. 'Did you tell any of them that we ran into each other yesterday?'

She shook her head.

'Interesting.' He grinned again.

'What's so interesting?'

'Well, they think this is the very first time we're meeting up since Amy and Mark's wedding.'

'Ha-ha, the joke's on them, then.' She laughed again. Oh God, she sounded like a hyena.

He eyed her in a way that sent quivers all over her. 'So why were you sneaking off? Trying to avoid me?'

No, I was actually going to freshen up so I looked tempting, she wanted to say, but instead she said, 'Oh no, what gave you that idea?'

'Maybe because you were tiptoeing down the hallway, *away* from the direction of the kitchen where you heard us all talking.'

'Oh, no, I um, thought better of going in there covered in dirt. Mum would have a fit. And I like to tiptoe over the floorboards that creak, that's all.' She knew she sounded like an idiot, and she felt like one too.

'Right.' He said it with so much scepticism she almost lost it laughing.

'I was just going to jump in the shower, and then I was going to join you guys and gals.'

'Well, in that case, I was just off to use the little boy's room, so I'll walk that way with you.'

'Oh, right, okay.' She felt so awkward, like a teenage girl.

They stepped in unison down the hall. 'You look good all roughed up, Soph.'

Her heart skipped a beat. She loved the way he shortened her name. 'You're a funny bugger.'

'I'm being serious. You're looking great. The unruly look suits you. Always did, and still does.'

She felt her cheeks flame bright. 'Well, thank you.'

He stopped at the toilet door and waved an arm in her direction. 'This reminds me of the Sophie I used to know before you met Zachary and became all hoity-toity. At Amy and Kurt's wedding you just didn't look like you.' He smiled. 'Welcome back, Firefly.'

Firefly? Her breath caught. Her heart tumbled towards him. That was the nickname he'd given her way before they'd become girlfriend and boyfriend, because he reckoned she always lit up everyone's life. With that he walked into the toilet and shut the door. She stood for a few seconds, dumbfounded. She loved the fact he appreciated her just how she came. The real her. The person she longed to be once again. She smiled, straightened her shoulders a little, and she felt a spring in her step as she strode towards the bathroom. She knew she shouldn't be basking in praise. But when it came from Dylan Stone, she just couldn't help herself.

CHAPTER

11

Rosewood Farm

Turning off the taps, Sophie stepped from the steamy shower cubicle and grabbed her neatly folded towel from the rack. Bless her mum for placing a fresh one there for her. She held it to her nose and inhaled the lavender scent of the fabric softener her mum had used for an eternity. The little things meant so much. She was sure Zachary wouldn't even know how to turn their washing machine on, the man never having done a load of washing in all the days she'd known him. How he was going to survive without her was beyond her, but then again it might not be long before he replaced her with a younger version – his secretary. The thought stabbed at her heart and not because she wanted him back, but because it made her feel insignificant and unlovable. Would she ever get to fulfil her dream of having a family? Time was ticking and her maternal clock was in overdrive.

She quickly dried herself. Then she wiped the mist from the mirror above the sink and tried to smile at her reflection, but instead tears filled her eyes. How Dylan could say she looked great was beyond her. She looked tired, exhausted even, spent, and way older than her twenty-nine years. Almost thirty if she was being truthful. The years were flying and she still hadn't found her happily ever after. What if Dylan had been the only man to bring her such joy, such love, such happiness? Had she gone and ruined her only chance at a forever kind of love when she'd walked away from him? The very thought felt like a sucker punch to her heart. As much as she didn't want to think ill of the dead, damn Grace and her threats. Maybe she was destined to die a lonely old woman who couldn't even own a cat because she was allergic to them … a depressing thought, but possible.

Huffing, she tried to push this feeling aside. Yes, Zachary had done the unthinkable, but that didn't mean she had to wallow in self-pity for the rest of her life. She really needed to find a way to snap out of it. She was stronger than this, better than this. Slamming her hands down on the bathroom sink, she glared at her reflection.

'Where's your fire gone, Sophie Copinni?' she growled. 'It's about time you found it again.'

Satisfied with her little pep talk, she unzipped her bathroom bag – a bit of gloss and a swipe of blusher would help perk her up. Her hand shook as she trailed over her lips with the cherry lip-gloss. As much as she'd tried to calm herself in the shower, to imagine her woes washing down the plughole with her soapsuds, she was nervous as hell. There was a magnetism lingering between her and Dylan. It was like a fire waiting for the right amount of kindling to burst back to life. But she didn't want to fan the flames, or her family to pick up on the attraction, because she didn't want to give the wrong impression. She'd already hurt Dylan once, and that was one too many times.

Running her fingers through her damp hair, she gave it a shake, deciding to leave it however it fell. As she touched a little blusher to her cheeks, painful nostalgia hit her again as she recalled the way Dylan had looked at her when she'd told him they were over. It had torn her heart to shreds walking away from him. But she hadn't had a choice. The fear that letter had instilled in her had been colossal. She took a deep breath in an effort to still her racing pulse. Leaning against the sink, she closed her eyes and allowed that night to replay as she had done a hundred times before.

'What are you saying, Soph?' The hurt in his beautiful blue eyes had almost killed her.

'I'm saying I don't love you anymore.' She had spat the words out before she could stop herself. And then she'd choked back sobs, not wanting him to see she was hurting so badly. She'd wanted him to hate her, to forget she ever existed. Not for her sake, but for his.

'Only yesterday you were telling me how much you love me. I don't understand. We're meant to be together forever. There has to be a reason, something you're not telling me. Please, Soph, what is it? Whatever it is, we can work through it together.' He'd grabbed her hands, but she'd tugged them away from him.

'We just can't do this, Dylan. I can't be with you anymore.'

He'd stood, his hands raking through his hair, blinking back tears. She'd never seen him cry. Ever. 'Please, Sophie, I love you. Don't do this. Don't give up on us. Please.'

Although already broken, her heart had smashed into smithereens right at that very moment. She'd ached to reach out to him. Ached to comfort him. Ached to tell him she was lying and that she loved him and couldn't imagine her life without him in it, but she couldn't. Without another word, she'd turned and walked away, every one of her footfalls feeling as though she were climbing Mount Everest in boots made of cement. She had fought with every inch of her being not to turn around and run back into his arms.

Flicking open her eyes, she returned to the present and wiped the tears from her cheeks. As much as Zachary had done the wrong thing, she couldn't blame him entirely for their relationship breakdown. If she were being completely honest with herself, she'd remained in love with Dylan Stone, and still was. She took in a shuddering breath and slowly blew it away. She needed to get dressed and go out to the kitchen and enjoy the dinner for Daniela and Mark's sake. This was their night, their time. She could crumble once she crawled into bed, in the comfort of the darkness of her room.

Dylan smiled. He'd really missed this. With Gina and Vinnie, Amy and Kurt, Daniela and Mark, Tania, Marie and Frank, and then Sophie, the table was almost full. As hard as it was sitting in the same room as her, and not being able to hold her hand beneath the table like they used to, or steal loving sideways glances, Dylan was enjoying the sense of family and unconditional love the Copinni household had always encapsulated. The four different conversations going on with voices getting louder and louder to be heard over one another would do most people's heads in, but his skill of being a part of the mayhem, learnt during the years he was with Sophie, made him an expert in taking part in four completely different conversations at once. It was a Maltese thing, Sophie had always said with a laugh.

As usual for a Copinni family dinner, there was enough food to feed an army, and then some. While he devoured his second helping of traditional Maltese beef casserole, Marie's cooking too delicious not to, he stole subtle glances across the table at the woman who had stolen his heart, and broken it, all those years ago. She was effortlessly beautiful, in so many ways. Occasionally, when she caught his eye, she'd smile softly at him and he'd return the gesture. Earlier in the kitchen, Mark had quietly mentioned something about her and Zachary's relationship going pear-shaped, and as much as he didn't want to know the ins and outs, especially second-hand, he hoped the bastard was suffering losing a woman like Sophie. He knew too damn well what it felt like. How any man could cheat on a woman was beyond him – it went against all his morals.

'Now that Zach's out of the picture, I wish you two would get back together,' Mark said, keeping his voice to a whisper so no one else around the dinner table could hear him.

'Never going to happen, buddy.' Dylan gave him a look as if to say *don't even go there*.

Mark grinned ruefully. 'Okay, all right. Just saying.'

'Well, you've said it, so now just drop it.'

'Gee whizz, don't get your knickers in a knot, mate.'

Dylan instantly regretted his harshness. 'Sorry, just a bit of a sore subject.'

'Righto, well let's change it. You up for a big night Saturday?'

His extra helping now eaten and the top button of his jeans about to burst, Dylan leant back in his seat. 'Of course ... what's the plan of attack?'

'Well, the girls are heading into the tavern for some karaoke, and we're going to the pub for a few bevvies and some pool. I just hope none of the guys have ordered me a stripper because Daniela will skin me alive and eat me for dinner.' He eyed Dylan suspiciously.

'Don't look at me. I'm not into watching some woman I don't know strip off, and I didn't think you'd be either.'

Mark took a swig from his beer. 'Speak for yourself.'

'Did I just hear the word "stripper"?' Daniela gave Dylan the death stare across the table.

Dylan held his hands up, laughing. 'I'm not getting him one, so don't blame me.'

Mark shook his head. 'Goddamn it, woman, you got some bionic hearing.'

Daniela smiled at him. 'And don't you forget it.'

'Look out, you're under the thumb now, Mark … your life will never be the same again.' Frank poured himself another glass of wine, grinning cheekily.

'Oi.' Marie slapped him playfully.

'Yeah, oi, all right,' Gina chimed in.

Everyone laughed, and amid the mayhem that was a Copinni dinner, Dylan's eyes met with Sophie's. And for a few brief moments it felt as if the past nine years had never happened, and they were back together, madly in love and hopeful for their future. But he snatched his gaze away and grabbed his beer to take a swig so nobody noticed his smile had all but vanished. As much as he still cared for her, he would never go back there with Sophie – his heart couldn't take another beating.

Stone's Throw

Dylan pulled on his board shorts, loving the fact he could wear the bare minimum of clothes – very different from the way it was in Sydney most of the time. A cold shower had been just what he needed after shoeing the horses, a job he'd been doing since a teenager. After hanging up his towel he stepped from the bathroom, looking for his mum – she'd called out for him while he was in the shower and he'd called back to say he wouldn't be long and to make herself comfortable. She was now sitting on the top step in the doorway, her feet bare and her guitar in her lap. He smiled at how the golden sunlight pouring through the open door of the old barn lit her up in an ethereal kind of way. Walking quietly so as to not disturb her, he sat on the arm of the lounge chair and watched her strum her pride and joy – her father's guitar. The melody of Pink Floyd's 'Wish You Were Here' carried across the room, her angelic voice bringing goosebumps to his skin.

Once she was finished, he clapped. 'You still got it, Mum.'

'Why thank you.' Grinning, Faith stood and carefully placed the guitar down.

As she'd stop playing, Dylan grabbed the moment. 'You and that copper looked mighty cosy the other day.' He noticed the subtle curl of her lips and the sudden rosiness to her cheeks as she sat back down.

'You mean Jim?' She kept her eyes firmly focused on the floor.

'No, I meant the other copper that came here … of course I meant Jim.'

'Don't be stupid, Dylan, we are just good friends.'

'If you say so …' He shrugged and gave her a yeah-whatever stare. 'But it didn't look that way to me.'

'You read too much into it then.' Faith returned his shrug and started humming to herself, her usual way of letting Dylan know a conversation was over and done with. He knew all too well she was the queen of distraction tactics.

He took a few moments to choose his next words wisely. 'I'm not telling you what to do, Mum, but it might be a bit risky getting too chummy with a copper, don't you think?'

She paused, but didn't turn to face him. 'How?'

'What do you mean *how*? You know exactly what I'm referring to.'

She turned to him, her usually sparkling eyes filled with what he could only describe as a deep sadness. 'Yes, I know all too well, Dylan. That's why I haven't let him any further into my life than as a friend.' She sighed, her shoulders slumping. 'Jim is a really lovely bloke, with a kind heart and a gentle soul. I know he likes me and I think he knows I like him too, but it can't go anywhere and as much as that really sucks, it's just the way it is.' She half smiled. 'Trust me to fall for the one guy in town I can't be with.'

'Oh, Mum, I'm so sorry.' Dylan hung his head, his heart heavy. 'You know, it wouldn't be the end of the world if we finally told the truth about what happened.'

'Don't even think about it, Dylan, it's too late for that.' She shook her head slowly. 'Just imagine what the townsfolk would say if it came out, and lord knows what the law would do about it. I won't allow you to risk that.'

'The locals might be sympathetic, Mum, and understand, and the law, well, only one way to find out.'

Her eyes turned fierce. 'I'm not allowing it, so don't even consider it.'

Dylan remained silent and walked over to the kitchen bench to get a glass of water.

'Okay, Dylan?'

He nodded. 'Yeah, okay, if that's what you want.'

'Yes, it is.' She gave his arm a gentle squeeze. 'We've kept it to ourselves for this long, so we may as well always keep it under wraps. Nothing to be gained from telling the truth.'

'Yeah, maybe, maybe not.'

'Let's not dampen our spirits by going on about it any longer.' Sighing, she stood up and walked around the room.

Dylan gave her a smile he wasn't feeling.

She returned an equally unnatural one before darting her eyes this way and that. 'It's the perfect bachelor pad. You're going to be a happy little camper in here.'

'For the next couple of weeks …' He hadn't mentioned that he'd quit his job, and wasn't intending to just yet. He still hadn't got his head around what he was going to do about it.

'Maybe longer, depending on your job.' She gave him a cheeky smile, implying that she knew something he didn't.

Grinning now, he rested his hip against the kitchen bench and eyed her suspiciously. 'Come on then, spill.'

'I just got off the phone to Kimmy.' Her smile went from ear to ear.

'Yeah, and?'

'Gary must have read our minds. He's handed in his resignation, and he and Kimmy are going to sell their house and buy a caravan to travel around Australia.'

'What?' The word came out in a whoosh. 'Wow!'

'I could hear a spark in Kimmy's voice that I haven't heard since before Grace passed away. I think this is going to be what helps her heal.' She smiled. 'Gary is a good man. She's very lucky to have him.'

'Got to agree there. Love Uncle Gary – he's certainly a man to look up to.' Dylan grinned. 'So I suppose this means I'm out on the street.'

'Of course not, Kimmy was calling to ask me to talk to you about it, to see if you wanted to rent the house off them while they travel. That's when I told her you will most likely want to move back up here.'

'Bloody oath I do!' He almost waltzed across the floor to give his mum a hug. 'This is the best news ever.'

Faith cuddled him tightly, and then pulled back. 'But what about your job … how's Angus going to take it?'

Dylan felt as if he'd just won the lottery. 'People come and go all the time there – he'll get over it.'

'Will he give you a good reference, do you think?'

'I don't need one. I'm going to open my own place, right here in Shorefield.'

'Oh, the empty menswear shop!' Faith was jiggling on the spot.

'I'll look into it.'

'I'm so happy right now.' She stood and spun in a circle, the anklet bells jingling at her feet.

'So am I, Mum, so am I.' One hurdle overcome, Dylan thought. 'I'll give Kimmy a call later, organise for my other things to be sent up. I'll put some money in her bank for it.'

'She'll like getting a call from you. She's been worrying herself sick about what you were going to do.' Faith smiled lovingly. 'See, the universe always has a way of making everything work out – you just have to trust in it.'

'Yeah, true, huh. And here I was worrying about her. Go figure.'

'Life works in mysterious ways, Dylan.'

'It sure does.'

'Right, well that's settled then, my son is home to stay.' She did another jiggle on the spot, her bangles in tune with her anklet. 'Just don't be bringing hordes of women home, will you, or I'll have to chase them away with my broom.'

'And the same goes for you, but I'll be chasing the blokes away with more than a broom.' Dylan gave her a wink.

'It's not like they're lining up to date me, so you won't have to worry about that.'

'Jim is.'

'Dylan, drop it.' Her tone was playful but cautionary.

'Sorry. I just want you to be happy, that's all. It's about time you had someone to love you for the amazing woman you are.'

'Aw, thanks, son, but to be honest I don't need a man to fulfil my life. I'm happy just the way it is.'

'Wouldn't you like someone to share all the ups and downs with, though?'

'Yes, sometimes.'

'If Jim wasn't a copper, would you let him into your life then?'

'I'd certainly be more open to the idea. But he is, and I don't like thinking about the *what ifs*.' She shrugged. 'Besides, I think I'm very set in my ways now, after living on my own all these years, so it would take someone extra special to break down my walls, so to speak.'

'I definitely know what you mean. I like my space and don't want just any woman coming in to fill it. She will have to be something else to get me to commit.'

'I'm glad you're being selective, but …' She gave his leg a pat. 'Just remember you aren't getting any younger and I want me some grandkids sometime over the next few years.'

'Cor, talk about no pressure,' he said with a laugh. He walked towards his bedroom and spun around to breathe in his new home. 'This old place has got so much character. I love it.' He straightened the western-print doona on the king-size bed he'd scored.

'So when are you going to call Angus and tell him?'

'In a little while, once I've let it all settle in.' Not wanting his mother to see through his white lie, Dylan momentarily gazed out the kitchen window.

'You reckon it's time to stop for morning tea yet? I have carrot cake with cream-cheese icing in the freezer; it won't take long for me to thaw some of it out.'

'You don't have to ask me twice when there's food involved, especially your cakes.'

'How about I go and get it from home and we have it here, at your dining table?' She looked to where they'd made a table out of an old wooden electrical spool, which they'd sat on blocks so it was high enough. That plus the four mismatched chairs around it added to the grungy-groovy style of the place. 'Kind of like a little house warming of sorts.'

'For sure. I'll put the kettle on.'

'Sounds like a plan to me.' She carefully picked up her guitar from where it was leaning against the wall. 'Back in two shakes of a lamb's tail.'

Fifteen minutes later they were seated at the table and Dylan was helping himself to a second slice of cake. Faith leant back with her cuppa cradled in her hands. 'So how did last night go? You haven't even mentioned it.'

Dylan licked the icing from his fingers. 'Yeah, really good … the Copinnis are always fun to hang with.'

'That's good, and how was it for you, being back around Sophie?'

Dylan's heart squeezed. 'Yeah, you know, a bit strange, but all good, considering.'

'It would be hard for you.' Faith smiled sadly. 'I know how much she meant to you back in the day. How's life going for her in the UK?'

'Not great … apparently Zachary did the dirty on her, the dickhead.' Dylan's jaw tightened. 'I just don't get men who cheat, and why would you cheat on a woman like Sophie anyway?'

'You never know what goes on behind closed doors, Dylan, so don't be too quick to judge their situation.'

'Yeah, true.' He shrugged. 'Not my concern either, I suppose.'

'No, it's not, so don't even think about needing to save her, will you?'

'Yeah, Mum, righto.' He shook his head, her directness throwing him off centre.

'Sorry, love, I just know you so well, and you're always wanting to take on other people's heartache and suffering. It's just who you are, and it makes you the wonderful man you've become.' Reaching across the table, she placed her hand over his. 'Don't get me wrong, Sophie is a beautiful woman, she and I were always so close. But being your mum, it's hard for me to get past what she did to you, and I don't want to see you heartbroken again because she might be on the rebound from Zachary.' She smiled and eyed him tenderly. 'Just be careful, okay?'

'Yeah, I will be.' He sighed heavily. 'You've got nothing to worry about when it comes to Sophie and me – we were done and dusted the day she broke it off. I have no desire to ever go back to what we had.' Even as he said the words Dylan wondered how much truth was behind them. He knew, deep within his heart, he'd never stopped loving Sophie.

Faith leant forwards and hugged her mug, her gaze now glued to the coffee within it. 'Okay, if you say so.' She paused and bit her lower lip before bringing her gaze back to his. 'I can still see it in your eyes when you mention her name, Dylan.'

'See what?' He half laughed, shaking his head. 'What are you on about?'

'You still love her.'

'Possibly, but I'm not *in* love with her ... there's a big difference.'

'Is that so?'

Dylan sat back and folded his arms. 'Gee whizz, Mum. Lay off a little, would you? Sophie and I have no intention of ever going back to what we were. We're just trying to be friends and move past it all. Why the hell can't everyone else?'

'Yes, you're right, sorry.' She offered him an apologetic smile. 'Changing the subject to a more positive one ... when are you going into town to meet the real estate guy?'

Dylan was glad for the diversion. 'I'll give him a call. You want to come with me when I do?'

'As long as you don't mind me tagging along, yes please.'

'Of course I don't mind. It'll be good to get your opinion on the place.'

'Count me in then.' She gave his hand a squeeze. 'I'm so glad you're back to stay. I've missed you.'

❧

'Morning, Soph, you've slept in. Was it a good sleep, love?' Marie said as Sophie padded into the kitchen.

'Morning, Mum. Yeah, it wasn't too bad.'

'Would you like some bacon and eggs?'

'No, thanks, I'll just have a bowl of muesli today.' She patted her belly. 'I'll become a fatty at this rate, with all your good cooking.'

Marie started to unpack the dishwasher and Sophie helped her. 'Oh, don't be silly,' she said. 'You've always been a Skinny Minnie.' Reaching up, she popped a bowl back in the overhead cupboard. 'So how was it, being around Dylan after all these years?'

'Yeah, a bit weird, but better than I'd expected.'

'Well, that's a good thing – but make sure you keep it platonic, won't you?'

'What?' Sophie felt as if her mother had just slapped her across the face.

'You've just come out of an eight-year relationship, love, and I don't want to see you jumping back into things with Dylan just so you don't have to deal with your heartache, that's all.'

'Oh, for goodness sake, Mum. I think I'm old enough and wise enough to not be so stupid, don't you think?'

'Sophie.' Marie's nostrils flared, as they always did when she was angry with her girls. 'Please don't speak to me like that.'

'Yes, you're right, sorry.' Sophie softened her tone. 'But for God's sake, Mum, Dylan and I can barely even class ourselves as friends right now, let alone look at rehashing an old relationship I ruined years ago.'

'I'm sorry you both went through that, love. I know it was hard on you and Dylan. Break-ups are never easy.' Marie gave her daughter a gentle smile before wiping her hands on a tea towel and turning to the sink. 'Life can be so damn confusing and unfair at times, but we always find our way through the fog.'

'What's so unfair?' Frank strode into the kitchen.

'Nothing, just girls' talk, love.' Marie leant in and met Frank for a welcome kiss on the cheek.

'Secret women's business, huh?' Grinning, Frank walked over to the radio and turned it on.

Sophie nodded. 'Yup.'

Frank raised his brows to his receding hairline. 'Interesting.'

'Would you like me to make us all a coffee?' Sophie asked.

'Yes, please, and make me an extra strong one, Soph. I feel like I need it.' Frank perched himself beside her, his arms crossed over his chest. 'I'm so bloody tired all the time lately.'

Sophie flicked the jug on and then lined the cups up in a row. Turning to her father, she took notice of the dark rings under his eyes and the slight hollowness to his usually full cheeks. Recalling the conversation with her sisters about Tania running into them when they were coming out of the doctor's surgery, and the oddness of the food in the fridge, she looked at him suspiciously. 'Is there anything going on with you that the girls and I should know about, Dad?'

From where she was placing bacon into the pan, Marie shot a subtle glance over her shoulder. Frank looked to her, shrugged, and then back to Sophie. 'Now that you've asked, I don't want to lie. Yes, there is something going on with me.'

Sophie stood up straighter, her heart suddenly in her throat. 'There is?'

'I wanted to wait until after the wedding so I didn't dampen everyone's spirits worrying about me.' Frank heaved a weary sigh. 'The doc has said I'll be okay, I just need to cut back on all the fatty food and get more exercise.'

'What are you talking about?'

'I had a heart attack three weeks ago, love, but please don't tell your sisters yet, because they don't know.'

'Oh my God, Dad.' The room spun and Sophie had to grip the kitchen bench to stay upright.

Rosewood Farm

Finally succeeding in giving her eyes a smoky appearance, the make-up accentuating the green, Sophie looked to where the straightening iron was heating. She switched it back off. To hell with the major effort of flattening out what God and Maltese genes had blessed her with. She'd always embraced her waves, up until she'd met Zachary. He was forever telling her how much better she looked with straight hair, and so she had spent ages doing it that way each and every time they were going out. All the effort she used to go to for him, and in the end it hadn't mattered a dime.

Feeling a little rebellious, she pulled the towel from her head and hung it on the rack. Grabbing the currycomb, she tugged it through her locks and then, tipping her head upside down, she gave it a shake and a scrunch with her mum's curl booster.

Now upright, she met with her reflection and smiled wickedly. It was liberating to feel a little wild, as though the shackles she'd worn for the past nine or so years were finally gone. Splashing on defiant red lipstick, she walked into her bedroom and rifled through her cupboard in search of her favourite little red number. Originally deciding she was going to wear jeans and a nice top, much to Amy and Tania's dismay, she was now opting for a risqué outfit topped off with her favourite black boots. The dress showed a little more cleavage than she was usually comfortable with, but she was in a brazen mood so why not flaunt it. Grabbing the feather earrings she'd discovered in her jewellery box from her dressing table, she slipped them on, liking how they matched her outfit. Tonight was all about having fun, and being herself – there was no smokescreen needed around her family. It was high time she let her hair down, so to speak.

Four hours later the group had finished dinner and Sophie, Tania, Amy and Daniela were each throwing back their fifth cock-sucking cowboy shot for the night. As did the three other women – Daniela's workmates – who were there for the festivities. After being out of the party scene for years, Sophie knew she had to work hard to keep up with them all, but she was going to give it her best shot, or shots, she thought with a chuckle. She looked to her now empty shot glass, her legs feeling a little wobbly. Gina and Marie sat at the end of the bar, sipping on their third glass of champagne and giggling like a pair of school kids. It was panning out to be a wonderful night.

Tania smacked her empty glass down on the bar. 'Who's up for some karaoke then?' There was a devilish grin planted on her pink painted lips. The tiny diamantes at each corner of her eyes glimmered.

'Me!' Amy squealed.

Daniela and the other women shook their heads. 'Count us out …' Daniela flashed a lopsided grin. 'We might go and play some pool while you ladies rock it out on stage.'

Amy pulled a pouty face. 'You lot are party poopers.'

'There's some talent over there we want to check out,' the tall blonde announced, grinning and licking her lips as though she were about to eat her prey.

'You lot just can't help yourselves, can you?' Amy said, laughing.

'Some of us are still single women, with needs to be met,' the redhead said with a grin.

'Oi, talk for yourselves, you three,' Daniela said with a laugh. 'I'm almost a married woman.'

'Off you go then, be gone.' Amy waved her hand in the direction of the pool tables.

The four women giggled as they sashayed off towards where a group of young blokes were huddled around the pool table – pool sticks and beers in hand. The women's arrival at the table stopped the game. The five men looked like their Christmases had all come at once as they said their g'days. Dressed in jeans, checked shirts and dusty boots, they looked like proper country boys in town from one of the neighbouring cattle stations.

The poor blokes, Sophie thought with a smile, they have no idea what they are in for.

Amy and Tania looked to Sophie. 'You keen to karaoke then?' Tania said.

'I'm in like Flynn ... as long as we get to sing up on the bar,' Sophie announced, surprising herself as much as her sisters. Talk about Dutch courage.

'Holy shit.' Tania reached out and felt Sophie's forehead. 'Are you feeling okay, blister?'

Amy threw her hands on her hips. 'Yeah, who are you and where have you put our big sister?'

'I'm fine.' Sophie playfully slapped Tania's hand away. 'I have a bucket list to tick off in less than four weeks, and one of the things is to dance and sing Coyote Ugly style on a bar. So if I'm going to embarrass myself trying to sing, I may as well go the whole hog and dance too.'

Tania leant into the barman. 'Hey, James, my sister here wants to do it Coyote Ugly style on the bar. Would that be okay?'

James grinned. 'Yup, as long as none of you fall off and break your legs.'

Tania returned a grin of her own. 'We'll try not to.'

Amy gestured to the bar with a tip of her head. 'You sure you'll be right up there, Soph?'

'Right as rain,' Sophie said with more confidence than she felt. Thankfully she'd worn boots and not her usual high heels.

'What are we going to sing?' Amy said.

The three girls smiled shamelessly at each other. Then said in unison, '"Sisters Are Doin' It for Themselves".' It had been their theme song when they were growing up.

Amy turned to the barman. 'Hey, James, can we be up next?'

James flashed a dazzling smile. 'There's another couple in front of you, then yup, the stage, or should I say, the bar, is all yours, lovely ladies.'

'Yay!' Amy squealed. 'I'm just going to duck off to the loo first; do either of you gals need to go?'

Tania crossed her legs. 'Nope, I'm determined not to break the seal just yet, otherwise I'll be running off every ten minutes.'

'I'm all good, strong bladder.' Sophie's legs were feeling the effects of the alcohol, and the realisation she was actually about to do something very out of character adding to her giddiness, she pulled up a bar stool. She shimmied onto it and then crossed her legs. She recognised James's face from high school, but as he'd been a few years younger than her, she hadn't known his name until now. The two women behind the bar had been in her year at school – some people didn't fly far from the coop. One she remembered very well, but for the life of her she couldn't even remember the name of the other woman. She also recognised most of the faces hovering over drinks and conversations in the packed hotel. Shorefield really was a small world and not many of the locals ventured far; even if they did, they always found their way back here. Just like she did.

And just like the dashing Dylan Stone.

She shook her head, not wanting to let her thoughts wander to him tonight, as they had been the past couple of days.

Tania held up twenty dollars. 'Can I order three vodka, lime and sodas, James?' He nodded as she pulled a stool up beside Sophie. 'Hey, blister, you recognise the brunette girl behind the bar?'

'Oh hell, yeah, how could I not? She was after Dylan like a dog on heat the entire time at high school.' Sophie half chuckled. 'She hated me for being his girlfriend.'

'Jealousy's a bitch, huh?'

'Sure is. Although she has nothing to hate me for now.'

Tania nodded. 'True that.'

As if sensing she was being spoken about, the long-legged stunner made her way towards them. 'Hey there, you two.'

'Hey,' Sophie and Tania said together.

'Long time no see, Sophie.' She leant on the bar, making her ample cleavage poking out of the top of her tight black singlet even more pronounced. 'Heard you've been hiding out in the UK.'

'Not so much hiding, more like living.'

'You back for the wedding?'

'Sure am.'

'Heard you and Dylan are both in the wedding party.'

'Yes, you heard right.' *You're all ears*, she wanted to add, but she bit it back. Barmaids always knew everything going on in town, and usually before anyone else did.

'That's gotta be a hard one, having to be around him again.' Sophie would have liked to wipe the smile off the woman's face.

'Why would it be?' Sophie did her very best to act nonchalant.

The woman smiled even wider, like the cat about to get the cream. 'Maybe because you didn't part on the best of terms.'

Sophie forced herself to shrug. 'We're all adults, and we know how to let bygones be bygones.'

'Well don't go trying anything stupid with him. You ruined your chances a long time ago, and he doesn't need his heart broken again. Leave him for someone that would treat him right, hey?'

Sophie flinched as the words stung. 'I beg your pardon.'

Heavily made-up eyes flashed disdain over her. 'You heard me.'

Tania shot to standing, her eyes fierce. 'Hey, back off, Leah.'

Leah straightened and folded her arms. 'What are you going to do about it if I don't, Tania?'

Gently nudging Leah out of the way, James plonked the three drinks on the bar and popped a straw in each of them. 'You better get back to it, Leah, there's a line-up over there.' He tipped his head to the corner of the bar, where it was now three rows deep with people waiting for drinks.

Leah flashed him a look worthy of killing and then stormed away.

'Thanks for that, James.' Tania smiled appreciatively.

'No worries, all part of my job, keeping the peace.' He smiled. 'We don't want any bar brawls tonight, thanks, ladies.'

'Please, as if that was going to happen.' Tania went to hand the money over but he shook his head.

'On the house.'

'Aw, thanks, James.'

'My pleasure.' James held Tania's gaze a moment too long.

Sophie noticed that Tania was the first to look away. Her curiosity was piqued.

When he walked off to serve another patron, Sophie elbowed her sister in the ribs. 'Oh my God, he soooooo has the hots for you.'

Tania's cheeks flamed red. 'Does not.'

Sophie grinned. 'Does too, and to top it off, he's a hottie pattotti.'

Tania stared at James pouring a beer, her gaze vacant. 'Yeah, I suppose he is. But I'm in a happy, loving relationship, remember.' Turning back to Sophie, she revealed a dreamy smile that spoke of how head over heels she was.

'Oh, shit yes, sorry, totally slipped my mind. Gee whizz, sorry, Tans – this is why I usually don't drink much.' Sophie placed a hand on Tania's back. 'So why haven't we met him yet?'

'Because you are all crazy and I don't want to scare Alex away.' She took a sip from her drink.

Sophie eyed her sister quizzically. 'Tania, come on, what's going on with you? I don't believe for a second that if you were madly in love you wouldn't want to show him off to us all.'

'Okay, here goes nothing.' Tania sighed and then took both of Sophie's hands in hers. 'Alex is actually a woman.'

Sophie stared in stunned silence. Tania gave her hands a firm tug, bringing her attention back to the conversation, and then gave her an I'm-not-kidding look.

Slack-jawed, Sophie tried to recover from the surprise. She sucked in a sharp breath and then unintentionally pulled her hands from Tania's to throw them over the place her heart had almost just jumped out of her chest. 'Holy shit, really? Like really *really*?'

'Yes, really *really*.' Tania was grinning now. 'And you're the first of the family I've told so please keep it to yourself until I find the right time to tell them all.'

Sophie's shoulders almost crushed with the weight Tania had just dropped upon all the secrets, big and small, that were already sitting there. It was one more to add to the load she was carrying … go bloody figure. She leant in and dropped her voice to a whisper. 'Even Amy doesn't know?'

'Nope.'

Sophie felt as if the entire bar was spinning. She grabbed hold of it to stop from falling off the stool. 'But I don't understand. How could you not like men?'

'Easily.'

'But what about getting married and having a family?'

'I can still do all that.'

'But ...'

'It's my life,' Tania said in quick dismissal of Sophie's concerns.

'Yes, true.' Sophie took another much needed deep breath. 'So is it really Alex?'

'Yes, her name is Alex.'

'Wow. Are you happy?'

Tania grinned like a lovesick teenager. 'Very.'

'Well then, I'm *very* happy for you, for both of you.'

'Thanks, blister, that means the world to me.'

'Are you bringing her to the wedding?'

Tania nodded. 'I sure am.'

'Are you going to tell Mum and Dad first, or are you just going to surprise them with it?'

Tania grimaced. 'Haven't decided yet.'

Amy came skidding in beside them. 'You two almost ready, 'cause we're up next.'

'Oh my God.' Sophie shook her head. The ground beneath her was still spinning from the shock of Tania's secret, or maybe it was the alcohol, or both. 'I don't know if I can do this.'

'Oh yes you can, sister.' Amy took her by the hands and dragged her to standing. 'You're not chickening out now.'

Less than a minute later the three girls were lined up on the bar, microphones in hand, with the entire pub now staring at them. Sure her face was glowing brighter than a beetroot, Sophie almost dived off to retreat behind the bar. 'That's a long way down,' she whispered to Tania, who was standing tall beside her.

'Only if you fall,' Tania said with a wink.

Sophie stared down, feeling as though she were peering off the edge of a cliff. 'Oh far out, Tans, thanks for pointing that out.'

The crowd clapped and cheered, urging them on. Necks cranked for a better look. Sophie groaned as she made a mental note to keep her legs together – she didn't really want blokes seeing her unflattering comfortable underwear. Feeling like a deer in the headlights, she grabbed Amy's arm, not only because she was nervous as hell but also for support to remain upright. How embarrassing would it be to tumble from the bar? Knowing her luck at the moment, she would most certainly break a few limbs in the fall, and in a town like Shorefield she'd never live it down. Another wave of dizziness engulfed her. She fought the urge to throw up as nerves ran amok in her stomach. Oh why had she suggested this? Damn bucket list!

The familiar beat of the song grabbed her attention and pulled her out of her internal terror. With a wobbly smile, she held the microphone to her lips. And then the lyrics started, as did Tania and Amy, matching Aretha Franklin word for word. She joined in, warily and as quiet as a mouse at first, but then thought what the hell and gave it all she had. Her voice sounded like she was being strangled, but she tried not to care and enjoyed the moment with her sisters. The crowd cheered even louder and some sang the words along with them. Blokes wolf whistled. Her mum and Gina applauded from the seats they'd basically glued themselves to all night – probably so they didn't fall over. Everyone, except for one particular person, was enjoying the performance.

Leah glared at Sophie, arms folded defensively. Then, looking away, a come-hither smile broke out on the barmaid's lips, and Sophie followed Leah's gaze. Her heart almost catapulted out of her chest when saw him, in all his masculine, muscled, tattooed glory, standing at the back of the crowd. His towering height allowed him to be a head above most and he exuded a charisma that was attracting looks from plenty of women. Although a tad jealous, Sophie revelled in the fact his blue eyes were glued to her and he was smiling, almost proudly. To her surprise, she didn't lose her courage. Instead she glanced back to the front row, to where the group of guys from the pool table now stood, cheering them on. It gave her the confidence to sing with even more passion. As her mind whirled, her body followed, and before she knew it she was swaying up on the bar in time to the music, the microphone pressed up against her lips. She caught Dylan's eyes again. He'd moved closer. So. Much. Closer. Now she could almost reach out and touch him. He gave the yobbo blokes at the front a cautionary sideways glance as he came nearer. Oh my God, was he jealous? She liked the thought, as much as she shouldn't. On cue, Leah shot to him like metal to a magnet. They leant into one another, saying something and then laughing like old friends. Then, turning to the side, Dylan leant on the bar as Leah started pouring his beer. When she handed it over, her smile let him know loud and clear that she wanted to tear his clothes off. Sophie felt a sucker punch to the stomach. Her heart squeezed tight. No way. She knew she could never have Dylan again, but please God, not Leah – of all the women.

Closing her eyes to block out the scene before her, she found herself trapped between the woman of now and the girl she once was – if only she could turn back time and make everything right. Would it ever be possible to undo what she'd done? Was it ever too late to right a wrong? And then before she knew it, the song was over and the crowd roared. Amy and Tania looked to her, their smiles wide. Amy's was a little lopsided, thanks to the alcohol. With the three of them grabbing each other's hands, they bowed. Then the spotlight was turned up to the stage and the next courageous trio took front and centre. The crowd turned to watch them, giving Sophie, Amy and Tania some privacy to climb down without showing too much. Sophie certainly wasn't in the state to do it gracefully, her legs going this way and that as she did her best not to fall flat on her face in the descent onto a bar stool and then to where her feet landed firmly on the floor. *Thank Christ for that.*

'I need the loo again, how 'bout you lot?' Amy crossed her legs tightly.

Tania let go of Jamie's hand, the barman having helped all three of them down. 'Count me in; it's about time I broke the seal.'

'Me too, Ames.' Sophie nodded as she gave a little grin at the way Jamie was still looking at Tania. The poor bloke had no chance. Her mind wandered to Tania and some unknown female, in bed, making out. Although she didn't judge, and in a way understood why a woman would rather another woman over the male of the species, she wouldn't be able to go there herself. Each to their own – love is love.

Making their way through the throng of happy pub goers, Sophie and her sisters bumped straight into the guys from the bucks' party. Amy threw her arms around Kurt's neck, kissing him smack on the lips in a way she wouldn't do sober. Tania gave their cousin, Gina's son Gino, a hello hug before beginning what appeared to be a deep and meaningful conversation, and that left Sophie, jammed between some bloke she didn't know and one she knew all too well.

'Hey, Soph …' Dylan gave her a little elbow nudge. 'You did really well up there.'

She leant in closer to him so he could hear her over the music, and so she could breathe him in. Good God he smelt divine. 'Thanks, although I know you're just being nice.' She laughed at her own expense. 'I sounded like I was being strangled.'

'Maybe, but it was still entertaining, and bloody well good on you for giving it a shot. I don't reckon I'd have the balls to get up there and do that.' He grinned before taking a swig from his beer.

With the mention of his balls, Sophie fought not to envision his nether region. 'It's a tick off my bucket list,' she replied with a smile, while at the same time trying to desperately rein in her wayward thoughts before she did something stupid.

His brows shot up, as too did the curl of his oh so kissable lips. 'You have a bucket list?'

'Yup.'

'What else is on it?' He took another gulp from his beer, eyeing her over the bottle with keen interest.

If only you knew, she thought, as she recalled the last thing on the list. She did her best to act blasé. 'Oh, just stuff like dancing in the rain, getting a tattoo, getting on the back of a motorbike, sleeping under the stars, those sorts of things.'

His smile widened. 'Ah, that's why you were swimming butt naked the other day – it was on your bucket list.'

She gave him the thumbs up. 'Spot on.'

'Well I'll be damned.' He shook his head, still grinning. 'I can help you out with the tattoo and the ride on the back of a motorbike sometime, if you like.'

'Hey, yeah, I hadn't really thought too much about it, but I'd have every confidence going with you on a bike, and I'd like you to be the one to tattoo me – at least I know I can trust you'd do a good job.'

'Do you have any idea what you'd like?'

Right now, you, she thought. 'Not really.' Damn the alcohol, it was making her irrational and way too hungry for his intimate, sensual touch.

'It's going to be on you for the rest of your life so make sure you think long and hard about it.'

Long and hard ... Her mind went haywire. 'Will do.'

'Once you've got something in mind I'll draw it up for you.'

'Groovy, thanks.'

'No wuckers.' He held up his empty schooner glass. 'I'm going to get another, you want a drink?'

'Oh, thanks but no thanks ... I've had my fair share tonight. If I drink any more I'm afraid I might not remain upright, or coherent.'

He chuckled, deep and low. It almost sounded like a growl, and it made her insides twirl and twist and tumble. 'You never were a big drinker, Soph. I still remember holding your hair back while you, as gracefully as you could, threw up in your mum's garden.'

'Oh shit, I'd forgotten about that.' She felt her cheeks scorch as she blushed beneath his devilish gaze. 'Trust you to remember something like that.'

'I remember a lot of the things we used to get up to.' He leant in closer to her. 'To be honest, I'm not really a big drinker anymore, either. I'm having a hard time trying to keep up with this lot.'

Sophie went to reply but was stopped when Amy grabbed her arm and gave it a firm tug. 'Come on, you, before I pee myself.'

Tania shook her head and laughed. 'Always classy, our sister.'

'Ain't she?' Sophie replied, smiling. She couldn't help but look over her shoulder as she was dragged away. Dylan graced her with an all too familiar smile, just before his handsome face vanished into the crowd.

By the time they had spruced up their hair and make-up, chatted about things that only get talked about whilst drunk in a ladies' loo, and then passed each other toilet paper beneath the doors because Tania was the only one who had any, the toilet trip took almost twenty minutes. They piled out behind another group of girls that had basically hogged the mirrors. The room felt a little as if it were spinning, so Sophie leant against a wall for support.

Pressing the home button on her mobile, Amy squinted into the blinding light of her screen. 'Holy crap, it's almost closing time. We better get our last round of drinks before the bar shuts shop.'

Tania clapped her hands. 'Sounds like a plan to me.'

With her legs feeling way too unsteady for her liking, Sophie held her hands up. 'Count me out. I've had enough for one night I think.'

'Spoil sport,' Amy slurred lightheartedly before dragging Tania towards the bar. 'If you change your mind, we're having shots,' she called out over her shoulder.

Now on her own, Sophie cast her eyes over the crowd that had seemed to thin dramatically while they'd been in the loos. She looked out for the other girls in the hens' night group, especially Daniela, but couldn't see any of them. And her mother and Gina had gone too. They must have all left while they were in the toilets. But to be honest, she was in search of only one person. Maybe, if she just walked right over there and kissed him, let him really feel how much she still loved him, all might be forgiven, and forgotten. Dutch courage was a godsend. Finding her object of interest, she sucked in a sharp breath and bit back tears. There he was, having a conversation with Leah on one of the cosy black leather couches. And they looked mighty comfortable with one another. It got her wondering whether something had gone on with them, after she had skipped town bound for London. With the sad, sorry state she'd left Dylan in that was very possible. Her heart sank, and that pissed her off. She shouldn't even be humouring the idea of ever being able to get back with him. They were well and truly over. Ended. Finished. She'd made damn sure of that. To hell with it, she was going to join her sisters in a shot, or maybe two. What did she have to lose? And in less than a minute, that was exactly what she was doing.

The DJ announced the final song of the night. Now propped up on a bar stool with her sisters on either side, Sophie turned and watched as Dylan and Leah put their drinks down and headed to the dance floor. Dylan kept his distance, but Leah inched her way closer and closer until she was almost upon him. Their eyes met and Leah wrapped her arms around his exquisitely broad shoulders. Sophie didn't feel the hand come reassuringly down upon her back, or Tania's voice asking if she was okay.

Her gaze stayed glued to the couple, as if mesmerised by the ache it triggered in her heart. Someone was saying something, Tania maybe, but she felt as if she was under water and they were above. Dylan stepped back and took Leah's hands, twirling her as though he were a rock-and-roll king. The pair moved in unison, annoyingly so. Sophie threw back another shot. After what felt like an eternity the song finished. Thank Christ. Dylan and Leah walked off the dance floor and retrieved their drinks. Leah placed her hand on Dylan's back, as if it belonged there, as if *he* belonged to *her*. Sophie struggled to inhale, to exhale. The room spun even more. She lost all sense of time, of what she was doing. Tania and Amy grabbed her arms but she shrugged them off and yanked herself away from them.

Next minute, as if she'd time travelled, she found herself at Dylan's side, with Leah's fierce gaze burning a hole into her. Sophie didn't give two hoots. Let the woman stare. She grabbed Dylan by the arm. 'I need to talk to you, right now, in private.' Her words were a little slurred. She now regretted the three shots at the bar. Immensely.

Dylan shook his head. He pulled his arm out of her grip. 'What about?'

'Oh come on, Dylan, you must have some kind of idea.'

He stared at her as though desperately trying to connect the dots.

She pulled him down so she could whisper in his ear. 'You were the best thing that ever happened to me and …'

He stepped away from her.

'Stop, Sophie. Don't say another word. You're too drunk to be thinking straight.' He kept his voice low so Leah wouldn't hear, and Sophie had to, at the very least, be thankful for that.

'But …' she stammered.

'No, Soph, I can't just let you waltz back into my life after what you did. It crushed me and tore my life apart, and it's taken me a fair bit to try and put it back together.' He sucked in a breath. 'How about we talk about it when you're sober.'

Sophie almost fell to her knees. His words held the strong tone of finality and there was an icy hostility in his eyes that stabbed a stalactite right through her heart. 'I'm not trying to just *waltz* back into your life, Dylan.'

With a heavy sigh he gently guided her away from Leah. 'Then what are you trying to do?'

'I honestly don't know.' She choked back a sob and looked down at the floor. 'Show you how sorry I am, and offer an olive branch, maybe?'

'An olive branch, are you kidding? It's going to take a little more than an olive branch to undo what you did, Sophie.'

Not getting the reassurance she craved, she remained mute. She dragged her eyes to his, and they were stormy, fierce, but also clouded with sadness. The shock of it almost knocked her to the ground. Her heart raced as fast as a bullet fired and she was now desperate to flee.

'I think you should go home and sleep it off. We can talk about this another time.'

'Yup.' She bit back hot tears. 'Just please, I'm begging you, don't go home with her.'

'With who?' He turned and looked at Leah who was now busy talking to another bloke from the bucks' party, the one Sophie didn't know. 'With her?'

Her eyes were waiting for his when he turned back to face her. 'Yes, her.'

'I wouldn't. Not interested.' He looked a little confused but then he recovered and straightened. 'But if I did want to, which I don't, why shouldn't I?'

'Because you're way better than that, than her. She's not good for you.'

'How would you know what's good for me?' He shook his head as though bitterly disappointed. 'Please, just go home, Sophie.' And with that he walked away, towards Leah and the bloke she was talking to, not once taking the time to glance back, to make sure she was all right. He'd thrown a verbal punch, and not cared where it landed. Sophie wanted to scream at him, tell him the real reason she'd left him all those years ago was to protect him and everyone else involved. Damn the letter. Damn her sisters. Damn her parents. Damn Faith. And damn Dylan. And while she was at it, damn Tania and her dad for telling her stuff and then asking her to keep it a secret too.

She was tired, so tired, of being everyone's confidant.

If only Dylan knew the truth, what would he think of her then? Why should she have to look like the bad guy when this wasn't even her doing? It was time she took hold of the reins of her life and did what she felt was right. But not tonight. Not now. Tomorrow would come soon enough. This was torture. Utter humiliation. She wanted nothing more than for the earth to open up and swallow her whole. Before she ended up in a flood of tears, she ran from the pub and out into the soothing darkness of night. She bent at the waist, trying to catch the breath Dylan had stolen with his dismissal of her. If only he knew the truth, if only everyone knew the truth – that would change everything. Maybe he'd even love her again.

Maybe …

Bed. She needed to go to bed. Daniela's cottage was only one street away, so it wouldn't take long for her to walk there. She wanted to get the hell away from Dylan, and Leah, too. She wanted to go to sleep and pretend none of this had happened. But it was too late. She'd done it. It was said. She'd made a complete fool of herself. How much lower could she tumble before she hit rock bottom? Because of everyone else's secrets her heart was broken and her life was in tatters. She couldn't do this any longer. Couldn't bear the burden of this anymore. Things had to change.

CHAPTER
14

Shorefield

A loud clap echoed through the dawn silence, stirring magpies from their perches in the gum trees surrounding the paddock between the pub and the four-storey apartment block. Thinking he'd heard gunshots, Dylan woke with a start, his heart in his throat. The men he'd watched exchanging drugs for a down payment from Angus claimed his mind's eye. What if they were after him now, because Angus was so hell bent on the idea that he had stolen the stash? Not daring to draw a breath, he listened intently, wondering if he'd dreamt it or if the sound was real. If they were out for blood, how would they know he was here of all places? Another clap echoed. The realisation it was a car backfiring allowed him to take a much-needed breath.

The room was still dark, the blackout curtains doing a damn fine job except for the tiny sliver of light peeking through. With his adrenaline waning, Dylan took a few moments to get his bearings. He was still fully dressed, on the couch, and not where Leah had so desperately wanted him to be. He hazily recalled walking out of the loo and her planting a kiss firmly on his lips. She'd then tried to drag him to her bedroom but he'd bluntly refused. He liked her as a mate, but any more than that, no thank you. Leah had laughed off his rejection, saying she was only kidding. Her body language spoke of the opposite. Sophie was right. He needed to steer clear of Leah.

The run-in with Sophie claimed his thoughts. His heart pinched when he recalled the distraught look on her face when he'd told her to go home. If only she knew it had taken every bit of his strength to walk away from her when all he wanted to do was take her into his arms and kiss her heartache away. The sensation had shocked him to the very core, as too did her open acknowledgement of her feelings for him, but he couldn't deny any of it, and in a way he couldn't be mad with her – because he still loved her. Immensely. He'd tried and tried to let her go, given it his best shot to forget she even existed, but no matter how much he tried to shake her off, she had a hold on him that was never going to ease completely. He was starting to believe he would never truly be able to move past her.

And if that were the case?

Melancholy hung over him like a black cloud. He grimaced from the pounding behind his temples but at the same time felt he deserved a hangover. After watching Sophie disappear out of the pub's front door, he'd stupidly drowned his sorrows. Turning on his side to ease out his aching lower back (couches were never a great place for a six-foot-something bloke to sleep), an empty pizza box tumbled to the floor and landed among a few empty beer bottles. Damn the taxis for not running all night here – otherwise he'd be home in his own bed. A groan pulled his attention to the left. Someone wriggled from beneath a checked blanket in the corner of the lounge room. Then they sat up, looking as bad as he felt. Dylan smiled when he saw it was his best mate. 'Holy shit, Mark, what the hell are you doing here?' He kept his voice low, not wanting to wake Leah. He wanted to get out of here before she woke up, so they didn't have to go through the whole elephant in the room thing after her trying to get him into her bed and being rejected.

'Morning to you too, buddy.' Mark's voice was croaky. He looked more than a little worse for wear with his hair flattened on one side from where he'd slept and creases lining his cheeks. 'I was following you. I thought we were walking home, which would have been a massive feat now I think about it, and the next thing I know we're back here eating pizza and playing truth or shots.'

'Hey, don't blame it on me. It was Makka that dragged us all here. I was following him.' Dylan stifled a chuckle. 'There was no way on this earth any of us would have made it all the way back out to the farm in the state we were in anyway.'

'Yeah, true … I was barely able to put one foot in front of the other without falling over.' Mark looked past Dylan. 'Speaking of Makka, the bugger's either made a run for it or got his wish since bloody high school.'

Dylan looked down the darkened hall and then back to Mark. 'Who knows, but I ain't going into her room to find out.'

'Neither am I.' Mark flopped backwards, groaning again. 'And just for the record, I'm never drinking again.'

'Yeah right, until the wedding night next weekend.'

'I might go cold turkey.'

'And hell might freeze over.'

'I'm being serious.' Mark rubbed his face. 'I feel like shit warmed up.'

'Some greasy bacon and eggs will fix you up, mate. Wanna head back to my place and I can rustle us up some breakfast?'

'Thanks, but nah, I might head home and go back to bed.'

'Man of strength and vigour you are, buddy.' Dylan stood and then straightened the cushions on the couch. 'Daniela is going to skin you alive once she finds out you crashed here.'

'Yup, and that's why you're going to tell everyone we went back to your place and crashed there.'

'Now you're being stupid.' Dylan shot Mark a wary glance. 'This is a small town, where people love to know other people's business. She's bound to find out sooner or later and then you'll be in even deeper water. And to be honest, I don't want to be in the shit for lying for you. Your woman is vicious when she's pissed off.'

'Ha-ha, yeah, she can be. No wonder she's a top lawyer. I love me a feisty woman. But if we hightail it before Leah gets up, she'll be none the wiser.'

'I reckon you'd be better off telling the truth and getting the blasting over with. Lying's not going to do you any favours in the long run.'

'I'm not in the right frame of mind to handle Daniela getting up me right now. I think my head would crack in two if she raised her voice.'

Dylan shrugged. 'Righto, buddy, I'm not going to tell you what to do.'

'Good, because I won't listen anyway.'

Dylan grinned and shook his head. 'You never do.'

'Yeah, you should know that pretty well by now.' Mark got on all fours, crawled two metres and then slowly came to standing with the aid of the couch. 'Oh, bloody hell, is the room spinning or is it me?'

'It's definitely you, buddy.'

A little unsteady on his feet, Mark headed towards the front door, his boots and socks in his hands. Dylan followed closely behind him, ready to catch his mate if he tumbled. Stepping out into broad daylight, both men squinted and held their hands up to ward off the glare.

Mark blinked, his bleary eyes watering. 'Holy snapping duck shit, that's one shiny arse sun.'

Dylan eased the door closed with a hushed click. 'It usually is pretty bright.' He gave Mark a friendly slap on the back. 'My God, you're really out of practice, aren't you?'

'Yup. I'm like an old married man already, and to be honest, I'd rather stay home and have a beer with Daniela than hang out at the pub all night like we used to.'

'Now that's a man in love if I've ever heard it.' Dylan tugged on his boots. 'You're one lucky bloke, having a good woman to love you like Daniela does.'

'That I am.' Mark succeeded in staying upright, only just, as he tugged one boot on and then the other. He smiled proudly. 'Now we just need to get you hitched and we can all play happy families.'

Dylan headed down the stairwell first, with Mark one step behind him. 'That's definitely not anywhere in the near future, or the distant one either. I have to find me the perfect woman first, and I'm not settling for second best.'

'You already have.'

'What, settled for second best?'

'No, you idiot, found yourself the perfect woman.'

'Who?' Dylan made his way across the paddock, towards the car park of the pub.

'Sophie.' Mark almost shouted it out.

'Oh, don't start on that again. Sophie and I were over years ago, and there's too much water under the bridge to go back. An ex is an ex for a reason.'

Mark was having trouble keeping up. 'I disagree.'

Dylan glanced over his shoulder. 'You might, so what.'

'You and Sophie were good together, Dylan.'

'We were, but she fucked it up, massively.'

They reached where Mark had parked his beefed-up four-wheel drive, with more aerials than there were radio stations. 'You know, there is such a thing as forgiveness, mate.'

Dylan knew Mark had a damn good point, but he wasn't about to give in to the fight he was having internally about Sophie. 'Far out, you've gone all soft on me.' He gave his best mate a slap on the arm.

'Not soft, just real, I suppose. We're not getting any younger and I want to see you happy, that's all.' He reached out and gave Dylan's shoulder a pat. 'And Sophie used to make you *real* happy.'

'Yeah, she did, and then she made me *real* unhappy.'

Mark sighed. 'It's your life and you've got to live it. I'm not going to tell you what to do.'

'Good, because I won't listen anyway.'

Mark grinned. 'Hey, that's my line.' He blipped his Landcruiser unlocked and went to climb in. 'You coming or what?'

Dylan shoved his hands in his pockets. 'Nah, I might go for a wander.'

'Where?'

Dylan shrugged.

Mark gave him a knowing look. 'Yeah, righto, happy wandering ... I'll catch you later.'

'Yup, catch ya.' Mark's little lecture had hit home, and Dylan knew he needed to go and apologise to Sophie, or he'd be pissed off with himself all day. She didn't deserve his cold shoulder, especially when she was so drunk. He waited for Mark to rev the old beast to life and then watched him drive off. He had to at least make right of his wrong if he and Sophie were going to be friends. For the first time in what felt like a lifetime, he could actually recall her with fondness, and that both delighted and scared him.

With one foot in front of the other, he headed in the direction of Daniela's cottage – because apparently that was where all the girls were going back to last night. He hoped Sophie was there. He felt a spring in his step as he recalled how hot she'd looked up on the bar, singing like a hyena but owning it all the same. The most fleeting of glances had connected them across the crowded room, making him feel as if it were just the two of them, alone. In that moment he'd hardly been able to breathe for wanting her. She could have strutted it out on a catwalk in her glove-like red dress. Adding to her allure were those knee-high black boots accentuating her perfect legs. Watching her dance Coyote Ugly style, her eyes closed so she was in a place no one else was privy too, and the way her chaotic curly blonde hair cascaded over her shoulders, and the swing of her hips way out of time with the music, did things to him they shouldn't have, or wouldn't have if it were another woman. He'd had to fight himself not to knock out every bloke that was looking at her in a way they shouldn't have been. It was weird, but she still somehow felt like his.

Turning down a laneway, he took the shortcut to Daniela's. His footfalls echoed in the quiet street. Shorefield was the quintessential little country town, a place so quiet on a Sunday morning you could hear the wind rustling through the leaves of the jacarandas that lined the pretty suburban street. Appearances could be very deceiving. He knew all too well the loudness of the whispers that went on behind his and his mother's back since his father's death. Everyone had their own take on the events that unfolded that night, even though none of them had been there. Some had it right, most had it wrong, but him, his mum and Aunty Kimmy were the only ones alive who knew the exact truth.

Amy and Tania had already left and now it was just Sophie and Daniela. It was nearing nine-thirty and the quaint two-bedder cottage was still silent apart from a kookaburra singing a familiar song from the backyard. It made Sophie smile through her wretchedness. It was such a typical Australian sound and one she hadn't realised how much she'd missed until now … just as she'd come to realise how much she had missed Dylan Stone. And what a heart of stone he'd had last night, turning his back on her as if she were nothing to him and leaving her standing there like the complete fool she was. She had been very drunk and out of line, but friends were meant to help friends, weren't they?

And weren't she and Dylan supposed to be trying to be friends? How stupid of her. Well, that would never happen again. She'd allowed herself to be vulnerable and he clearly didn't give two hoots. As mad as she was at him for that, she also knew she had to try to understand his side. But not this morning – for now, she wanted to stay mad so it didn't hurt so much.

Rolling on her side, she flinched from the gloriously bright sunshine streaming through the parted curtains as if reaching out to her. The day was beckoning, but she needed a few more moments just to get her bearings. Now sober, albeit very hungover, and with a clearer mind, she was mortified by her actions and regretful that Dylan now knew she still thought of him in a romantic way. Damn alcohol and the false courage it had given her – she should have known better. Her face had blazed so hot as she'd watched him walk back to Leah that she was sure a three-course meal could have been cooked up on her cheeks. There was that horrible moment in time, between action and consequence, where she'd just wished she could curl up and die. She wasn't sure how she was ever going to face him again, let alone be glued to his side for the entire wedding ceremony, and the photos afterwards. *Oh lord, just kill me now*, she thought. But, as hard as it would be, she was just going to have to grit her teeth and do it for Daniela's sake. At the very least, all this drama took her mind off her woes with Zachary.

Not wanting to bash herself up any longer – what was done was done – she pulled off the thin cotton sheets and sat on the edge of the bed. Her mouth felt drier than the Simpson Desert and her head thumped relentlessly – a ripper of a hangover in the making. Grabbing her hair tie from around her wrist, she pulled her knotted hair up and hobbled over to the full-length mirror. She grimaced at the sight. Black mascara was smudged under her bloodshot eyes and two unsightly pimples seemed to have appeared on her chin overnight. They looked bigger than Mount Everest. Leaning in closer, she squeezed one at a time, determined to make them pop, jiggling on the spot with the pain. Job done, she grabbed a tissue and dabbed them, although now they appeared twice the size. She would be putting make-up on before leaving the house today. With a weary sigh she straightened the sexy silk and lace PJs Daniela had lent her because she'd forgotten to bring her own, liking the way they made her feel all womanly and empowered – and then made her way towards the kitchen where she craved a stand-her-spoon-up kind of coffee. She hoped her cousin had some bacon and eggs on hand too, because she was hankering for a greasy breakfast.

Twenty-five minutes later she was on the couch, her legs curled up beneath her with a romance novel she'd plucked from Daniela's overloaded bookshelf in her lap. Reading always made her feel better. A chapter in and she was hooked. Sophie and Daniela's parents all loved to read and it was a pastime instilled into their children, although Tania hadn't taken a shine to it. The black sheep of the family, now in more ways than one, her darling baby sister had always danced to the beat of her own drum. Sophie was just finishing her coffee and was considering checking if Daniela was still alive in her bedroom when a knock at the front door brought her to her feet. Placing the book on the coffee table, she walked over and opened it. She smiled, expecting to see Mark standing there.

Another familiar face stared back at her. His gaze flashed over her, from head to toe and back again. He looked so devastatingly handsome. Her smile faded. Her heart slammed hard against her chest. Her breath caught in her throat. His eyes, a sea blue beneath a cloudless cobalt sky, shimmered and crashed and churned all at once. She had to fight not to be pulled into their hypnotic power as she gripped the door. She noticed he was still wearing the clothes from last night, and the realisation that he possibly hadn't gone home almost buckled her legs beneath her.

'Dylan, what are you doing here?'

'Hey, Soph, nice to see you too.' He tried to smile but faltered. His voice was hopelessly husky. He cleared his throat, not once but twice. 'How'd you pull up?' There was apprehension in his words. His eyes rested on hers as if they were home, but only briefly, before he looked down at his boots.

She suddenly remembered how awful she looked, how big the two pimples were on her chin, and how risqué her pyjamas were. She quickly wrapped her arms around herself, knowing she looked ridiculous in doing so but what else was she meant to do? 'I'm a bit hungover but not too bad, considering how much I drank.' She spoke to his chest, not daring to look into his eyes for fear of falling too deeply into them. She reminded herself she was mad with him. Very mad. But her body was betraying her. She ached to reach out and draw him to her.

'Yeah, you were knocking them down like water. No wonder you were trashed.' He looked at her and succeeded in smiling this time but she didn't return the gesture.

He'd hit a raw nerve. And it stung like hell. 'You come over to rub a little more salt into the wound, have you?' She was surprised she'd squeezed the words past the boulder in her throat, and she could tell by the wounded look in his eyes they'd hit their mark.

Dylan rubbed his five o'clock shadow. 'No, pretty much the opposite really ...'

'Is that so.' She was intrigued. Enormously. His gentle voice made her pulse race.

'I've come with a peace offering.' His hands going behind his back, he grabbed something from his back pocket and revealed a dusky pink rose. 'It's not much, but it's as fresh as can be.'

Sophie recognised the rose from the house three doors down. 'You're game; Mrs Barrington would knock you out with her broom if she caught you picking that.' She didn't reach out to take it from him.

'It would have been worth it if she did.' Still holding it out to her, he shook his head. 'I'm so sorry about last night. I should never have fobbed you off like that. You were pouring your heart out and trusting me to take care of it, and instead, I crushed it.'

'Thank you, Dylan, it's beautiful.' She accepted the rose and, holding it to her nose, breathed in the heady scent, her heart welling. It was such a simple gesture yet it brought tears to her eyes. 'I deserve worse than what you did last night, after what I did to you nine years ago.'

He went to respond but stalled. He shook his head, his eyes sad.

Sophie's heart reached for his. He was the first man who'd ever woken her body to life and lit the flame in her heart. The first man, and the only man, to show her what true love felt like.

He cleared his throat. Again. 'Let's not go back there, huh. There's nothing to gain from it. Can we have a fresh start, from right now?'

'Of course.' She nodded as she vividly recalled how it felt to be kissed by him. Her lips tingled with anticipation. She stepped out of the doorway, allowing him inside the cottage. 'You want to come in?'

'Thanks, but no, I better get home. Mum will be getting worried.' He chuckled a little uncomfortably. 'That made me sound like a teenager then, didn't it?'

'A little.' She grabbed the opportunity to ask him the question burning a hole in her heart. 'You haven't been home yet?'

'I um, well … we, hmm.' He shifted from foot to foot, looking mighty guilty.

She held up a hand. 'You don't owe me an explanation, you're a big boy.'

'It's not what you think.' He was rocking back and forth on his heels now, and couldn't meet her gaze.

'Like I said, not my business.' She itched to throw the rose in his face.

He leant in close to her and dropped his voice to a whisper. 'If I tell you something do you promise to keep it a secret?'

'Oh sweet baby Jesus, not you too?' She spoke the words before she could stop herself.

'What do you mean?'

'Oh, nothing, don't mind me … yes, I'll keep your secret.'

He hesitated, eyeing her cautiously. 'Well, you know how much Daniela dislikes Leah?'

'Yes.' *Not as much as I do*, she wanted to add, but zipped it.

'Well, we all ended up back at Leah's, including Mark. And then it was too late to catch a taxi home. I slept on the couch and Mark on the floor. And I think Makka is still shacked up in the bedroom with Leah.'

Sophie instinctively glanced over her shoulder to make sure Daniela hadn't walked out from her room. 'Oh shit, Daniela's going to kill him.'

'Yes, correctomondo … exactly why we can't tell her.'

Sophie gave him an I'm-not-too-sure-about-that look.

'We don't want them fighting the week of their wedding, do we?'

'No. So what's Mark going to tell her?'

'That we stayed at my place.'

'Right.' She groaned inwardly. Another bloody secret she had to keep. This was getting ridiculous. Although she completely agreed with Dylan – this was something Mark and Daniela could talk about *after* the wedding was over. She pretended to zip her lips. 'Not a word.'

'Thanks, Soph.' Dylan drew in a deep breath as he shoved his hands in his pockets. 'Will you have dinner with me tonight?' He spat the words out in haste, as if he were a fifteen-year-old boy asking a girl out on a first date. Her mouth must have dropped open because he quickly followed that up with, 'Nothing fancy, maybe just a burger or a pizza or something, and then I thought we might go and catch a movie at the drive-in.'

'Yes, I'd love to.' A feeling of warmth spread throughout her.

'Great. Excellent. Fantastic.' A broad smile lit up his face. 'I'll pick you up at your place at six?'

'Perfect, see you then.'

'Oh, and one more thing.'

'What's that?'

'I only own a motorbike so I hope it's okay to pick you up on it?'

'Oh, great, yeah, sure … I'll be able to tick it off my bucket list.'

'Oh yeah, that's right, the ol' bucket list.'

'Yup.' She was smiling from ear to ear now.

'Trust me, it's just like riding a horse, only better.'

'I don't know about that but I'll have to take your word for it.'

'Don't worry, I'll bring you home in one piece. Promise.'

'It'll be fun.' Her concerned expression said otherwise. 'You only live once, right?'

'Very true, so best to make the most of it while you can.' He nodded and then turned away, this time making sure to glance back at her, his smile sending her insides into a beautiful tumble.

Rosewood Farm

Sophie grabbed her old but well-loved riding boots from the assortment of shoes and boots lining the bottom of her cupboard. They could use a little bee's wax to shine them up, but all in all they still looked in good condition. Sitting down on the edge of her bed, she tugged them on. They fitted like a glove. Now with not much to do but wait, she contemplated what it would be like climbing onto the back of the motorbike and the very thought made her inner conformist scream blue murder. What if she slipped off, what if another driver ran into them, what if a cow appeared out of nowhere? She mentally slapped herself. She had to stop. It was just like riding a horse, only faster … apparently. Anyway, she trusted Dylan to take care of her.

Walking over to her full-length mirror, she turned this way and that. Her hair loose and only a little bit of blusher and light lippy on, it felt good to be going out *au naturale*; unlike the times she'd had to dress up to the nines to accompany Zachary when they'd entertained his clients. Even so, she'd spent a good part of the afternoon trying on every combination of outfits imaginable before deciding on a pair of jeans and a boho-style top. It had been forever since she'd been on a date, especially one with a man as handsome as Dylan. She felt the same as she had all those years ago, when they were about to go on their very first date to the school disco. This time it was burgers and then the drive-in. She had no idea what movie they were going to but it didn't matter – the company was all she cared about.

Making sure she had everything she needed in her handbag – lip-gloss, perfume, chewies, phone and wallet – her belly filled with even more butterflies. A knock at the bedroom door startled her. 'Come in.' She expected it to be her mum but her father opened it.

He leant on the doorframe and folded his arms. 'Hey, love.'

Sophie smiled. 'Hey, Dad.'

His expression turned serious. 'Are you sure this is the right thing to be doing?'

'I'm not *doing* anything, Dad, other than going out with a friend for a burger and a movie.'

'You've just come out of a long-term relationship and had your heart broken, and now you're running back to the man you left years ago.'

'I'm not running back to Dylan, Dad.'

'Sophie, it's clear as day what's going on between you two.'

'Is it, Dad?' She couldn't help the irritation creeping into her voice.

'Yes, Sophie, it is.' Frank's tone became sterner.

Sophie bit back the words trying to leave her lips. 'Please, I don't want to talk about this right now, so save it, Dad.' Her pulse quickening, she slung her handbag over her shoulder and went to make her way out. Then she stopped just shy of him. 'I know this is your way of looking out for me. But I'm a big girl now and I can sort my own life out, okay?'

Frank heaved a sigh. 'Please don't treat me like I'm the enemy, Sophie.'

'I know you're not the enemy, Dad, but please, let me make my own decisions, how I see fit.'

He looked at her indignantly. 'And let you make your own mistakes too, I suppose.' He sighed as if she were a naïve teenager. 'I wish you would learn instead of making the same one again.'

'Dylan and I were not a mistake.' Something inside her snapped. 'To set the record straight, I never should have left him in the first place.'

Frank flinched, his bushy grey brows furrowed. 'Well why did you?'

The rumble of a motorbike alerted her that Dylan was almost here. 'I had my reasons.'

Frank looked flabbergasted. 'And you don't want to tell me what they were?'

'No, I don't. Sorry, Dad.'

He glanced out the window to where a headlight blazed down the driveway. 'Good lord, he's picking you up on a motorbike?'

'Yes, he is, and I can't wait to feel what it's like on the back of one.' Sophie noticed she didn't sound as confident as she wanted to.

Frank shook his head. 'Oh, love, what happens if you come off it?'

'Dad, lighten up, would you? Millions of people ride around on them every single day.'

'You will always be my little girl, so no, I will never lighten up.' Hands on hips now, Frank turned back to face her. 'Make sure he doesn't speed, and you wear a helmet and jacket.'

'Yes, Dad, I will make sure of all three.'

'Good girl.' His tone was still stern but a smile was tugging at the corners of his lips.

Leaning in, she kissed his cheek. 'As annoying as you can be, I love you, Dad.' And with that she turned and raced down the steps.

'Sophie …' Frank leant over the railings. 'As annoying as you are, I love you, too.'

She flashed him a wide grin.

The rumble got closer, louder, and then stopped. Dashing through the lounge, she paused at the couch and gave her mum a peck on the cheek. 'Enjoy your *Game of Thrones* marathon.'

'Yes, I'll try to keep my eyes open for just one more episode. I wish you hadn't introduced me to it, sweetheart, I'm an addict. And Jon Snow …' She sighed dreamily. 'He is just divine.'

'Told you you'd love it, and him. Almost every woman I know does.' Sophie smiled. 'Catch you in the morning.'

'You're not intending on coming home?' Marie's eyes went from sleepy to saucer-wide.

Sophie forced her groan back down. 'Yes, Mum, but I'm guessing you'll be in bed by then.'

'Oh, right, please be careful on the back of that motorbike, won't you?'

'I will be.' She could almost picture Dylan climbing from it, his leather jacket hugging his gorgeous tattoo-adorned muscles. She arrived at the front door just in time to hear his heavy footfalls thud across the timber floorboards of the verandah.

The sensor light fired to blinding life as she swung open the door. Dylan's hand was raised to knock. 'Howdy doodie, Dylan.' He smelt of leather and spice and all things naughty and nice. With him only two feet away from her, she had to fight not to rest her head against his broad chest so she could breathe more of him in.

His lips curled ever so sexily into a cheeky smile. 'Howdy doodie to you too, Firefly.' He looked her up and down appreciatively. 'I have to say, you look very nice tonight.'

'Why thank you.' Closing the door behind her – before her dad had another chance to add his two bobs' worth – she stepped out beside Dylan. Like a bee to honey, her eyes were drawn to him, head to toe and back again. She loved how he looked in his well-worn jeans and button-up black shirt, open just enough at the top to tease her into wanting to see more of the chest she longed to rest her head against. 'You scrub up pretty damn good yourself.' The black boots, shirt, and leather jacket suited him. It gave him a dark, slightly threatening edge, and she loved it. What woman didn't love a bit of a bad boy?

He held out a leather jacket. 'You and Mum are both little itty bitties, and even though you're taller than her I think this will fit you perfectly.'

Another compliment, boy oh boy she wasn't used to this. She took it from him and slipped it on. His smile let her know in no uncertain terms just how much he thought it suited her.

'Very nice,' he said with a satisfied nod.

Her body heated beneath his warm gaze. She needed to move before her face flushed any redder. 'Well, come on then, we better get a move on if we want to catch the start of the movie.'

'Yup, we should.' He gave her another heart-stopping smile.

They walked side by side towards the impressive motorbike, aglow beneath the light of the moon. Its sleek lines made her think of a powerful animal ready to chase its prey. She ran her fingertips over the shiny steel-grey tank, embossed with a golden eagle with its wings spread. 'She's very nice.'

'Yes, she is. It took me a year to restore her and it was worth every bit of blood, sweat and tears, and every pretty penny, I might add.' He passed her an open-faced helmet. Watching her pull it on, he then took the liberty of tightening her chinstrap. 'Comfy or too tight?'

'All good.' She struck a pose. 'How do I look?'

'You look like a very cute biker chick.'

'I do?'

'Uh-huh.' He grinned as he got his helmet secured.

It was the third compliment in less than five minutes – more than what she'd got from Zachary in the past year. She smiled coyly as she watched him straddle the bike and then motion for her to join him. Before she could second-guess herself, she grabbed hold of his shoulder and hiked her leg up and over. Once settled behind him, he shoved the kickstand back and balanced the bike with a boot on either side.

The Indian Chief Vintage grunted as Dylan revved it to life. 'Hold on tight,' he called back to her.

With the bike vibrating between her thighs, she wrapped her arms around his waist tentatively – she would wait until their speed justified a tighter grip before she closed the gap between them. Even though Dylan now had a very good idea how she felt about him, she didn't want to be so hopelessly obvious. Friends, they were trying to be friends – nothing else, she reminded herself firmly. Her voice of reason laughed hysterically in her head.

A fool could see the chemistry between them, but until the truth was revealed, come hell or high water whatever this was between them could go no further. Dylan deserved to know the truth this time round. The possible bad consequences were scary, but she'd just have to find it within herself to live with it. Because she just couldn't continue to keep the secret in her closet, not when she was going to be living back here.

Trying not to let the fear of what she was going to do overwhelm her, she focused on the moment – there was no use living in the woes of tomorrow. She was back in Australia, without a high-rise in sight, going out for burgers and a movie, on the back of a motorbike with the one and only true love of her life. The reality of it made her smile from the inside out. Never would she have believed it if someone had told her it would be. She ached to be closer to Dylan. Craved it. Craved him. Giving in to her longing, she slid forwards a little more. His back felt so deliciously solid against her chest. She wondered how it felt for him, having her breasts lightly pressed into him. A quick but firm squeeze on her thigh told her he liked it. She shouldn't have taken so much gratification in the fact, but she couldn't help herself. The heart wants what the heart wants.

The moon bathed the dirt road in silvery light. And with nothing but the simplicity of Mother Nature surrounding them she allowed the luxury of being alone with him to sweep over her. Dylan took the corners slowly, changing gears smoothly. He occasionally placed his hand on her thigh to press her more firmly into him. Little bit by little bit, they were edging closer and closer. She could tell he was being extra careful with her on the back, and that made her want him all the more. They reached a T-intersection. Left was out of town, right was to the heart of it. Dylan came to a complete stop, his foot balancing them as he waited for a lone car to pass. Traffic was never a problem here.

'Can we go faster now?' She felt a little rebellious asking, but loved the thrill of it.

'You're going to have to hang on tighter if you want faster.'

She didn't need to think about it twice. She slid in tight, closing any space between them. Dylan placed his hand over hers, pressing it in even more snugly to him. His touch sent searing heat throughout her body. With the tyres meeting the bitumen, he hit the throttle and the bike lurched forwards like a launched rocket. Adrenaline rushed through her, and she loved it. The white lines turned into one as they tore along the highway. Sophie clamped her thighs to his hips, the sensation making her nether regions tingle. The sea air felt cool on her face and tears formed at the corners of her eyes with the whip of the wind. She pressed her cheek against his back. The leather jacket kept her warm, as did being so close to Dylan. She glanced down at the moonlit water, glittering as if it were dusted with diamonds. It was so vast it stole her breath away. The waves folded over one another, embracing the shore in a fleeting moment before flowing back into the arms of the ocean. Salt spray sparkled in the moonlight and when she licked her lips she felt she could taste it. The coastline was so achingly familiar, as was this feeling she was getting from Dylan. It was as if no time had passed between them. A sigh travelled all the way from the depths of her soul.

In the blink of an eye, the ocean was gone, replaced by paddocks dotted with the glowing lights of the houses. Leaning them into a turn, Dylan defied gravity. The road brushed past only inches from her as she gripped him even tighter. One bad move and they'd be goners. Knowing that Dylan was in control of that outcome was hotter than hot – it was scorching. Bringing them back upright, he handled the bike with ease as they hit the road straight into town. Seeing him in such control made him even more desirable than he already was.

Slowing, they passed the bank, hardware store, butcher's and green grocer's. Much too soon he was pulling up outside of the local burger joint – Sophie didn't want to let go of him. She begrudgingly unclasped her hands from around his waist. Gripping his shoulders, she climbed off and then removed her helmet. Aware of how flattened her hair would be, she gave it a shake before he turned to face her.

'You like?' His grin was wicked.

She stepped onto the curb. 'Like? I love! That was awesome.'

'Great to hear.' He stood and straddled the bike. 'It soothes the soul, huh?'

Her eyes travelled to where his thighs squeezed the fuel tank. Her breath hitched as she imagined it being her between them. 'It sure does.' She desperately wanted him to lean in and kiss her.

Climbing off the bike, he took her helmet and sat it alongside his on the seat. 'You want me to order the usual for you?'

She cocked her head to the side. 'The usual?'

'Yeah, a steak burger with the lot minus the pineapple but with extra cheese.'

'Holy shit, you remember all that?'

He tapped his head. 'It's like a vault in here.' He grinned. 'And I even remember you like tomato sauce and mayo, and hate barbeque sauce.'

She felt her heart skip a beat. 'I'll have all of that minus the extra cheese.' She tapped her belly. 'Gotta watch the waistline, now I'm getting older.'

'Come on, live a little.'

'Oh, okay then, double cheese it is.' Even though he was ordering for her, she followed him in, not wanting to be too far away from him for even a second.

Twenty minutes later and they were heading into the drive-in. The bike caught the attention of other moviegoers as Dylan weaved through the parked cars and to the front of the open-air cinema. Parking off to the side, he gestured for Sophie to hop off before doing the same. After pulling her helmet off, she passed it to him. 'I can't believe this place is still going.'

'I know, me too. It's the last of three drive-ins in Australia.'

'Seriously?'

'Deadly.' His smile was wide. He pointed to what looked and smelt like freshly mowed grass up front under the screen. 'You happy to swag it over there?'

'For sure ... we can have ourselves a little picnic while we watch the movie, like we did in the good ol' days.'

'That's the plan.' He rifled through his saddlebags, bringing out a blanket and a bottle of red wine along with two plastic cups. 'Sorry about the drinkware, but you got to make do in these kinds of situations, huh?'

'I'm just stoked you thought to bring wine.'

'Of course I did. What's a picnic without wine?'

'Hear, hear,' she said, following closely behind him while admiring how perfect his arse looked in his worn jeans.

Tossing the blanket onto the grass, they settled down and started tucking into their burgers and a side of chips. The screen fired to life and the trailers began, followed by the main event, a romcom Sophie had been dying to see back in the UK, but Zachary had refused to go to it with her. And by the time she'd organised a friend to go with her the movie had run its course at the theatre. The country drive-in was a little behind the times, but it had worked in her favour.

Scrunching up the wrapping of her burger, she wiped her lips with the napkin. 'Did you know this one was on?' Following movie etiquette she kept her voice to a whisper.

'Nope, but I don't care. I just wanted to hang out with you.'

'Aw, thanks.'

He gathered their rubbish and shoved it into the bag the burgers came in. Tying it up, he plonked it on the grass beside them to throw out later, and poured them both a cup of wine. Passing one to Sophie, he held up his cup. 'To being friends and good times ahead.'

She chinked his cup. 'To being friends and *many* good times ahead. Oh, and the perfect wedding day for Daniela and Mark.'

'That too,' he said before taking a swig.

'Ooooo, nice drop,' Sophie said.

Dylan lay back on the blanket and stretched out. Although Sophie ached to join him, she remained sitting. He smiled at her as though he knew exactly what she was thinking. 'Come on, I'm not going to bite.' He raised his brows. 'Or maybe I might.'

She slapped him playfully and then lay down beside him. She rolled from left to right, trying to get comfortable, and just when she thought she was, a part of her neck or back would ache and she'd wriggle again. She tried resting on her arms, propped up on her elbow, lying on her side, her back, her stomach with her hands propped beneath her chin …

Dylan chuckled softly. 'You right there, Soph? You got ants in your pants or something?'

'This isn't like it was when we were teenagers.' She laughed. 'I can't get comfy.'

'Sorry I didn't bring pillows, couldn't really fit them on the bike, but you can use my chest if you like.'

Her heart stalled, and then, when she remembered to breathe, her heart took off in a gallop as if launching from a starting line. 'You sure you don't mind me cramping your space?'

'If it'll stop you wriggling around, I don't mind at all.' He snaked his arm out and around her shoulder, pulling her into him before she could say any more.

'If you insist,' she said softly as she tucked her head beneath his chin, every curve and plane of their bodies fitting together perfectly.

'I insist.' His voice was husky and low.

Watching the movie now, she listened to the comforting sound of his heart, liking the way his chest would move when he chuckled. It felt like the good old times, cuddled up together at the drive-in. They used to do this kind of thing before they'd even thought about becoming girlfriend and boyfriend all those years ago. If only they could wake up tomorrow and have this feeling all over again, but she doubted that would be possible. It was Murphy's Law that life would somehow get in the way of whatever this was.

The velvet blanket of night settled over them. Diamond-sparkling stars were painted across the sky. Sophie felt torn, lying like this, as if she were somehow taking advantage of Dylan and his willingness to try to be friends, to let the past go, to forget the heartache she'd caused him. He deserved to know the truth. Maybe it was wrong of her to like this so much. They weren't teenagers anymore so she couldn't use her youth as an excuse to be swept away in the moment. She knew better. Life wasn't a fairytale, and the fact she and Dylan still clearly loved each other didn't guarantee a happy ending. Life and love were hard and challenging and filled with rocky paths that sometimes led nowhere. But for now, just for tonight, she just wanted to walk along this path with Dylan right beside her.

CHAPTER
16

Shorefield drive-in

Dylan glanced down at Sophie wrapped in his arms, her cheek against his chest as she slept. He bit back emotions he didn't dare acknowledge for fear of them overwhelming him. What in the hell was the universe playing at? It felt as if they had unfinished business, like their fates were forever entangled. He was the master of blocking out love and trying to pretend Sophie didn't exist. It had been his way of dealing with the hurt of losing her. He'd come to accept she was never going to be a part of his life ever again – had even forced himself to believe he disliked her – but there was a fine line between love and hate. And now here she was, all flesh and bones and gorgeous curves, and close enough for him to kiss her. The hidden part of himself he'd turned off, the one he'd let no other woman come close to, had been switched on again by the mesmerising Miss Copinni without her even trying, or realising what she was doing. They'd always been that way, so easy and free together, before everything had turned sour. This, right here, just felt so damn right. Too damn right. All his happy thoughts of her were rushing back into his consciousness, and he couldn't help but love the feeling. It was like coming home after a long, long time away.

But was he just stepping back into dangerous territory, where he risked being hurt again? It was on the cards ... but being a man to take a chance, he was leaning towards dealing them. Staring into the night, he watched a colony of fruit bats swoop across the sky, their vampire-like silhouettes enhanced by the silvery moonlight. The movie screen was black now, the last of the cars having left over an hour ago, and even though his arm was dead, he didn't want to move. Sophie looked so peaceful, so beautiful, so ... his. One of her arms was slung over his waist and her other hand was tucked beneath her chin. He watched her chest rise and fall, her breathing slow and rhythmic. He liked imagining, if just for a little while, that they were together and everything was effortlessly perfect. If only it were that simple. He longed to know why she'd left him all those years ago, especially now he could feel the love she still harboured for him; love that was visible each and every time he caught her gaze.

Had she seen it in his eyes too?

A sugarcane train approached on the tracks behind the open-air cinema, the rumble a familiar one for locals this time of the year, although, having been away for a while, it seemed louder and more invasive than it had when Dylan had called Shorefield home. He smiled down at Sophie when she stirred.

'Howdy, Firefly.'

'Hey there, you.' Her voice was soft with sleep, and her gaze unconsciously provocative. 'How long was I out for the count?'

Those delicious full lips, he so wanted to kiss them. Heat swirled inside of him as he imagined claiming them with his. 'A good couple of hours.'

Sophie's eyes widened. 'Holy crap. Really?' She unravelled from his arm, sat up, and then crossed her legs.

Dylan almost pulled her back to him but instead flexed his hand open and closed to get the feeling back in his arm. 'Yes, really, and you were snoring a little too.'

'I didn't, did I?' She looked so distraught it was gorgeous.

'Maybe you did, maybe you didn't.' He tucked his hands behind his head and grinned. 'You'll never know and I'll never tell.'

'Well, if I did, I think it was those two glasses of wine that made me do it.' Her smile was wickedly playful.

'Ha-ha, maybe.'

'Oh well, I missed half of the movie but it's a small win for the fact I can wipe another thing off my bucket list.'

'Falling asleep at the drive-in?'

'No, you tripper, sleeping beneath the stars.'

'Ah, cool, and speaking of your bucket list, we need to organise that tattoo for you, too.'

'When you're ready, just give me the word.' She smiled softly, sleepily.

He returned her smile. 'I'm ready whenever you are.' A shooting star shot across the sky, leaving a fiery trail. He made a silent wish. One he never thought he'd make.

'Cool, thanks.' She hugged her knees to her chest. 'Why didn't you wake me up?'

'With you being asleep I could watch the movie without you yabbering on.'

A sassy smile played on her lips in the most erotic of ways. 'Oi, that's not very nice, Mister Stone.'

'I'm always nice, Miss Copinni.' He skilfully dodged a slap as he sat up beside her. 'I better take you home before your father gets his shotgun out.'

'Oh no, he's not that bad.'

'I caught him looking out the window as we rode off,' Dylan said. 'If looks could kill, I would have been dead on the spot.'

'He was just worried about me getting on the back of a motorbike, that's all.'

'I can understand that. You'll always be his little girl, no matter how old you get.'

'Yeah, true ... as much as it drives me nuts I know he means well.' She stretched her arms high, yawning. 'Sorry I fell asleep. So much for being great company.'

'Awake or asleep, you're good company.'

'Aw, that's sweet of you to say. And ditto.'

Yes it was sweet, too sweet. The energy shifted, intensified, as she held his gaze with one he could so easily fall into. Good God, he needed to get a grip. He stood. He had to get away from her before he did something stupid, something that would give her the right to step back into his life as more than just a mate. But it was bloody hard. It had felt so right having her in his arms, so close to his heart, he'd wanted her back there. He wanted to stake his claim, and make her his. Again. Like two pieces of a puzzle, they belonged together – but it just wasn't that cut and dry.

Sophie held out her hand. 'Help me up, would you, cowboy?'

'That'd be my pleasure, ma'am.' He mocked a southern drawl.

'Why, thankya.'

Her southern drawl was so much better than his. Her hair was tousled and her eyes glimmered with waywardness as she looked up at him beneath long lashes, and he liked it. Liked it one hell of a lot. Maybe too much for his own good. Definitely too much for his own good. He pulled her to standing and then quickly uncurled his hand from hers, at the same time reminding himself of the reality of their situation, of the past he so longed to forgive and forget. But like the desert needed the rain, he needed Sophie Copinni. Yin and yang. Ebb and flow. Soul mates.

But she'd gone and ruined everything ...

Dylan's voice of reason snapped him to attention.

Wandering over to the bike, Sophie picked up her helmet and tugged it on.

In four strides Dylan was standing only inches from her. She smelt so good, like wildflowers on a warm summer's day. As if on autodrive, he fastened her helmet. His fingers brushed the side of her neck as he pulled away, the very place where he could see her pulse racing. She caught his eyes with hers yet again. Her gaze filled with what looked like soul-deep love. But it couldn't be. Not after how easily she'd walked away from him. Yes, she had feelings for him, but true unconditional love? He just couldn't believe it. He couldn't let this, whatever it was, fool him into believing they could go right back to where they used to be, before she fucked everything up.

Snap out of it, man ... pull yourself together.

As much as he wanted to, he couldn't drag his eyes from hers. Something unfathomable passed between them. Desire lingered. Enflamed. Sizzled. Arousal pumped into his loins, hot and heavy. The flare of her pupils told him she was feeling the same.

He almost didn't know how to breathe anymore. Damn her for being so irresistible. Her lips parted as if she were about to say something. He hung on the moment, waiting for the words to tumble from her lips, waiting for the declaration of an acceptable reason why she left him, one that would allow him to take her into his arms and freely love her again. *Please, Sophie, just say it …*

She shook her head, as if telling herself to remain quiet. Long lashes feathered her cheeks when she fleetingly closed her eyes. He grabbed the opportunity to step away from her, and then straddled his bike. He gripped the handlebars not only to steady himself but also to stop himself from tearing every inch of clothing from her delectable body. The primal urges she stirred, just by looking at him the way she did, were out of this world. It was exactly how it used to be – she always knew just how to woo him, how to win him over. It actually made him angry that she had this power over him. But try as he might he couldn't shake her off. The way her arms had embraced him on the blanket, the way her head had rested against his chest right atop where his heart beat wildly. How was he supposed to ignore her mesmerising beauty, or the touch of her soft skin beneath his fingertips, or the invisible thread that connected them? If it were any other woman, he would have never allowed history to repeat itself, but with Sophie it was as if it were out of his hands.

She gently touched his shoulder, making him jump. 'All good for me to hop on now?' Her voice sounded a million miles away.

'Yup.' He cleared his throat.

She slid on behind him. The feeling of her breasts pressing into his back almost rendered him senseless. Her arms reached around his waist and tightened. He longed for her to slide her hands under his leather jacket and shirt, to leave marks on his skin as she clawed him in ecstasy. To take the edge off, he closed his eyes and breathed in deeply. He tried not to think about riding back to his place, about carrying her through the front door and tossing her onto his bed so he could bestow pleasures upon her that hopefully no other man had. He tried not to think about how she would look naked on his sheets, her limbs curling tightly around his as he climbed on top of her and slowly slid inside of her. His jeans grew tighter against his crotch. Revving the bike to life, the growl of it only added to his yearning for her. He needed to hit the road and let the ride take his thoughts away.

Five minutes later he was doing just that, the white lines a blur beside him. He slowed as he reached a turn-off. Up ahead the faint glow of an approaching car shone over the summit. He had plenty of time. Pulling out and onto the highway, the rumble of the bike helped soothe some of his frayed edges. Before he knew it, headlights were looming from behind, bigger and brighter with every heartbeat, and quickly closing the distance until it was no longer safe.

Some arsehole kids, he thought.

He kept one eye on the road and one on his rear-view mirror. Sophie's arms tightened even more around him, and he gave her hands a quick pat to reassure her that everything was okay. But he wasn't sure of that himself. He slowed, but the car didn't pass. He sped up, and the car did too. His gut squeezed. Angus's harsh words slammed to the forefront of his mind. *You better not have taken my gear, Stone …*

Was this really happening? Had Angus put the heavies onto him? Or could it even be Angus himself? The black Ford swerved to come up beside them, so it was now on the wrong side of the road. Dylan inched away as far as he safely could, aware he couldn't go any further with the guardrails now right beside him. They were trapped. One movement from the driver and they'd be crushed up against the rails. Dead in an instant. Sophie, he had to protect her at all costs.

She leant right into him. 'What the hell are they doing?' Fear dripped from her every word.

'I have no idea, just hold on tight.'

The driver of the car matched their speed. Sophie's embrace intensified as did his on the handlebars. The brief glow of a lit cigarette was the only thing he could make out behind the tinted glass of the car's window. He shifted down a gear, and slowed. The car slowed too. He tried to make out someone, anyone, but the tinted windows were too dark. He wanted to speed off, to get away from whoever it was, but he couldn't risk doing that with Sophie on the back. The car edged closer. The handlebar tagged on the guardrail and sparks flew. He kept the bike up and stayed in control – but it was a fight. And then, just as he was starting to really freak out, the car sped up, moved in front of them, and then took off down the road like a bat out of hell. He sucked in a deep breath, willing his racing heart to slow to some sort of normal rhythm. Damn kids. If it had been Angus or a couple of his thugs, they wouldn't have driven off.

He thought about pulling over to make sure Sophie was okay, but he was too afraid of her seeing through his facade, and he was also worried the car would return. The next ten minutes felt like the longest of his life, as he made his way back to Sophie's place. He kept the bike in low gear as he approached the house, not wanting to wake Frank or Marie.

He pulled to a stop in the shadows of a towering gum and then switched off the ignition. The silence made his ears ring. He didn't bother taking off his helmet, hoping it would help to conceal some of his lingering anxiety. Sophie climbed off and passed her helmet to him. He shoved it on the seat in front of him for now, wishing he could see more of her face to gauge how she was, but shadows made it impossible.

He forced a smile. 'Bloody idiot kids, scared the bejesus out of me.' He needed to bounce this off and pretend it hadn't bothered him in the slightest … a major omission on his behalf. As soon as he left here, he'd be dialling Angus's number, and if he didn't answer, he'd be ringing the tattoo shop first thing in the morning. This shit needed to be sorted before someone got seriously hurt, or worse. There was no way in hell he was going to risk harm to his mum or Sophie.

Sophie remained silent. The front verandah light flickered on, bathing her face in soft light. Dylan could tell she'd been crying, but before he could comfort her, Frank stepped out of the screen door, wrapped in his robe.

'I'm heading to bed, love.'

'Hi, Dad, okay, I'll be in in a minute.'

'Hi, Mister Copinni.'

'Hi, Dylan.' Frank gave a curt nod before disappearing back inside.

'And he waited up for you, bless the old bugger.'

'Yeah, it was sweet of him, but it makes me feel like I'm a teenager again.' There was a tremor in her voice.

His heart aching to reach out and soothe her, he took her hands in his. They were shaking, and cold. 'Are you okay, Soph?'

She edged a little closer to him. 'Not really ... I thought we were going to be crushed up against the guardrail.'

He rubbed her hands between his, trying to warm them up. 'Sorry the night ended on such a sour note. Try not to let it worry you too much, though, okay?'

She released a slow, measured breath, and shook her head as if dazed. 'I want to ask you a question, and I hope you're going to answer me honestly.' A sliver of moonlight lit her face now. Her gaze reached into his and tugged at his heartstrings.

'Of course, shoot.' He held his breath.

She dropped her head to the side, assessing him in a way that made him extremely uncomfortable. 'Are you in some sort of trouble?'

'No.' It was said way too fast.

'You sure about that?'

'One hundred and ten percent positive ... They were just some hoodlum kids, Soph, nothing more sinister than that.'

She bit her lip, hesitated, and then nodded. 'Yeah, you're probably right.'

He could tell she didn't believe a word. 'I wish I'd thought to get their numberplate, but I was too busy trying to keep you safe on the back.' He hated lying, but in this case he had to.

'Well it's a good thing I got it, isn't it?' She slipped the leather jacket off.

'You did?' He swore beneath his breath.

She handed the jacket over. 'Yes. And I'm going to call the police in the morning and report it.'

'You are?'

'I am.' She was looking at him as if waiting for a confession of sorts.

He wasn't about to give it to her. 'Do you think it's worth it? It's not like the police can do anything about it now; the car would most probably be long gone.'

'Bloody oath it's worth it. Why wouldn't it be, Dylan?'

He knew that tone. Knew it very well. She was trying to get something out of him. He wasn't about to tell her that he'd witnessed a drug deal. How in the hell would he explain himself out of that one? 'Righto, yes, you're right. Sorry.'

Worry lines etched her forehead. 'I'll give you a call tomorrow and let you know what they said.'

'Better still, why don't you give me the rego number and I'll call the police tomorrow. I should be the one to do it, not you.'

Her expression was deadpan. She folded her arms. 'You promise you will?'

'Cross my heart.'

There was a moment's hesitation before she nodded. 'Okay, I'll text you the details once I get inside, before I forget it.'

'Great, thanks.' He sighed weightily. 'I feel shitty that tonight ended so badly. Why don't you come to my place tomorrow night; I'll do your tattoo and cook you dinner?'

A soft, coy smile curled her quivering lips. 'A tattoo *and* dinner, how could I refuse?' She leant in and gave him a hug, her lips trailing across his cheek as she pulled away. 'Night, Dylan.'

'Night, Firefly.' He watched her walk down the garden path, up the front stairs and then disappear into the house.

CHAPTER

17

Stone's Throw

The minute Dylan woke he recalled coming home to find his front door wide open. Not that he locked it when he went out, he never did on the farm, but he did remember shutting it. His mother might have come in to get something, or then again there was a chance the wind had blown it open. Nothing had been moved or taken, but he'd been left with an eerie feeling that someone uninvited had been there, making the incident with the car even more chilling. Was he overreacting? Possibly.

He needed to talk to Angus.

He reached for his mobile phone, knocking it off the bedside table. Hanging over the edge of the bed, he scrabbled around for it, and once he'd retrieved it he flopped back onto his pillow. Blinking, he tried to force his body to catch up to his already racing mind. He checked the screen. There was nothing. No missed calls, no text messages. He called Angus's phone five times before giving up. Groaning, he sat up and slung his legs over the side of the bed. It was too early to call the tattoo shop. It didn't open until ten. He flicked through the texts between him and Sophie, the first the details of the numberplate.

Please don't wake up and shrug off what happened, Dylan. It was serious, and very scary.

Promise I'll take care of it first thing in the morning.

Good, thank you. Hope you're okay, and not too shaken up from it.

I'm all good, tough as nails.

You might be on the outside but I know you're a big softy on the inside.

Shh, keep that a secret. I don't want to ruin my reputation round these parts. It was nice hanging out, Soph. Thanks for tonight.

Thanks for asking me out. I really enjoyed myself, even though I fell asleep. I've missed you, Dylan.

I've missed you too. I'm glad we can be friends again.

Yeah, me too ... Night. Xo

Night, Soph. Xo

He scrolled back to the text about the numberplate. He couldn't call the police. Couldn't tell them everything. He'd be charged as an accessory and do jail time. Goddamn it. So, he did the next best thing and called one of the staff.

'Johnno speaking.'

'Hey, Johnno, it's Dylan.'

'Hey, Dylan ... hear about the break-in at the shop?'

'Yeah, Angus told me. The thieving bastards.'

'Got that right. Apparently they got off with a few grand from the safe. Angus is hell bent on catching whoever it was.'

Dylan had to bite his tongue. 'Can't blame him.'

'Yeah, hey, I heard you moved back to the sticks. That was a bit sudden, wasn't it?'

'Yes and no … I've been wanting to come home for a while now.'

'Fair enough. Can't blame you when you're not used to the city lifestyle. So what do I owe this phone call to, buddy?'

'Not much, mate, just trying to get in touch with Angus but he's not answering his phone. You going to be seeing him today?'

'Nah. The break-in has stressed him out to the max, so he's taken a week off. And you're not the only one having trouble getting hold of him; the bugger has basically gone off the grid.'

'For Christ's sake, Johnno, you serious?'

'Yup.' Johnno chuckled. 'Thank fuck all of us know how to do our jobs, because with you gone and now Angus going MIA, we'd be up shit's creek without a paddle otherwise.'

A pounding headache arrived in full force. Dylan slammed his eyes shut and pinched the bridge of his nose. 'So who's looking after the two shops?'

'Nobody at Kings Cross, it's closed until Angus gets back. And he's got me managing the one in the city while he's away … the drive there is an absolute bitch.'

'Yeah, with all that city traffic to wade through, damn right it is. So what are the artists doing for work?'

'A few of them are taking shifts here when they can, and a couple of them have decided to take time off.'

Dylan leapt to his feet. He needed to pace. 'What a fucking mess.'

'Tell me about it.' There was a weighty sigh. 'Is Angus in some sort of trouble, Stone?'

'No idea.' He straightened, his jaw muscles clenching. 'Why you asking?'

'I had some seedy looking blokes turn up at the shop yesterday, demanding to know where he was.'

Dylan rubbed a hand over his stubble. 'What did you tell them?'

'The same I told you, that he's gone on leave.'

'Suppose that's all you could tell them, huh.'

'Yup, so, is he in some sort of trouble?'

'How would I know, Johnno?' It was said way too defensively.

'Shit, calm your farm, buddy. I just thought you might know something, that's all.'

'Sorry, just got a ripper of a headache.' He made a conscious effort to soften his tone. 'I don't know anything about any trouble.'

'Okay, well, if you hear from him, can you tell him to call me?'

Dylan stopped pacing. 'Will do, and same goes. If he calls, tell him to give me a holler.'

'Roger that … anyways, better run, buddy, got shit to do before I head to work; make sure you keep in touch from time to time, hey?'

'Okay, will do, Johnno, catch ya.'

'Yup, on the flip side, Stone.'

Dylan hung up and then, striding to his window, pushed it open. Gulping in the fresh country air as if he'd been drowning and just resurfaced, he tried to slow his racing pulse. Just how in the hell this was going to play out, he hadn't a clue, but one thing was for certain, with all the weird shit going on and with Angus MIA, he needed to watch his back, and the backs of those he loved – and that included the beautiful Miss Copinni. If somebody was trailing him, they'd now know he was close to her after seeing her on the back of the motorbike – it wouldn't take much for them to figure out who she was and where she lived. His jaw clenching, he stared out at the horses in the adjacent paddock. A gallop was going to be first on his list after he'd done a few odd jobs around the place for his mum. He needed to clear his head, to get a grip on not only the situation with Angus, but also the one with Sophie, and getting his butt in the saddle was going to be the best way to do it.

A distant crack of thunder announced the imminent arrival of a tropical storm. Sophie grabbed her jacket from where she'd left it slung over the hat rack near the front door. Her father passed her the keys to his car. His face was solemn and his eyes were full of concern. 'I hope you know what you're doing, Soph.'

Sophie shook her head. 'I beg your pardon?'

Frank sighed through his nose. 'You and Dylan tried and failed, and I don't want to see you hurting even more than you already are after what Zachary has done to you.'

Sophie's hackles rose but she fought to keep her fiery Maltese temper at bay. She loved her father with all her heart, and she knew he was only looking out for her, but she wanted her own life, her own path. If only he knew the real reason she'd run from Dylan, and Australia, all those years ago, what would he have to say to her then? The urge to tell him what she knew overcame her. 'Actually, to be honest, no I don't know what I'm doing, Dad, but for once in my life, I'm going to go with my gut and my heart, instead of worrying what's best for everyone else and hurting myself in the process, and that includes you and Mum, *and* my sisters. It's time I started thinking about myself and what I want from my life.'

Frank said nothing, but looked her dead in the eye.

There was a stand-off.

Sophie wondered if he knew exactly what she meant.

Frank broke the silence. 'What was all that supposed to mean?'

Sophie shoved the keys in her pocket and then reached out to gently touch his arm. 'Please, Dad, just trust in my choices, okay?'

'Your choices?' It was said with caution.

She lowered her voice to a whisper and dropped her arm back to her side. Maybe it was time she told him. Without taking any more time to consider it she said, 'Dad, I know.'

Slack-jawed, Frank's eyes widened to saucers, but he quickly composed himself. 'Know what?'

'Do I really need to spell it out?' Her voice was low, measured. She didn't want to say it out loud, and was finding it hard to draw breath.

'I haven't the faintest idea what you're on about, Sophie.'

'I think you do, Dad.' She sighed heavily. 'I can't just sweep everything under the rug and pretend life is peachy perfect anymore.'

Her father looked at her as if she were crazy.

Irritation filling her, Sophie glanced left and right, making sure her mother wasn't in earshot. 'I know what happened … with Faith.'

'Do you now?'

Sophie stood her ground, her gaze stern. 'Yes, I do.'

Frank instantly paled. He took a step back, shaking his head. He squeezed his eyes shut and took a deep breath. When he opened them again there were welling tears but he blinked them away quick smart. 'And what is it that you know about Faith?' Every single word was forced, measured.

'I know what you and Mum, and Aunty Gina for that matter, did all those years ago.' She ached to look away from his eyes, the fear and sadness within them tearing at her heart.

'How?' he stammered out.

'I overheard you and Mum arguing about it one night, when I was seventeen.' She held her breath as she waited for Frank to catch his.

'Why didn't you say something back then?'

She shrugged and then shook her head, wrapping her arms around herself. 'I was in so much shock I didn't know what to say at first, and then I thought it was best to keep it to myself, for everyone involved.'

'So you didn't talk to anyone about it?'

'I only ever told one person, and they told me to keep it a secret.'

'Oh, who?'

'Grace.'

'I see.' Frank paused, briefly. 'Did knowing have anything to do with the reason you left Dylan?'

'Yes, in a roundabout way.' Clutching the moment and hoping her father would understand now, Sophie powered on. 'I really think everyone deserves to know the truth, Dad, so we can all move on with our lives.'

'I don't know about that, Sophie.' Frank looked as though he was carrying the weight of the world on his shoulders as he leant against the wall. 'We all make choices in life and we have to deal with the consequences of them as best we can, and we all agreed it would be kept under lock and key.'

'Okay, but I shouldn't have to deal with the consequences of your and Mum's decision.'

'You shouldn't have been eavesdropping on our conversation that night, and then you wouldn't be in the predicament you're in.' His tone rising a little, Frank's gaze darted to the left, as if making sure Marie wasn't going to overhear them.

'I wasn't eavesdropping … I couldn't help that I needed a drink of water. How was I to know I was going to overhear you saying all those things on my way to the kitchen?' Sophie made sure to keep her voice low, although her tone was sharpening.

'I don't know what to say, Soph, other than I'm sorry you heard what you did.'

Sophie huffed. 'I'm tired of keeping it a secret. It's too much to carry around every day, especially now I'm staying in Shorefield.'

'Don't even think about it, Sophie … especially when we haven't got your mother's or Faith's agreement to bring it all out in the open.'

'Well, Dad, what do you suggest I do?'

'I don't know. But why now, Sophie? After all these years of keeping it a secret.' He shook his head. 'I'm sorry, but I just don't understand.'

'Living in the UK made it easier, like I could pretend it wasn't true, but now I'm here, amongst you all again, I can't stop thinking about it. When the time is right, I'm going to talk to Mum.'

'It could break up this entire family. You do understand that, don't you?' Frank said.

'Of course, but I also don't want to sit back and keep something so important from those who should know, and that includes Dylan. We have to give people the benefit of the doubt, give them a chance to let it sink in and accept it.'

Frank regarded her with suspicion. 'So this is what it's all about. You want to clear the air so you can get back with Dylan?'

'Yes and no.' How could she explain she'd kept her mouth shut because Grace not only threatened to reveal what she'd overheard, but also said that she would tell the police about what she witnessed the night Dylan's father was killed if Sophie didn't leave him?

'That's very selfish of you, don't you think?'

'Selfish? Of me? Really? Don't you think it's you and Mum, and Faith as well, who are the selfish ones keeping something like this hidden? I can kind of understand it when we were young, but now?'

Frank's shoulders slumped. He hung his head in his hands and then sighed. When he brought his gaze back to Sophie's there were tears welling again. He gruffly wiped them away. 'I'm sorry you've been put in this position, Soph. I really am. Believe me when I say I understand what you're saying, I really do, but this doesn't just involve you and me.'

'I know, Dad, I do, but … this might be a good thing.' She reached out and placed her hand on his arm, almost feeling his inner turmoil. He was usually so strong, so composed. 'I think the time has come to tell the truth, and if you're not prepared to do that, then I will do it for you.'

'You don't have the right to make that decision, Sophie.'

'You don't have the right to make me keep it a secret, Dad.'

He held up his hands in surrender. 'All right. This isn't getting us anywhere. How about we sit down and talk to your mother tomorrow? See how she feels about it, and then take it from there.'

Sophie released the breath she'd been holding. 'I think that's a very good idea.'

Footsteps came up behind them and Marie appeared. 'Frank. I've been calling you for five minutes. Dinner's on the table and it's going cold.'

'Sorry, I didn't hear you. I'm coming now, love.' His voice held none of the strength it usually did.

Marie placed her hand on his shoulder. 'Frank, are you all right? You're not having a turn again, are you?'

'I'm fine, Marie.' He patted his chest. 'The old ticker's all good.'

Sophie tried to hide her emotions as Marie looked from her to her father and back again. 'What's going on here?'

Sophie planted a smile on her lips. 'Nothing, Mum, Dad's just being over-protective again.'

Marie visibly relaxed and gave him a playful slap. 'Oh lighten up, Frank, and let the girl go and have some fun. Lord knows, she needs it.'

'I'm trying to, Marie, but it's not that easy.' He turned on his heel and headed off down the hallway.

Marie rolled her eyes. 'Men. You can't live with them and you can't live without them.'

'Very true, Mum.' Sophie leant in and gave Marie a kiss. 'Night, catch you later.'

'Night, love, have fun, but please bear in mind what I said, about not jumping into anything with Dylan. You need time to get over Zachary.'

'Yes, Mum.' Sophie couldn't get outside quick enough.

Minutes later and she was behind the wheel of her dad's pride and joy, and with the rain bucketing down she was driving at a snail's pace to avoid hitting any roos. She tried to leave all her troubles behind as she made the short trip over to Dylan's. Being next-door neighbours had its advantages, although it had been quite a big disadvantage when they'd broken up – there'd been no avoiding him or the guilt she'd felt with leaving him the way she had. She thought about what they'd had as teenagers, all the dreams they'd had for their future and the deep love they'd shared. She thought about the good times and the rare bad times, when they would argue over something stupid, but then make up not long after. Neither of them had ever been able to stay mad at the other for too long, and the making up had been oh so beautiful. Even now, remembering how he used to kiss her melted her heart. That had been true love – the need to be together more primal than thirst or hunger. Dylan had been the only man who had ever made her feel that way, and now she was spending time with him again she wanted that feeling back. She had to tell him what she knew, and show him the letter from Grace to prove why she did what she did, but first she had to speak with her mother. She knew it was wrong of her to allow this, whatever it was between them, to keep going before she told him the truth, but he was like a drug she couldn't get enough of.

A crack of thunder boomed, quickly followed by a flash of lightning that lit up the landscape around her like a photographer's flash. The raindrops continued, big and heavy, making it almost impossible to see ten feet in front of the car. Sitting forwards, she drove even slower, smiling at her own expense – she was sure she looked like a little old lady. Turning down the driveway of Stone's Throw, her stomach somersaulted – she couldn't wait to lay her eyes on Dylan again. Passing Faith's cottage, she reached the old tobacco shed. She pulled to a stop and tried to see through the raindrops, cursing for not thinking to bring an umbrella. Through the window she saw the flicker of what appeared to be candlelight. The thought Dylan may have lit candles for her arrival stoked her own flickering inner flames to blazing life. His towering silhouette appeared in the doorway and then an umbrella shot up. Quickly getting her handbag, she smiled as she watched him race out to meet her.

As soon as he reached the car door she jumped out, laughing as she tried to avoid getting wet. 'Howdy, cowboy. Thank you for coming to my rescue.'

'My pleasure, ma'am.' His dazzling smile was knee-buckling. He pulled her close and left his hand resting on her hip, his other arm around her waist. 'Squeeze in so you don't get too wet.'

So she did, close enough for his freshly showered scent to thread into her sharp intake of breath. Goddamn he smelt good. Good enough to eat.

'So what's cooking, good looking?'

'A good old-fashioned lamb stew … you dig?' His voice was low and husky.

'Oh yeah, I'm digging.'

'Good, because I've been slaving over the stove all afternoon.'

A gust of wind ripped the umbrella from his hand. Sophie shrieked and Dylan swore as he took off after it. Sophie tried to help him but just made things worse. She stopped and watched him crash tackle the brolly like a footballer until he finally had it in his hands. He stood, triumphant. When he turned back to face her, they both burst out laughing. Soaked through to the skin, Sophie tucked her wet hair behind her ears. So much for all the time she'd spent in front of the mirror, making sure every piece of hair was in place and looked good, and she honestly didn't care.

Dylan folded the umbrella up and strode back towards her like a man on a mission. He dropped it to the ground at their feet and held out his hands. 'Dance with me.'

Sophie wiped the water from her cheeks, laughing. 'Have you happened to notice it's raining?'

'Is it?' Raindrops clung to Dylan's lashes. He chuckled, so damn sexily. 'Didn't you say one of your things on the bucket list was to slow dance in the rain?'

'Oh yeah, I did.' Her heart beat faster.

'So come on then, dance with me.'

'But there's no music.'

He shrugged. 'We don't need music.'

Sophie's heart somersaulted in the most beautiful of ways. How she had ever found the strength to walk away from this heavenly man was beyond her. She imagined his arms around her as they danced. Pinpricks of delight raced through her. She obliged and placed her hands into his, loving the way his fingers curled around hers possessively. He looked into her eyes, a suggestive smile curling the corners of his oh so kissable lips. Shyness swept over her. With a playfully gentle yank he pulled her to him, not leaving an inch between them, and she tumbled into the dreamlike moment.

Wrapping her arms around his neck, she rested her head on his chest, loving the way she could feel the beat of his heart beneath her cheek. Dylan's hands found the small of her back, and stayed there, pressing ever so gently. They swayed, sharing a silent song, their feet moving together effortlessly. She felt a stirring inside her, beyond the pleasures of the flesh. It was as if her heart and soul were reaching for his, and she could almost say it was reciprocated. Memories of them dancing together at the school discos made her heart skip beat after beat after beat, until she felt a little breathless. The poignancy tugged hard at her heartstrings. Tears stung her eyes and her throat choked with emotion. Truth be told, she had never stopped loving Dylan Stone. Not for one second. She had given up so much, all for the sake of other people, and as she just told her father, it was about time she started thinking of herself.

They remained like this for a few minutes, wrapped in a comfortable silence. The rain had eased to a faint sprinkle. With the atmosphere intensifying, Dylan stopped swaying, as did she. He looked down at her and she smiled. Desire rushed through her. They shared a lingering gaze filled with possibilities and promises. But could they ever be together again? Maybe. Maybe not. For fear of bursting into tears, she looked away. The energy between them shifted and became more intense. Placing his finger beneath her chin, he gently tipped her face to his once more. His lips parted. She waited for him to say whatever was on the tip of his tongue. He hesitated, and then shook his head softly. She felt his laboured breath on her cheek, hot and heavy. His blue eyes deepened their hold on hers. His back muscles tightened beneath her fingertips. She forced her legs to support her and her breathing to continue. But before she could draw another breath his mouth was upon hers, dominating her in a way that made her ache to be naked with him. The whole world reduced down to just him and her. His tongue dipped past her lips, meeting and dancing with her own. She melted into him. He tasted as good as he had all those years ago. Smelt as good. Felt as good. No. Actually. Now a whole lotta man and muscles, and delectable tattoos, he felt, and tasted, even better.

Stopping mid-kiss, he withdrew, but thankfully his hands remained clasped behind her back. There was something indecipherable in his gaze. Her heart beat crazily. The mouth he'd just kissed couldn't form a word. Was this the moment he'd voice his regret in throwing caution to the wind? A whimper escaped her. Sadness tightened her throat. She didn't want to hear it. She almost covered her ears so she couldn't. He closed his eyes and sighed, and when he opened them again they were glistening with tears. His arms dropped from her, and then stepping away, his thumbs hooked through the belt loops of his jeans. His gaze wandered, absorbing all of her like a warm caress. It wasn't the kind of look a remorseful man would give. It was hungry and primal. Hopeful, she allowed herself a half smile. Heat engulfed her, as did the longing to tear every scrap of clothing from his magnificent body. She wanted to straddle him, and feel him shudder beneath her as she brought him to the edge of euphoria.

'I don't want you to stop.' It was whispered, almost unintentional.

'Neither do I, Soph … but … I need you to …' He cleared his throat, seemed to choke on his words.

'What is it? What do you need me to do?' *I'll do anything*, she wanted to say. She struggled for some kind of control.

'I can feel how much you still care for me, Sophie.'

'Yes, I do, so very much.'

He looked torn. 'It just doesn't make sense.'

She took a tiny step towards him. 'What doesn't?'

'This.' He gestured between himself and her. 'Us. What's happening here. None of it makes any sense.'

She felt as though he'd just driven a stake through her heart. 'I'm not playing with you, if that's what you mean?'

'No, that's not what I'm trying to say.' He huffed, shaking his head. 'I need to know why you left me, Sophie. The truth. There has to be something you're not telling me. It's like we've picked up right where we left off, apart from one minor detail – you crushed me somewhere in between.'

Not able to hold his anguished gaze any longer, she focused on the stars appearing on the horizon, the rain clouds now giving way to a clear black sky. 'I'm sorry, Dylan, I never meant to hurt you so badly. It's just …' She choked on her words.

'Just what, Sophie?'

She remained silent. She promised to talk to her mother first, so what was she meant to say right now?

'Look at me, goddamn it.' His words were stern, passionately demanding.

She wrenched her eyes back to his. She had to continue the lie, just for a little longer, and as soon as she'd spoken with her mum, she would run right over here to tell him the truth. 'I was young and stupid and made a bad decision. I wanted to spread my wings and travel. I wish I could rewind time and take back what I did, but I can't. All I can do is try to make up for it now.'

'So it didn't run any deeper than that? There's nothing you're not telling me?'

Clamming her mouth shut, she forced herself to shake her head.

'So you wanted to test the waters and make sure the grass wasn't greener on the other side?'

'No, it wasn't like that. It was more about travelling, and finding myself.' She shivered, not only on the outside. 'If it's any consolation, I never stopped loving you, Dylan.'

He sucked in a sharp breath. 'Say the last bit again.'

'I've never stopped loving you.'

He half smiled, but there was lingering sadness in his eyes. 'But you stayed with Zachary for years. Why, when you were in love with me?'

She looked away again.

'Look, Sophie, I'm laying all my cards on the table here. What you see is what you get with me. You haven't done that, and I reckon I deserve better. Talk to me, please.'

'Okay, all right, I stayed with him because I thought I'd made my bed, so I had to sleep in it, basically.' She couldn't hold back the tears any longer. Dylan took a step towards her but she held her hands up. 'Please, don't comfort me. I don't deserve it after how much I hurt you.'

'Soph, I can't just stand here and let you cry; you mean too much to me for that kind of bullshit.' He ignored her plea and, closing the distance, pulled her to him. 'I've missed you, my beautiful Firefly,' he said soothingly.

She hid her face against his chest and hugged him tight. 'I missed you too.' She looked up at him beneath wet lashes. 'I didn't think you'd ever be able to forgive me.'

He didn't answer but she could feel his heartbeat quicken beneath her hand resting on his chest. 'I can forgive you, Soph, but I can't forget. I'm hoping time will help me with that.'

'I hope so too.'

'Did you cheat on me … is that what you can't tell me? Is that why you left?'

'No way, I could never do that to you.'

'I suppose that's a bit of a relief.' He took her hand in his and ran his thumb over her palm. 'I don't want anything between us anymore. No lies, no secrets, nothing. So if there is something, spill …'

'Nothing to spill.' Terrified to say any more in case she blurted it all out, she gave his hands a squeeze in response.

'There's something else, Soph, that we need to talk about.'

Oh dear lord. She almost fell to the ground. 'What is it?'

'I *really* don't want any clothes between us either.' A wanton smile claimed his lips. He traced his fingers over the tautness of her nipples through the sheer material of her top. 'I know I shouldn't say this out loud, but I want to make love to you. I have since the moment I laid eyes on you at the beach.'

A helpless gasp escaped her. 'I *want* you to make love to me.'

His eyes were clear and intent as they searched her face. 'You sure?'

'Yes, surer than I've ever been about anything.' Her hunger-filled gaze caught his eyes before she kissed him again, this time hot and hungry and demanding. The feminine roar she'd buried the day she'd walked away from him erupted from deep within, and she embraced the rush with vigour.

Clutching her tightly, Dylan matched her passion and sent her tumbling over the peak he'd brought her to. But she knew all too well there were many more pleasure-filled summits to climb when it came to Dylan Stone, and she was hungry to ascend them with him so they could fall into ecstasy together. Winding his arms around her waist, he greedily pulled her closer. Heat rushed through her, from head to toe, igniting sparks in places that had long ago dimmed. She felt alive, free, and like a woman wanted. It had been a long time. Way too long. Wrapping her arms around his neck, she pressed harder into him, letting him know in no uncertain terms that she didn't want him to stop, loving how their bodies seemed to mould into one. Trailing his lips over her cheek, he continued on a downward path. He buried his face against her neck, nipping at her skin, sending her to the brink of pleasure and pain perfectly – as only he knew how to do. His hands dragged down the length of her, stopping to cup her behind. She smiled with memory. He'd always loved the voluptuousness of it.

'I want you. Now. Please.' Her voice was rasping, breathless, beseeching.

Picking her up from the ground, he obeyed her demand and carried her across the front lawn, up the few steps and into the old tobacco barn. Inside, her breath caught at the sight of all the candles. The flicker of the flames danced over everything in sight, including Dylan's face. The television was on and the country music channel was playing, the country love song one she was very familiar with.

'Oh my God, Dylan … do you remember this song?'

'Of course I do. It was one of our favourites.' He paused, watching Tim McGraw and Faith Hill belt out the lyrics – their love for each other undeniable as they looked deeply into one another's eyes.

A smile twitched at the corner of his lips. 'I think the universe is telling us something.'

'Damn right it is.' She grinned suggestively.

'I like your way of thinking, Miss Copinni.'

He carried her to the bed, but instead of placing her upon it, he guided her to her feet right beside it. He pulled her wet top up and over her head, dropping it on the floor. Hooking his finger beneath her bra he undid the clip and then flicked it off her shoulders with effortless sexiness.

He shuddered when he laid his eyes on her breasts. 'Just beautiful.'

The blaze in his eyes spoke of how much he wanted her. Needed her. She felt no shame standing half naked, only the thrill of pleasure to be bestowed by this gorgeous hunk of man. Her nipples ached for his touch, for his lips to be upon them. She could feel her pulse fluttering wildly in her throat. The world around her turned a passionate blazing red. She wanted more of him. All of him. Now. This might be her only chance to show him just how much she loved him. She undid the buttons on her shorts and let them drop. Slipping her fingers beneath the thin straps of her lacy G-string, she provocatively slid it down her legs. Her gaze locked onto where his fingers hovered over the zipper of his jeans, the denim taut. He struggled out of them and threw them aside. Next were his jocks, which were off in seconds. Her eyes widened as she witnessed the evidence of his desire for her. She closed the distance between them. Urgently, she ripped at his shirt, the buttons popping off in succession. Fiery hot, their skin met. She pressed against the weight that was hard and heavy between his legs.

Dylan dropped to his knees, and then slowly, from her knee, he followed the route upwards with soft, open-mouthed kisses. His tongue traced her skin like a lit match. She writhed in mindless pleasure. She gripped the back of his head, her fingers entwining in his hair. His mouth journeyed up, lingering, pausing, tasting, and teasing, until he found her centre. She shuddered, gasped, and pushed his head in closer. Hard ... so beautifully hard. She almost wept as he brought her to the brink. His name spilled from her lips. She begged him not to stop. She was almost there. But then he paused. Stood. Her legs were shaking, quivering. She could barely stand. He smiled rebelliously as he pressed her backwards and onto the bed. He made sure her head rested against a soft pillow. There were more kisses, more teasing touches. Then they were kneeling, facing one another, and for a few brief moments, did nothing else but breathe each other in. Her hands rested against his bare shoulders. Their eyes searched over one another. Their breaths, heavy, mingled as if dancing.

Dylan cupped her cheek. His thumb traced her parted lips. 'You're so damn magnificent, Soph.'

His eyes were deep and demanding, sending her heart into a wild gallop. She swallowed, sensing his struggle for control. 'And you, Dylan, are damn magnificent yourself.'

Their lips met, softly, their kisses featherlike. Dylan's hands came possessively upon her hips, his fingertips digging into her as he pulled her closer to him. His kiss deepened until it was devouring. She clung to the wildness of it. His scorching touch made her nerve endings tingle. She followed his cues. Just like his kisses, his touch grew rough and reckless, raw and greedy, but she loved it. Her lioness roared. Enraptured moans escaped her. Easing backwards, she brought him with her.

Clasping her hands in his, he pressed them to the bed, so she was at his mercy. The tip of his longing pressed into her. He held her gaze. Slowly, gradually, he slid inside her, until she was filled with him. Tightening around him, she raised her hips to bring his heat even deeper inside. He slid in and out, long and deep and slow. Leaning in, he kissed her. She could feel his love for her with every stroke, every kiss, and every touch. Her breath quickened, as too did the rise and fall of her hips. He let go of her hands and she brought them to grasp his back, her nails digging into him. Warm solid muscles tightened beneath her touch. She could feel the desperate race of his heart and hear his ragged breath against her ear. The crescendo built. They moved in unison with one another. There was the hint of fireworks. They began to move frantically, each lost in their own world of passion yet connected on a level way beyond the flesh. Her body trembled and tensed. She reached the summit, as did he. The fireworks exploded. She soared high, her body shaking with glorious trembles. Clutching one another they toppled, crying out in rapture. She felt the surge of pleasure, the quivering release and the rippling aftershock. Reaching the finishing line, she was dizzy from where he'd taken her. A glow swept throughout her and in that moment she contemplated her promise to him. He deserved to know the truth, and nothing was going to stop her telling him … she just needed to talk to her mum first. And he also deserved to know that the very secret he'd kept hidden from her was one she already knew.

CHAPTER
18

Stone's Throw

Dylan smiled to himself. Sophie was curled tightly to his side. Glorious silence lingered between them. They lay in a delicious, spoon-style embrace, the velvet black of night surrounding them, interrupted only by the soft flicker of candlelight. Having succumbed to the temptation to make love for the third time, slowly but still passionately, it took him a good while to return to earth. The way she had hungered for his touch, the way she'd trembled when she'd toppled over the edge along with him, made his heart beat faster. No other woman had ever made him feel the way she did. If he weren't so spent he'd wake her up in the most delicious of ways and send her to the brink with his tongue again. But his sensual contemplations clashed with the realistic side of his brain, and as much as he tried to shrug off the negative, he couldn't deny it was there, hovering like an ominous cloud just off in the distance. Were they simply two ships passing in the night, trying to recapture the love of their youth, or did this have the potential to bring them back together, back to how they used to be? How could he deny the coincidence of he and Sophie both arriving at a crossroads at the same moment, with both of them in situations where they were considering staying in Shorefield indefinitely? That had to mean something, had to count for something. Didn't it?

Or maybe it was all just going to fall to shit again …

Closing his eyes, he memorised the silkiness of her skin, the scent of her, the way she felt pressed up against him, because he was all too aware this might be the only time they made love. The dawn of the new day would bring with it the realities of their lives, and send his misgivings into overdrive. Trust, once broken, took time for him to regain, if he ever regained it. He'd been burnt by her, so his protective wall was still standing, albeit a little less impenetrable. There was something about her that he couldn't keep himself away from. Where he'd found the strength to get through a single day without her the past nine years, he hadn't a clue. But he'd done it, and he could do it again if he had to.

Placing a soft kiss on Sophie's back, he breathed her in – she smelt of everything good in the world and he wanted more of it, more of her. She calmed him, made him feel whole. Half asleep, she nestled in closer, with his arms around her. He put his hands over hers – they felt so small, so soft, in his. A smile claimed his lips. He found it hard to believe the charismatic Sophie Copinni was wrapped within his arms once again; her soft, supple body meeting his as though they were the only two pieces in an intricate puzzle. Ask him last week if this was possible and he would have laughed it off. Life certainly worked in mysterious ways, and although he had many reservations about them ever making it past this night together, for now, he just wanted to hang his hat and live in this very moment.

Needing to touch the spot he knew made her nerve endings fire to life, he brought his lips to her earlobe. 'You awake yet, sleeping beauty?'

She squirmed, her skin instantly covered with goosebumps. 'I am now.' She laughed softly, sexily. 'You are the ultimate tease, Dylan Stone.'

'I do my best.'

Untwining from him, she rolled onto her back, her perfect breasts rising and falling with each breath, and her grey-green eyes lusty and heavy. 'FYI, your best is beautiful.' She gave him a smile that seemed to come from her soul. Her hair, on the other hand, was in bedlam and it looked devilishly sexy.

Reaching out, he pushed a lock of it from her face and traced her high cheekbones. 'Just for the record, I didn't bring you here to have my way with you.'

'Now you tell me.' She smiled and playfully batted her eyelids.

His heart skidded. 'Ha-ha, you did a good job of seducing me, too, Soph.'

'I did my best.'

He chuckled at her banter.

Her smile faltered and seriousness claimed the sparkle from her eyes. 'I honestly never thought we'd ever make love again.'

Leaning in, he kissed her delicious mouth as softly as he could. 'Neither did I, but I'm glad we did.'

'Me three.' She was smiling again. Her belly growled.

He tapped the tip of her nose. 'And speaking of the real reason I asked you here, sounds like we should eat some dinner.'

'I must admit, I'm famished.' Her hands going to her belly, she looked to where his bedside clock glowed red. 'It's almost midnight, but better late than never.'

'True that, and I'm starving too.' Still naked, Dylan climbed from the tousled sheets and retrieving his boxers from the floor slipped them on. He picked up the red and black lacy bra he'd torn from her and dangled it from his finger, his expression one of approval. 'Very nice choice of underwear, Miss Copinni.'

'Thank you, sir.' She lifted her head from the pillow and propped up on her elbow. 'I wore it just for you.'

'So you had me in your sights before you even got here.' He couldn't help the wicked smile that claimed his lips.

Sophie matched it. 'I sure did.'

'I love your sass.' His eyes wandered to the dip of her supple stomach, and then down her gorgeous legs. 'Back in a sec, with some well deserved sustenance.'

'I can get up and join you at the table, or on the couch, like normal people would, if you like?'

He dragged his gaze back to hers, the glint in her eyes letting him know she liked the fact he was taking in the view. 'Nah, stay there and relax. We're not normal anyway, so let's just eat in bed.'

'Perfect.' She rolled onto her stomach so she was facing the kitchen and propped a pillow beneath her chin. He found it hard to tear his eyes from her voluptuous rear and fought the urge to go back to bed to kiss every beautiful inch of it. 'I'll just stay here and watch you, you sexy hunter gatherer,' she purred.

Heating up the stew on the stove, Dylan felt her eyes on him the entire time. They didn't speak. There was no need to. Like the old times, just being with one another was enough. Leaning against the bench as he waited, their eyes met, the intensity making his soul feel as if it were exposed. And it scared him. Terrified him. Was he really ready to leave the past where it belonged? Could he? If he couldn't, it would spell disaster sooner or later. Relationships needed faith, and he wasn't sure he had that in her, now or ever. Regardless of his inner turmoil, he smiled and she returned it. His mind went back to the conversation they'd had outside, to when he asked her to tell him the truth. His instincts screamed out that she wasn't telling him everything. There was something more, maybe something he wouldn't like hearing, but had the right to know. Was she lying about not cheating? What else could it possibly be? Were they heading into dangerous territory where the facts would eventually explode in their faces, and ultimately leave him wounded and having to pick up the pieces of his shattered heart all over again? Her feelings for him felt tangible, straight from the heart, but there was a part of him that just wasn't prepared to let all of her in. He needed honesty and truth, and he wasn't sure she was giving him that. Without them, this was never going to work. He groaned inwardly. He didn't want to torment himself right now; he'd have plenty of time for that in the light of day.

Live in the moment …

With the stew heated, he dished it up. Carrying the bowls back to the bed, he took in his fill of the goddess before him as she sat up and brought the sheet with her. He waited until she was settled and then passed her the bowl and a spoon.

Balancing the bowl on a pillow in her lap, she tucked her hair behind her ears. 'Oh my God, Dylan, this smells divine.'

He snuggled in beside her. 'I hope you like it.'

She took a mouthful and her eyes almost rolled back in her head. 'It's amazing.'

'Glad you think so.'

Silence settled as they ate their food as though it were their first and last meal. Five minutes later, they were both scraping the bottom of their bowls to get the last of the tasty morsels.

'Damn, you can cook.' Sophie took his empty bowl from him, and before he could object, was out of the bed and padding towards the sink, gloriously naked.

Tucking his hands behind his head, he enjoyed watching the way her body moved and flowed in the flicker of the candles as she washed up the bowls and spoons.

Picking up the bottle of pinot noir he'd chosen for them to enjoy over dinner from the bench, she held it up. 'Do you want me to pour us both a glass?'

He shrugged casually. 'Why the hell not?'

Glasses filled, she joined him back in bed, her curves fitting perfectly in his hands as he reached out to steady her while she climbed in beside him. Settled, she passed him his glass and he took a sip, as did she. They both stared out the window opposite, where a star-speckled sky dazzled.

'I suppose I should get home soon. I told Dad I'd bring his car back tonight.'

'You could always go back first thing in the morning.'

'Yeah, but he'd be pissed off.'

'It's not like he needs his car right now.'

She nodded, biting her bottom lip in a way that made him crave to lick and kiss it. 'True.'

Companionable silence reigned once more.

Sophie's hands came down upon his. They caressed each other's fingers. 'I love spending time with you, Dylan, you've made me feel young again.'

He turned to her. 'You are young, Soph.'

'I'm thirty in just over two weeks.'

'So what? I'm thirty in two months' time. We're spring chickens in the big scheme of life.'

'Yeah, I know, but I always dreamt I'd be married with a couple of kids by now.' Her eyes glazed with tears. 'But clearly it wasn't to be.'

'Oh, Soph, try not to get upset about it. You've still got plenty of time for all of that.'

'Yeah, maybe.'

'If you'd stayed with me, I would've made damn sure we were surrounded by a tribe of kids by now, and I would have put a ring on it too.' The words tumbled out of his mouth before he'd had time to think and stop himself.

Her hand drifted from his. She looked down at the glass cradled in her other hand. 'I wish I could have stayed, I really do. You're everything I ever wanted, and more. Hindsight's an absolute bitch.' She tried to laugh but failed.

Dylan's heart squeezed. He hated seeing her upset. Leaning in, he kissed her cheek.

Placing her empty glass on the bedside table, she shifted so she was straddling him. Her mesmerising eyes were fleetingly concealed as a shield of long dark lashes covered them. When she opened them again, he almost lost himself in their fathomless depth. Emotions danced like fire within … anguish, loneliness, longing and desire, mirroring his own sentiments. She drew in a slow, steady breath, and then with a suggestive smile her arms snaked around his neck and her lips joined his for a scorching, sensual kiss. It was as if every time their lips met, it was the very first time he'd tasted her.

Reaching out blindly, he fumbled to place his glass down without spilling what was left of the wine. Once both his hands were free, he grabbed her, possessively. Her skin begged for more of his touch. He obliged her silent demand, trailing his hands over her breasts and down her stomach until he met with her warmth. She did the same, her skilful fingers enticing him to throbbing hardness within seconds. As torn as he was, his body heated with renewed desire.

Begrudgingly, he pulled his lips from hers, ignoring her little whimper of protest. 'So I'm gathering you're going to stay the night?' His voice was rasping, as if he'd been running a marathon.

'Only if that's okay with you.' It was said breathlessly. She chewed her bottom lip, waiting for him to respond.

He took his time, teasing her. 'Sure is, but only …' He tipped her over and climbed on top of her, pinning her down by the wrists. 'If you let me tie you up this time.' Her approving smirk fired his soul to blazing life.

Leaning over, he grabbed his belt from where he'd dropped it to the floor. Sitting back up, he was careful not to hurt her as he fastened it around her wrists and then latched it to his bedhead. Sophie writhed beneath him, her nipples hardening even more. Her gaze was soul stroking, immeasurable. He closed the gap between them, pressing his body into hers as he slowly slid inside of her.

༄

Sophie woke with a start. It felt as though someone other than Dylan was in the room. Flicking open her eyes, she half expected whoever it was to be standing beside the bed, staring down at her. Her heart hammered madly with the possibility. But instead, bright sunlight poured through the open windows opposite, and the curtains fluttered in the soft breeze. Her eyes gravitated to the front door, which was half open. She couldn't recall it being open last night, but then again she hadn't been taking much notice of things like that; her entire focus had been on Dylan and the mind-blowing things he was doing to her. She was sure they'd shut it, for privacy and to also keep out the wind and rain. Maybe the breeze had blown it ajar? Although it wasn't a big deal, she felt a little uneasy about it. Her mind already in a spin with her and Dylan connecting beyond a level she ever thought possible again, she tried not to add to her thoughts by making a mountain out of a molehill. And that reminded her, she'd forgotten to ask him what the police had said about the numberplate.

She tried to switch her mind off by focusing on the sounds coming from outside. Birds chirped, welcoming the brand new day, a dog barked off in the distance, and there was the faint hum of a tractor. She turned to look at Dylan. He was still asleep. Goddamn he was handsome, and the tattoos snaking around his strong body made his bad-boy edge even badder. Her body responded to his magnetism, the flood of heat sending her nether regions ablaze once more. She pressed her thighs together in a bid to ward off the longing. She didn't have the time, or the heart, to indulge in his magic again. She had to make right of her wrong, today. But first, she was going to read the letter from Grace again for the first time in years. It would be her proof; something to show Dylan to help him understand why she did what she did. The lingering smell of his spicy aftershave, along with what she could only describe as him, made her want to rest her head against his delicious chest. But she couldn't. She had to get up, get dressed, and get home. She needed to talk to her mother and tell the truth. Her heart cracked and crumbled just thinking about doing so. But it was the only way for her to be able to live a guilt-free life, hopefully alongside this majestic man lying naked next to her.

Turning back towards the doorway, in her mind she was measuring the distance she was going to have to cross in the bright sunlight to retrieve her clothes. She didn't feel so sexy in the light of day, and all her flaws would be on display. Would she make it and be able to get dressed and outside before he woke up? Her heart thumped, and not just because of her dilemma right now. Last night, her decision to keep the truth from him until she spoke to her parents seemed so logical, so right, but now everything seemed wrong. So. Very. Wrong. Her belief that she and Dylan would ever be able to fully work things out wavered. Massively. Boy, oh boy, what had she been thinking, succumbing to her sexual urges? This was dangerous territory. She needed to sort her life out once and for all, no matter the consequences. The harsh reality of it all hit her like a thunderclap. The urgency to get out of Dylan's bed overcame her. She felt torn, confused, bad. Her heart and soul ached painfully. She squeezed her eyes shut, willing the tears to go away. She didn't want him waking to find her crying, because she wouldn't be able to explain why. Not yet anyway.

Carefully, she pulled back the covers. She fleetingly pondered wrapping a sheet around herself but then that would leave Dylan lying gloriously exposed. And he'd be bound to wake up. Making a conscious effort, she edged to the side of the mattress and then slid one leg out. Dylan stirred and turned towards her. His arm flung over her stomach. She held her breath, watching his face for any sign of consciousness. If he caught her trying to sneak off, it wouldn't end nicely. He'd think she was making a run for it, which she was, but not for the reason he'd believe. Cautiously, she lifted his hand and placed it back on the mattress. He didn't stir. She silently thanked the powers that be. Edging her other leg out, she moved cautiously but quickly, planning her escape route before her feet had even hit the floor. Tiptoeing across the room, she made her way towards her pile of clothes, forgetting to breathe.

'Where are you going, Firefly?' Dylan's voice, dripping with husky morning sexiness, forced her heart into a wild gallop.

She didn't stop walking, didn't miss a beat. *Act natural* … 'I'm just going to the bathroom.'

'Oh, good, I thought you might have been making a run for it.' He chuckled and then cleared his throat. 'Make sure you come back to bed. I want to give you a morning cuddle.'

Her body responded to his promise, but she didn't allow herself to hesitate. 'Only if you're lucky, Stone.' It was said with a confidence she was far from feeling. Thank goodness he couldn't see her face, for it would have been filled with shame and remorse. Scooping her clothes up, she didn't dare turn to look at him. The temptation to join him back in bed would be all too much.

Knowing he was watching her the entire way, she had to stop herself from running to the bathroom. Once there, she quickly closed the door behind her and then leant against it, her legs weak. Last night had been dreamlike, but she couldn't help but wonder what would come next, especially when she told him the truth behind her urgent departure from Shorefield almost nine years ago. Would he hate her for keeping it all from him? Possibly. She caught sight of herself in the mirror and almost laughed out loud at her god-awful bed hair and the mascara smudged beneath her eyes, but the seriousness of the situation stopped her. She washed her face and then searched for a hairbrush, but with Dylan having clipped short hair he had no need for one. Trying to rake her fingers through her mop, she tamed it somewhat before finding the hair band on her wrist and tying her hair up into a messy bun. Grabbing the toothpaste, she squeezed some onto the end of her finger. Baring her teeth, she rubbed her fingertip along them a few times before spitting the toothpaste and washing her mouth out. Now all she had to do was get dressed and make a gracious exit.

She dressed and left the bathroom; her plan was to say a quick goodbye to Dylan before heading home. She could feel the truth suspended on the very tip of her tongue as she approached him, and she was terrified that in a moment of utter weakness, she was going to blurt it all out before she took the right first step in going home and talking to her parents about it. And then there was also Faith to think about, a woman she cared for after the years of her treating her like a daughter when Sophie was growing up … it was all too much.

She stopped just short of the bed. The covers rode low on his hips, and the fine dark hair that led beneath the white sheet made her flush with longing.

Looking to where her gaze had fleetingly settled, he smirked. 'Come back in here with me, I promise I'll make it extra warm and cosy.' He reached out and grabbed her hand before she had a chance to step back.

'I'm sorry, Dylan, but I really have to …'

'Come back to bed.' He finished her sentence. Before she knew it she was on the bed with his arms wrapped around her, and although it felt so damn good, she just couldn't force her body to melt in his arms like it had last night.

With his finger travelling from her cheek and beneath her chin, he lifted her gaze to his. 'What's wrong, Soph, are you regretting what happened?'

A golf ball of emotion lodged itself firmly in her throat. Unable to edge a word past it, she shook her head.

'Okay, well, I can tell something's bothering you.' He smiled sadly. 'So, please, tell me what it is … remember we promised we'd keep nothing from each other this time round.'

This time round? So he *was* looking at something long term. Maybe she could tell him, should tell him right now? Panic sent her pulse into a frenzy. She hoped he couldn't hear her pounding heartbeat. Her mind was screaming all the possible scenarios, but she remained silent.

He brushed a kiss over her lips and then cupped her cheek. 'Soph, you're really freaking me out. What is it?'

She swallowed and drew in a deep calming breath. 'I …' She stumbled over her words. 'I told Dad I'd bring his car back last night, and I'm worried he's going to hit the roof when I get home.'

Big. Fat. White. Lie.

But what else was she meant to do?

His frown was replaced with a knee-buckling smile. 'Oh God, Soph, is that all? Phew, for a minute there I thought you were going to tell me something I didn't want to hear.'

If only you knew, she thought. She forced a chuckle, making sure her face was hidden against his chest so he couldn't see through her laugh. 'Yeah, I feel stupid, but seeing as I'm staying under his roof, I need to respect his rules. He can be a right pain in the arse when he's got a bee in his bonnet.'

'Fair enough.' He cuddled her in closer. 'We didn't do your tattoo.'

'That's okay, we were a little sidetracked.' She smiled through her wretchedness.

'Yes, we were.'

'Hey, did you call the police station about the numberplate?'

'I did, and they're looking into it.'

'Oh, good, hopefully they'll find out who it was.' Begrudgingly, she slid from his arms. 'I really have to get going.'

He pushed up to sitting. 'Come back tonight and I'll make sure we do it before anything else.'

'Do what?'

'Your tattoo.'

'Oh.' She laughed a little nervously. 'I'd love to.'

'Good. It's a date.'

She leant in and gave a quick kiss on his enticing lips. 'Catch you later.' She took measured steps towards the front door and out into the sunshine.

⁓

He hated lying to her about reporting the numberplate, but he had to. He was just glad she didn't ask anything more about it. She gave him one last look before disappearing out the door, the depth of her eyes stoking the smouldering fire she'd started in his soul. It took every bit of his resolve not to jump from the bed and lure her back to it. He just couldn't get enough of her.

Outside, the car door slammed and the engine revved to life. He waited until the sound of tyres on the gravel drive faded before dragging himself from the bed to begin his day. He wanted to service his mother's car before heading into town to have lunch with Mark. There were a few more minor details of the wedding day they needed to wrap up, and it was a good excuse to catch up for a couple of light beers over a counter meal.

Wandering towards the kitchen, he thought about how awkward Sophie had seemed before she'd left. He wanted to believe her story about her dad and the car, but his instincts were telling him there was something else way deeper than she wanted to let on. Maybe it had something to do with him, maybe it didn't, but all in all he didn't like the fact she was keeping something from him. Sighing, he flicked the jug on and brought his eyes to the window. His heart missed a beat. Just a day or two ago his mum had polished the glass windowpane to a shine when she'd helped him tidy up the place. Now the glass was marked with a handprint and a grimy smudge above it, as though someone had been trying to peer in. Had somebody been watching him and Sophie make love? The very thought made the hair stand up on the back of his neck as Angus McDonald's face came to mind.

A knock at the door made him jump. Turning, he watched his mother walk in.

'Morning, Dylan.' She smiled, but there was a hint of apprehension hidden behind it.

'Hey, Mum, I'm just about to make a cuppa, want one?'

'Yes, please.' She pecked him on the cheek, her amber-oil perfume lingering. 'Nice night?'

Dylan glanced over his shoulder before adding a teaspoon of sugar to each mug. 'Yeah, it was.'

She pulled up a chair and sat. 'Sophie stay the night, did she?'

'Yeah.' He didn't like his mother's tone. He was a big boy and could do what he wanted. Especially when he wasn't living underneath her roof.

There was a moment's silence, a jingle of her bangles as she sat down at the dining table, and then a soft sigh. 'Do you think that's wise, letting her back in after what she did to you?'

Dylan bit back irritation, partly because his mother had a fair point and had hit a raw nerve, but also because it really wasn't anyone else's business what he did. Taking a breath, he tried to calm himself before he turned to face her. He knew she only meant well and was worried about him. 'That was a long time ago, Mum.' He carefully carried the coffees to the table. 'And remember you were the one who taught me it's best to learn to forgive, rather than carry it around and be bitter and hateful.'

'I don't want to see you fall down that dark hole again, if things don't work out, that's all.' She graced him with what he could only describe as a sad smile.

Reaching out, he gave her hand a gentle squeeze. 'I'm not thinking that far ahead right now, but I promise I'll be able to deal with whatever comes of it.'

'Good. That makes me happy to hear.' She looked down at her cup and sniffed. When she lifted her eyes to his again they were filled with tears.

His heart sank to his bare feet. 'What is it, Mum?'

'Oh, nothing, just having one of those days where my menopause hormones are running amok.' She wiped at her eyes with the back of her hand and then shook her head and laughed it off. 'I can be a right sook with it sometimes.'

'Are you sure that's all it is?'

'Yes, positive.' She looked over his shoulder, for some reason not able to meet his eyes.

He didn't believe her for a second. 'That's good then.' Taking a sip from his coffee, he considered her over the rim of his cup. He knew her like the back of his hand, and there were shadows in her eyes that spoke of something more troublesome than hormones. Surely it couldn't only be because Sophie had stayed the night, could it? He groaned inwardly, feeling as if everyone around him knew something he didn't, and it was really starting to get on his nerves.

Rosewood Farm

Sophie had spent a good part of the morning shovelling manure into a wheelbarrow. Not her most favourite of jobs, but she'd needed to do something physical to burn off some of the restless energy pent up inside her. It had done the trick, somewhat, and the company of the horses had helped take her mind off the outside world, if only for a little while. Now showered and feeling more human, she finished getting dressed and then ran a brush through her hair. She tried to distract her thoughts from what she was about to do by thinking about Dylan and the dizzying heights he'd sent her to, and then tumbling again while encompassed in his arms. And the way he'd held her after they'd finished making hours of love, as though she was the most precious thing in the world. It had left her on a high, despite the anxiety of what awaited her today – with her family, Dylan and his mother. She glanced at her watch. Her parents would be home from town any minute. How was her mum going to react? What was she going to say when Sophie told her there was no talking her round? That she'd made up her mind about revealing the truth?

She sucked in a shaky breath. As sick as it would make her feel, it was time she sat down and read Grace's letter again. Opening the cupboard, she pulled it out from where she had hidden it away. Then, sitting on the edge of her bed, she unfolded it as if it were made of glass.

Sophie,

For years I've sat back and watched you woo Dylan with your coy looks and sweet, innocent smile. But we both know you're not that sweet and innocent, don't we? He deserves better than you. Keeping what you know from your sisters, and Dylan, is so wrong of you, in so many ways. Yes, I told you to keep it a secret because I didn't want to hurt Aunty Faith, but now I'm a grown woman I have my own wants and desires to think about. I love Dylan, more than you ever will, and I know, deep down, he loves me too. It's just that he's a good man, and because he feels committed to you, he won't allow his true feelings for me to be known. So, I have a proposition for you. Well, more of a demand really ... depends which way you want to look at it.

I want you to STAY THE HELL AWAY FROM HIM!! Break it off with him, break his heart, do whatever you have to do to make him hate you ... or I will make you pay, in more ways than one. AND YOU WILL DO AS I SAY ... you want to know why?

The night my uncle died, I was there and I saw everything. Aunty Faith told the police it was her who shot him, in self-defence, but it was a lie. Yes, Uncle Don was going to kill her if she didn't stop him, but it was Dylan who picked up the gun and shot his father dead. He was only doing what he had to, to keep his mother alive – I get that. It only makes me love him more, to know the lengths he will go to to protect those he loves. And Aunty Faith did what she did to protect her son, and I've kept the secret safe to protect him too, but if you don't leave him, I will go to the police and tell them what he did. If I can't have him, I don't want anyone else to – he can go to jail and never be touched by another woman for as long as he lives. And if you even dare try and tell Dylan about this, I will make sure your sisters find out who they really are.

So, there you have it. The choice is yours, but make sure you choose wisely. If you don't do as I ask, I will make sure every single person that means the world to you pays in one way or another.

Life is a bitch, and I've learnt you have to be a bitch to make it through.

Grace.

Sophie wiped the tears from her cheeks. There was so much to be sad about within this letter. Grace had been such a beautiful soul when they'd first become friends, and they'd shared so many wonderful moments together in the school holidays. But from her late teens drugs had stolen Grace's sanity, and in the end, her life. Sophie had tried time and time again to talk Grace out of partying so hard down in Kings Cross, had begged her to stop hanging around the people she'd met there, but to no avail – it only made Grace hate her, and then do this.

She heard the crunch of tyres and then a car coming to a stop. Her heart landed in her throat. Folding the letter up and tucking it in her pocket, she glanced out her bedroom window, watching her mum and dad get out of the Landcruiser. Her mother lifted out a handful of shopping bags from the back seat, and her father lobbed a bag of magnesium over his shoulder. Sophie remembered that they always kept a bag of it beside the bathtub – a much cheaper way to enjoy bath salts. They were home. This was real. She was going to do this. Her stomach somersaulted and her heart beat wildly, as if a shot had just been fired. Fear of what she was about to do to her family, to Dylan's family, trickled down her back like an ice cube. Would they all end up hating her? The fear almost rendered her motionless. She couldn't back out of this. She had to move before she backed down. As if on autodrive, she swung open her bedroom door, strode along the hallway, down the steps and towards the kitchen. Before she knew it she was standing in there with her parents.

Her mum was at the fridge, unpacking a bag of groceries. 'Hi, love.'

'Hey, Mum.' She turned to her father. 'Hey, Dad.'

'Hi, Sophie. I needed my car this morning but it wasn't here.' His voice was stern, terse. 'You promised me you'd be back last night with it.'

'Yes, I know. I'm so sorry, I fell asleep.'

His brows almost disappeared over his disappearing hairline. 'Did you now?'

Her mouth feeling drier than the Simpson Desert, all she could do was nod. Her cheeks flamed what she imagined to be a bright shade of red. For God's sake, she was almost thirty.

'Can we please all sit down and have a chat?' She blurted it out, her voice squeaky.

Her father folded his arms across his broad chest. 'Now?'

'Yes, now.'

'I've got to go and clean up the stables.'

'Already done it for you.'

'Oh, thanks, well, I still need to do a few other things … money doesn't grow on trees, you know.'

'This is important, Dad.'

'So is working, Sophie Copinni.'

The shopping bag unpacked, Marie came to Sophie's side. 'What is it that you'd like to chat about, love? Has Zachary upset you again? Is everything okay?'

'Not really, Mum,' she said, and then a sigh from her father made her turn to him.

His expression had changed from one of annoyance to one of alarm. He eyed her as if to say, *It better not be what I'm thinking it's about.*

She quickly looked away from him. Her legs went weak beneath her. The room started to spin. She suddenly felt as if she were about to throw up. She grabbed hold of the kitchen bench to steady herself, taking a few deep breaths to fight off the nausea.

Marie took her by the hand and led her to a chair at the dining table. 'You look very pale, love.' Once she got her seated, Marie dashed to the sink, filled a glass with water, and handed it to her. 'Here, drink this.'

After sculling the water, Sophie placed the glass down. 'Thanks, Mum.'

Marie looked extremely worried. 'Would you like another?'

'No, thanks.'

Frank stood beside his wife, looking deathly pale. Sophie felt terrible doing this, but it just had to be done. His phone chimed from his top pocket and he pulled it out. 'It's Amy, I'll just take this quickly.' He took a few steps towards the kitchen sink and leant on it. 'Do you have me on loudspeaker, Amy?'

There was a short pause, and then, 'Well, I can't hear you properly. Can you take me off it, please?'

Another short pause.

'Oh, you're driving. Fair enough then.'

Marie tipped her head to the side. 'You're not about to tell us you're pregnant, are you? As much as I'd love a grandchild, it wouldn't be good timing with you and Zachary …'

Sophie cut her off with a shake of her head. 'No, nothing like that.' She pressed her hands to her rib cage and tried to draw a long, steady breath to settle herself.

'So what is it then?' Marie pulled up a chair and sat down beside her. Frank returned, placing his phone down on the table. Marie gestured for him to sit down and join them, but he remained standing.

'Um …' Sophie bit her lip and turned to the window. The sky was clear. The sun was bright. She wanted to be out there, enjoying the simple beauty of it all, not in here with the roof and walls feeling as if they were about to cave in on her. Her eyes welled with tears. She blinked them back.

'Sophie, you're scaring me.' Marie turned to Frank. 'Well, say something instead of standing there mute, would you, Frank?'

He pinched the bridge of his nose and sighed heavily. He dragged a chair out, the legs scraping along the floor, and then sat down heavily. 'Do you really think this is wise, to go stirring up a past that is best left where it is, Sophie?'

'As I've already explained to you, Dad, yes, I do.'

Marie shot him a look that could kill. 'You know what this is all about?'

'I'm afraid I do, Marie. Sophie spoke to me about it last night, before she went to Dylan's place.'

Sophie felt bile rise in her throat. She had to get the words out. Now. 'I know, Mum.'

Marie half laughed. 'Know what?' She warily looked to Frank. 'I know about the girls.'

Marie scrunched her face up. 'What girls?'

'Amy and Tania.' Sophie drew in a breath.

'What about them?' Looking towards Frank, Marie chuckled awkwardly and shrugged. Frank remained pokerfaced. Bringing her gaze back to Sophie, Marie tilted her head slightly, as if trying to gain some perspective.

'Mum, please stop … you know exactly what I'm talking about.' The budding tears fell, but this time Marie offered no comfort. Instead, she shook her head slowly, her face now a deep shade of red.

'No, Sophie, I don't.' She folded her arms.

'You don't, or is it more like you don't want to admit you know?' Sophie wished she didn't have to say the words out loud, that her mother would spare her that pain.

'Sophie.' Frank's tone was cautionary. 'Explain yourself to your mother, please. This is not a time for stupid games.'

Sophie shot her father a glower. 'I'm not playing games, Dad.' She turned back to her mother, heaved in another much-needed breath, and then forced the jumble of words on her tongue to spill out. 'I came downstairs one night, to get a drink of water, and I overheard you and Dad quarrelling about it. I was standing in the dark, stuck between the stairs and the kitchen, and I couldn't go either way, so I heard everything.'

Marie was staring at her, wide-eyed. 'This happened while you've been here?'

'No, I was seventeen at the time and I stupidly thought I could keep it a secret. But I can't live with the guilt of it anymore, Mum. I just can't. People deserve to know the truth.' She could almost feel the letter burning a hole through her pocket, but her parents didn't need to know about it just yet – the damning information was for Faith and Dylan to do with as they saw fit. One step at a time.

'I see.' Marie's frown deepened and spread. She tugged at the hem of her blouse and then smoothed her already impeccably ironed trousers. Her thin lips all but disappeared as she pressed them together. She drew in a shuddery breath and then delicately blew it away. She blinked faster. Tears formed. Reaching across the table, she plucked a paper napkin from the holder. 'All this time and you thought it best not to tell me, Sophie? And you, Frank, keeping this from me … I'm disappointed in both of you.'

Frank and Sophie remained silent, although they shared a regretful stare.

Marie pressed the way-too-cheery-patterned napkin over her eyes. There was a twitch at the corner of her mouth as she shook her head. When she looked back up at Sophie, her expression was deadpan. 'So what would you like to tell me, other than you knowing about it?'

'I think they should both know.'

'You do, do you?' Marie's dark eyes grew darker, stormy.

Sophie tried to sit up straighter. 'Yes, Mum, I do. It's not right to keep something like this from them.'

'I don't think that's your decision to make, Sophie.'

'I'm sorry, Mum, but I can't keep it from them any longer. If you and Dad don't tell them, I'm going to.'

'Have you really thought about this and what it might do to this family?' Marie's voice went up a few notches.

'Yes, Mum, I have, for twelve long years, and enough is enough.' Sophie released a pent-up sigh. 'Can you just, for one minute, imagine what it's been like for me, keeping this from them, and you and Dad, all this time?'

'Yes, I can, and yes, I understand it would have been extremely hard, as it has been for your father and me.'

'What's the worst that could happen, Mum, by letting them know?'

'They might want nothing to do with any of us.'

Frank cleared his throat, attracting both Sophie's and her mother's attention. 'I don't think that would be the case, Marie. I think they'll both be upset at first, and rightly so, but in time they'll understand. We are their parents.'

'You are, Frank, by blood, but I certainly am not.'

A sucker punch hit Sophie in the chest. She looked from her mother to her dad. 'What do you mean Dad's their blood?'

'Your father is their father, Sophie.'

'But, how?'

'He gave his, you know what, for the fertilisation.'

'You mean scientifically.'

Marie and Frank shared a glance that spoke volumes. 'No, we didn't have the money for that at the time.'

'You mean he slept with Faith?'

Marie nodded, her bottom lip quivering.

'Oh my God, Mum, that would have been terribly hard.'

'It was. It almost broke your father and me, but we stuck through it.' Reaching across the table, Marie patted Frank's folded hands. 'Didn't we, love?'

'We sure did, Marie.' Frank looked to Sophie. 'It wasn't something I wanted to do, or enjoyed doing … but it had to be done. Your mother and I were desperate for more children and for you to have a sibling.'

Sophie couldn't wipe the shock from her face. 'And here I was, thinking you'd adopted them.'

'Well, we didn't really need to go down the adoption route, Soph, seeing as your father is their father.'

The room spun. Gravity seemed to tip. Sophie clamped a hand over her gaping mouth. Closing her eyes to block out the wretched looks on her parents' faces, she shook her head. She'd always thought Amy and Tania's father was Dylan's dad, all the more reason she'd battled with telling the truth of what she knew. Don Stone wasn't a father to be proud of. This made things a little easier in the long run, but it was a shock all the same. Gathering strength from God knew where, she met her father's sad eyes. 'I don't understand why you had to sleep with Faith to have more children. You had me?' Her stomach pitched and rolled as she held Marie's gaze. 'Didn't you? Wasn't I enough?'

'Yes, love, you're our God-given child.' Marie heaved a weary sigh. 'I had a scare, after having you, with uterine cancer, and I had to have a full hysterectomy, so I couldn't have any more children.' She smiled sadly at Frank. 'And your father and I had always dreamt of having an army of children.' She shrugged. 'One day, Aunty Gina was telling me how Faith wanted to get away from an abusive relationship, but she needed money, so she suggested we ask her to be a surrogate and carry the baby. In turn we would give her money, to help her and Dylan get away from Don. It was a win-win situation for all of us.' Marie smiled sadly. 'Little did we know she would fall pregnant with twins.' She sniffled and wiped at her eyes. 'Faith made us promise we would never tell a soul about adopting the girls, and we agreed that it would be for the best, for everyone concerned, so we kept it our secret.'

'But how come you looked pregnant before the girls came home with you and Dad from the hospital that day?'

'I wore a fake pregnancy belly, so our secret was safe.'

Sophie was struggling to piece everything together. 'So Faith was pregnant when Don died?'

'Yes, she was trying to protect the babies growing inside of her, your sisters.'

'So that explains why Faith and Dylan went to stay with his Aunt Kimmy for almost a year after Don died.'

Marie nodded. 'Yes, Faith wanted to keep the fact she was pregnant hidden, and with Kimmy being a midwife, she was there to help Faith through the pregnancy and the birth. We had to cover all bases, seeing as we wanted the locals to think Amy and Tania were my biological children.'

'Oh, poor Faith. So what did she tell Dylan, then, about the babies? He would have been old enough to know she was pregnant? As Grace would have been.' She shook her head.

'She told him and Grace they'd been stillborn.'

'Oh my God. Dylan has never ever mentioned any of this to me.' And neither had Grace, Sophie thought, when she had confided in her about what she'd heard. 'It's no wonder Faith doesn't want him finding out, seeing as she lied to him.'

'Yes, that's right, Sophie. What a terrible mess.' Marie leant on the table, her head cradled in her hands. 'I can't believe this, and of all the times for it to come out, just before Daniela's wedding.'

Frank reached over and rubbed her back. 'We'll deal with this together, Marie, as a family. I promise we'll make it through this.'

Marie looked to Frank. 'So you agree we should tell Tania and Amy?'

'Yes, Marie, I do, if not for our sakes, so we don't have to carry the burden of the secrecy any longer, then for the sake of the girls and especially for Sophie. It's not fair for her to have to hide our skeletons.'

'But what about Faith?'

Frank rubbed his temples, sighing. 'I'll go over and have a talk with Faith, if you like, before we tell the girls.'

Marie sobbed now, hard and loud, to the point she was struggling to draw a breath. Frank knelt before her, taking her in his arms.

Guilt almost suffocated Sophie as she sank further into her chair. 'I don't think we should tell them before the wedding, otherwise we might ruin the day for Daniela and Mark.'

'When then?' Marie straightened up in her chair and gave Frank an appreciative, loving smile.

Sophie shrugged. 'I don't know, the next day, maybe?'

Marie folded her arms once more. 'How do you think this is going to impact on Tania? She's not really got herself together. Your father and I both know she's teaching pole dancing at the gym, even though she told us otherwise, and telling her something like this might be the straw that breaks the camel's back. We want to see her settle down with a nice man and have some children, and this is certainly not going to help.'

Sophie wrung her hands on the table as she recalled the secret Tania had told her on the hens' night. It was not her place to reveal that one either. 'I think Tania will handle it better than Amy, to be honest.'

'I tend to agree with Sophie, Marie,' Frank said.

Marie took a deep breath, and then exhaled as if measuring what she was about to say next.

'Is this possibly why you left Dylan, Soph, because you couldn't handle keeping what you overheard hidden from him?'

'Yes.' She could say no more, emotion lodging in her throat.

Reaching out, Marie took both her hands and gave them a squeeze. 'Oh, love, I'm so sorry. If I had known, I wouldn't have let you go through with it. I honestly thought you and he had had a falling out, and you were keen to travel. And I wasn't going to argue with that, given the circumstances. It did worry your father and me, and Faith, with you and Dylan being together, but we weren't going to come between young love either. And besides, Dylan is a good boy, always has been, your father and I both like him a lot.'

'He is a good man.' Sophie nodded and offered a small smile. 'But we can't dwell on the past, Mum.'

'I'm sorry, Sophie. I had no idea.' Frank looked devastated.

Marie placed a hand on Sophie's cheek, wiping away her tears. 'You're right, Soph. It's time to tell the girls the truth, and the sooner the better. We'll deal with the consequences as best we can. I don't want you giving up your one true love for your father and me, or your sisters. You've done that once, and you don't deserve to have to do that again. I can see the way Dylan looks at you, and the way you look at him – you're made for each other.'

'I do really love him, Mum. I just hope he doesn't hate me for keeping this from him.'

'Well, there's only one way to find out, isn't there?'

Sophie sucked in a shaky breath. The first step was taken, and now there was no turning back. Although terrified of how Dylan was going to react to this, and the fact she knew he'd pulled the trigger on his father, she just had to keep moving forwards.

CHAPTER
20

Rosewood Farm

The sound of a car speeding up the driveway and then coming to a skidding stop brought Sophie to her feet. She tossed the horse magazine she was reading to try to distract her thoughts onto the lounge chair and dashed towards the front door, worried, but at the same time thankful for the distraction from her distraction. Nothing seemed to be easing her mind from thinking about how her sisters would react to the news, and also her concern for Dylan and Faith. She knew they'd be mad at first, all of them, and they each had a right to feel so. But she just prayed that none of them would hold it against her in the long run. She sure as hell didn't judge Dylan for what he did that night, in protecting his mother and killing his father, and nobody else should either. If she had been in that situation, she would have done the same thing.

Opening the flyscreen door and walking out, she held her hand up to shield her eyes from the bright sunshine. Amy stepped from her four-wheel drive and Tania got out from the passenger side. She gave them a wave but they didn't return it. As they came closer she realised they both had tear-stained faces. She rushed forwards and was down the front steps in seconds.

'Oh my God, what's wrong?'

Neither Amy nor Tania answered. And they both looked pissed off, to say the very least.

Sophie's heart smashed wildly and then landed in her throat. Only finishing their heart-wrenching conversation just over an hour ago, there was no way her mum and dad could have told the girls already, and they'd promised they wouldn't be doing so without all of them together in the first place … after the wedding, and after speaking to Faith about it.

Sophie looked from one to the other. Tania shook her head and then looked away, her chin quivering. 'What is it?' Reaching out, she took hold of Amy's hand. 'Has something happened to Kurt?'

Amy tugged her hand free and then fisted it at her side. 'Where are Mum and Dad?' The words were angry, fierce.

Oh my God, they know. Play it cool, just in case they don't.

'Why?' It was said with absolute caution.

'Because I think we all need to have a *family* chat, don't you, Sophie?'

Sophie noticed how Amy had emphasised 'family', and her mouth dried up. 'They've just headed down to the stables. What's happened, Ames?' It felt as if her tongue was sticking to the roof of her mouth.

Amy's dark brown eyes bore into her as she folded her arms across her chest, her hands still fisted. 'Please stop playing games with me. I think after all these years enough is enough, don't you?'

Sophie lost all ability to speak and instead stared wide-eyed at the pair of them.

Tania stepped forwards, slightly in front of Amy, as if to stop a fistfight. 'Amy overheard everything, Sophie.' Her lips quivered as she clamped them shut.

'What do you mean?' Sophie mentally slapped herself – she was doing exactly what her mother had just done by playing ignorant. Like mother like daughter.

'When I rang Dad before, he didn't end the call. I heard everything that was said between you all, as if I was sitting right at the table with you.'

There was suddenly not enough oxygen to breathe. Sophie wished the ground would open up and swallow her whole. The shit had hit the fan way too soon, and here she was, on her own, having to explain it all. 'Oh, Amy, I'm so sorry.' She looked to Tania, who was now sobbing. 'Tania, I'm sorry.' She took a step forwards, wanting to comfort her little sister.

Tania took a step away. 'Save it, Sophie.' She couldn't even look at her and instead focused on the garden path and at her bare feet as she padded towards the front steps. She was so much like Faith, all hippy and free spirit. Amy was exactly like their dad, feisty and hot headed.

Feeling a part of her heart going with her, Sophie brought her gaze back to Amy's and met a glare worthy of killing.

'How could you keep something like this from Tania and me? I thought you were my sister, my best friend. We kept nothing from each other growing up, Sophie. Nothing. But this, you go and keep *this* from me, from Tania? Who in the hell do you think you are?'

Unexpected anger bubbled up inside of Sophie. Anger with Grace. Anger at her father. Anger at her mother. Anger with herself. Anger with Dylan. With Faith. With the whole damn messy situation. Before she could stop herself, her defences fired to life. 'I understand you being upset, I really do. But this isn't fair, you taking this out on me, Amy.' She matched her sister's stance. Hands fisted and arms folded.

'You've got the audacity to get mad at me right now? Seriously?' Amy roared.

'Yes, seriously … believe me, I wanted to tell you both when I found out, but I was too scared to. I'd just turned seventeen, Ames, and I didn't know what the right thing to do was, so I kept it quiet.' Sophie's whole body was shaking with adrenaline and nerves. 'I know now that it was wrong of me.'

'Well, you've been a big girl for quite a few years now, Sophie, with a mouth and mind of your own. So what you're saying is a damn cop-out in my opinion.'

'You can't just hold me culpable for this, Amy. There are a few other people involved too, don't forget.'

'Oh trust me, I'm not. Dad, and Mum, will both be getting a piece of my mind, but for now, you're the one standing in front of me, so you're the one I'm holding culpable.'

Sophie didn't know what to say. She'd blamed herself all these years, so why could she hold it against Amy or Tania for doing the same? She swallowed down a sob.

'So much for always having each other's backs … now I know you've never really had mine, or Tania's for that matter. If the shoe had been on the other foot, I never would have kept something like this from you.' Amy shook her head, disappointment tugging her features into a miserable frown. 'You're no sister of mine.'

Sophie felt as if a dagger had just been speared through her heart. 'You don't mean that.'

'Oh, yes I do.'

'But Amy ...'

Amy couldn't look more furious if she tried. 'No buts about it.'

'Okay, I understand.' Sophie's voice trembled as she fought back deep, heaving sobs. Heaviness settled within her heart. This was the worst outcome possible.

'Will you two please stop it?' Tania's voice was filled with pain. 'Aren't we going through enough right now, without adding in being nasty to one another?'

Sophie and Amy turned towards her.

'Fighting isn't going to get us anywhere, and it's not going to change the fact that Mum's not really our mother, and that Dylan is actually our half brother.' Her face contorted and she leant forwards, her hands resting on her knees as she took in deep heaving breaths.

Seeing Tania so weak and vulnerable, Sophie felt instantly responsible. 'I'm so sorry, Tans.'

'I honestly don't know how I'll ever be able to forgive you for this, Sophie.' Amy stormed past her, quickly closing the distance between her and her twin sister. She reached Tania and took her in her arms, comforting her as she stroked her back. Tania sobbed into her shoulder, her arms entwined tightly around Amy. 'Everything's going to be okay, sis,' Amy soothed. She pulled back a little so she could look Tania in the eyes. 'We'll get through this, together, okay? You and me.'

Tania nodded and breathed in a shaky breath.

Sophie wanted to join them. Wanted to wrap her arms around them and say how *they* were going to get through this – the three of them. She wanted to be part of their togetherness. She wanted to comfort and support and be there for them, just as they'd always got through everything else in their lives, by sticking together. But this time it was very different. She was part of their heartache, and that tore her into a million tiny pieces.

Without even a look over their shoulders, Amy and Tania walked across the verandah, through the doorway, and out of sight. Watching them disappear, for the very first time in her life Sophie felt like an outsider in her own family. She wasn't following them in there. They clearly didn't want her around, and she had to respect that. Without thinking, she turned away from the homestead and stumbled along the path, out the little front gate, and down the gravel driveway, not caring that her feet were bare and the rocks were piercing into her soft skin. In a way, the pain felt good. Somehow satisfying, like she deserved it. She had no idea where she was going or what she was about to do, all she knew was that she needed to get away from what was about to unfold when her parents came back in from the stables. She'd played her part, and she'd witnessed the abhorrence in her sisters' eyes because of it. She didn't need to see any more to know exactly where she stood.

Stone's Throw

Almost two hours later, and after an unhurried walk through scrubland and along the stretch of beach that separated Rosewood from Stone's Throw, Sophie found herself at the front door of the old tobacco barn. The wander through nature had done her the world of good, as did putting her feet into the ocean. Although she was still deeply wounded, and worried about what the future held, her head felt a little clearer and her spirit a little cleansed. There was nothing she could do to help the situation back home now; it was in God's hands. She'd made sure to leave a wide berth around Faith's cottage, not wanting to have to stop and chat if she were spotted.

Before she'd even raised her hand to knock, Dylan appeared in all his handsome glory. With tanned skin and muscles rippling around his broad torso and sculpted arms, he looked sexy as hell with only a towel wrapped around his waist.

'Hey, Soph. I wasn't expecting you so early.' He pushed the flyscreen door open. 'I just got home from fixing the horse paddock fencing, and jumped in the shower. I was just about to have a shave.'

She eyed the razor in his hand. 'Sorry, I can come back later if you're busy.' She couldn't help but watch the path of a water droplet as it rolled from his damp hair, down his smooth chest, and then disappeared into the material of the towel.

'Don't be stupid. I'm never too busy for you.' He stood aside. 'Come in, would you, you're making the place look untidy.'

She tried to laugh, but it came out as a squeak.

He cast her a concerned glance. 'Are you okay, Soph?'

'Kinda sort of.' She wrinkled her nose. Until her father spoke to Faith (which wouldn't be long given what had just happened back home) she couldn't go telling Dylan everything. She owed Faith that much – to give her a chance to tell her son in her own words. As much as it wounded her, Sophie had waited this long, another few hours weren't going to make the world of difference. 'The girls and I just had a bit of a fight.'

'Oh shit, really?' They had walked over to the kitchen and he now leant up against the bench. He tossed the razor on the bench. 'Everything okay now?'

'Not really.' She sniffled, trying to ward off another flood of tears.

'Come here, you.' Grabbing her by the hand, he pulled her to him. She stood between his legs. His bare thighs brushed against hers and his arms embraced her tightly. She tried not to imagine what lay beneath the towel, only inches from her. Making love with him would certainly help take her mind off everything. 'Do you want to talk about it?'

'Not really ... it'll all be okay, they just need some space. Amy can get really heated if you keep pushing her buttons.'

'Yeah, probably a good idea coming over here while it cools off. Better to walk away from an argument than let egos win over.' His hand smoothed her hair, making her feel safe, warm, loved ... very unlike the way her sisters were making her feel right now. 'Was it about the wedding?'

'Mmm.' She was thankful her face was hidden against his chest because she didn't want him to see that she was holding back the truth. She was going to tell him everything, and show him the letter from Grace, but just not right this very second. She couldn't handle him hating on her too. Not yet.

'It'll all blow over, you'll see. Weddings are stressful times.' Pulling back slightly, he gave her a gentle smile – one that led her to believe everything *really* was going to be okay. If only that were the truth.

She offered a small smile. 'Yeah, I hope so.'

'How'd you get here anyway? I didn't hear a car pull up.'

'Walked.'

He looked down at her feet. 'You walked all the way here without any shoes?'

'I didn't want to go back into the house to get them.'

'Shit, it must have been a doozy.'

'It was.'

'I remember how you and Amy used to fight when you were teenagers.' He brushed a strand of hair from her face and gently tucked it behind her ear. 'It was always really heated, but you both got over it pretty quickly, so don't let it worry you too much. Okay?'

'I'll try not to.' A whiff of something delicious, other than Dylan's mixture of soap and what she could only describe as him, grabbed her attention. She used the distraction to veer the conversation away before she blurted everything out. 'So what's cooking?'

'Our dinner.' He looked proud as punch.

'Already?' She glanced at the clock on the microwave. It was just past three-thirty. 'What is it?'

'Maltese casserole.' His grin widened. 'Needs to cook for six hours on low and slow, so I put it in the oven before I headed out to fix the fences.'

'Are you kidding me? That's Mum's specialty.'

'I know. After eating at your place the other night, I googled Maltese casseroles and this one looked good, so I thought I'd try it out. But I know you prefer lamb to beef, which is what the recipe called for, so I'm making it my own by using lamb.'

She placed her hands on his cheek, liking the tickle of his five o'clock shadow. 'You really are a sweetheart, Mister Stone.'

'I do my best, Miss Copinni.' He wrapped his arms around her waist and pulled her so close to him she could feel his building hunger for her. 'So, do you want to get the tattoo done and out of the way, just in case we get sidetracked again?' His voice was husky, raw.

'Sounds like a plan.' The curl of his lips was so deliciously suggestive Sophie almost floated to cloud nine on the spot. Suddenly, everything beyond the walls of the barn faded away, leaving just him and her, here, together, safe from the treacherous world outside. She wished to God she could rip off all his clothes and then her own, so she was free to straddle him and slowly make love. She ached to be at one with him. His hands moved to cup her butt cheeks, and she almost gave in to her burning desire then and there. 'Did you get the pic I emailed to you this morning?'

'Sure did, and I've drawn it up, made it a little more personal for you.' He dropped his arms from around her waist and walked over to the open laptop on the dining table. Beside it sat a couple of drawings. He spread the sheets of paper out, and she gazed at them over his shoulder as he sat down. The last one stole her breath away. Staring back at Sophie was a lifelike drawing of herself – her eyes vivid, her smile soft yet evocative, and her body stripped, supple and curved. She was lying on her side, looking up intently, strands of hair falling across her cheeks. She reached out to pick it up, but before she could, Dylan plucked it from the table and flipped it over.

He cleared his throat. 'You weren't meant to see that one.'

'But why? It's amazing. I can't believe it's me.' She tried to move around him to get to it. 'Is it me?'

'It's definitely you, Soph.' Blocking her path, he slid it further away from her reach. 'And you can't get a better look at it because it's my personal way to remember how beautiful you were, lying on the bed while I was heating dinner up last night. I don't ever want to forget it.'

She tucked her hand back in her shorts' pocket. 'There'll be plenty more moments like that.' Her voice didn't hold the confidence she wanted to convey.

Dylan swivelled in his seat and seized her gaze. 'You don't sound too sure of that?' He folded his arms across his tattooed chest.

'I *am* sure.' She dropped her eyes from his. 'I'm sorry, I'm just shaken up from the fight with my sisters, that's all.' As if dragging a chain, she met with his baby blues again, the few seconds giving her enough of a reprieve to try to steady herself.

'Fair enough.' He gave her a smile that spoke of the uncertainty he had in what she'd just said. He hesitated for a moment – for Sophie the seconds felt like hours – before turning back to his sketches. He picked one and held it up. 'This is my favourite. You like?'

'Oh my God, yes, that's my pick of the bunch too.' She took the piece of paper from him and stared in awe. The Om symbol she'd chosen was drawn amid a beautiful blossoming pink lotus flower. 'I can't wait to see it on me …' She grinned sheepishly. 'But I'm also very nervous.'

'I promise I'll be gentle.'

'Uh-huh.' Her nether region ached for his touch as she recalled just how gentle he could be, especially with the tip of his tongue. 'I know,' she added with an involuntary wayward smirk.

He graced her with a grin that hinted at everything she was imagining. 'Are you happy with the colours? I made sure to put in as much of the aqua as I could, without it looking overdone.'

'It's perfect, Dylan. Thank you.'

'Have you decided where you want it?'

She pointed to her thigh. 'Right here.'

He took the drawing from her and placed it back on the table. 'Great. Just give me a few minutes while I get some clothes on, and get everything ready and sterile, and then we'll get started, huh?'

'Okay. Where would you like me to sit?'

'Seeing as you want it on your thigh, probably best if you get comfy on the couch, lying on the side you don't want tattooed.'

Nerves crashed and bashed in her belly. 'Yup, right.' She made her way to the couch and went to lie down.

'You'll have to take those sexy little shorts off, Firefly, or I won't be able to get to where I need to.'

She remembered the god-ugly polka-dot cotton undies she had on, and then laughed nervously. 'Oh, silly me, of course.' She quickly whipped the shorts off, and then dropped onto the couch, glad the back of it gave her some privacy while she got comfortable. She shoved a cushion over what she could of her undies.

Propped up on her elbow, she watched as Dylan pulled the coffee table up beside her, and then an office chair.

He followed her gaze. 'Pinched this chair from Mum. I need to be at the right height or my back kills me.' He looked to where the cushion balanced on her hip. 'I actually saw you naked last night, you know, so no need to be modest.'

Sophie's cheeks flamed. 'Yeah, I know, but I'm not wearing the most attractive of undies.'

Without a word, he leant in, and with the speed of a shooting bullet he ripped the cushion from her. He nodded and smirked. 'They're actually very sexy.'

'Are not.'

'On you they are.'

'Yeah, whatevs.'

'You'd look good in a paper bag, Soph.'

'I don't agree, but thank you.'

'You're most welcome.' He said it in the worst English accent she'd ever heard, just before heading back into the bathroom to get dressed.

Lying in silence, and without Dylan to help distract her thoughts, Sophie tried to imagine the conversation, or argument, that would be going on between Amy and Tania and her parents right about now. Worried about the strength of her family's usually unbreakable bond, she wished she were a fly on the wall so she could see how they were all coping. As bad as she felt for pulling the damn rug up and revealing what had been brushed beneath it, she stood steadfast in the fact that she truly believed this was for the best. Secrets led to lies and more secrets and more lies, a vicious circle until there was nothing left of the strong foundations of a relationship in the first place. And didn't she know that all too well when it came to Dylan. A rush of fear swept over her, and she fought to shake it off. If these were going to be the very last hours she spent with him, she wanted to enjoy every second she was blessed with.

Swaggering out of the bathroom and gracing her with a megawatt smile, Dylan opened a stainless-steel box and started to take out the tattoo gear. He dropped a few different coloured inks into little paper cups, and pulled out a box of disinfectant wipes and the tattoo gun. *Holy shit*, Sophie thought. Then he started to hold up a few different needles. *Holy snapping duck shit*, she thought then. He settled on two that he placed on a tray now lined with a paper towel. A wave of nausea washed over her, but soon ebbed away. She breathed a sigh of relief just as another wave hit, this one more intense. Oh God, she just wanted this over with. Her anxieties getting the better of her, she almost bailed, but she reminded herself of the bucket list, which she was hell bent on completing.

Dylan breathed in deeply, methodically assessing everything once more, and then, shoving his hands in the pockets of his board shorts, he blew the breath away. 'Right, I think we're good to go.'

'Great, let's get cracking then.'

Dylan sat and all her senses fired to life. He remained bare-chested, and she found it a nice distraction from the nerves dancing like billyo in her stomach. She tried to shift her thoughts away from the impending pain of the tattoo – she could smell freshly cut grass, could hear the sound of cattle carrying on the wind and the ticking of a clock somewhere in the room. She squeezed her eyes shut, feeling as if she were about to jump off a cliff. Her heart pounded against her rib cage and she was struggling to draw a breath. She was silently telling herself to pull on her big-girl boots when the hum of the tattoo gun made her jump. Her eyelids flew open and she met with the sky blue of Dylan's eyes. He smiled the most charming of smiles as he gently placed his hand on her leg. 'You okay?'

'To be perfectly honest, I'm shitting myself.'

'It's all good. I promise not to hurt you too much. And if you need me to stop, just say so, and I will, okay?'

'Thank you.'

Dylan got back to work. Tearing a disinfectant rub open with his teeth, he wiped it over her skin, leaving a cold trail. Carefully lifting up the transfer sheet, he pressed it against her thigh, making sure to smooth out any creases. Satisfied it was perfect, he slowly peeled it back to reveal the sketch of her tattoo. Sophie quickly pulled her eyes away. She didn't want to see it until it was completed.

'Right, you ready?'

'Ready as I'll ever be.' Closing her eyes, she heard the buzz of the tattoo gun, like the sound of a drill when she was in the dentist's chair, and then felt the needle press against her skin. It felt like the tips of a razor's edge biting into her flesh. She winced as Dylan dragged it upwards in one smooth stroke, the pain almost pleasurable in a weird kind of way. His movements were practised, quick and precise, and after only a few short moments, she grew accustomed to the sting. There would be no turning back now, this tattoo would sit on her skin for eternity, and forever remind her of this moment with the one and only man she had ever truly loved with all her heart and soul. God, she prayed these wouldn't be their final moments together – just how he was going to react to her secrets was anybody's guess.

She glanced at his face. He appeared lost in his work, and looked so damn handsome doing it. Her body relaxing into the experience, she closed her eyes and floated off into the abyss between sleep and wakefulness, hovering there for an incalculable time. Finally, the weight of his hand upon her thigh eased and the buzzing stopped. He wiped some tissue over her skin, dabbing up the speckles of blood across the tattoo.

His blue gaze snapped to hers. 'All done.'

'Is that it?'

'I can do more, if you like.'

'I might hold you to that in the future.'

'Really? You liked getting one that much?'

'It wasn't as bad as I thought it was going to be.' She peered down at where her thigh felt as if it had been sunburnt, and smiled. 'Wow, I love it.' She tried to twist a little more so she could see it properly.

Dylan rolled away from her on the office chair. 'Go and check it out in the bathroom mirror.' The smile on his lips made her want to kiss him.

'Yeah, might be easier.' She stood, acutely aware of her Bridget Jones style knickers, and made a mad dash for the bathroom, feeling Dylan's eyes on her the entire way.

Standing in front of the mirror, she smiled from ear to ear. It was all that she had imagined it would be, and then some. The dilemma back home tried to claim her mind, but she mentally pushed it away – there was nothing she could do to change the outcome now, the ball was in motion and hammering down the hill at top speed. Having revealed one of her secrets, and got a tattoo, she'd almost completed the entire bucket list. All that was left was walking down the aisle with Dylan Stone. She almost snorted with laughter, as if that was going to happen within the next two weeks, if ever.

Leaving the bathroom and padding back towards Dylan, she stopped just shy of him and tugged her shorts on, wincing as the material brushed her tattoo. 'Thank you, I love it.'

'It was my pleasure.' Still sitting on the office chair, Dylan rolled towards her and held up some plastic wrap and tape. 'We'll have to cover it for now; you can take it off in a couple of hours and give it a wash with some soap.'

'Oh, groovy.' Not bothering to do up the fly of her shorts just yet, Sophie positioned her leg for him. Watching his hands work so close to her inner thigh made her shiver with longing. 'How much do I owe you for it?'

Dylan looked up at her. 'Are you kidding, I'm not going to charge you, Soph.'

'Why not?'

'Because I can think of other ways you can make up for it.' He placed some tape either side of the plastic wrap to keep it in place. Wrapping his hands around her, so he had a firm grip on her behind, he tugged her to him. She folded her arms around his neck. Leaning in to her, he placed a kiss on the cotton of her knickers, pausing to breathe hot air through the thin material before trailing his lips upwards and to her belly button.

She gasped, his gesture catching her off-guard. Straddling him, she sat in his lap. His smile was wicked as he met her eyes. 'Do you mind if I have my way with you?' His voice was dripping with dominance in the most erotic of ways.

Sophie's breath caught in her throat.

The air shimmied between them, growing thicker by the second.

'I'll take that smile as a yes.' Bringing her closer to him, he trailed a necklace of kisses over her neck, down to her shoulders, and then tracked his lips down to where her nipples pressed through her t-shirt. She let her head drop back, giving him better access. He bit down softly, sending shudders throughout her body, and then brought his lust-filled gaze back to hers. 'You're so damn sexy, Soph. I know we're supposed to be working on being friends for now, but I just can't seem to keep my hands off you.'

She loved the way his longing for her had roughened his voice and made it low and raspy. An equally wicked smile curled her lips. 'Is that so?'

'Very much so.'

'Well, FYI, I like that you can't keep your hands off me.' She felt like a thief in the night, taking his affection and revelling in it before telling him the truth of her sisters, of his sisters, of the fact she knew it was he who killed his father. But she couldn't help herself.

'Good, because I'm going to make mad, hungry love to you right here, right now on the lounge. And then after that I'm going to wine and dine you. A bit back to front, but that's me. I never do things by the book.'

'I love that you rebel against the norm, Dylan.'

'Good. And I love the way you try to be a good girl, when deep down you're actually a very, *very* bad one.' Lifting her as though she were the weight of a feather, he placed her down amongst the scattered cushions, ripped her shorts and then her god-awful undies off, pulled her t-shirt over her head, revealing the fact she hadn't been wearing a bra, and then dropped his board shorts to the ground. Last were his jocks, which he playfully twirled on his finger and then let fly. Dark and dangerous, muscular and tattooed, a bad boy but a good, *good* man, she could have eaten him alive.

Stepping to the side of her, he pulled a lever that turned the reclining lounge into an almost flat bed, and then climbed on top of her, his longing for her hard and long and deliciously thick. She went to touch him but he grabbed her wrists, just firm enough to let her know he was in control without hurting her, and then pinned her hands above her while his lips came to meet hers. His manhood pressed into her wetness. Needing more of him, she pushed her hips up, and he groaned in pleasure. With their need building fast, he slid inside her, making her cry out. He fitted perfectly as she clenched around him. They didn't take the scenic route this time, and there was no stopping to smell the roses. It was raw and hungry and hard and fast, the climb to the summit more of a sprint than a leisurely wander. Peaking together, they tumbled, holding tight to one another, trembling and quaking and crying out each other's names.

Breathless and sated, they lay like rag dolls on the couch, limbs entwined. As she always did, she savoured the sound of his heart beating against her cheek. She was just about to cuddle in tighter and tell him how much he meant to her, when a loud, urgent rap at the door brought him rushing to his feet.

Whoever it was tried to push it open. The handle jiggled. 'Dylan, are you in there? Why have you locked the door?'

Oh my God, it's Faith …

'Hang ten, Mum, I've got company in here.' Covering his manhood, he began gathering strewn clothes from the floor, gently tossing Sophie's to her.

'Sophie's in there, isn't she?'

'Yes, Mum, she is.'

'Oh, I see.'

Sophie felt impending dread. Faith knew. This was not how she wanted things to play out. Not one little bit – story of her damn life the past few weeks.

Dylan grinned the kind of smile that would usually send Sophie's insides fluttering, but she couldn't get past the feeling of her heart leaping into her throat. 'I've got everything but my jocks … any idea where they might be, Soph?'

'Um …' Her knickers and shorts now on, she tugged on her t-shirt and then struggled to standing. Walking on shaky legs, she hurriedly tried to find his underwear. She happened to glance upwards, spotting his jocks hanging from the ceiling fan. She pointed and he followed her gesture, bursting into laughter. She wished to God she could join in his mirth but instead she clamped her lips shut to stop them from quivering.

'Oh come on, Dylan.' Faith's voice carried beneath the door.

'One sec, Mum.' He tugged his jocks on and then followed up with his board shorts. 'You okay, Soph? You look like you're about to pass out.'

'Oh, yup, right as rain. Just a little embarrassed your mum has caught us out, that's all.'

'We *are* consenting adults, you know.'

'Yeah, I know, but I haven't had time to catch up with her since I arrived home, and this isn't really the most comfortable of get-togethers.' Folding her arms around herself to try to stop from shaking, she watched Dylan race towards the front door. Once open, the distraught look on Faith's face told her everything she needed to know.

Dylan's broad smile vanished. 'Mum, what's wrong?'

Sophie braced herself for the inevitable. She tried to remain calm on the outside while her insides crashed and tumbled like a ship on a storm-ravished sea.

'Quite a lot, actually, Dylan.' Tugging her shawl in tighter, Faith brought her sorrow-filled eyes from Dylan's to Sophie's. Sophie squirmed, wishing she could look away, but Faith's eyes held her captive.

Dylan noticed the shared glance as he looked from Sophie to his mother. 'Mum, please, what is it?'

As if dazed, Faith shook her head and then tried to smile, failing miserably. 'This is not something I can tell you standing at the door, Dylan.'

He jumped aside. 'Oh right, yup, sorry, come in.'

With her fight or flight senses kicking into full force, and with flight winning over almost immediately, Sophie took long strides to make a speedy exit. 'I think I'll leave you two alone and come back later.'

'You won't do any such thing, Sophie.' Faith reached out and firmly took Sophie by the hand. 'This involves you too.'

Sophie tried to swallow the lump in her throat that was making it almost impossible to draw a breath. 'You know about it?' Her voice was a mere whisper.

'Yes. I just got off the phone to your father. He was worried sick about where you'd gone off to, especially without transport and leaving your mobile phone behind. He's told me everything.'

'I'm so sorry.' Sophie choked out every word as she bit back hot tears.

'Why are you sorry, Soph?' Dylan shifted from foot to foot, his arms now folded tightly. 'Mum?'

Neither woman answered.

Faith reached out and tenderly touched Sophie's shoulder. 'I know you're sorry, sweetheart. But in a weird way, I'm not sorry this has happened. I've battled with this secret for too many years. You shouldn't have to bear the weight of your parents' decision and mine.'

'What's going on here?' Dylan looked from one to the other, his brow furrowed.

'How about we all sit down with a cuppa, and then Sophie and I will explain everything.' Faith switched her gentle touch to Dylan's shoulder. 'It's time you knew the truth, son.'

CHAPTER

22

Stone's Throw

With both women now sitting down, Dylan noticed that Sophie was avoiding meeting his mum's gaze, and instead focused on the view out the kitchen window. He had to admit the sight was a mesmerising one, with the rolling landscape and the beginnings of a jaw-dropping sunset that was hinting at shades of orange and red, but it made him nervous that neither woman spoke or even dared look at each other. This was bad. What if this had something to do with his father's death? What if Sophie knew the truth of that night and just hadn't told him? Could that have been the real reason she'd left him all those years ago? A light bulb flicked on in his head. It would make some kind of sense, but then why would she choose to invite him back into her heart now, without making mention of what she might know? Had she been sworn to secrecy, as he had been by his mother? Did she judge him for what he'd done? God, how he wished he could just tell the truth and get it all over with, get this weight off his shoulders and deal with the consequences. But out of respect for his mother and concern for what may happen to her because of her false statement to the police, he couldn't.

After heaping a spoonful of coffee in each of the three cups, Dylan drummed his fingers on the sink. The jug felt as if it were taking forever to boil. To calm himself as he waited he stared at the horses way off in the distance. He could just make out their silhouettes, heads down with their long, elegant necks glistening in the last rays of sunshine – such majestic creatures with a commanding air of grace. What he'd give to be galloping through the scrub on one right now, instead of standing here, both ready and not so ready to hear what was about to be said.

With the coffee finally made after what felt like an age, he carefully placed two cups down on the table, and then plonking his own cup down, and cursing beneath his breath when he spilt some, he pulled up a chair. 'Righto, ladies, I'm all ears.' He fought to keep his voice calm and his breath steady.

To his exasperation neither Sophie nor Faith said a word. The tension in the room was so thick he felt as if he could cut it with a knife. 'Oh, come on, for God's sake. This is ridiculous, you two. Has someone died?' It was said a little lightheartedly, but he held his breath regardless.

Sophie shook her head, her focus locked on something over his shoulder. 'No, it's nothing like that.' He could barely make out the words she spoke so softly.

'What is it then?' He couldn't help the sternness of his tone.

Sophie's gaze finally skidded over his. Her lips opened, the words obviously fighting to be spoken, but then she clamped her mouth shut. He could see her quickened pulse at the side of her throat and he ached to reach out and somehow soothe her anxiety away. What was she so afraid of? Nothing could be that bad, could it? She looked as though she was about to pass out. Anxiety surged through him, fuelling his need to know what in the hell was going on. He fought expletives back – he wasn't going to disrespect the two women who meant more than life to him. Holding her eyes, he silently pleaded with her to tell him what was on her mind. Sophie looked to his mother for some kind of guidance, but instead Faith was concentrating on her hands wrapped around her cup, her bottom lip clasped between her teeth.

His heart hammered faster. The silence of the room was almost deafening.

As if conjuring up as much courage as she could, Sophie straightened her shoulders and released a long breath. 'Do you want me to tell him, Faith?'

Faith snapped to. She graced her with a humble smile. 'No, sweetheart, I think it's my place, I'm just finding it hard to think of the best way to explain it, that's all.'

'Probably from the start ...' Dylan's tone was curt, tense, and although he regretted it, it was out of his control.

'Yes, I know, Dylan, it was just so long ago, and I don't know how much Sophie knows, how much her parents have told her ... Frank only had time to run through the main details over the phone just now.' Faith's voice faded away, as if she'd gone back to the time and place she was speaking of. Tears welled, and she blinked fast to get rid of them.

Reaching out, Dylan gently prised her hands free from her cup and gave them a reassuring squeeze. 'Mum, whatever it is, you can tell me. Please …'

'I'm not too sure about that.' She smiled woefully. Her bangles chinked as she lifted her hand to wipe a stray tear away from her cheek.

'Try me.' His voice was soft now, full of the compassion he felt with seeing his mum so upset.

She nodded and drew in a shuddering breath. 'I wish I'd told you years ago, but I buried it all down, shoved it into some godforsaken corner of my soul, because that was the only way to deal with it …' Her voice broke and she took a few moments to try to control her emotions. 'But now that it's out in the open, it's brought up all the heartache, all the guilt and shame, as if I were back there, living it all over again. But I know it's time, it's time that you learned the truth of what I've done.'

Dylan's heart almost exploded from his chest. She was referring to his father and what happened that night. What else could it possibly be? But there was nothing she could tell him that he didn't already know. He was there. He saw everything. As did Grace – God rest her soul. Did Sophie know his and his mother's deepest, darkest secret? He sat back abruptly, as though he'd just been slapped hard across the face. 'This doesn't have anything to do with Dad, does it?' He nervously rubbed his five o'clock shadow as he waited for a reply.

Sophie gasped beside him.

His mother seemed to step out of her hazy cloud. She sat up straighter, and gave him the same smile she always did when she was protecting him from that night. 'Oh no, love, nothing of the sort. That's all well and truly behind us.' She reached out and tapped the hand now gripping the edge of the table, his knuckles white. 'There's nothing more that needs to be spoken about that night.'

'Oh, right, well, what is it then?' He desperately tried to shake off the unease sitting lead-heavy in the pit of his stomach. Fear coiled throughout him, not allowing room for anything else.

'Of course, sorry ...' Faith nodded and then drew in another slow, steady breath. 'Remember when I went off to hospital that night?'

Dylan was fighting to catch his breath. 'What night?'

'When my waters broke in the kitchen at Aunty Kimmy's.' She gave him a delicate smile, one that would be easily shattered.

'*Yes.*' It was said with absolute caution. He cleared his throat as he waited.

'And then I came home and told you I'd lost the baby.' Her jaw clenched, as did her hands in her lap.

'Of course I remember, Mum. How could I forget? You were so sad for so long, I didn't think I was ever going to see you smile again.'

'Well, I was sad for a different reason to what I led you to believe ...' Colour drained from her face, leaving her ghostly white. 'I didn't lose the baby.'

Head swimming and mouth dry, Dylan forced the words out. 'You didn't?' He had to remind himself to keep breathing. In. Out. In. Out.

'No, I didn't. I gave birth to a very healthy little girl.' She forced a weak smile from her trembling lips.

'You did?' He was shell-shocked, barely able to breathe.

'Yes, and she was followed by another equally healthy little girl.'

What the fuck?

The room spun. The walls started to cave in on him. Sophie came in and out of focus, her expression grim. He fought to keep control. None of this made any sense. 'Hang on a minute.' He groaned as he gruffly rubbed his face once again. 'You're telling me you gave birth to twins? And they lived?' His brows came together in a scowl as anger won out over his anxiety.

'Yes, I did, and yes, they lived.'

His heart nosedived. Tears stung his eyes but he blinked them back. Men weren't supposed to cry, especially not in front of women. 'I have twin sisters?'

Faith nodded. 'You do.'

A wave of emotions – anger, hurt, disappointment, bewilderment, and everything in between – overcame him. 'Why did you lie to me?'

'I had to, to protect you, and the others. I had no choice.'

'No choice?' He shook his head. 'Everybody has a choice. And what do you mean to protect me? I can protect myself.'

'You'll always be my boy, Dylan.'

'Where are they?'

'They were adopted by a lovely family.'

'Adopted.' The word felt like poison on his tongue. 'But why would you do that?'

'We were broke and I was offered good money to be a surrogate.'

Dylan went to retort, but bit the words back. He needed to hear her out, to try to somehow understand.

'I wanted to give you a good start in life, and not live on struggle street anymore. And I had to get us away from your father before he killed me, or heaven forbid, you, so I agreed to do it. But believe me, it was the hardest thing I've ever done.'

Her eyes were filled with sadness. 'After I'd given birth, I almost backed out of the deal, but I'd made a promise and needed the money desperately – with your father gone and me trying to make ends meet. The bank was going to take the farm off us, and I didn't want to lose it and make you have to move to Sydney permanently because the only other option we had was to move in with Kimmy. No matter how much I liked visiting her there, I didn't believe the city was the right place for a lad like you, a country boy, to grow up. You have no idea how hard that was for me, giving both girls up, but what else was I meant to do?'

Dylan tried to understand what his mother was saying, but instead he felt as if he were treading water, barely able to keep his head above the surface. He needed to be honest, needed to say what was in his heart right at this second. 'You're right, I have no idea how you would've felt, because I just can't comprehend giving away your own flesh and blood like that, and even worse, coming home and lying to me about it all. You knew how much I'd longed for a sibling, and you kept that from me, denied me the right to have a sister, or should I say two sisters.' He watched as Sophie raised her cup to her lips, her hands trembling worse than his mother's.

Tears gathered and then rolled down Faith's cheeks, but as much as he wanted to comfort her, as much as he wanted to retract his harsh words, he sat stone still. He had nothing to give right now. 'Who adopted them? And how does Sophie have anything to do with this?'

Faith looked to Sophie, the unspoken message loud and clear. Knowingness punched him in the chest. 'Are you fucking kidding me? Amy and Tania are my sisters?'

Faith nodded. Sophie didn't move.

'Who's the father?'

'Frank.'

'Dad.'

Both women answered in unison.

'Artificial insemination?'

'No, we couldn't do that because it wasn't above board. It's illegal to pay someone to be a surrogate.'

'Oh my fucking God … you slept with him?' He couldn't hide the disgust from his face.

'I had to.'

'For Christ's sake.' Drawing in a deep breath, trying his best to remain as calm as possible, Dylan looked from one woman to the other. 'And you both thought it was best to keep this from me?'

Sophie looked desperate, her gaze imploring him to pardon her. 'I only found out when I was seventeen. I was young and stupid, and scared out of my wits.' The words rushed from her lips.

'Oh, righto, just because you've kept it from me for …' He paused briefly as he calculated the time. 'Almost twelve years, that's supposed to make it easier to swallow, is it, Sophie?'

She sat, mute, tears now sliding down her cheeks.

To see her upset sliced at his heart like jagged glass, but he wasn't about to comfort her. 'You betrayed me, Sophie.'

She dropped her eyes to her lap. 'I'm so sorry, Dylan. I didn't mean to.'

'So is this why you left me, left Shorefield, to run away from it all, to run away from having to tell me, and my sisters, the truth?'

She stared at him for a long moment. 'Yes, in a roundabout kind of way.'

'You ruined us, ruined our future, ripped my heart to fucking shreds, and all to keep a secret from me that should have been told to me by my own mother?'

She nodded and then stared down at the floor.

'And if that wasn't bad enough, you lied to me, again and again. You told me that your leaving had nothing to do with me, and everything to do with you. You pretended that everything between us could be worked out, and we could maybe make it through to the other side and be in a relationship again …' He laughed almost mockingly. 'I don't fucking think so. A person needs trust to be in love, and we ain't got that.'

'You can trust me. I didn't lie, I just didn't tell you, and not by choice either. I was going to tell you, once Dad had spoken to your mum about it all, I swear.'

'Oh that's a cop-out, Sophie. Stop fucking lying to me, please.'

'I'm telling you the truth, Dylan.'

He didn't believe a word. Couldn't believe a word. He eyed her suspiciously.

'I've got something that might help you to understand why I did what I did.'

'Really, and what's that?' He watched as Sophie dug in her pocket and then pulled out a tattered-looking note. She placed it on the table and pushed it towards him.

He refused to pick it up. 'What does it say?'

'Just read it, Dylan, please.' Sophie turned to Faith. 'And you might want to read it too.'

Huffing, he picked it up and opened it. 'Well, I may as well read it out loud, save Mum the trouble.' He began reading it word for word, his breath snagging when he got to Grace's threats, but as much as his hands shook with both shock and rage, he pushed on until he'd read to the end. His mind whirling, he looked up at Sophie. 'What the hell?'

Sophie offered him a wobbly smile. 'Hard to comprehend, isn't it?'

In a daze, he nodded, and looked to his mother. She was staring straight ahead, a hand over her gaping mouth and her face paler than before.

'Oh, Dylan, I can't believe it.' Faith was shaking. 'I can't believe Grace would do such a thing. It must have been the drugs talking.'

'Definitely.' Dylan carefully folded it back up. 'You knew all this time, Soph, that it was me who pulled the trigger?'

'Yes, but please don't think I ever judged you for it.'

Her words jolted him. He hadn't thought anything of the sort. 'I'd hope not.'

Faith placed a hand on Sophie's arm. 'Thank you, love, for keeping our secret safe.'

'You're welcome, Faith. As hard as it was to leave Dylan, to break his heart, at the time I thought it was for the best for both of you, and for my sisters.' Sophie turned and caught his eye. 'So now do you get why I left without any explanation? I had no other choice.'

Dylan ran a hand over his dark stubble. 'This is all too much.' He groaned, shaking his head. 'As much as I can understand your dilemma at the time, Soph, it's hard for me to accept you didn't tell me. You should've known I would've found some way to work it out … I would have done anything if it meant not losing you. I would never have let Grace get her own way.' Numb with shock, he passed the note back to Sophie, and stood. 'I don't know what else to say right now.' His hands flattened on the table. 'I want you both to leave, please, before I say something I might regret. I need time to think.'

'I understand you need time to let it all sink in, but please don't let the hurt overrule your thoughts, son.' Faith's voice was soft, beseeching. 'Sophie did what she did to protect us, and her sisters.'

With so many raw emotions vying for his attention, Dylan found himself at a loss for words.

Faith nodded, painfully slow, as if the last bit of life had drained out of her. 'Just remember, while you're trying to understand it all, we all have our secrets, Dylan. Nobody can say they don't.'

Dylan felt it was a low blow. His deepest darkest secret, that it was he who took his father's life, was one he'd kept for his mother's sake, not his. If he had his way, he would have told the truth that night, twenty-odd years ago. 'Yeah, Mum, very true, but some secrets are necessary, aren't they? Whereas some others aren't. You should have told me I had two sisters.'

Faith's lips parted to speak, but as if thinking better of it, she closed them again.

Both women remained sitting, looking to him for reassurance he wasn't ready to give. He fought back tears, willing himself not to cry. He was stronger than this. 'Leave, now, both of you, please.' He watched Sophie choke back a sob, his heart shattering even more. Tears filled her eyes and ran down her face. He took steps away from her before he gave in and wrapped her in his arms. He headed towards the sink, where he stared out the window.

'I love you, Dylan, don't forget that in all of this, will you?' His mother's voice wrapped itself around his aching heart. 'And I think I'm right in saying Sophie does too.' She touched him gently on the back. 'Neither of us meant to hurt you. Please try not to take it out on Sophie. It's not her fault. It's mine.'

Unable to wade through his jumble of thoughts and feelings, Dylan fought the urge to shake his mother's hand from him. His laboured breathing and the rhythmic tapping of his fingers on the steel of the sink were the only sounds to be heard over the silence of the room.

'Come on, Sophie, I'll drive you home,' Faith said, her voice trembling.

Out of the corner of his eye, Dylan watched Sophie grab a tissue from the box on the kitchen bench just as someone bashed impatiently on the front door. Groaning, Dylan stormed past them. 'Oh, what the fuck is it now?'

The door was barely ajar when Angus stumbled through, pistol raised. Faith and Sophie screamed and grabbed hold of one another.

'What in the hell?' Dylan immediately pulled the two women behind him. He widened his stance and folded his arms. 'What do you want, McDonald?'

'Don't play dumb, Stone …' Angus grinned, the tip of a gold tooth showing. He looked worse for wear and his breath reeked of alcohol. 'You know damn well what I've come here for, and you better give it back to me.'

'You should have saved yourself the trip. Because like I've already told you, I haven't got your shit.'

'Dylan …' Sophie's voice trembled.

'What's going on?' Faith's was equally shaken.

Dylan quickly glanced over his shoulder. 'Just stay calm. I got this. I'm not going to let anything happen to either of you, okay?'

Faith and Sophie nodded. A whimper escaped Sophie and Faith did her best to comfort her, her words hushed.

Angus tipped his pistol to the side and waved it at the three of them. 'All of you, down on your fucking knees, and your hands where I can see them. And no funny business ... got it?' His words were a little slurred, and his Scottish accent more pronounced.

They dropped down and did as they were told. Dylan made sure he remained in front. 'Why don't you let the women go? This is between us.'

'Is it now?' Angus walked towards Dylan, and then shoved the pistol hard up against his cheek. The glint in his eyes showed just how much he meant business. 'Where's my gear, Stone?' His thin lips pressed together. 'I ain't going anywhere until you give it back.'

'I didn't steal your gear.'

'Liar!' Angus roared.

Stifled sobs came from behind Dylan. He felt like the biggest arsehole on earth, putting his mum and Sophie in this position. He should've taken all the warning signs seriously – the black Ford almost ramming them off the road, finding his front door open, the smudges on the kitchen window ... it had been Angus all along. The muzzle of the pistol felt cold against his skin. A bead of sweat rolled down his cheek as he tried not to imagine the bullet flying into his skull. Angus was clearly drunk as a skunk, and the crazy look in his eyes made Dylan wonder if he was high on drugs too.

'Like hell you didn't.' Angus shook his head. 'Do you really think I'm that fucking stupid?' His tone was heightened by impatience. He sucked air through the gaps in his teeth, eyeing Dylan maliciously. 'You got two choices. You give me my shit, or I shoot all three of you.'

'I. Haven't. Fucking. Got. It,' Dylan said through clenched teeth.

'Well, if you haven't got it, where's the money you made from it, huh?'

'Oh, for Christ's sake, Angus, you're barking up the wrong tree.'

His eyes growing wilder, Angus's finger pressed a little harder into the trigger.

'You wanna go to jail for murder, Angus?' Dylan was desperate to keep him talking, so he could somehow find a way, a fleeting moment in time, to get the gun out of Angus's hands. With the state the man was in, he had no doubt in his mind Angus was prepared to use it, on all of them.

Angus shrugged, his grin ominous. 'I won't go to jail.'

'Pretty bloody sure of yourself, aren't you?'

'Yup ... because if I don't get the drugs back and pay off the debt I owe to the boss man, I'll be a dead man anyway. I got to get my revenge somewhere, and what better way than making you watch me shoot the women you love, before killing you?'

'Why didn't you just go to the cops with what you knew, like you said you would? Send me to jail for shooting my father? Isn't that vengeance enough?'

Angus guffawed. 'I considered it, but then I thought, if I do that, I'll never get my stuff back ... and then I'm back to square one. A dead man walking.' He pushed the pistol in harder. 'Now, go get what you stole, or the money you've made from it, arsehole, and give it the fuck back.'

Grabbing hold of the hope that Angus's reflexes were slow, given the stench of alcohol clinging to him, Dylan acted quickly and knocked the gun away from his cheek, catching Angus unawares. Jumping to his feet, he protectively barred Angus's path from his mother and Sophie. Time slowed. The muscles in his jaw clenched, as did his hands into fists, before he thumped a right-hander to Angus's jawbone.

Flying backwards, Angus landed in a heap. He rubbed his jaw, blood seeping from his split lip. 'You're gonna be sorry you did that, Stone.' Teeth bared in a snarl, Angus got back to his feet, the gun still in his hand, and went to close the distance, his steely gaze on the women.

Panic fuelled Dylan into action. He had to do something. Now. With Angus at arm's length, like lightning he grabbed the man's wrist, twisting it upwards. The pistol fired and the bullet smashed the roof. Sunlight speared through the hole. Stumbling, Angus tried to free himself. They struggled, tumbling backwards and slamming into the wall. Dylan brought his knee up and slammed it into Angus's groin. It hit its mark. The man's face twisted in agony. A sneer curled his lips as he wiped blood from them and flicked it away. Fists flew. Grunts matched each bone-shattering strike. Somewhere amongst the mayhem, the pistol dropped to the floor. Dylan went to grab it but Angus got him a beauty. Blood dripped from his nose as he staggered sideways. Both men dived towards the gun, each of them getting to it at the same time. They fought for it, the silver metal gleaming.

Gaining the upper hand, Angus tried to pin Dylan's hands to the floor while his knees dug into his chest. Dylan won out and rolled away, his fist connecting with Angus's cheek. But as if he'd hit a brick wall, Angus barely flinched and retaliated with wild force, punching Dylan in the stomach. Desperate to gain control, Dylan reached for Angus's hands, now clutching the pistol. Another shot fired, but this time, it hit Angus's target.

Bright red blood splattered the wall as she crumbled to the floor. Unmoving. Lifeless. Red rage filled him as Dylan cried out her name, and in one ferocious, deadly punch sent Angus flying into the wall, where the mammoth of a Scotsman crumpled in an unconscious heap. Crawling through her blood, Dylan arrived at her side. There was no life in her eyes. He grabbed her wrist and tried to feel for a pulse, praying with everything he had he was going to get the chance to tell her just how much he loved her.

CHAPTER
23

Shorefield

Sophie woke to inky darkness, the kind of deep black that makes it impossible to see a hand in front of your face. But then she realised her eyes weren't open. Wouldn't open. Her head throbbed. Her throat hurt. Where was she? She tried to blink but her eyelids felt as if they weighed a tonne. Her memory of the last few minutes she'd been conscious flooded back to her. The bullet, piercing through her flesh, had felt like fire slicing her skin. The pain had been excruciating. And then the darkness had overcome her, the very same darkness she was experiencing now. Was she dead and having an out of body experience? Fear settled in the pit of her stomach. She desperately tried to resurface from wherever she was. Her mind tried to catch up. Her eyes refused to open. She fought on. She wasn't giving up. Dylan. Was he alive? She tried to say his name, but her mouth was too dry to form the word. Her lips felt as if they'd been glued together. There was a hand on her arm. Was Angus going to finish her off? As if forcing a door ajar, she finally heaved her eyes open. Her focus was blurry. The lights were blinding. Beeps sounded beside her. The stench of antiseptic almost choked her, although it was much better than the smell of gunfire.

'She's waking up.'

The voice was familiar but distant, as if it were a thousand miles away. Her eyes drifted closed again. She dragged in a ragged breath. 'Dylan?' With supreme effort she forced them back open.

'I'll call the nurse.' Kurt's deep voice was unmistakable.

'Sophie, it's Dad. Can you hear me?'

'Soph?' It was her mother's voice. 'Oh, Soph.' Sobs followed.

She tried to nod. She was in hospital, with her family. But where was Dylan? And Faith?

'Do you know where you are, love?' Her father's voice was like a warm blanket.

'Um, I …' She felt a sob rising in her chest.

'I love you, sis.' Amy's voice carried deep into her heart. As did Tania's.

'We all love you, blister.'

Strong chiselled features finally came into focus, as did the familiar crystal-blue eyes. 'Dylan?'

'Oh my God, Soph, I thought we'd lost you.' Dylan gently took her hand in his.

'Your mum, is she okay?' She peeled each word from the roof of her mouth.

'Yes, she's shaken up, but all good.' He leant in and kissed her cheek, pausing by her ear. 'I love you so much, Firefly.'

Tears filled her eyes. 'I love you too,' she whispered from her heart, her soul finally wrapping itself around his.

On the other side of the bed, her family was lined up, huddled around her, even Gina and Vinnie, and Daniela and Mark; all of them looking down at her as though she was an angel sent from heaven.

Marie was crying and her father had his arm around her shoulder, cuddling her to him. 'Oh, Sophie, it's so good to see you open your eyes, love.'

Plucking a tissue from her bosom, Gina passed it to Marie. If Sophie weren't feeling like death warmed up, she would have smiled. She licked her lips. 'Can a girl get a drink of water around here?'

Five sets of hands reached for the jug.

With the straw pressed to her lips, she sucked. The water was the best thing she'd ever tasted.

'Where was I shot?' she said softly, every word taking all of her strength.

Dylan looked across the bed at her father.

'You were shot through the shoulder, love. Your collarbone and humerus are shattered. The bullet lodged so they had to operate to remove it. You …' He paused as if fighting off tears. 'We were very lucky you survived. If it hadn't been for Dylan stemming the blood …' He shook his head, weeping now. Marie took him into her arms, soothing him.

The reality of how close she'd come to death overcame her. 'How long have I been out for?' She looked to Dylan for the answer.

'Almost twenty-four hours.'

'Have you been here the entire time?'

He shrugged. 'Nowhere better to be.' He grinned a wobbly smile, clearly trying to make light of the awful situation.

'You've got a really lousy bedside manner, Stone.'

'I think you're going to have to get used to my lousy bedside manner, because it looks as though I'll be here a fair bit.' She tried to move and winced. Pain shot down her left side. Dylan placed his hand on her right arm. 'Steady up there, Soph.'

'How long are we talking about here?'

'Not really sure, maybe a week or two.'

Panic shot through her. 'A few weeks, but what about the wedding?'

'It's okay, sweet pea ...' Gina smiled from the foot of the bed. 'Don't worry yourself about that right now. You just focus on getting better.'

'Oh, Daniela and Mark, I'm so sorry if this has mucked everything up.'

'Don't be ridiculous, cous!' Daniela looked at her like she was crazy. 'I don't care if we have to wheel you down the aisle in your hospital bed ... you're going to be a part of the bridal party come hell or high water.'

A dishevelled doctor bustled in, a stethoscope around his neck. Everyone backed away from the bed. 'Hi, Sophie. I'm Doctor Jules. How do you feel?'

'Like a million dollars.'

'A sense of humour is good medicine, but so is plenty of rest. And that's what you're going to be doing for the next few months.'

'Months?'

'Yes, months.' He offered a small smile, displaying perfectly white teeth as he pressed the stethoscope against her chest. 'We have a heartbeat, so that's a good start.' He grinned now.

'Excellent.' She smiled back at him, ignoring the pain starting to pulse through her arm and chest.

Lifting her chart from the end of the bed, he ran his eyes over it, nodding and mumbling to himself before he wrote something down. Coming back to her, his eyes fixed on hers. 'Now, how's the pain, on a scale of one to ten?'

She thought about it. 'Maybe a five or six.'

'Good, that means the painkillers are working. Although, they are going to make you very tired, so please sleep as much as you can.' He held up the call button. 'And if it starts to get too much, you just holler, and we'll up the dose, okay?'

She nodded. 'So how long is my recovery going to be?'

'The skin wound will take about three to six months, and hopefully there'll only be minor scarring. The bones will take about the same amount of time. You'll be wearing a sling for around three months – give or take, depending on how quickly you heal.'

'Wow, that long, huh?'

'Afraid so.' His friendly eyes turned serious. 'But just be thankful you're alive, Sophie, you came very close to not being here.'

Death suddenly became so terrifyingly real. Emotions welled and choked her. She couldn't fight back the tears as they filled her eyes and rolled down her cheeks. Her mother jumped to her aid with a tissue, dabbing them up, as every member of her family closed in on the bed, their hands touching some part of her. Dylan entwined his fingers in hers.

'Sorry for the scare, everyone,' she choked out.

There was a chorus of replies telling her basically to stop being so silly and no more apologising.

The doctor gave her a caring smile. 'It's very normal to cry after coming so close to death, so let it out when necessary, okay? We don't want you bottling everything up.'

'Oh, I'm a good crier, so I'm sure I'll be letting it all out.' She smiled through her tears as tiredness overcame her, her eyelids suddenly heavy as lead once again. And although she wanted to fight off the sleepiness, and talk to Dylan and her family, she just couldn't.

❧

When Sophie opened her eyes again, there was no sunlight shining through the small hospital window. It looked as though everyone had gone, when a noise pulled her gaze to the other side of the bed. Dylan was curled up as best he could in a chair, fast asleep. Seeing him made her smile from the inside out.

As if sensing her looking at him, Dylan stirred. He blinked his eyes open and rubbed them, yawning. Spotting she was awake, he brightened. 'Hey there, beautiful, how are you feeling?'

'Hey, handsome, a little groggy, but okay.'

'You've had quite an entourage here all day; most of them only left a little while ago. Your poor sisters, well, our sisters, they feel terrible about the fight you all had and the things that were said before everything went belly up. They said to tell you as soon as you woke up again that they love you.'

'Aw, I love them too. I hope they know just how much.' Sophie sniffled back tears.

'They know, Soph.' Leaning in, he took her by the hand. 'Even though it's good to see how much love they all have for you, it's actually nice to have a little bit of time on our own.'

'I'm hearing you.' Sophie met his eyes, which were filled with so much sadness it tore at her heart. 'What is it?'

'I'm so sorry I put you in that position. It's my fault you were shot, Soph.' He blinked back tears. 'I don't know how I'm ever going to forgive myself.'

'Don't you dare blame yourself. If anything, you saved me.'

'Thanks, Soph, but I don't see it that way.'

'Well, you're going to have to, because I'm not going to have you beating yourself up over it every day if I'm around.'

He smiled softly. 'You want to be around me every day?'

'Of course I do, why wouldn't I?'

He looked down at their entwined fingers. 'Why would you?'

'What do you mean?'

'I reacted really badly to Grace's letter, when all in all, I should have wrapped my arms around you and thanked you for what you did, for me, and Mum … and Amy and Tania. You're so selfless, Soph, and always have been.'

'I understand it was a lot for you to take in at the time, Dylan. So no hard feelings.' She watched him fight off emotions. If she had been fit and able, she would have embraced him, but she could barely move. She gave his hand a loving squeeze. 'So what drugs was Angus on about?'

He drew in a deep breath. 'Long story short, Angus forced me to watch him do a drug deal in the office of the tattoo shop I managed, so he had a witness to what was said and exchanged. And then the night I left Sydney, someone broke into the shop and stole the stash out of the safe. Angus blamed me because I apparently was the only person, other than him, of course, who knew the combination to the safe.'

'You've always hated drugs, so I know you wouldn't have had anything to do with it. Did they find out who did take them?'

'Sure did. Sergeant Tucker arrested Angus, and then he gave the Kings Cross coppers the lowdown. They raided a few places and that's when they found the stash.'

'So don't leave me hanging, who was it?' Sophie found herself holding her breath.

'It turned out to be one of the staff from the tattoo shop. Johnno Sturt, the conniving bastard. I'd given him the combination once, when I'd had to have a few days off with the flu. He didn't have a set of keys so he had to bash the back door in and, of course, he knew where the security cameras were. I only spoke on the phone to him last week, when I was looking for Angus so I could sort all this rubbish out. I didn't pick up on it at the time, but Johnno was fishing for information the entire conversation.'

'Shit, hey? Keep your enemies closer and all that.'

'Exactly.' Dylan paused. 'I'm so sorry I never told you the truth about the night my father died, and you had to hear it from Grace.'

'Please don't apologise. I understand you wanting to keep it a secret.'

He nodded then cleared his throat and twirled his thumb around hers as though a million miles away.

Sophie waited for him to regroup.

'I've wanted to go to the police about it for years. But I was protecting Mum. With her lying and saying in the statement to the police that she had shot Dad, I was worried that if it came out she'd be charged with something. For giving a false statement or something like that.'

'You weren't worried about what would happen to you?'

'Yes, but not as much as what could happen to her. I had no choice at the time, Soph. I had to take his life before he took Mum's. The bastard was going to kill her that night.'

'You did a very brave thing, at only nine years old.'

'I don't know about brave, it was more of a natural reflex to protect Mum.'

'I can only imagine how horrific it must have been for you.'

'It was, but the good thing now is that I've finally broken my silence, as has Mum, and we've made a statement to the town sergeant, Jim Tucker, about what really happened that night.' He breathed a sigh of relief. 'I feel like a massive weight has been lifted off my shoulders, by being honest.'

'Wow, no wonder.' She drew in a slow, steadying breath. 'So what does this mean for you legally?'

'Jim has been brilliant about it all. He says I won't be held culpable because under ten years of age you're deemed too young to be charged with murder. And Mum, well, he says she did what any mother would do, in protecting her child. She was diagnosed with battered-wife syndrome at the time when Dad was shot, and deemed not culpable because of all the abuse she'd endured.'

'Oh thank God for small mercies, hey?'

'Absolutely,' he said, with a loving smile.

She returned it with one of her own. 'So, are all our skeletons out of the closet now?'

Dylan chuckled, his laughter soothing her soul. 'I bloody hope so. I don't reckon you and I need any more shocks to the system.'

'I'd have to agree with you on that one, Dylan.' It hurt to laugh, but she couldn't help herself. 'I really need to wriggle, my back's killing me.' She grimaced as she tried to move to relieve the pain.

Dylan shot to his feet to help her, and then rearranged the sheet and pillow so she was comfy. Dragging his chair as close as he could to her, he sat down again.

Cuddling into her pillow, she smiled dreamily. 'What would I do without you?'

'Not sure, but I'm not going to let you find out.' He placed a kiss so tender yet so passionate against her lips. 'Love you, my beautiful Firefly.'

'I love you too, my gorgeous man.'

A sense of absolute peace washed over Sophie as she drank in the love shining in his eyes. Together, they were finally home.

EPILOGUE

Having given up on the fact her sling really didn't match her teal bridesmaid dress, Sophie readjusted it to stop her shoulder aching. Thankfully, the bouquet of flowers she was holding was small, especially compared to Daniela's huge bunch of white roses. The painkillers she'd taken half an hour ago were kicking in nicely, although maybe she shouldn't have had them with a glass of champagne. Her legs were feeling a little wobbly, or perhaps that was because she was about to meet her handsome man at the altar – although she was not marrying him, her bucket list would be completed, and only four days before her thirtieth birthday. The chapel was full to the brim, with some people having to stand at the sides for lack of seats – a typical Maltese wedding. It was nice to see Faith sitting alongside her parents, and with her boyfriend, Jim Tucker, proud as punch beside her. They made a lovely couple.

With her sisters in front, and Daniela being fussed about by Gina behind, Sophie leant in to whisper to Tania. 'Are you sure Alex feels okay sitting with Mum and Dad?'

'Oh God yes, they're all getting on like a house on fire. Who would have thought it?'

'Yeah, I can't believe Mum and Dad took the news so well yesterday,' Amy chimed in as she readjusted her boobs in her skin-tight bridesmaid gown.

'Tell me about it, Ames, I almost passed out from shock. Maybe the fact she's a doctor helps,' Tania said with a hushed chuckle. 'But seriously, it's nice to see them so genuinely happy for me.'

'We all are.' Sophie smiled lovingly.

Tania returned it. 'Thanks, sis.'

Caught up in the poignant moment, all three sisters hugged.

The song Daniela had chosen to accompany her as she walked down the aisle began.

'Okay, Mum, you really need to go to your seat now,' Daniela said while trying to peel an emotional Gina from her.

'Okay, all right, I'm going.' Gina retrieved a tissue from her bra. 'I love you, darling.'

'Love you too, Mum.' The two women kissed.

'Now go, before you steal my limelight.' Daniela grinned cheekily.

Gina dashed past them, dabbing her eyes as she took her seat at the front of the chapel, beside Frank and Marie.

Vinnie smiled and offered Daniela his elbow – a proud father if Sophie had ever seen one. Her heart swelled with love and pride for her amazing family, and the way they'd all worked through the turmoil of secrets being revealed. It had taken some big deep and meaningfuls, for all of them, but they had embraced the truth and that was the most important thing. She blinked back emotional tears, not wanting to walk down the aisle with her mascara running. Each of the six bridesmaids in front of her began rhythmic steps. Then it was her turn. Sophie felt a rush of nerves as all eyes fell upon her, but then her gaze zeroed in on Dylan and everything and everyone faded away. He mouthed, 'I love you,' and she mouthed it back to him. Goosebumps covered her. Their very own moment, suspended in time, silently, yet a thousand words were spoken in their gazes. She imagined what it would be like if this were her very own wedding, with Dylan standing there waiting for her to join him, and her heart sang. One day, she just knew it would be so. There'd be no keeping them away from each other now.

It was two in the morning when Sophie and Dylan finally made their way back to the hotel room, and within minutes, they were both undressed and helping each other to the bed, their lips pressed hard up against one another's. As always with his touch, Sophie's heart welled. Dylan was careful not to hurt her as he climbed on top. Sliding downward, making sure his mouth and tongue trailed her tingling skin the entire way, he stopped to savour between her legs, his strokes long and slow – exactly how she liked it. She writhed in gratification, her bottom lip caught between her teeth. She was so close, and God, how she just wanted him to take her, to make her his, like only he knew how. Bringing her to the brink and then stopping, he came back to meet her mouth, his kisses hungry, demanding, but his touch tender and gentle. Sliding inside her, he reached underneath her and arched her hips up so he could go even deeper. Her body tightened, trembled. Heat rose to her face. His pace built the crescendo she could feel hurtling throughout her body in mind-blowing, euphoric waves. He watched her, took pleasure from her pleasure, burning her flesh with his blazing blue eyes.

She reached for him, her fingernails scraping down his chest as she arched even harder into him. She clenched around him, teetering, as fireworks hinted their explosion inside of her. And then together, they flew off the edge and into ecstasy. Her body shook as she gripped tightly to him, her hips not stalling until his did. Sated, she wrapped her legs around him, letting him know she wanted him to stay right where he was, above and deep inside her, just until they caught their breath. It was only then that she felt her shoulder hurting. The pleasures he bestowed on her were the perfect drug to take the discomfort away, if only for a little while.

Finally tumbling to the side of her, Dylan stroked her hair now damp with sweat. 'God you're beautiful, Soph.' His voice was raw and husky.

She caressed his shoulders and chest with a gentle trail of her fingertips. Smiling, she collected what she wanted from him, a soft, tender, lingering kiss. 'I couldn't imagine my life without you. Thank you for loving me the way you do. I'm one lucky lady.'

'You're damn easy to love, Soph. And I want to go on loving you the way I do, and fall even more in love with you, every day, for the rest of my life.' He rolled to the side of the bed. 'And just while we're on the subject ...' He leant over the edge, giving Sophie the perfect view of his perfect butt. She couldn't help but reach out and pinch it. 'Oi,' he said with a chuckle. And then, 'Ahhh, there it is.' He came back to face her, his playfulness now replaced with a look so intense and unfathomable it stole her breath.

She looked to his hands and her heart stalled.

He flipped the little box open, revealing the most beautiful, glimmering diamond ring she'd ever seen. He took her hand in his. 'Sophie Copinni, I love you with all my heart and soul. Will you make me the happiest man alive and be my wife?'

She cried and laughed all at once.

'So that's a yes, I'm hoping?'

'Yes, yes, yes!'

With shaking hands, he slipped the ring on her finger. She squealed, wincing when she launched herself on top of him, feathering kisses all over his face and lips. 'I love you so much, Dylan Stone.'

'We never stopped loving each other, Soph, and we never will.' He pulled her closer to him, closing any gap, kissing her in a way that sent her soaring above the clouds.

If you loved *A Country Mile*,
please turn over
for a taste of Mandy Magro's
most recent bestseller

Out October 2022

Rose Jones lifted her dark sunglasses to the top of her head, took a shaky breath and braved a glance left and right. All around her, the pews of the church were packed with mourners, from near and far. Her beautiful great-grandmother had touched many hearts over the years. Elizabeth Jones was going to be deeply missed.

Bringing her attention from where her stepfather, Heath, had his arm wrapped tightly around her grieving mother, Rose looked to the mahogany casket adorned with flowers through tear-blurred eyes. She jumped as her father, Mark, placed a reassuring hand on her shoulder. Swivelling in her seat, she graced him with an appreciative glance over her shoulder. His kind eyes were filled the same sadness she carried in her heart.

She was grateful for his comfort, especially as the poker-faced man beside her was cold as ice after an argument this morning, and had offered her no support. It showed to Rose how insensitive her fiancé had become. Rose and Finley Cole had been together for years, sharing dreams, fears, goals … and yet, she felt as if she didn't know him at all anymore. Cracks were appearing in every part of their relationship, but after months of trying to be the only peacekeeper, she just didn't have the energy anymore, and they were sinking, fast.

Watching GG, her great-grandfather, shuffle up to say his final words very nearly had her sobbing uncontrollably. But with her mother squeezing her hand tight, she held it together, just. She also felt consoled in knowing her great-grandmother was no longer suffering from the cancer that had stolen her bright spirit and riddled her body with pain, even if it didn't curb the fathomless anguish of her loss. Never had she thought her heart could break like this; it was as if she could barely draw a breath.

Taking a moment to gather himself, David Jones cleared his throat before leaning into the microphone. 'Elizabeth was the absolute light, and love, of my life. She was a wonderful wife, a devoted mother, a loving great-grandmother and a loyal friend to many. She always believed that love was the greatest of gifts, and we all know how much of it she gave to each and every one of us.' His chin wobbled, and he paused, gripping the lectern tightly. 'Excuse me for a minute.' Closing his eyes, he turned his back to the mourners, his burly shoulders shaking.

Unable to sit back and see her hero in so much pain, Rose shot to her feet, disregarding her wobbly legs, and rushed to his side. 'It's okay, GG. I can finish your speech if you like,' she whispered, rubbing his back.

'Thank you, little one, but I want to try to do this. For her.' Wiping his eyes with a handkerchief, he brought his big hand to her cheek. 'But can you stay here with me, just in case?'

Biting her trembling lip, Rose bit back a sob. 'Of course I can.' In her line of sight, her mum, Molly Jones, offered her an appreciative look.

After a few breaths, her great-grandfather turned back to the sea of mourners, and she slipped an arm around him. Together, somehow, they got through it. As they always had, and always would, no matter what life threw at them. Then, taking his hand in hers, she led him back to his seat, beside her stepfather. Step by step, they had been moving through the motions of death as the tight-knit family they were. Day by day, they now had to find a way to get thorough their mountains of sorrow. She didn't know how it was going to be possible, but one thing was for certain, she was going to make sure she was there for her family, just as they'd all been loyally by her side throughout her twenty-one years of life.

CHAPTER

1

One month later – Jacaranda Farm

Dumping the grooming bucket onto the timeworn timber workbench, Rose stole a moment to ease out her tight neck. Tossing and turning all night long while she worried herself sick was doing her no favours. She really needed to get back to her yoga and meditation; it would help her to relax and to switch off her overactive mind. With the new year only weeks away, maybe that could be her resolution to welcome the next year in? Not that her one for this year had come to fruition – with her busy lifestyle, taking better care of herself had proved difficult. Between teaching kids how to ride, meeting her writing deadlines, keeping in touch with family and friends, being a good fiancé/ homemaker and the intense training and competition schedule that came with her barrel racing, she barely had time to stop and take a much-needed breath. If only she had the chance to slow down and smell the proverbial roses, just for a little while. Now, wouldn't that be nice?

Pigs might fly too.

Sighing, she looked at the two posters her great-grandmother had made, which she'd pinned to the tack shed wall as an eleven-year-old girl. Now faded – even the tacks that held the laminated placards in place were rusting – the posters had been a way to encourage her big dreams of becoming Australia's barrel-racing champion, just like her great-grandmother had once been. She remembered working with her GG, hammering each pin into place – her up on the bench with swinging legs, GG with hammer in hand, the next tack held between his teeth.

She quietly read each inspiring quote for the umpteenth time in her life.

'I figure if a girl wants to become a legend, she should just go ahead and be one.'

– Calamity Jane

And

'Courage is being scared to death but saddling up anyway.'
– John Wayne

She softly smiled to herself. This kind of encouragement and inspiration was what pushed her through the hard times and lately, she'd had many challenging times. Sure, barrel racing was tough – the hours on the road were gruelling and the injuries could sometimes be excruciating – but it was all worth the blood, sweat and tears. Not that Finley shared her opinion. And to prove the point, he'd stopped showing any interest in her endeavours. Sure, it would never make her a millionaire, but between the prize money, the income from her horse-riding school, occasional jillarooing jobs and the royalties from her barrel-racing guidebooks, she was living comfortably doing something she was passionate about. Yes, she was juggling a few balls, but she always found a way to fit everything in, and to put time aside to spend together as a couple. Although, for the past few months, he didn't seem keen to be on her company. It felt like he was avoiding her.

With a heavy heart, her thoughts drifted back to their argument yesterday. She plucked her mobile from her pocket and re-read the text message he'd sent her last night.

You're going to be my wife in six months' time, Rose, and you know I want a family sooner rather than later. You really need to start looking towards motherhood, which means letting go of your barrel racing and riding school. You can't ride a horse like that when you're pregnant. That would just be stupid, and selfish.

No mention of 'I love you', or 'We will work this out'. Just demands. That had become Finley's way. And she didn't like being told what to do.

Cursing beneath her breath, she grit her teeth as she shoved the phone back into her jeans pocket. It was a given that she'd never compete while she was pregnant – she'd never dream of endangering her unborn child's life. But wasn't it her choice too, as to when she and Finley had children? She wasn't ready yet. Especially considering she was just shy of twenty-two. Yes, Finley was seven years older, but that gave him no right to pressure her into his timeline – one that she'd known nothing about until recently – and she'd said as much in her reply text to him, to which she'd received no response. Nor had he answered her three calls this morning. Her annoyance rose another notch just thinking about it. Hopefully, when he arrived home tonight, they could have a calm conversation, like the adults they were supposed to be.

You're kidding yourself, Jones. He's never going to listen. You should've learnt that by now.

Rose huffed her voice of reason away. Love was unconditional, uplifting, and encouraging … wasn't it? But since getting engaged five months before, the rose-coloured glasses had tumbled off and been crushed beneath her boots. The position Finley had taken at his father's insurance firm meant many nights away from home, and he was gradually turning him into a person she didn't know and, at times, didn't like very much. Not to mention his outdated expectations had thrown her off-kilter, with him transforming suddenly from an easygoing larrikin who laughed a lot to a suit-wearing solemn man who lived to work.

If they could only iron out the matters that were causing their recurring arguments, she truly believed they could be happy again. She was asking much. He wanted four children; she'd be happy with one or two, and she didn't want any for a few more years. He wanted her to stay home, but she didn't want him to be the only breadwinner; she believed in mutual contributions. She didn't believe he needed to know where she was all the time because she was as loyal and trustworthy as a person came, and she thought it was a double-standard that he expected her to give him complete freedom to do as he wished, whenever he wanted, without question. It just all seemed a little one-sided, and it was beginning to wear her on patience and optimism.

Heaving another weighty sigh, she tried to shake the contemplations from her mind. There'd be plenty of time for her to mull it all over later, like she'd been doing all week, with Finley away on yet another work trip. Right now, she needed to put one hundred and ten percent focus into her barrel racing. She couldn't risk an injury to herself or Buck, especially when it was so close to the end of the rodeo circuit. She needed top points to walk away Australian barrel-racing champion for the second year running – handing the trophy over to her arch-nemesis would be an utter nightmare. Madeline Hew might have been an excellent rider, but she was a horrid human being, a bad sport and a shocking loser.

Leaning in, Rose placed a hand on her great-grandmother's cursive writing. 'I'm going to make you super proud this weekend, Great-Grandma,' she said quietly, blinking back tears. 'I just wish you were here to watch.' She bit down on her bottom lip to stop from crying. 'But I know you'll be cheering me on from heaven.'

Running at her dreams head-on had been a trait the strong women of her family had taught her – her grandmother, her mum and her aunties. She wasn't about to let go of that, not even for Finley. She just hoped he loved her enough to accept who she truly was.

Taking a breath, she turned and gathered her emotions before stepping from the shade of the leather-scented tack shed. Having made the effort to dress in her competitive gear – it always gave her that extra oomph – she looked every part of the champion barrel racer, with her diamanté-studded jeans, blingy belt, pink and purple checked western shirt and timeworn Ariat boots.

Hands on hips, her wide-brimmed hat pulled level to her brows and her long brown hair pulled into a tightly plaited ponytail, she narrowed her gaze and looked towards the arena that she'd spent countless hours in over the years. Heath had positioned the three barrels perfectly for her cloverleaf pattern. She adored that he cared enough to know that every second counted.

The terrain underfoot was a little soft after the overnight rain – something to take into consideration. With her trained eye, backed up by a nudge with the toe of her boot, she could tell if an arena was going to be shallow or deep or have a deceptively hard pan underneath which could injure a horse. And even though winning was important, she'd prefer to knock back a race than risk hurting her beloved gelding.

As if sensing her thoughts were on him, Buck turned and whinnied from where he was patiently waiting for their training session to begin. His red chestnut coat glistened beneath the midmorning-morning sunshine, and he looked mighty dapper in his new set of splint boots and glittery halter. Shoving her hands into her pockets, Rose forgot about everything that had been weighing her down and smiled from the inside out. Three turns, two hearts and one pair of tightly united souls – that was her and Buck down to a tee. God, how she loved him. In thirteen years, they'd been through so much together and knew each other like only best mates could. He made her laugh with his playful antics, and had taken her on many adventures, while his mane had wiped away many of her tears. She couldn't imagine life without him.

The crunch of gravel under tyres pulled her gaze down the earthy track. Spotting Molly climb from her new LandCruiser Sahara, she instantly felt the familiar peace her mother had always brought into her life.

'Hey, Mum.' Rose gave her a wave as she took steps to close the distance.

'Hi, sweetheart,' Molly hollered back as she ambled towards her with her six-year-old sister, Lizzy, in tow. 'Sorry I'm a little late, but this munchkin was a right Little Miss Grumpy Pants this morning.'

Lizzy glanced up at her mum, her face crumpled with characteristic Miller rebelliousness. 'It was Angus's fault for eating all the peanut butter.'

'Yes, so you've said.' Molly offered a playful glance to Rose. '*Many* times.'

'Wowsers.' Rose had to fight to curb her laughter. 'Sounds serious.' She forced a frown in Lizzy's direction.

'Oh, trust me, Rose, it was almost World War III.' Molly rolled her eyes. 'Thank god Heath came to the rescue with one of those little sachet thingies of peanut butter he gets from the breakfast bar at the mine.'

'Ha, yeah. At least now you'll live to fight another day.' Grinning at her mum's exasperated expression, Rose brushed a kiss on her cheek then bent to do the same to Lizzy. 'You're going to turn into a tub of peanut butter one of these days, my little ferret.'

Lizzy giggled. 'You're so silly, sis.'

'I try to be.' Ruffling Lizzy's platinum blonde ringlets, Rose straightened.

'Right then.' Molly clapped her hands together. 'Let's get this show on the road, shall we? Before it gets too hot to think.'

'Yes.' Rose nodded. 'Let's.'

Though she hadn't carried on in her mother's vein of horse whispering, the love of these magnificent creatures ran deep in her blood. She adored teaching kids to ride, found the thrill of rounding up cattle and wayward bulls addictive, and sharing her wealth of knowledge in her bestselling guidebooks was such a blessing – she wasn't about to put all of that on hold for the life Finley had apparently chosen for her. He was clearly counting on her to be the stay-at-home wife and mother, and although she wanted to make him happy, the thought of being housebound for the next twenty-odd years terrified her. That was where one of her favoured lines from her favourite Nicholas Sparks movie, *The Longest Ride*, about love requiring sacrifice came into play. If only it was as easily done as said.

Rose couldn't wait to be in the saddle – it's where she lived to be – and she was eager to get into the last training session before the annual Mareeba Christmas Eve Rodeo on the weekend.

Reaching Buck, Rose pecked him on the muzzle. 'Right, my boy. Let's do this.' She vaulted into the saddle. Locking her boot heels into the stirrups, she quickly got settled as she studied the cloverleaf pattern she was about to make around the three barrels. With Buck eyeing the path too, the gelding pushed into the bit as she got him into starting position. His body twitching with anticipation, he snorted and stomped his hoof. Ears forward and muscles coiling tightly beneath the saddle, Rose knew every bit of Buck's powerful build was honed and ready – she treasured how he was always as keen as she was to reach the finishing line. It's what made them a team to be reckoned with.

Standing on the bottom rail with her arms resting on the top one, Molly held the stopwatch up. 'You two ready to go, sweetheart?' Her singsong voice carried across the yard.

Rose flashed her a smile. 'Yes.'

'And.... go.'

Rose barely twitched the reins and Buck exploded like a missile fired. Eyes intent on making the sharp turn, they shot towards the first barrel. Dirt flew out from Buck's hooves as he dug down and curved around it. She watched where his feet were going, one powerful stride after the other. Clouded by dust, she maintained her core and kept her hips ground evenly into the saddle as she cut him tight around the second one. Relaxing her midsection, she encouraged him to shorten his stride as he approached the final one. Like a bolt of lightning, he shot around it, swiftly and smoothly, careful not to tip it. Then, with one last burst of speed, he galloped for the finishing line.

'Wow, Rose.' Molly danced on the spot as she bellowed out, 'Fourteen point two seconds.'

'Woohoo.' Rose exhaled. 'Did you hear that, Buck? We just cut point three seconds off our record.' She gave him a rub for a job well done. 'Yay for us, my clever boy! I reckon we might have this in the bag.'

Buck bobbed his head then whinnied animatedly, enticing a wholehearted giggle from Lizzy.

Finding her little sister's laughter addictive, Rose smiled even wider as she gently pulled Buck to a stop just short of Molly and Lizzy. 'Of course you agree with me, hey buddy? You always do.' She dismounted in one graceful movement and collected a kiss on the cheek from her Mum. 'I love you, so much, mumma bear. Thank you for everything you do for me. I honestly don't know where I'd be without you.'

'Pfft, don't speak of it.' Waving a hand through the air, Molly smiled like only a mother could towards a daughter. 'I love you to the moon and back, my sweet girl.' She tucked a wisp of hair behind Rose's ear before bringing her hands to her cheeks. 'You're looking a little weary today, love. Make sure you rest up before the weekend, won't you?'

'I'll try to, I promise.' Rose bit back the urge to spill anymore about her and Finley's troubled relationship. Her mum had enough emotional baggage to deal with right now.

'Glad to hear it, sweetheart.' Molly held her gaze with matching-coloured eyes for a moment longer, then looked to Lizzy, who was now drawing circles in the dirt with a stick. 'I best get a move on. I have to get this little one to her dance class at twelve-thirty.'

'Okey-dokey. I'll call you tomorrow.' Rose started to lead Buck towards the stables. 'Bye, Lizzy.'

Lizzy waved enthusiastically. 'Bye, sissy.'

An hour later, Rose was stepping through the doors of her second favourite shop in Mareeba, the first being the western clothing store with all its leather goods and sparkly tops. She breathed deeply; she'd always loved the smell of the local feed store, Stockman's Hall of Hay. Striding towards the back of the building, she went in search of golden yolk chicken feed, the secret behind the almost orange hue of the eggs she consumed every morning. Fried, poached, scrambled, the occasional omelette, you name it – eggs were her go-to. Ironic that Finley was allergic.

Turning a corner while lost in her thoughts, she ran smack-bang into a big, burly chest. The owner of said chest instantly grabbed her arm as if to steady her, his hold strong yet gentle, cool but heated. And holy moly, he smelt good – leather and spice and all things horsey nice.

'Oops, sorry about that.' Shamefaced, she stepped back and her skipped a beat as she peered up into the bluest eyes she'd ever seen, ones that contrasted with the bloke's shaggy black hair and the equally dark five o'clock shadow that dusted his square jaw.

In a single breath, his gaze raked over her, paused on her lips then back to her eyes. 'Equally guilty for the collision.' Balancing a twenty-kilogram bag of feed on each of his wide shoulders, the towering bloke flashed her an apologetic grin. 'So no worries at all.'

'Oh, okay, cheers.' Remembering to blink, she smiled as she stepped aside to let him pass. And that was when it hit her – she'd just collided with the one and only Ty Parker, champion bull rider. She'd seen him atop a bull quite a few times, but never had she been so up close and personal. By god, his presence was emanating masculinity in spades. For some strange reason, she felt the need to look around and make sure nobody was watching them. She shook herself. What was that all about?

Out of the corner of her eye, she watched him walk away quickly, disappearing except for his wide-brimmed hat. She observed it hovering across the store then, after pausing at the cash registers, out the front doors. She knew that he owned a cattle station a few hours west of Townsville, nearer Charters Towers, and that was about it. With one of the biggest rodeos of the calendar on this weekend, he was no doubt here to jump aboard a bucking bull.

Remembering what she'd come in here for, she got back to her list of errands. Even though they were in a hard place right now, she was looking forward to seeing Finley and hoped they could find a way to move past all the drama. Maybe she should cook his favourite of grilled garlic Moreton Bay bugs with a side of her rocket, pear and blue cheese salad. Washed down with a good bottle of wine, of course, to soften the mood. Yeah, that's exactly what she was going to do. The very thought made her steps a little lighter. All she wanted was a happy life with him – surely it couldn't be that hard? She swallowed down another wave of hurt, wishing he'd call her back.

As if on cue, her phone chimed from her pocket. She plucked it out, breathing a sigh of relief when Finley's handsome face lit up her screen. 'Hey you.' She stepped into a quiet aisle, keeping her voice low.

'Hi, Rose.' The line was crackly, distorting his voice a little.

'I was getting worried, seeing as you didn't return any of my calls.'

'Yeah, sorry. I've been flat-out.' Finley's tone was curt and cold.

Not wanting to bite, Rose pushed past her anger and reached inside her heart for the love she felt for him. 'I can't wait to see you tonight.'

'Yeah, about that.' More crackles sounded. 'I'm not going to make it to the airport in time.'

Her heart sank to her scuffed boots. 'Why, what's happened?'

'I've been caught up at a meeting, and I've had to rebook my flight, so I won't be home until tomorrow, around lunchtime.'

Rose almost protested but stopped herself, knowing from experience it would be a waste of her breath, and would only add fuel to their heated fire. 'Oh, okay. Well, it can't be helped, I suppose. I'll see you tomorrow then.'

'Yup.'

'Okay. Well, have a safe flight.' Tears threatened and she blinked faster.

'I will. Bye, Rose.' He hung up before she could even tell him she loved him.

Dropping her phone from her ear, she stood there for a few long moments, trying to gather her emotions. She didn't want to cry – not here, not now. Having spent so much time alone over the past few months, she'd cried rivers over her bumpy relationship with Finley.

On the way home, she pulled into the McDonald's drive-through. With nobody to cook for, a Quarter Pounder and chips washed down with a sugar-free frozen Coke was on the menu. Hell, she might even grab herself an apple pie to munch on later, when she wanted to drown her lonesome sorrows. It would go well with the tub of cookies and cream Connoisseur ice-cream she had stashed in her freezer for just such an occasion.

Twenty minutes later, driving past the sign that read *Cole Estate*, she slowed and turned left. It had taken her a while to get used to her future in-laws' flashy fifty-acre Mareeba property – she'd always envisioned growing old on the unpretentious family property, Jacaranda Farm. But then she'd met Finley on the night of her seventeenth birthday and, after four and a half years of dating, he'd shocked the hell out of her and everyone who knew him by getting down on one knee. She'd moved in with him a few months later.

His parents made their disapproval of their engagement known whenever the chance arose, jibing about everything from the way she chose to dress to how she placed her knife and fork on her plate after eating. They were subtle, but it was passive aggression in its ugliest form. Finley chose to not see what they did to make her feel uncomfortable, and unwelcome, which caused more arguments.

If only she could talk him into returning with her to Jacaranda Farm, where life was peaceful, her family loved unconditionally, and the future seemed bright.

*   *   *

Rose couldn't believe what she was hearing. She carefully placed her knife and fork down, trying to reel in her anger while death-staring Finley. 'What do you mean, you think we need to take a *break*?'

Sitting opposite her at the dining table, his garlic Moreton Bay bugs barely touched, Finley shrugged. 'I just think it would do us good to, you know, see how we really feel when we're apart, before we go committing our entire lives to each other.'

For goodness' sake, he'd been her first date, her first kiss, her first ... *everything*. And now he was worried about commitment?

He pushed his salad around the plate with his fork. 'Maybe we're not as compatible as we first thought we were.'

'Not compatible?' She blinked faster – she was not going to cry. She'd done enough of that, especially since losing her beloved great-grandma. Besides, Finley didn't deserve her precious tears.

He lifted his gaze to hers. 'Come on, Rose. We aren't on the same page about a lot of things. I think all our arguing lately has proven that.'

'Couples are meant to work through their differences, Finley, not just shrug and give up when the going got tough.' Instead of replying, he once again shrugged. It was as if he'd already given up on her, on them. 'I don't understand the sudden change of heart.' She sniffled, blinking away instant tears. 'Has something happened to make you like this?'

'Nothing I can pinpoint. It's just a feeling.' He sat back and folded his arms. 'I honestly don't know if I'm in love with you anymore.'

Shell-shocked, heartbroken, and so damn angry, Rose couldn't summon a reply that wasn't filled with expletives so, in the vein of not saying anything if she had nothing nice to say, she remained silent.

As if becoming impatient with her, Finley drew in a breath, held it, then huffed it away. 'I don't think it's a good idea for you stay here while we figure things out either.'

Rose shot to her feet, tugged off her engagement ring, and thumped it on the table. 'Then I'll pack my things and be out of your hair.' Shoving her chair back, it tumbled as she stormed off down the hallway. Thank god she'd left Buck over at Jacaranda Farm – it meant she didn't have to hitch the trailer and load him before getting the hell out of here.

'Rose.' Finley's voice carried after her. 'I'm sorry.'

After packing what little she could claim as her own, the drive to her childhood home flashed by in a tear-hazed blur. Her relationship was in tatters, but so was the business she'd put so much time and effort into – her students weren't going to drive the forty-five minutes to Dimbulah for their lessons. And it wasn't like she could move the riding arena she'd had built at Cole Estate to Jacaranda, even if they would. Talk about everything blowing up in her face. At least she still had her writing and jillarooing. Thank goodness.

With her mind all over the place, Rose slammed on the brakes when she almost missed the turn that she'd taken countless times before. The back end of her Holden Colorado fishtailed as she took the corner and her tyres left the bitumen, meeting with loose gravel. Glancing in her rear-view mirror, she was thankful there'd been nobody behind her.

Pulling to the side of the road, she heaved breaths in. Her fingers tightened around the steering wheel as she fought not to shatter. She had to find a way to deal with this. Giving herself a firm pep-talk, she pushed the despair down as best as she could and pulled back out, her high-beam headlights making it look as if it were daylight. Heading down the long dirt road, she felt a wave of relief when she turned into the front gates of Jacaranda Farm. Pulling up beneath a towering paperbark, she killed the engine, kicked her door open, and jumped out.

Her mum's border collie, Ralph, dashed to her side, his big brown eyes seeming to know she was upset. 'I'll be right, buddy.' She loved the fact he was a pup of Mack and Sasha, who'd been gifted to her as puppies by her great-aunt, Cheryl. It made him all the more special.

Trev and Kenny, who'd worked on the farm as long as she could remember, were sitting on the patio of their workers' cottage – their usual spot for the evening – beers in hand. They both grinned and waved and she tried to do the same, but with her smile faltering, she quickly turned away. She needed her mum, now.

'Hey, is everything okay, kiddo?' Trev called out to her.

'Not really.' She called over her shoulder. 'But don't worry, I'll be fine Uncle Trev.'

'We got your back.' Kenny hollered.

'Thanks Kenny.' She shouted back to him, their show of support choking her up even more.

Kicking her boots off at the back door, she strode into the homestead to the cheery chatter of family and the smell of her mum's midweek roast – it had become a tradition over the years to have a roast twice a week, to bring them all together more often. The only reason she hadn't come tonight was so she and Finley could try to sort things out.

She followed the scent down the hallway, past the line-up of family photos, and into what her great-grandmother had always called the heart of the home: the kitchen. Happy conversation halted. Five sets of eyes looked up at her from the table – Mum, Heath, Angus, GG and Lizzy. She didn't need to say anything – they could all tell she was upset, with the tears now pouring down her cheeks.

Molly was the first to feet. 'Oh, sweetheart, what's happened?' She dashed to her side and took her into her arms. 'Are you okay?'

'No.' Rose clung to her. 'Finley just broke up with me.' The sobs she'd been keeping at bay escaped.

'Oh, sweetheart. I'm so sorry.' Molly hugged her tighter. 'He doesn't know what he's giving up.'

'He's a damn fool,' GG firmly stated. 'Our girl deserves better.'

'Do you want me to go and kick him in the nuts?' Angus groused.

Lizzy gasped. 'Angus, don't talk like that. It's rude.'

'My heart hurts so much, Mum,' she finally said, as she untangled her arms and looked into her mother's kind eyes. 'Even though we were having a bit of a rough time, I thought he and I were going to be forever.'

'Oh, darling, I know you did.' Reaching out, Molly cupped her cheeks. 'Somehow, everything will work out exactly as it's meant to. You'll see.'

Nodding, Rose sucked in a shaky breath. 'I hope you're right, Mum.'

'Your mother is always right, Rosie,' GG said gently. 'She's wise, just like your great-grandma.' Coming to her side, he gave her shoulders a squeeze. 'You're a beautiful young woman, with so much to light and love to give. You deserve great love.'

'Thanks GG,' Rose squeezed past the emotion lodged in her throat. She appreciated how the menfolk in her life showed their love and support in their own masculine ways – she could only guess how infuriated her father was going to be.

Lizzy clambered from her chair and wrapped her arms around Rose's legs. 'We all love you, sissy,' she said, looking up at her.

'Yes, we do,' echoed Heath, wrapping a comforting arm around her.

Leaning her head against her stepfather's shoulder, Rose couldn't help but smile through her tears. 'Thank you all for loving me like you do.' If only she could one day cross paths with a man who would love her like this lot, she'd be a very happy woman.

talk about it

Let's talk about books.

Join the conversation:

 facebook.com/harlequinaustralia

 @harlequinaus

 @harlequinaus

harpercollins.com.au/hq

If you love reading and want to know about our authors and titles, then let's talk about it.